Co-President/Editor-in-Chief:
Victor Gorelick

Co-President/Director of Circulation:
Fred Mausser

Vice President/Managing Editor:
Michael Pellerito

Cover Art: **JOE STATON & AL MILGROM**
Cover Colorist: **Rosario "Tito" Peña**
Script: **MELANIE J. MORGAN**
Pencils: **JOE STATON**
Inks: **Al Milgrom**
Letters: **JOHN WORKMAN**
Colors: **Stephanie Vozzo**

Art Director: **JOE PEPITONE**
Production: **STEPHEN OSWALD,**
CARLOS ANTUNES,
PAUL KAMINSKI,
JOE MORCIGLIO

www.archiecomics.com

Dedicated to the memories of:
Michael I. Silberkleit 1932-2008   Richard H. Goldwater 1936-2007

Archie New Look Series Book 2, Jughead "The Matchmakers" 2009. Printed in Canada. Published by Archie Comic Publications, Inc., 325 Fayette Avenue, Mamaroneck, New York 10543-2318. Archie characters created by John L. Goldwater; the likenesses of the Archie characters were created by Bob Montana.

ISBN-13: 978-1-879794-38-2   ISBN-10: 1-879794-38-1

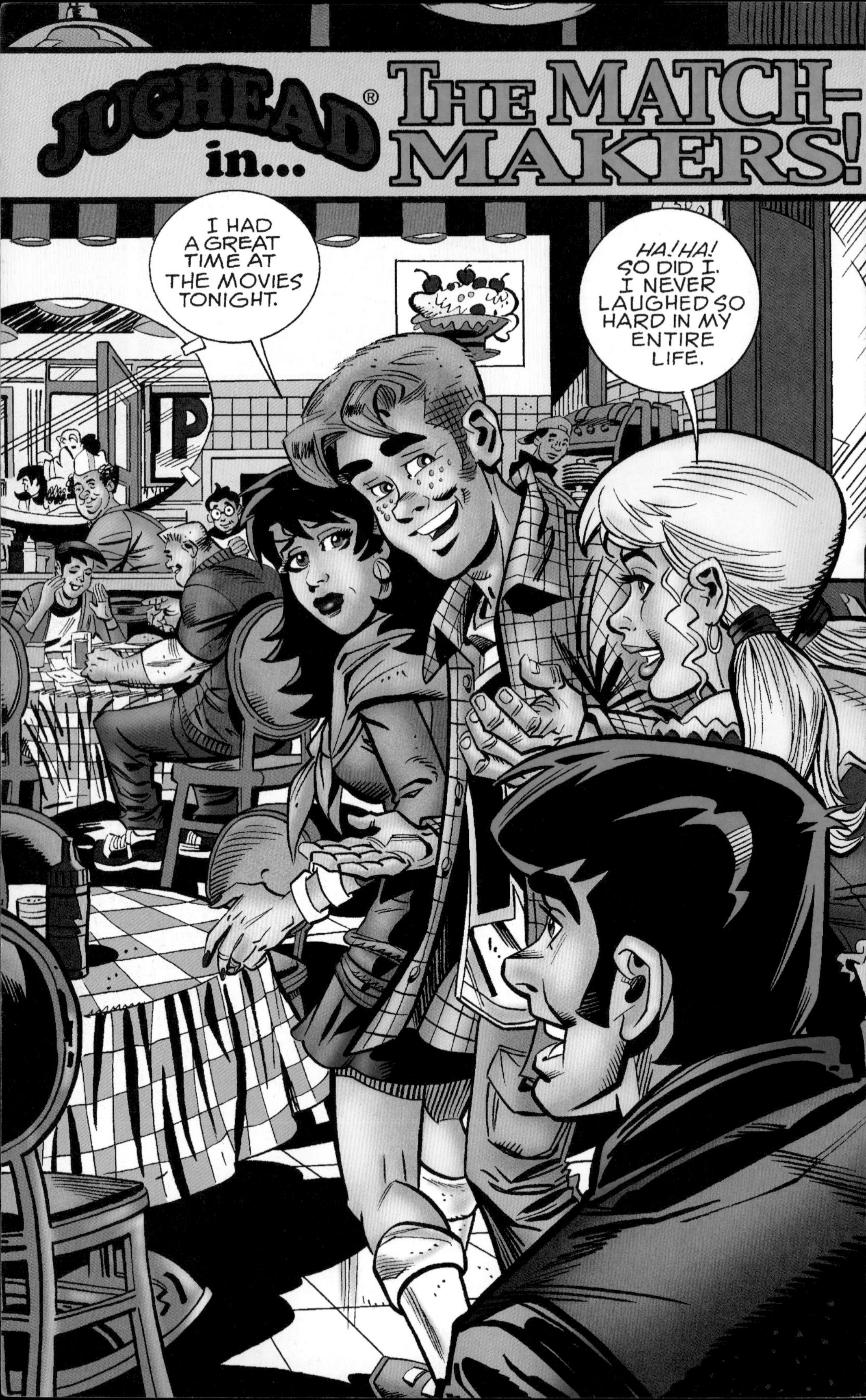
JUGHEAD® in...
THE MATCH-MAKERS!
I HAD A GREAT TIME AT THE MOVIES TONIGHT.
HA! HA! SO DID I. I NEVER LAUGHED SO HARD IN MY ENTIRE LIFE.

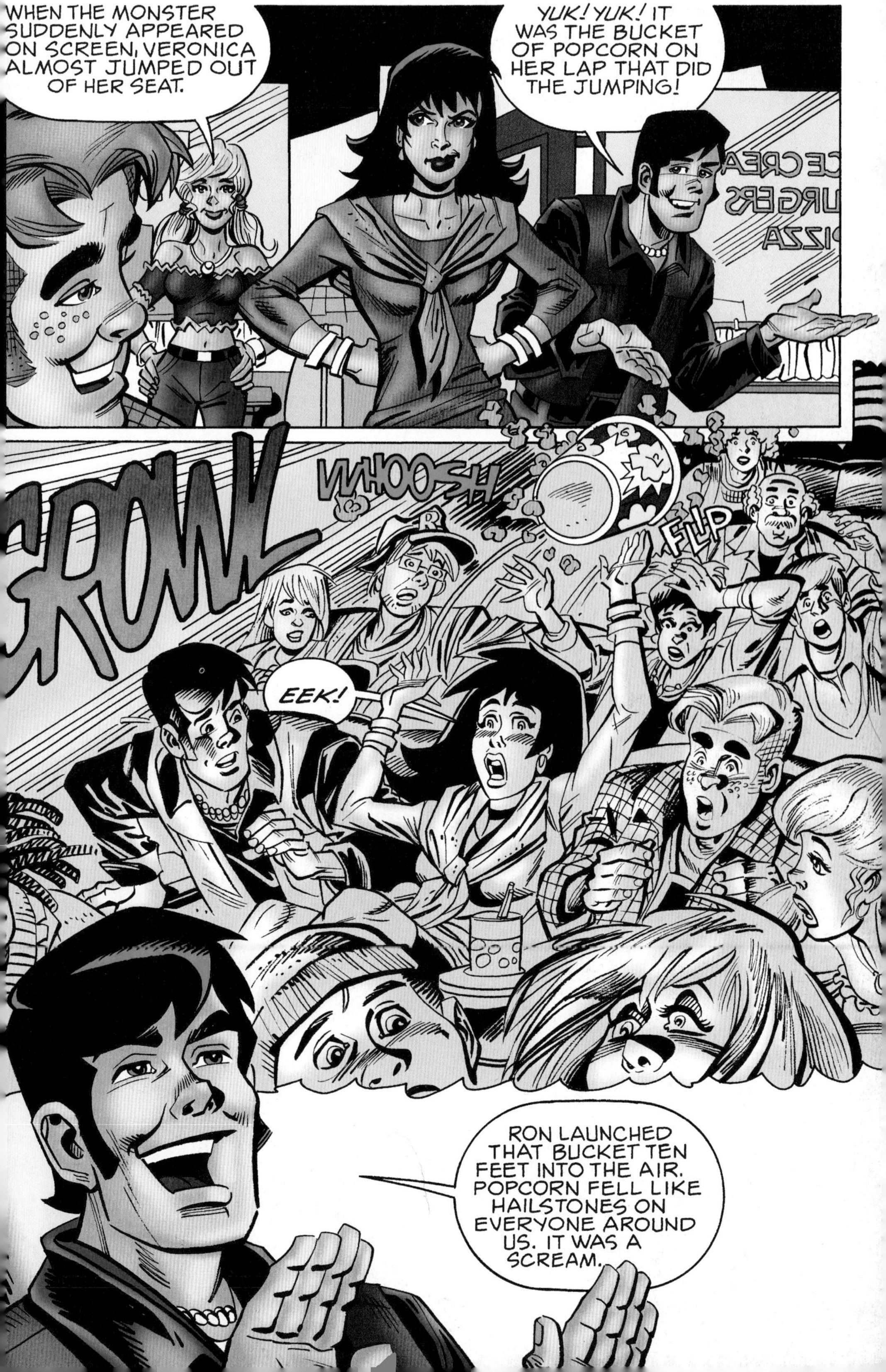
WHEN THE MONSTER SUDDENLY APPEARED ON SCREEN, VERONICA ALMOST JUMPED OUT OF HER SEAT.
YUK! YUK! IT WAS THE BUCKET OF POPCORN ON HER LAP THAT DID THE JUMPING!
GROWL
WHOOSH
FLIP
EEK!
RON LAUNCHED THAT BUCKET TEN FEET INTO THE AIR. POPCORN FELL LIKE HAILSTONES ON EVERYONE AROUND US. IT WAS A SCREAM.

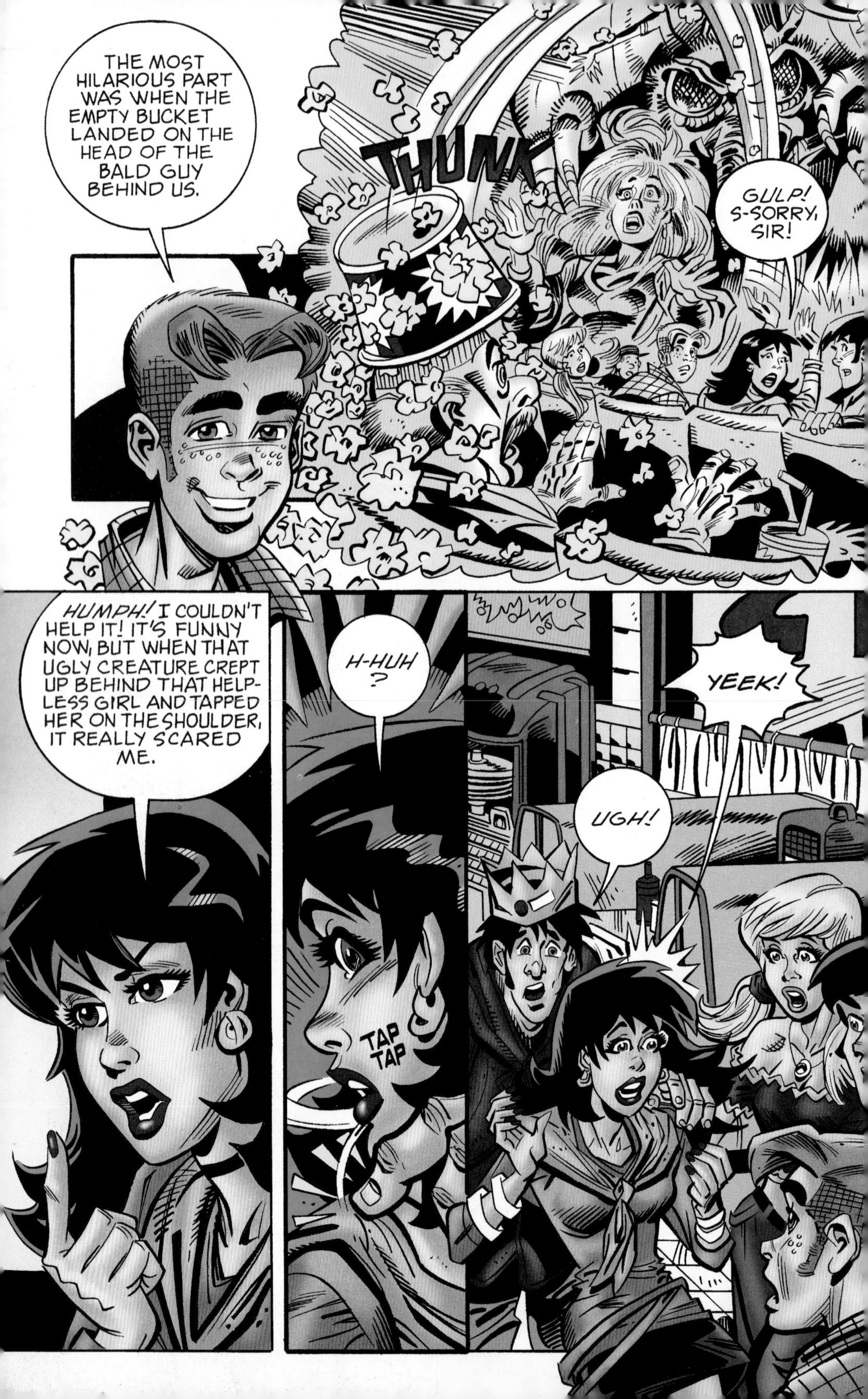
THE MOST HILARIOUS PART WAS WHEN THE EMPTY BUCKET LANDED ON THE HEAD OF THE BALD GUY BEHIND US.
THUNK
GULP! S-SORRY, SIR!
HUMPH! I COULDN'T HELP IT! IT'S FUNNY NOW, BUT WHEN THAT UGLY CREATURE CREPT UP BEHIND THAT HELP-LESS GIRL AND TAPPED HER ON THE SHOULDER, IT REALLY SCARED ME.
H-HUH ?
TAP TAP
YEEK!
UGH!

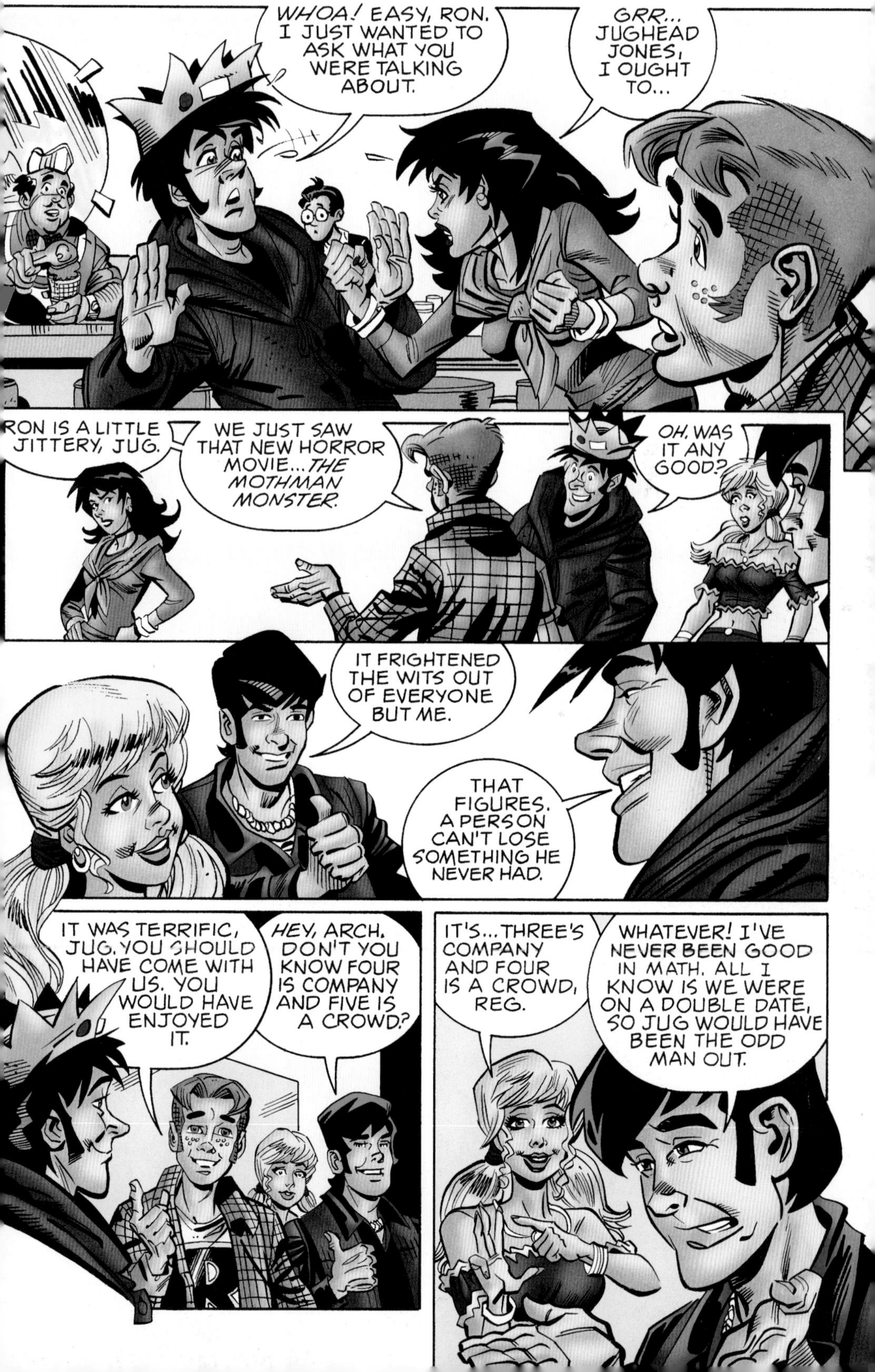
WHOA! EASY, RON. I JUST WANTED TO ASK WHAT YOU WERE TALKING ABOUT.
GRR... JUGHEAD JONES, I OUGHT TO...
RON IS A LITTLE JITTERY, JUG.
WE JUST SAW THAT NEW HORROR MOVIE... THE MOTHMAN MONSTER.
OH, WAS IT ANY GOOD?
IT FRIGHTENED THE WITS OUT OF EVERYONE BUT ME.
THAT FIGURES. A PERSON CAN'T LOSE SOMETHING HE NEVER HAD.
IT WAS TERRIFIC, JUG. YOU SHOULD HAVE COME WITH US. YOU WOULD HAVE ENJOYED IT.
HEY, ARCH. DON'T YOU KNOW FOUR IS COMPANY AND FIVE IS A CROWD?
IT'S... THREE'S COMPANY AND FOUR IS A CROWD, REG.
WHATEVER! I'VE NEVER BEEN GOOD IN MATH. ALL I KNOW IS WE WERE ON A DOUBLE DATE, SO JUG WOULD HAVE BEEN THE ODD MAN OUT.

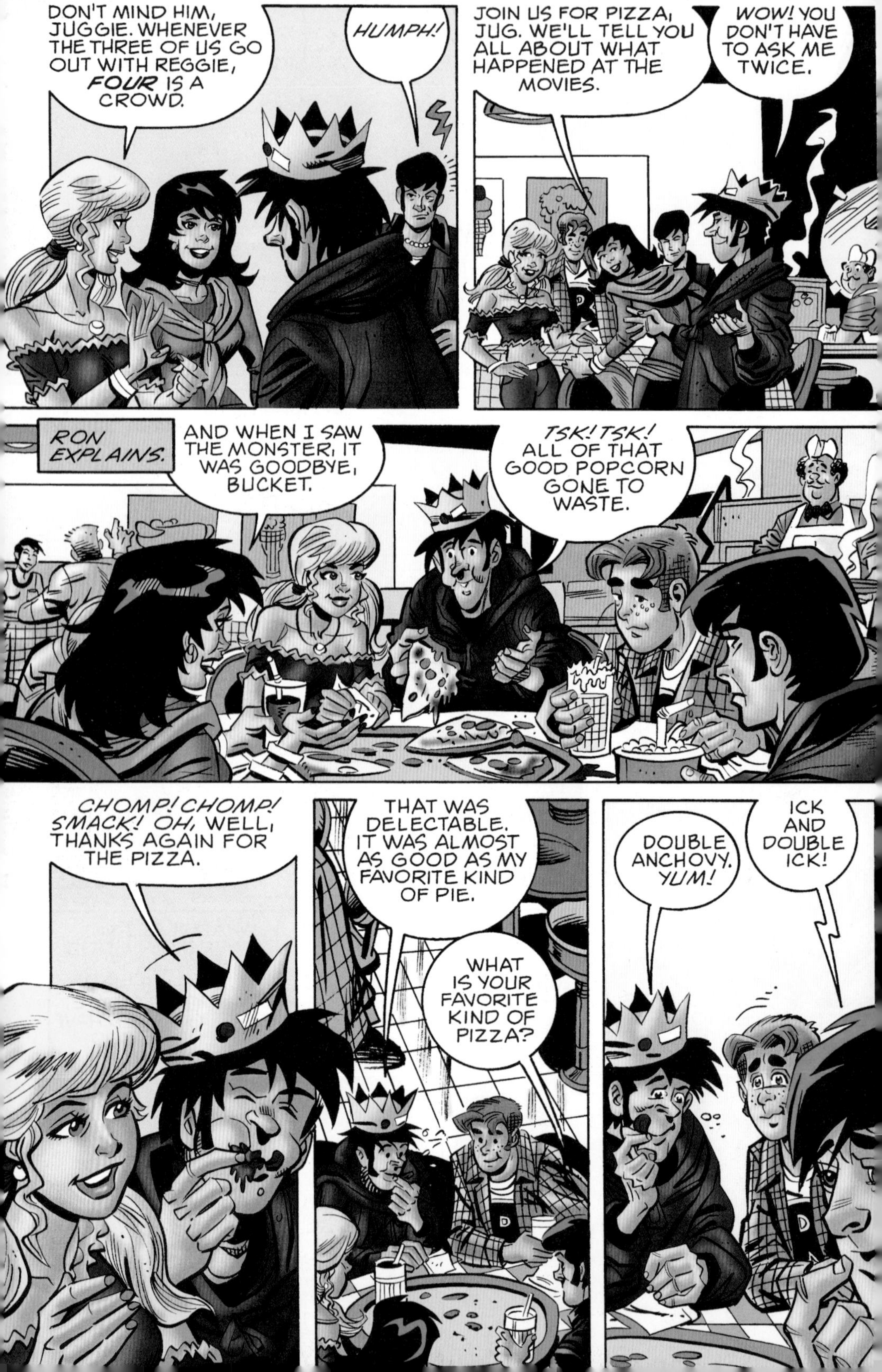

DON'T MIND HIM, JUGGIE. WHENEVER THE THREE OF US GO OUT WITH REGGIE, FOUR IS A CROWD.
HUMPH!
JOIN US FOR PIZZA, JUG. WE'LL TELL YOU ALL ABOUT WHAT HAPPENED AT THE MOVIES.
WOW! YOU DON'T HAVE TO ASK ME TWICE.
RON EXPLAINS.
AND WHEN I SAW THE MONSTER, IT WAS GOODBYE, BUCKET.
TSK! TSK! ALL OF THAT GOOD POPCORN GONE TO WASTE.
CHOMP! CHOMP! SMACK! OH, WELL, THANKS AGAIN FOR THE PIZZA.
THAT WAS DELECTABLE. IT WAS ALMOST AS GOOD AS MY FAVORITE KIND OF PIE.
WHAT IS YOUR FAVORITE KIND OF PIZZA?
DOUBLE ANCHOVY. YUM!
ICK AND DOUBLE ICK!

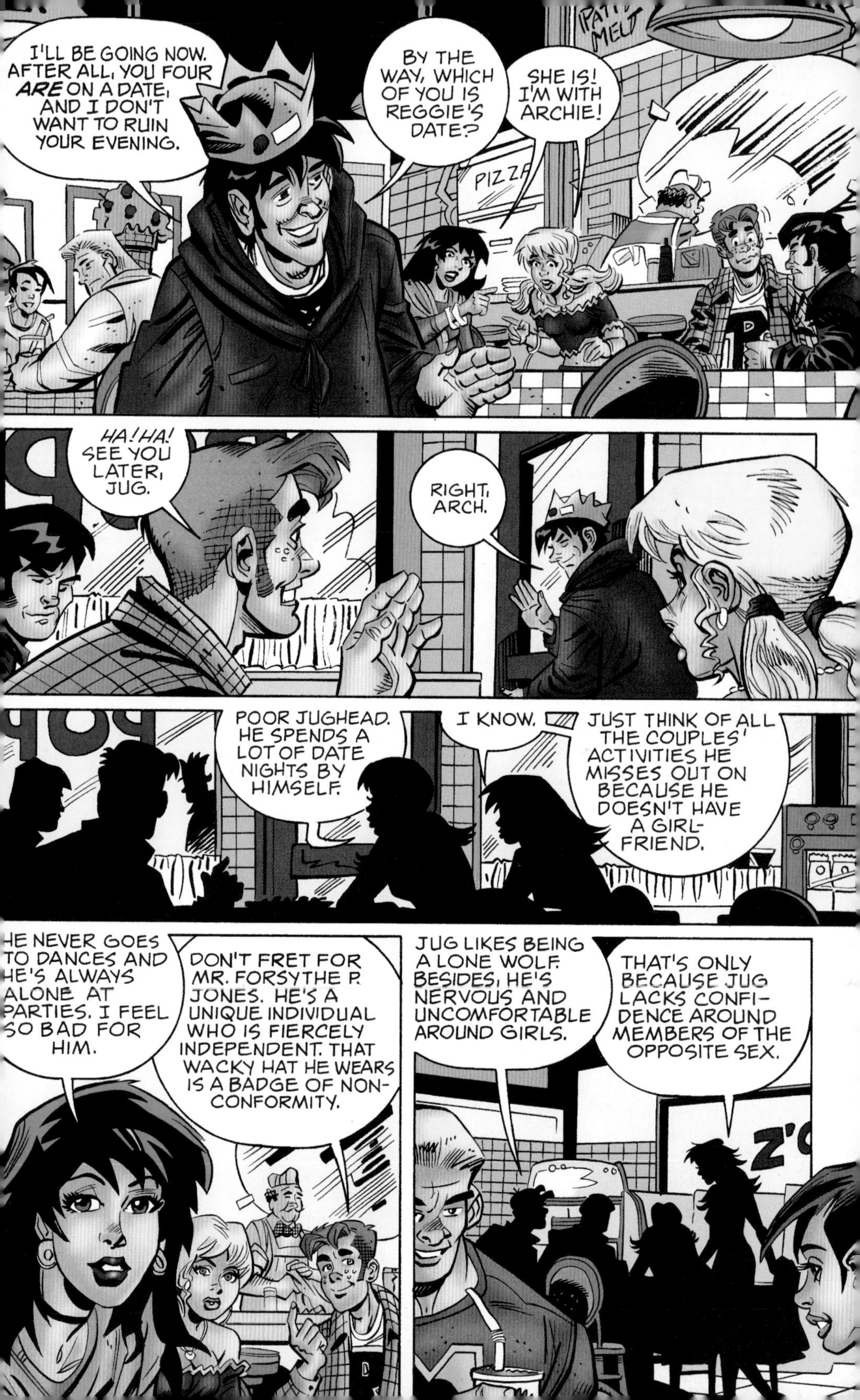

I'LL BE GOING NOW. AFTER ALL, YOU FOUR *ARE* ON A DATE, AND I DON'T WANT TO RUIN YOUR EVENING.
BY THE WAY, WHICH OF YOU IS REGGIE'S DATE?
SHE IS! I'M WITH ARCHIE!
PATTY MELT
PIZZA
HA! HA! SEE YOU LATER, JUG.
RIGHT, ARCH.
POOR JUGHEAD. HE SPENDS A LOT OF DATE NIGHTS BY HIMSELF.
I KNOW.
JUST THINK OF ALL THE COUPLES' ACTIVITIES HE MISSES OUT ON BECAUSE HE DOESN'T HAVE A GIRL-FRIEND.
HE NEVER GOES TO DANCES AND HE'S ALWAYS ALONE AT PARTIES. I FEEL SO BAD FOR HIM.
DON'T FRET FOR MR. FORSYTHE P. JONES. HE'S A UNIQUE INDIVIDUAL WHO IS FIERCELY INDEPENDENT. THAT WACKY HAT HE WEARS IS A BADGE OF NON-CONFORMITY.
JUG LIKES BEING A LONE WOLF. BESIDES, HE'S NERVOUS AND UNCOMFORTABLE AROUND GIRLS.
THAT'S ONLY BECAUSE JUG LACKS CONFI-DENCE AROUND MEMBERS OF THE OPPOSITE SEX.

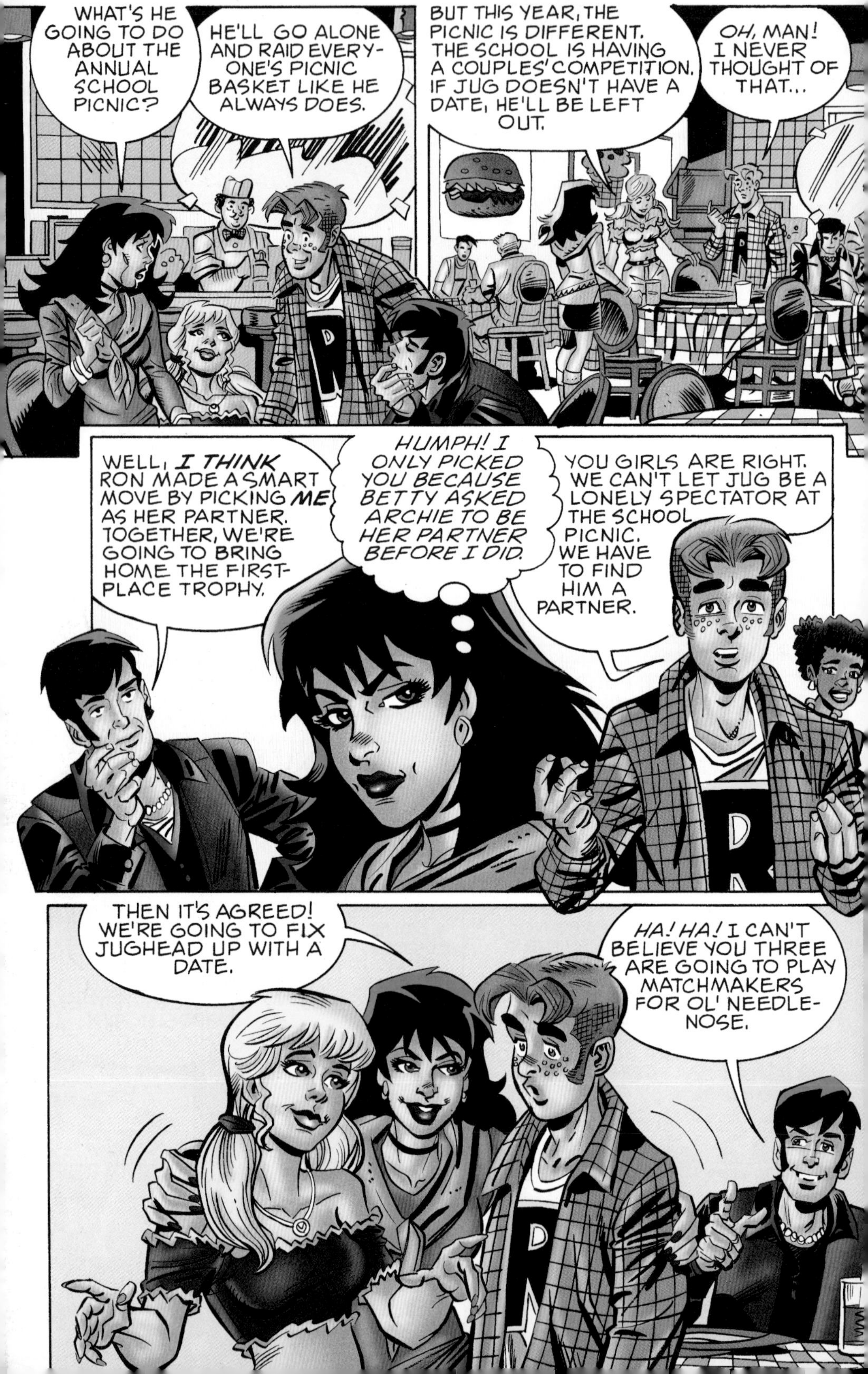
WHAT'S HE GOING TO DO ABOUT THE ANNUAL SCHOOL PICNIC?
HE'LL GO ALONE AND RAID EVERY-ONE'S PICNIC BASKET LIKE HE ALWAYS DOES.
BUT THIS YEAR, THE PICNIC IS DIFFERENT. THE SCHOOL IS HAVING A COUPLES' COMPETITION. IF JUG DOESN'T HAVE A DATE, HE'LL BE LEFT OUT.
OH, MAN! I NEVER THOUGHT OF THAT...
WELL, I THINK RON MADE A SMART MOVE BY PICKING ME AS HER PARTNER. TOGETHER, WE'RE GOING TO BRING HOME THE FIRST-PLACE TROPHY.
HUMPH! I ONLY PICKED YOU BECAUSE BETTY ASKED ARCHIE TO BE HER PARTNER BEFORE I DID.
YOU GIRLS ARE RIGHT. WE CAN'T LET JUG BE A LONELY SPECTATOR AT THE SCHOOL PICNIC. WE HAVE TO FIND HIM A PARTNER.
THEN IT'S AGREED! WE'RE GOING TO FIX JUGHEAD UP WITH A DATE.
HA! HA! I CAN'T BELIEVE YOU THREE ARE GOING TO PLAY MATCHMAKERS FOR OL' NEEDLE-NOSE.

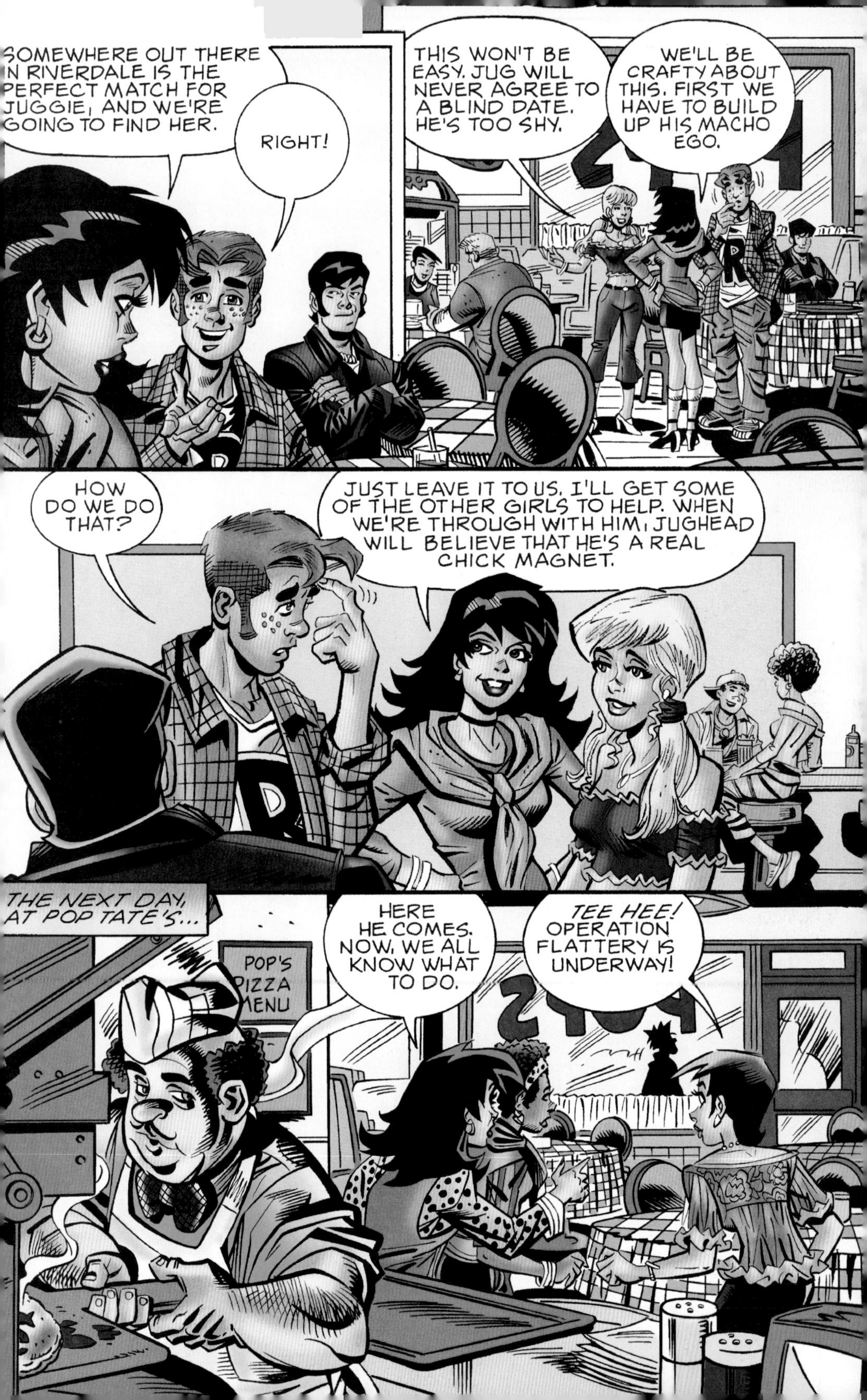
SOMEWHERE OUT THERE IN RIVERDALE IS THE PERFECT MATCH FOR JUGGIE, AND WE'RE GOING TO FIND HER.
RIGHT!
THIS WON'T BE EASY. JUG WILL NEVER AGREE TO A BLIND DATE. HE'S TOO SHY.
WE'LL BE CRAFTY ABOUT THIS. FIRST WE HAVE TO BUILD UP HIS MACHO EGO.
HOW DO WE DO THAT?
JUST LEAVE IT TO US. I'LL GET SOME OF THE OTHER GIRLS TO HELP. WHEN WE'RE THROUGH WITH HIM, JUGHEAD WILL BELIEVE THAT HE'S A REAL CHICK MAGNET.
THE NEXT DAY, AT POP TATE'S...
POP'S PIZZA MENU
HERE HE COMES. NOW, WE ALL KNOW WHAT TO DO.
TEE HEE! OPERATION FLATTERY IS UNDERWAY!

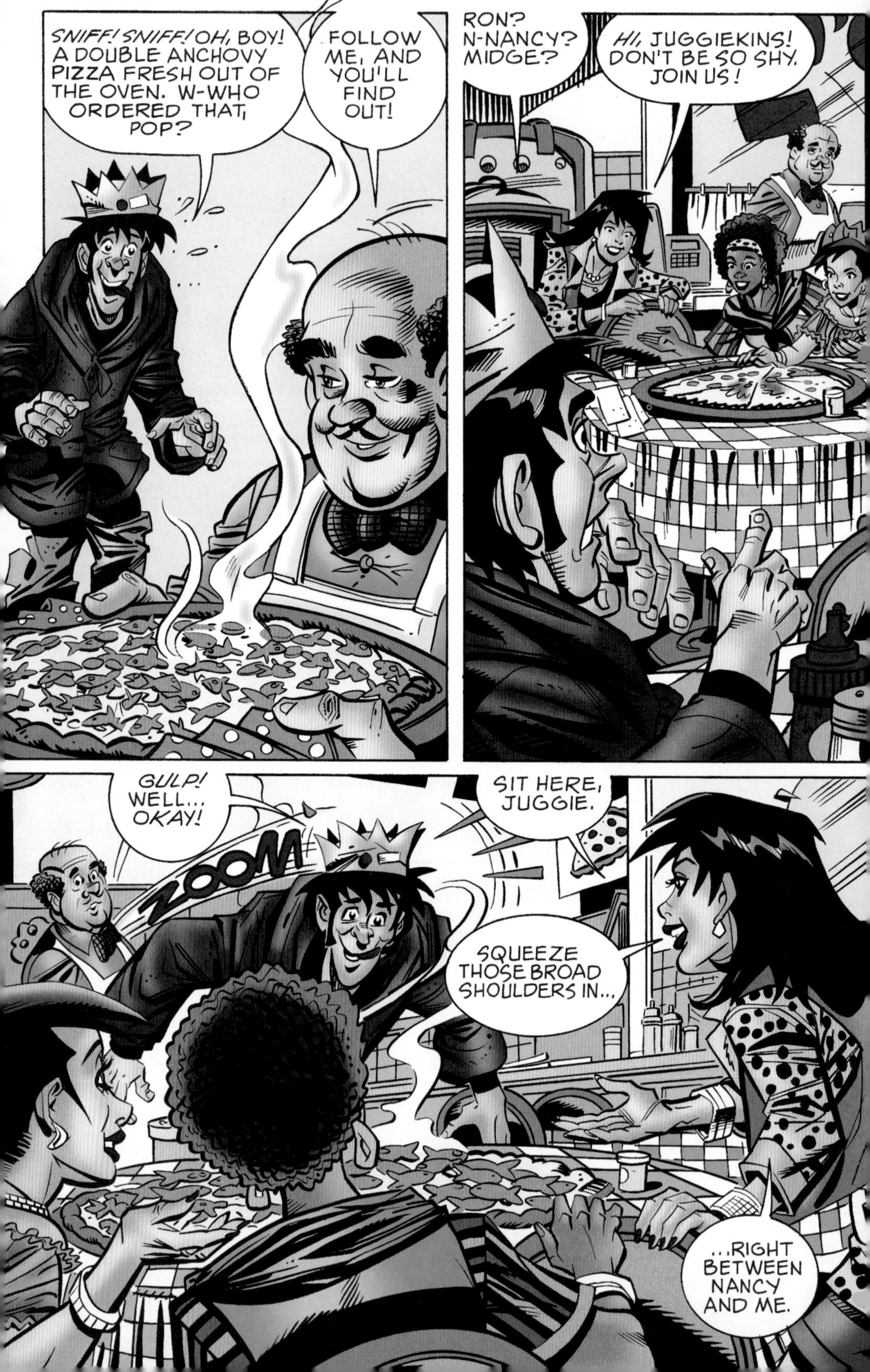
SNIFF! SNIFF! OH, BOY! A DOUBLE ANCHOVY PIZZA FRESH OUT OF THE OVEN. W-WHO ORDERED THAT, POP?
FOLLOW ME, AND YOU'LL FIND OUT!
RON? N-NANCY? MIDGE?
HI, JUGGIEKINS! DON'T BE SO SHY. JOIN US!
GULP! WELL... OKAY!
ZOOM
SIT HERE, JUGGIE.
SQUEEZE THOSE BROAD SHOULDERS IN...
...RIGHT BETWEEN NANCY AND ME.

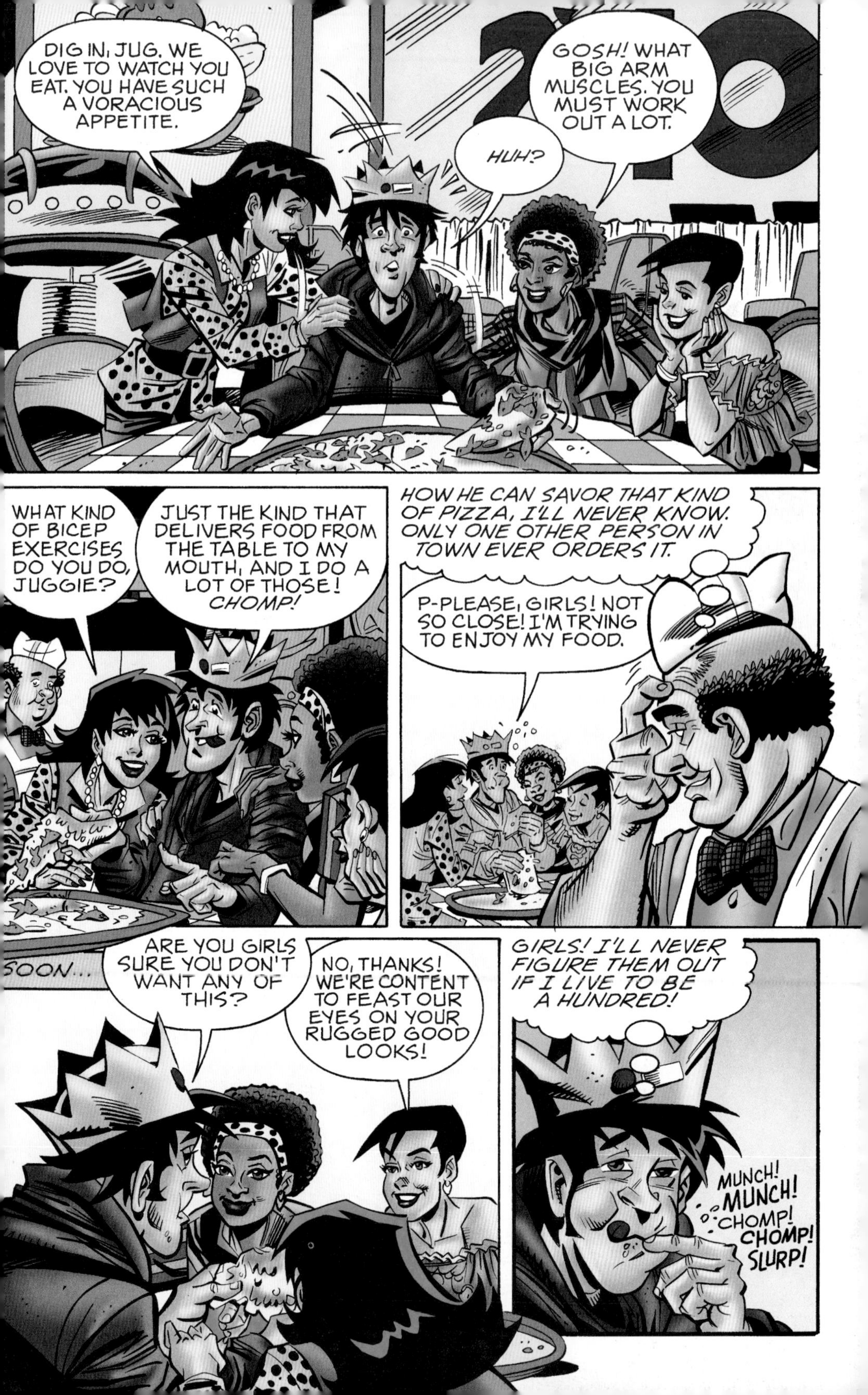
DIG IN, JUG. WE LOVE TO WATCH YOU EAT. YOU HAVE SUCH A VORACIOUS APPETITE.
HUH?
GOSH! WHAT BIG ARM MUSCLES. YOU MUST WORK OUT A LOT.
WHAT KIND OF BICEP EXERCISES DO YOU DO, JUGGIE?
JUST THE KIND THAT DELIVERS FOOD FROM THE TABLE TO MY MOUTH, AND I DO A LOT OF THOSE! CHOMP!
HOW HE CAN SAVOR THAT KIND OF PIZZA, I'LL NEVER KNOW. ONLY ONE OTHER PERSON IN TOWN EVER ORDERS IT.
P-PLEASE, GIRLS! NOT SO CLOSE! I'M TRYING TO ENJOY MY FOOD.
SOON...
ARE YOU GIRLS SURE YOU DON'T WANT ANY OF THIS?
NO, THANKS! WE'RE CONTENT TO FEAST OUR EYES ON YOUR RUGGED GOOD LOOKS!
GIRLS! I'LL NEVER FIGURE THEM OUT IF I LIVE TO BE A HUNDRED!
MUNCH! MUNCH! CHOMP! CHOMP! SLURP!

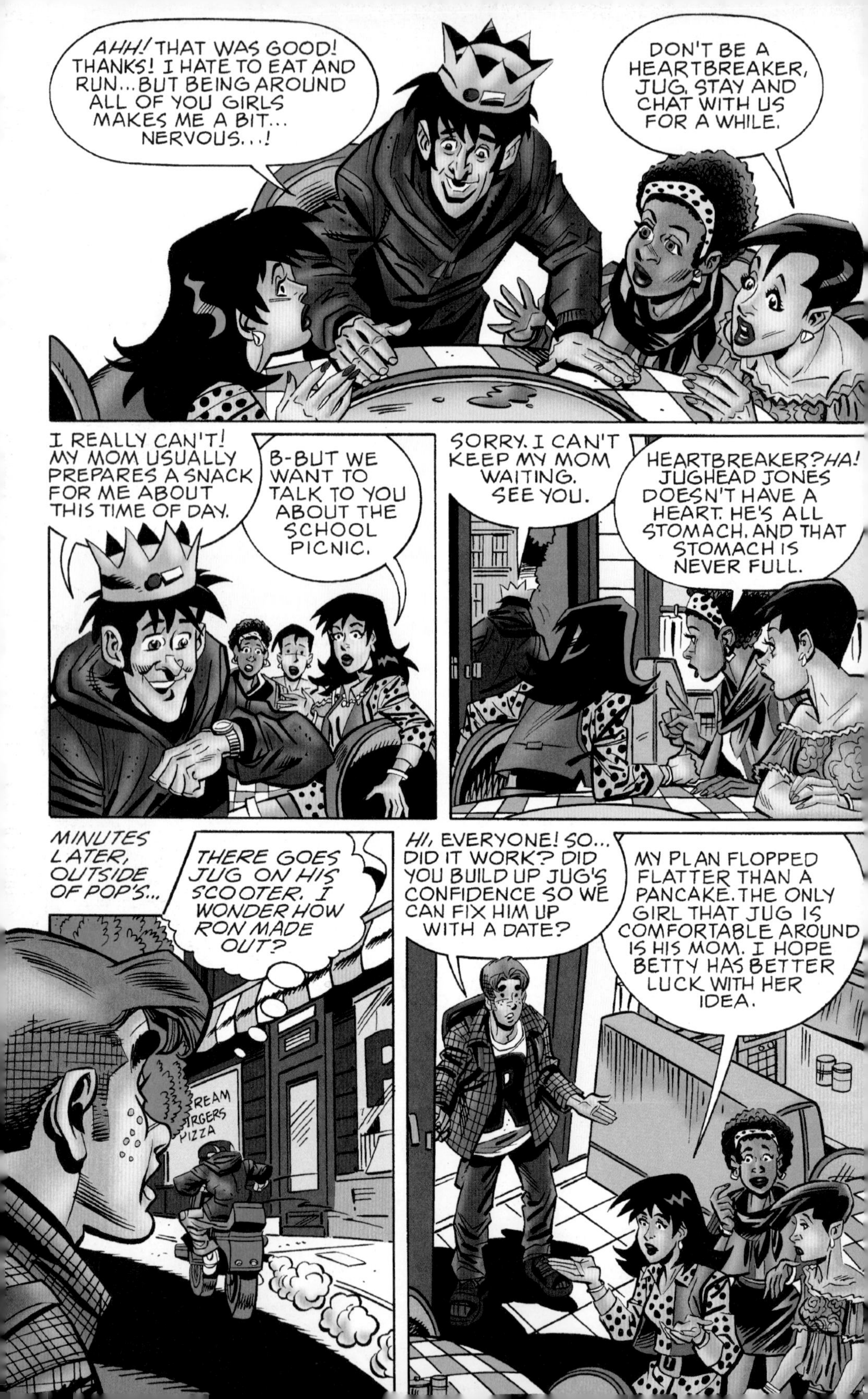
AHH! THAT WAS GOOD! THANKS! I HATE TO EAT AND RUN...BUT BEING AROUND ALL OF YOU GIRLS MAKES ME A BIT... NERVOUS...!
DON'T BE A HEARTBREAKER, JUG. STAY AND CHAT WITH US FOR A WHILE.
I REALLY CAN'T! MY MOM USUALLY PREPARES A SNACK FOR ME ABOUT THIS TIME OF DAY.
B-BUT WE WANT TO TALK TO YOU ABOUT THE SCHOOL PICNIC.
SORRY. I CAN'T KEEP MY MOM WAITING. SEE YOU.
HEARTBREAKER? HA! JUGHEAD JONES DOESN'T HAVE A HEART. HE'S ALL STOMACH. AND THAT STOMACH IS NEVER FULL.
MINUTES LATER, OUTSIDE OF POP'S...
THERE GOES JUG ON HIS SCOOTER. I WONDER HOW RON MADE OUT?
REAM
RGERS
PIZZA
HI, EVERYONE! SO... DID IT WORK? DID YOU BUILD UP JUG'S CONFIDENCE SO WE CAN FIX HIM UP WITH A DATE?
MY PLAN FLOPPED FLATTER THAN A PANCAKE. THE ONLY GIRL THAT JUG IS COMFORTABLE AROUND IS HIS MOM. I HOPE BETTY HAS BETTER LUCK WITH HER IDEA.

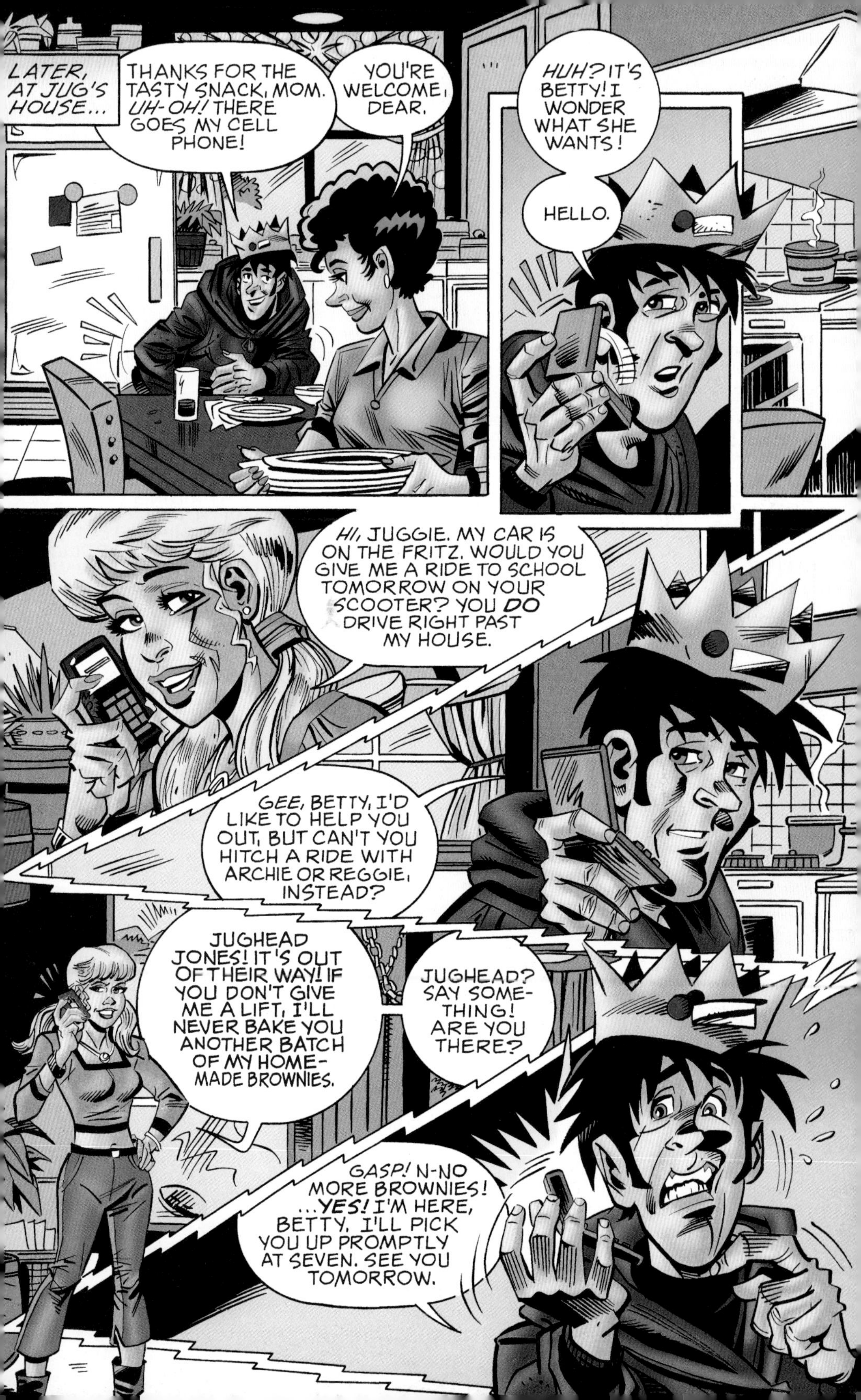
LATER, AT JUG'S HOUSE...
THANKS FOR THE TASTY SNACK, MOM. UH-OH! THERE GOES MY CELL PHONE!
YOU'RE WELCOME, DEAR.
HUH? IT'S BETTY! I WONDER WHAT SHE WANTS!
HELLO.
HI, JUGGIE. MY CAR IS ON THE FRITZ. WOULD YOU GIVE ME A RIDE TO SCHOOL TOMORROW ON YOUR SCOOTER? YOU DO DRIVE RIGHT PAST MY HOUSE.
GEE, BETTY, I'D LIKE TO HELP YOU OUT, BUT CAN'T YOU HITCH A RIDE WITH ARCHIE OR REGGIE, INSTEAD?
JUGHEAD JONES! IT'S OUT OF THEIR WAY! IF YOU DON'T GIVE ME A LIFT, I'LL NEVER BAKE YOU ANOTHER BATCH OF MY HOME-MADE BROWNIES.
JUGHEAD? SAY SOME-THING! ARE YOU THERE?
GASP! N-NO MORE BROWNIES! ...YES! I'M HERE, BETTY. I'LL PICK YOU UP PROMPTLY AT SEVEN. SEE YOU TOMORROW.

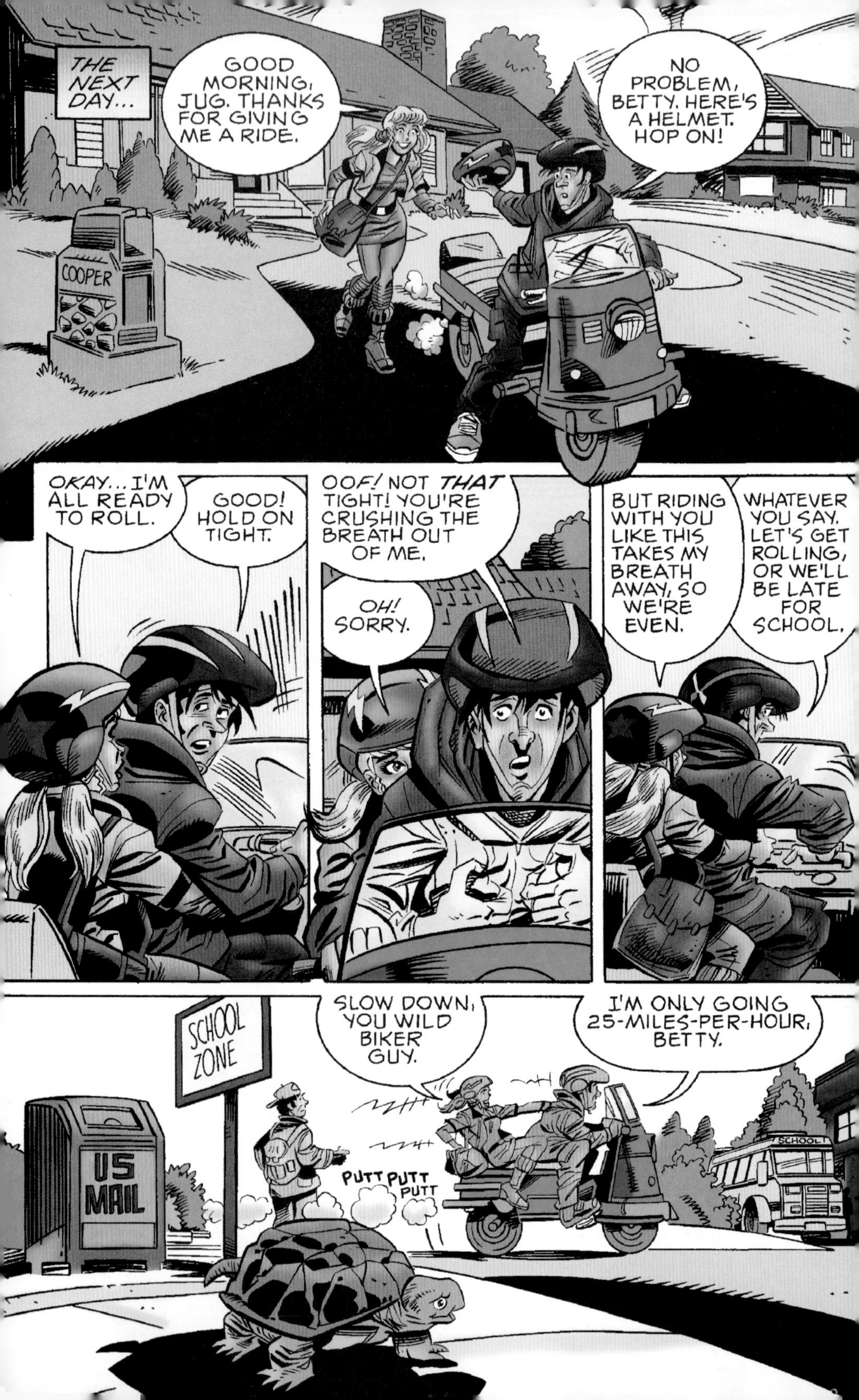
THE NEXT DAY...
GOOD MORNING, JUG. THANKS FOR GIVING ME A RIDE.
NO PROBLEM, BETTY. HERE'S A HELMET. HOP ON!
COOPER
OKAY... I'M ALL READY TO ROLL.
GOOD! HOLD ON TIGHT.
OOF! NOT THAT TIGHT! YOU'RE CRUSHING THE BREATH OUT OF ME.
OH! SORRY.
BUT RIDING WITH YOU LIKE THIS TAKES MY BREATH AWAY, SO WE'RE EVEN.
WHATEVER YOU SAY. LET'S GET ROLLING, OR WE'LL BE LATE FOR SCHOOL.
SCHOOL ZONE
SLOW DOWN, YOU WILD BIKER GUY.
I'M ONLY GOING 25-MILES-PER-HOUR, BETTY.
US MAIL
PUTT PUTT PUTT
SCHOOL

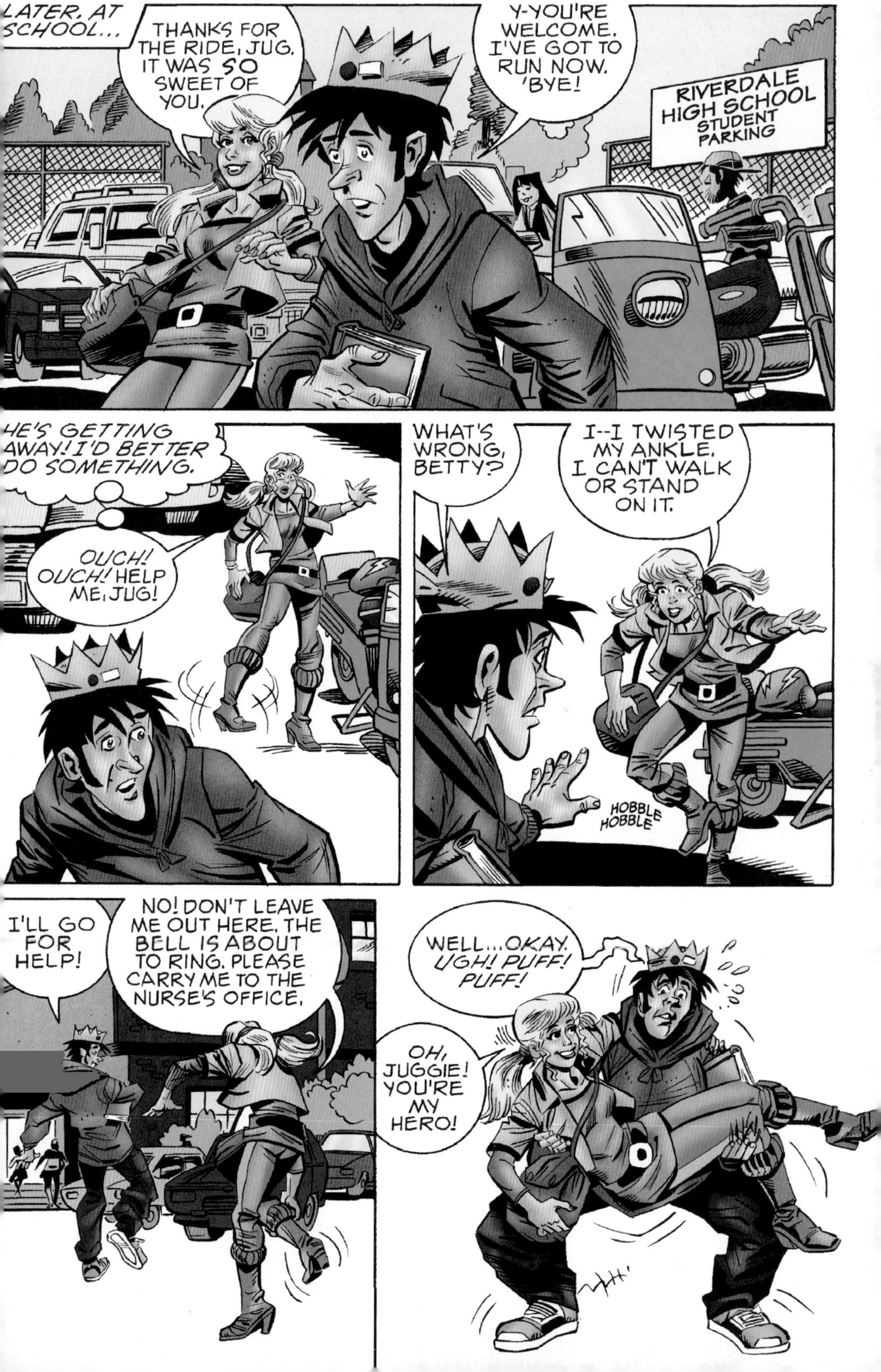
LATER, AT SCHOOL...
THANKS FOR THE RIDE, JUG. IT WAS SO SWEET OF YOU.
Y-YOU'RE WELCOME. I'VE GOT TO RUN NOW. 'BYE!
RIVERDALE HIGH SCHOOL STUDENT PARKING
HE'S GETTING AWAY! I'D BETTER DO SOMETHING.
OUCH! OUCH! HELP ME, JUG!
WHAT'S WRONG, BETTY?
I--I TWISTED MY ANKLE. I CAN'T WALK OR STAND ON IT.
HOBBLE HOBBLE
I'LL GO FOR HELP!
NO! DON'T LEAVE ME OUT HERE. THE BELL IS ABOUT TO RING. PLEASE CARRY ME TO THE NURSE'S OFFICE.
WELL...OKAY. UGH! PUFF! PUFF!
OH, JUGGIE! YOU'RE MY HERO!

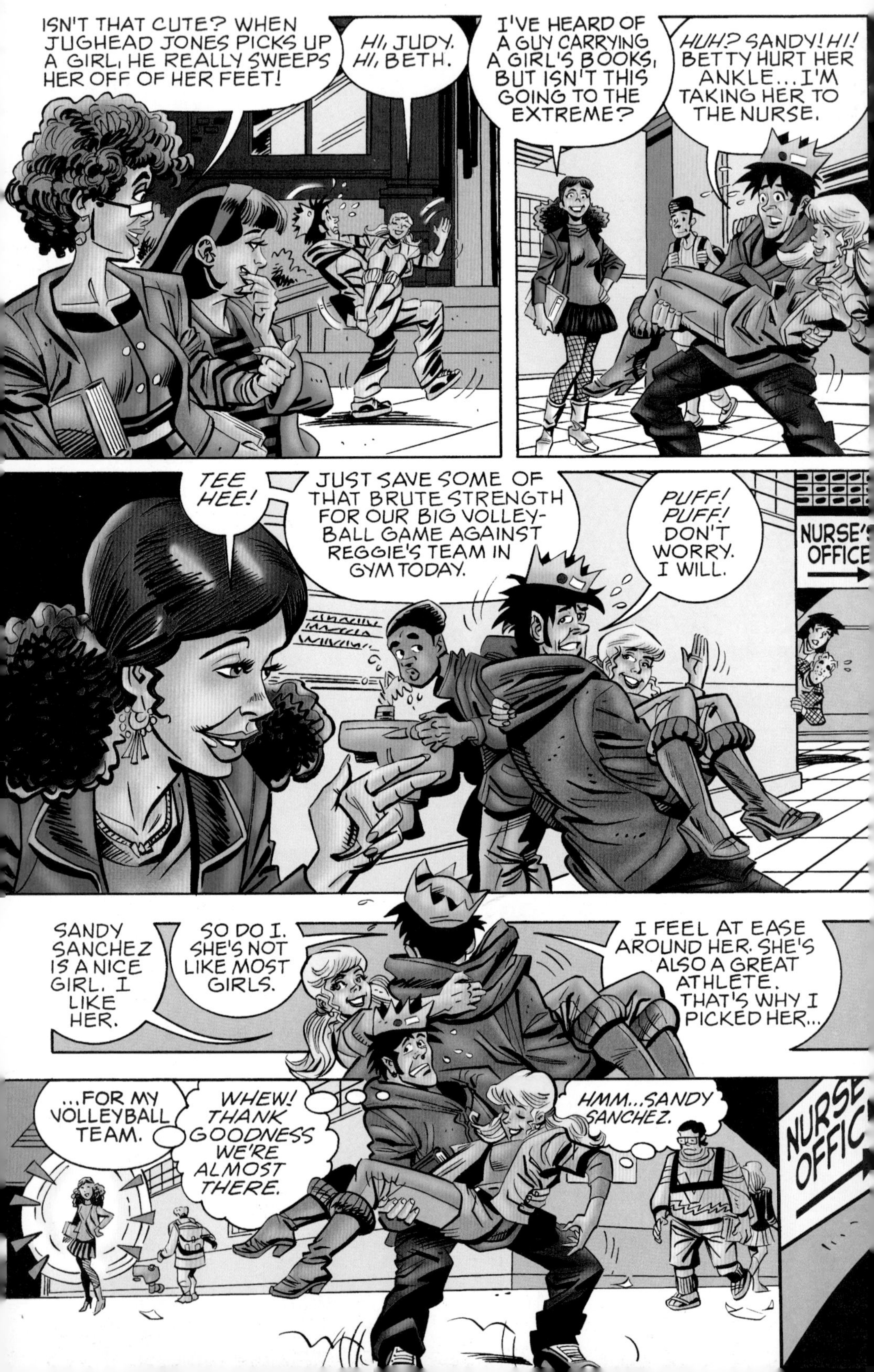

ISN'T THAT CUTE? WHEN JUGHEAD JONES PICKS UP A GIRL, HE REALLY SWEEPS HER OFF OF HER FEET!
HI, JUDY. HI, BETH.
I'VE HEARD OF A GUY CARRYING A GIRL'S BOOKS, BUT ISN'T THIS GOING TO THE EXTREME?
HUH? SANDY! HI! BETTY HURT HER ANKLE... I'M TAKING HER TO THE NURSE.
TEE HEE!
JUST SAVE SOME OF THAT BRUTE STRENGTH FOR OUR BIG VOLLEY-BALL GAME AGAINST REGGIE'S TEAM IN GYM TODAY.
PUFF! PUFF! DON'T WORRY. I WILL.
NURSE'S OFFICE
SANDY SANCHEZ IS A NICE GIRL. I LIKE HER.
SO DO I. SHE'S NOT LIKE MOST GIRLS.
I FEEL AT EASE AROUND HER. SHE'S ALSO A GREAT ATHLETE. THAT'S WHY I PICKED HER...
...FOR MY VOLLEYBALL TEAM.
WHEW! THANK GOODNESS WE'RE ALMOST THERE.
HMM... SANDY SANCHEZ.

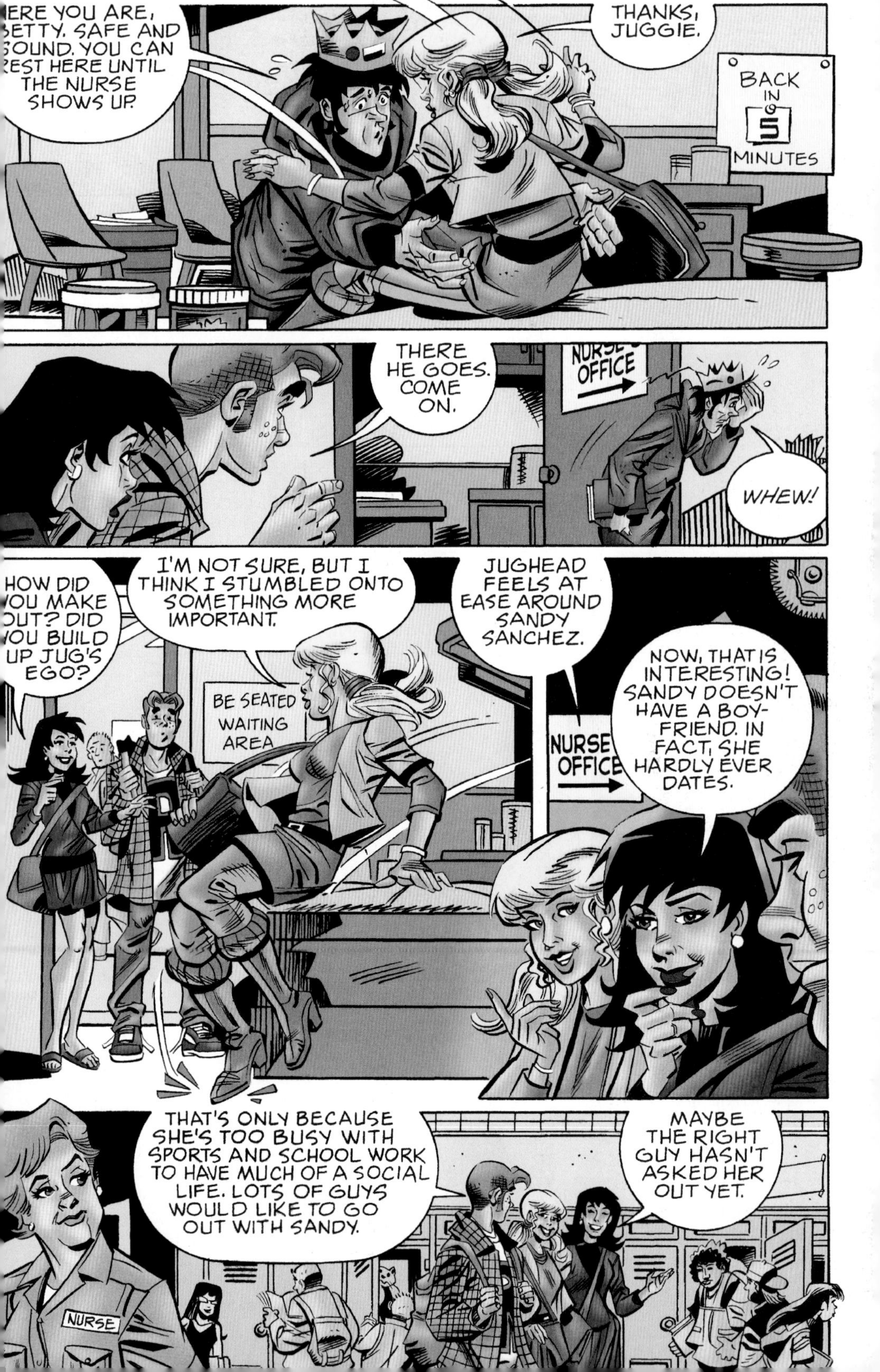
ERE YOU ARE, ETTY. SAFE AND OUND. YOU CAN EST HERE UNTIL THE NURSE SHOWS UP.
THANKS, JUGGIE.
BACK IN 5 MINUTES
THERE HE GOES. COME ON.
NURSE'S OFFICE
WHEW!
HOW DID OU MAKE UT? DID OU BUILD UP JUG'S EGO?
I'M NOT SURE, BUT I THINK I STUMBLED ONTO SOMETHING MORE IMPORTANT.
BE SEATED
WAITING AREA
JUGHEAD FEELS AT EASE AROUND SANDY SANCHEZ.
NURSE OFFICE
NOW, THAT IS INTERESTING! SANDY DOESN'T HAVE A BOY-FRIEND. IN FACT, SHE HARDLY EVER DATES.
THAT'S ONLY BECAUSE SHE'S TOO BUSY WITH SPORTS AND SCHOOL WORK TO HAVE MUCH OF A SOCIAL LIFE. LOTS OF GUYS WOULD LIKE TO GO OUT WITH SANDY.
MAYBE THE RIGHT GUY HASN'T ASKED HER OUT YET.
NURSE

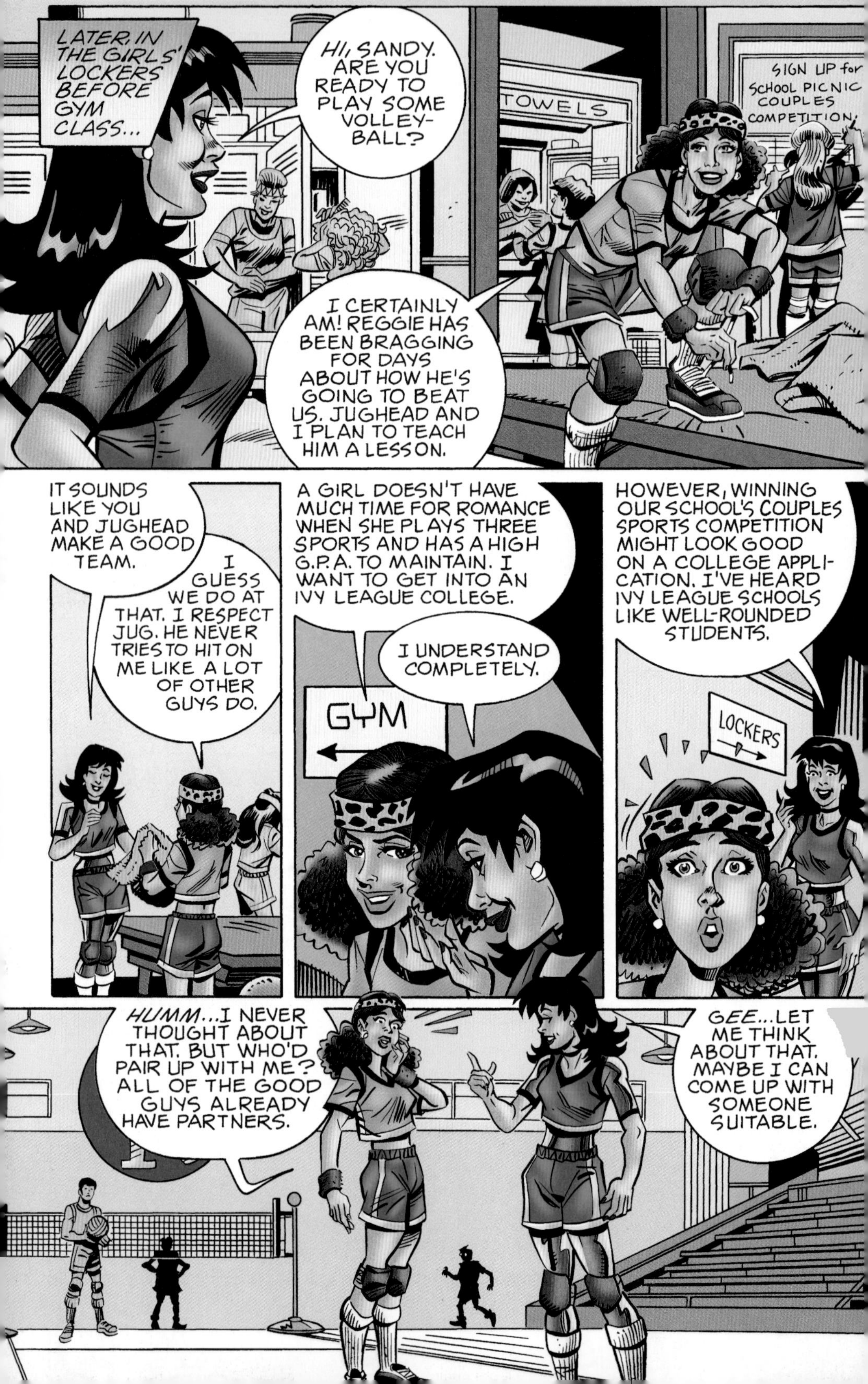
LATER, IN THE GIRLS' LOCKERS BEFORE GYM CLASS...
HI, SANDY. ARE YOU READY TO PLAY SOME VOLLEY-BALL?
TOWELS
SIGN UP for SCHOOL PICNIC COUPLES COMPETITION.
I CERTAINLY AM! REGGIE HAS BEEN BRAGGING FOR DAYS ABOUT HOW HE'S GOING TO BEAT US. JUGHEAD AND I PLAN TO TEACH HIM A LESSON.
IT SOUNDS LIKE YOU AND JUGHEAD MAKE A GOOD TEAM.
I GUESS WE DO AT THAT. I RESPECT JUG. HE NEVER TRIES TO HIT ON ME LIKE A LOT OF OTHER GUYS DO.
A GIRL DOESN'T HAVE MUCH TIME FOR ROMANCE WHEN SHE PLAYS THREE SPORTS AND HAS A HIGH G.P.A. TO MAINTAIN. I WANT TO GET INTO AN IVY LEAGUE COLLEGE.
I UNDERSTAND COMPLETELY.
GYM
HOWEVER, WINNING OUR SCHOOL'S COUPLES SPORTS COMPETITION MIGHT LOOK GOOD ON A COLLEGE APPLI-CATION. I'VE HEARD IVY LEAGUE SCHOOLS LIKE WELL-ROUNDED STUDENTS.
LOCKERS
HUMM...I NEVER THOUGHT ABOUT THAT. BUT WHO'D PAIR UP WITH ME? ALL OF THE GOOD GUYS ALREADY HAVE PARTNERS.
GEE...LET ME THINK ABOUT THAT. MAYBE I CAN COME UP WITH SOMEONE SUITABLE.

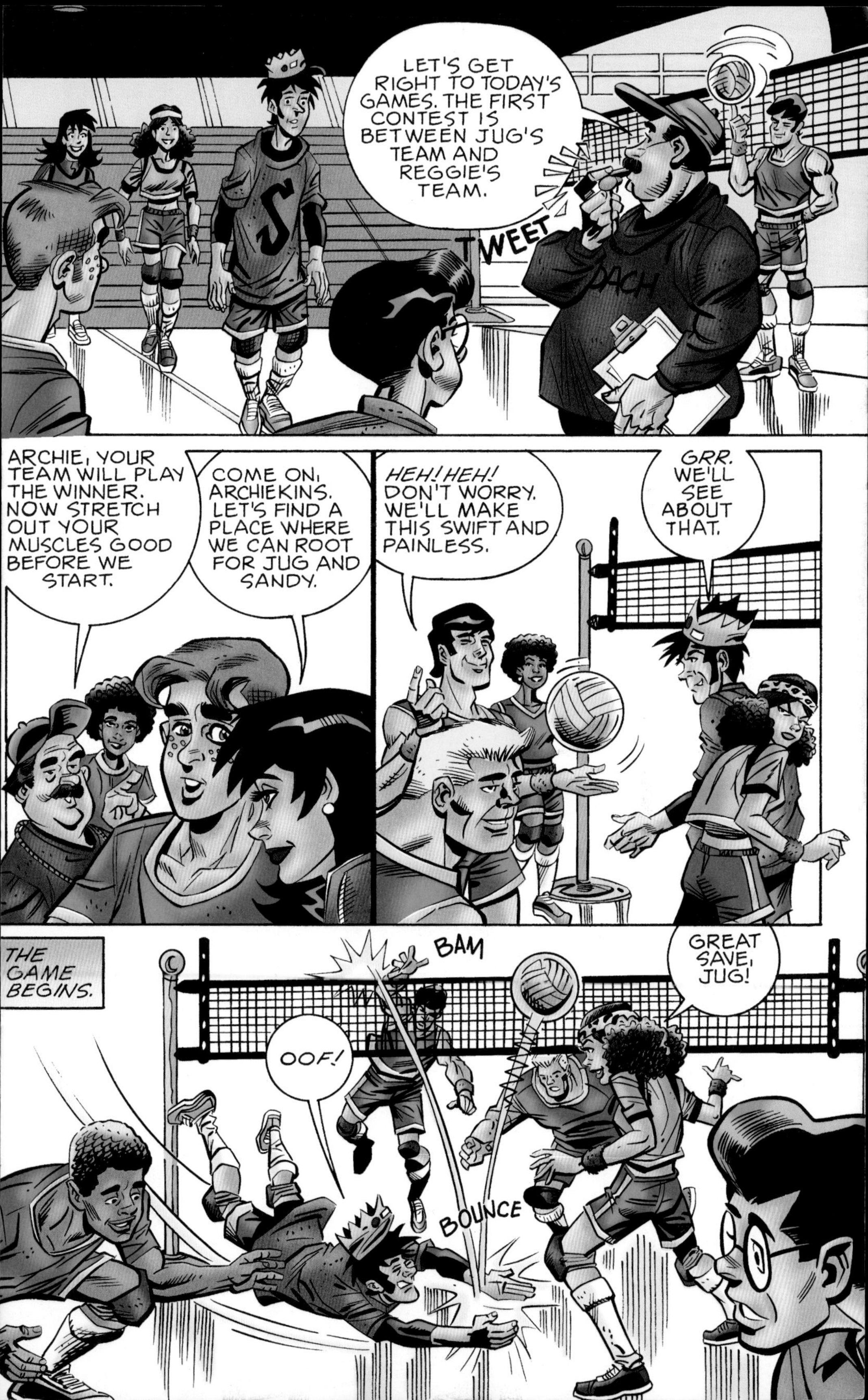

LET'S GET RIGHT TO TODAY'S GAMES. THE FIRST CONTEST IS BETWEEN JUG'S TEAM AND REGGIE'S TEAM.
TWEET
ARCHIE, YOUR TEAM WILL PLAY THE WINNER. NOW STRETCH OUT YOUR MUSCLES GOOD BEFORE WE START.
COME ON, ARCHIEKINS. LET'S FIND A PLACE WHERE WE CAN ROOT FOR JUG AND SANDY.
HEH! HEH! DON'T WORRY. WE'LL MAKE THIS SWIFT AND PAINLESS.
GRR. WE'LL SEE ABOUT THAT.
THE GAME BEGINS.
BAM
GREAT SAVE, JUG!
OOF!
BOUNCE

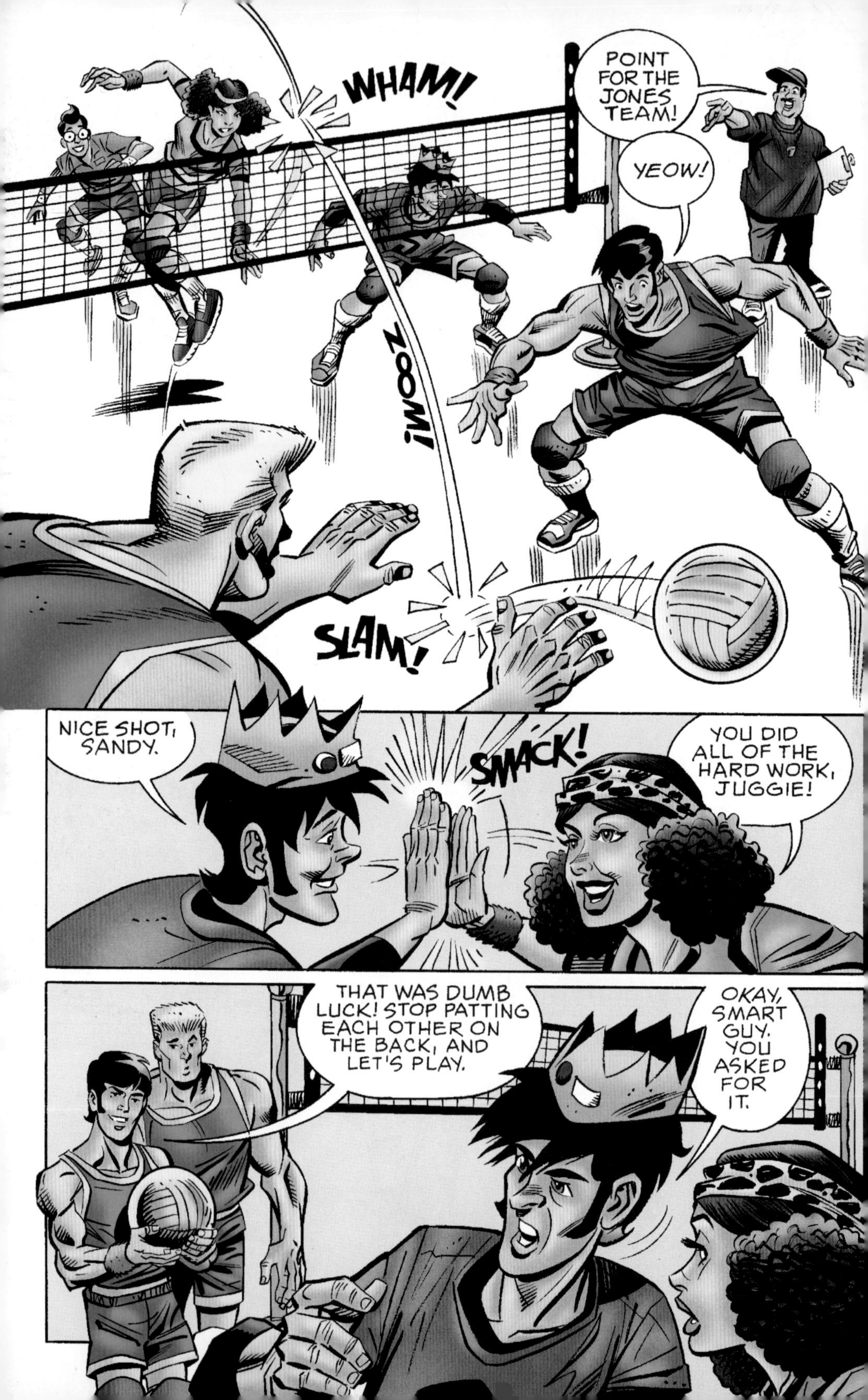
WHAM!
POINT FOR THE JONES TEAM!
YEOW!
ZOOM!
SLAM!
NICE SHOT, SANDY.
SMACK!
YOU DID ALL OF THE HARD WORK, JUGGIE!
THAT WAS DUMB LUCK! STOP PATTING EACH OTHER ON THE BACK, AND LET'S PLAY.
OKAY, SMART GUY. YOU ASKED FOR IT.

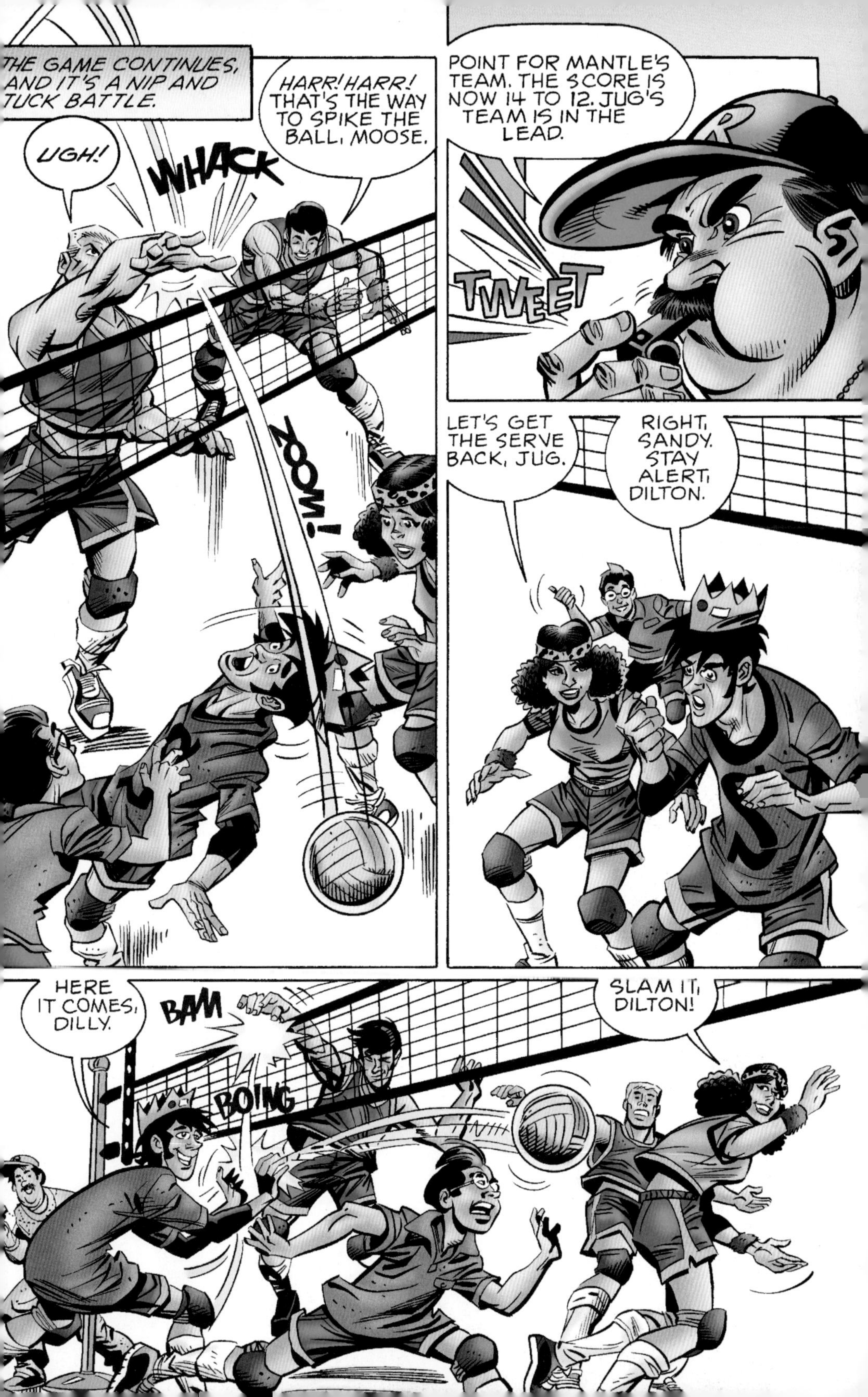

THE GAME CONTINUES, AND IT'S A NIP AND TUCK BATTLE.
UGH!
HARR! HARR! THAT'S THE WAY TO SPIKE THE BALL, MOOSE.
WHACK
ZOOM!
POINT FOR MANTLE'S TEAM. THE SCORE IS NOW 14 TO 12. JUG'S TEAM IS IN THE LEAD.
TWEET
LET'S GET THE SERVE BACK, JUG.
RIGHT, SANDY. STAY ALERT, DILTON.
HERE IT COMES, DILLY.
BAM
BOING
SLAM IT, DILTON!

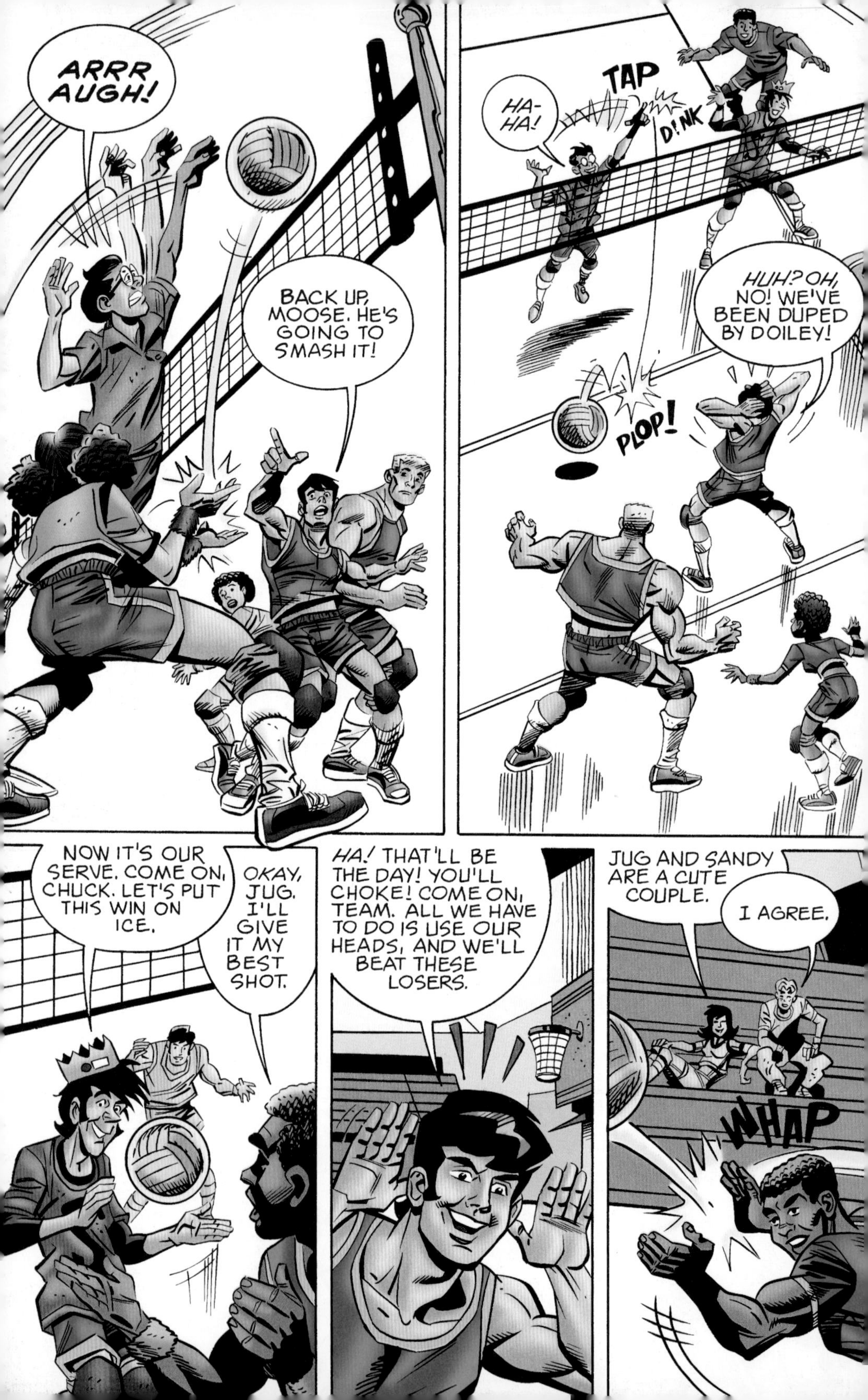
ARRR AUGH!
BACK UP, MOOSE. HE'S GOING TO SMASH IT!
TAP
HA-HA!
DINK
HUH? OH, NO! WE'VE BEEN DUPED BY DOILEY!
PLOP!
NOW IT'S OUR SERVE. COME ON, CHUCK. LET'S PUT THIS WIN ON ICE.
OKAY, JUG. I'LL GIVE IT MY BEST SHOT.
HA! THAT'LL BE THE DAY! YOU'LL CHOKE! COME ON, TEAM. ALL WE HAVE TO DO IS USE OUR HEADS, AND WE'LL BEAT THESE LOSERS.
JUG AND SANDY ARE A CUTE COUPLE.
I AGREE.
WHAP

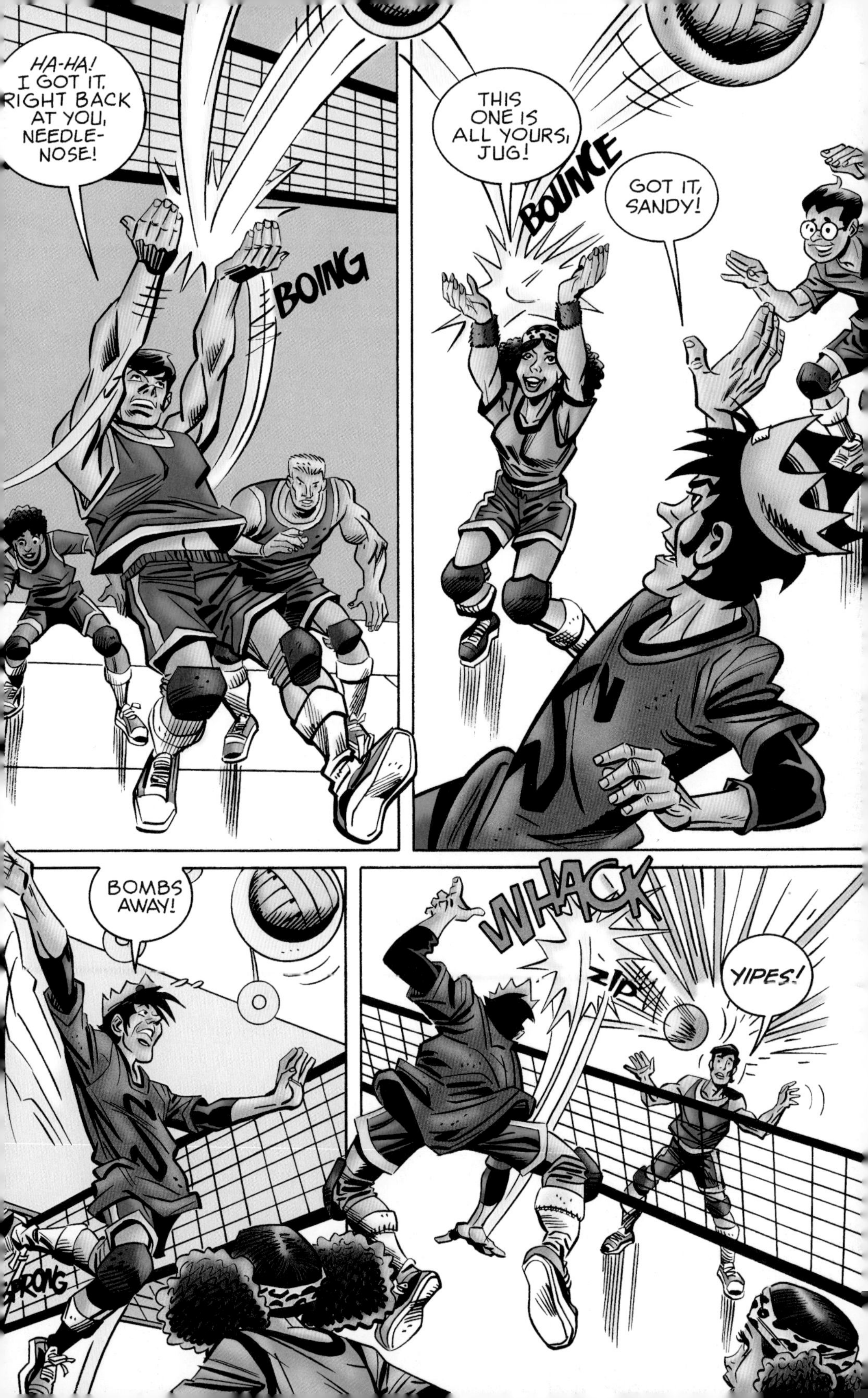
HA-HA! I GOT IT. RIGHT BACK AT YOU, NEEDLE-NOSE!
BOING
THIS ONE IS ALL YOURS, JUG!
BOUNCE
GOT IT, SANDY!
BOMBS AWAY!
SPRONG
WHACK
ZIP
YIPES!

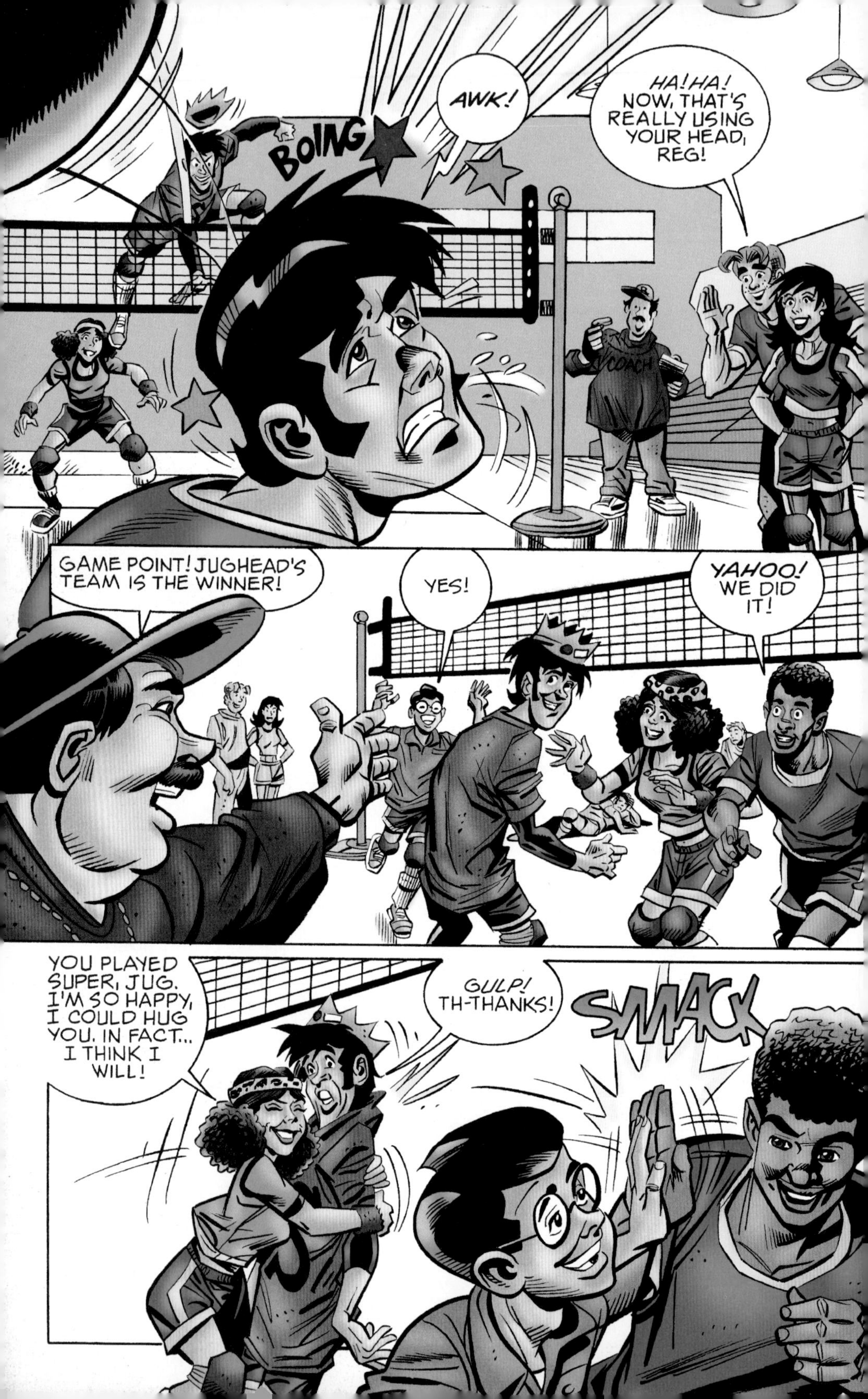
BOING
AWK!
HA! HA! NOW, THAT'S REALLY USING YOUR HEAD, REG!
COACH
GAME POINT! JUGHEAD'S TEAM IS THE WINNER!
YES!
YAHOO! WE DID IT!
YOU PLAYED SUPER, JUG. I'M SO HAPPY, I COULD HUG YOU. IN FACT... I THINK I WILL!
GULP! TH-THANKS!
SMACK

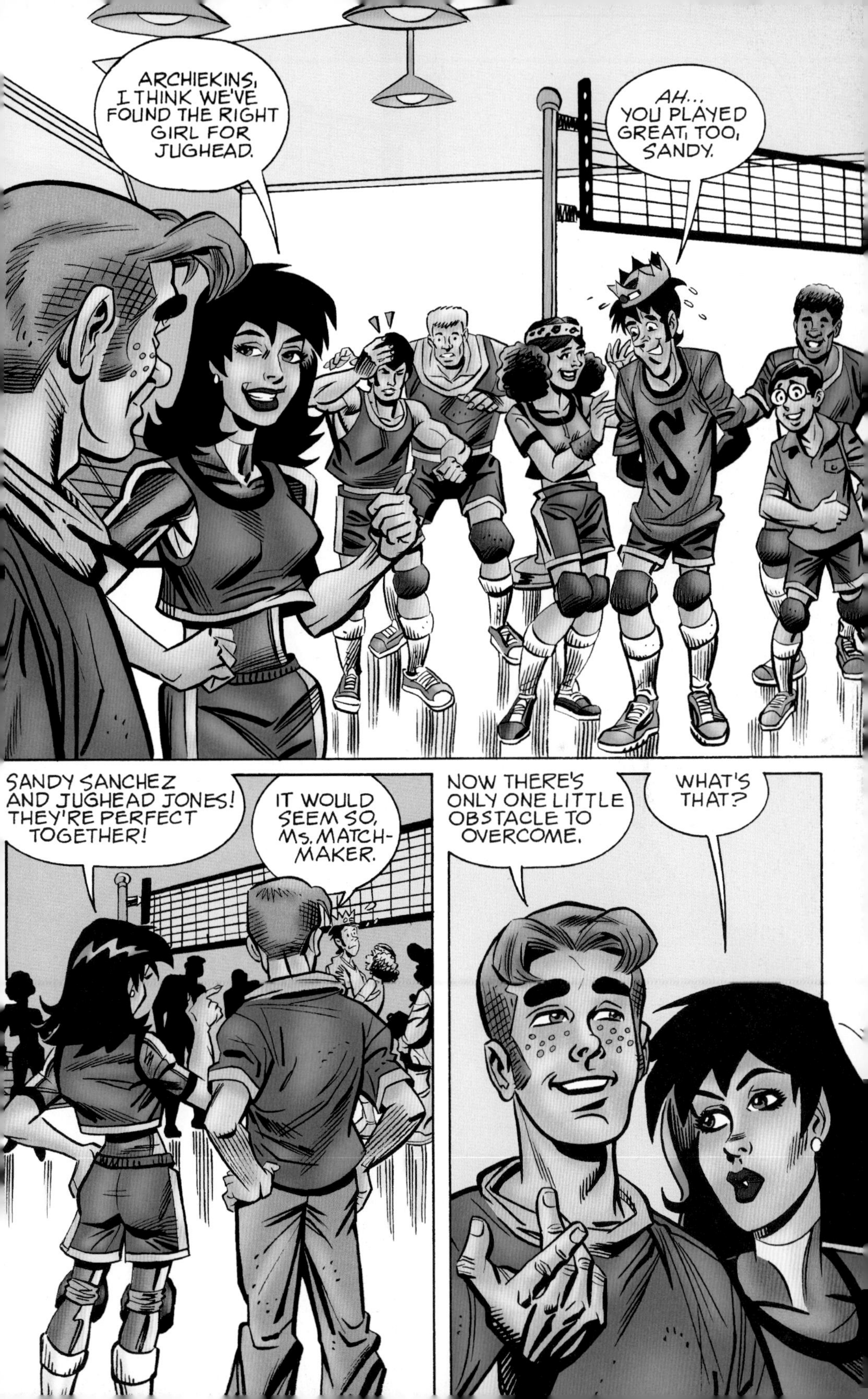
ARCHIEKINS, I THINK WE'VE FOUND THE RIGHT GIRL FOR JUGHEAD.
AH... YOU PLAYED GREAT, TOO, SANDY.
SANDY SANCHEZ AND JUGHEAD JONES! THEY'RE PERFECT TOGETHER!
IT WOULD SEEM SO, Ms. MATCH-MAKER.
NOW THERE'S ONLY ONE LITTLE OBSTACLE TO OVERCOME.
WHAT'S THAT?

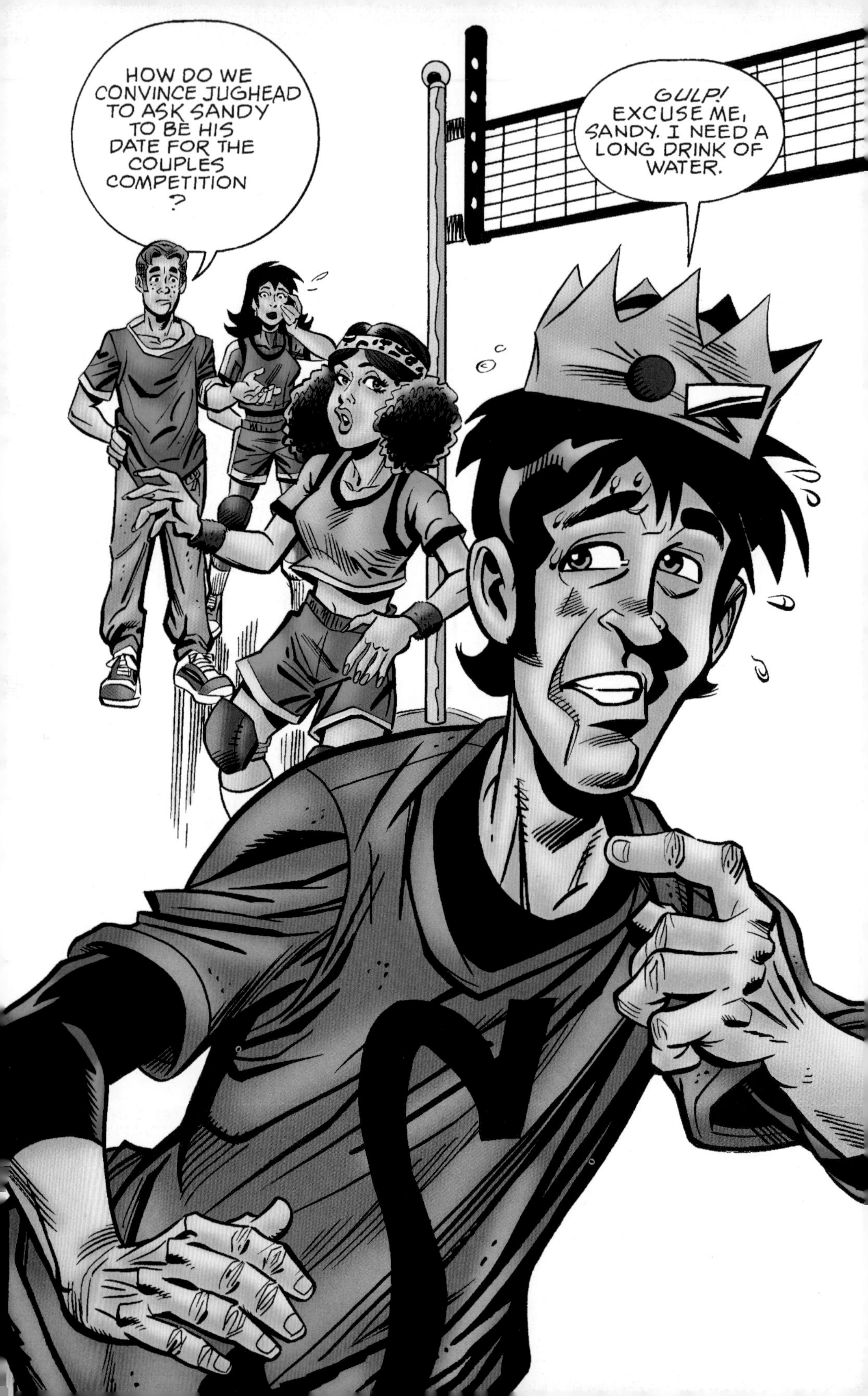
HOW DO WE CONVINCE JUGHEAD TO ASK SANDY TO BE HIS DATE FOR THE COUPLES COMPETITION ?
GULP! EXCUSE ME, SANDY. I NEED A LONG DRINK OF WATER.

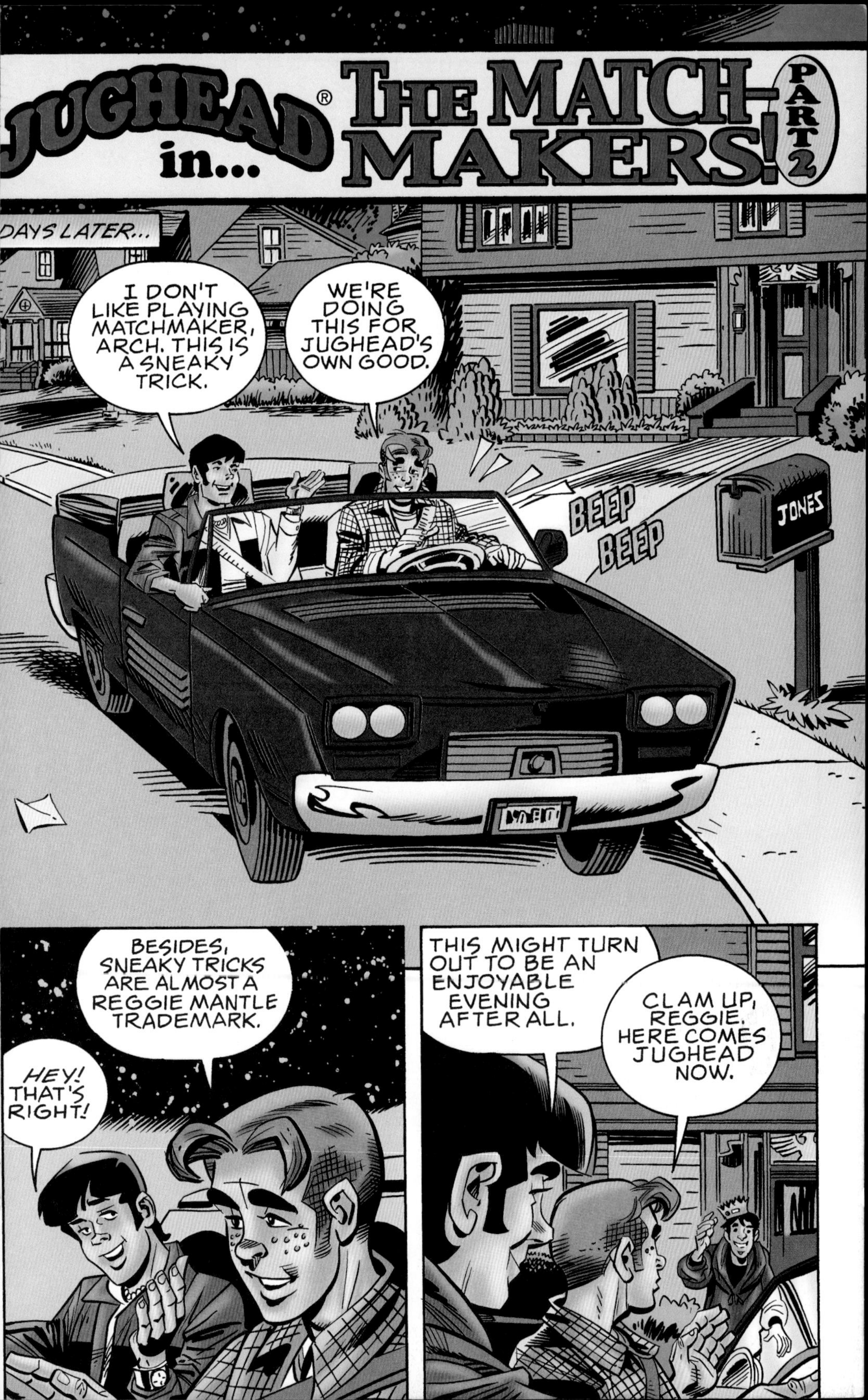
JUGHEAD® in...
THE MATCH-MAKERS! PART 2
DAYS LATER...
I DON'T LIKE PLAYING MATCHMAKER, ARCH. THIS IS A SNEAKY TRICK.
WE'RE DOING THIS FOR JUGHEAD'S OWN GOOD.
BEEP BEEP
JONES
BESIDES, SNEAKY TRICKS ARE ALMOST A REGGIE MANTLE TRADEMARK.
HEY! THAT'S RIGHT!
THIS MIGHT TURN OUT TO BE AN ENJOYABLE EVENING AFTER ALL.
CLAM UP, REGGIE. HERE COMES JUGHEAD NOW.

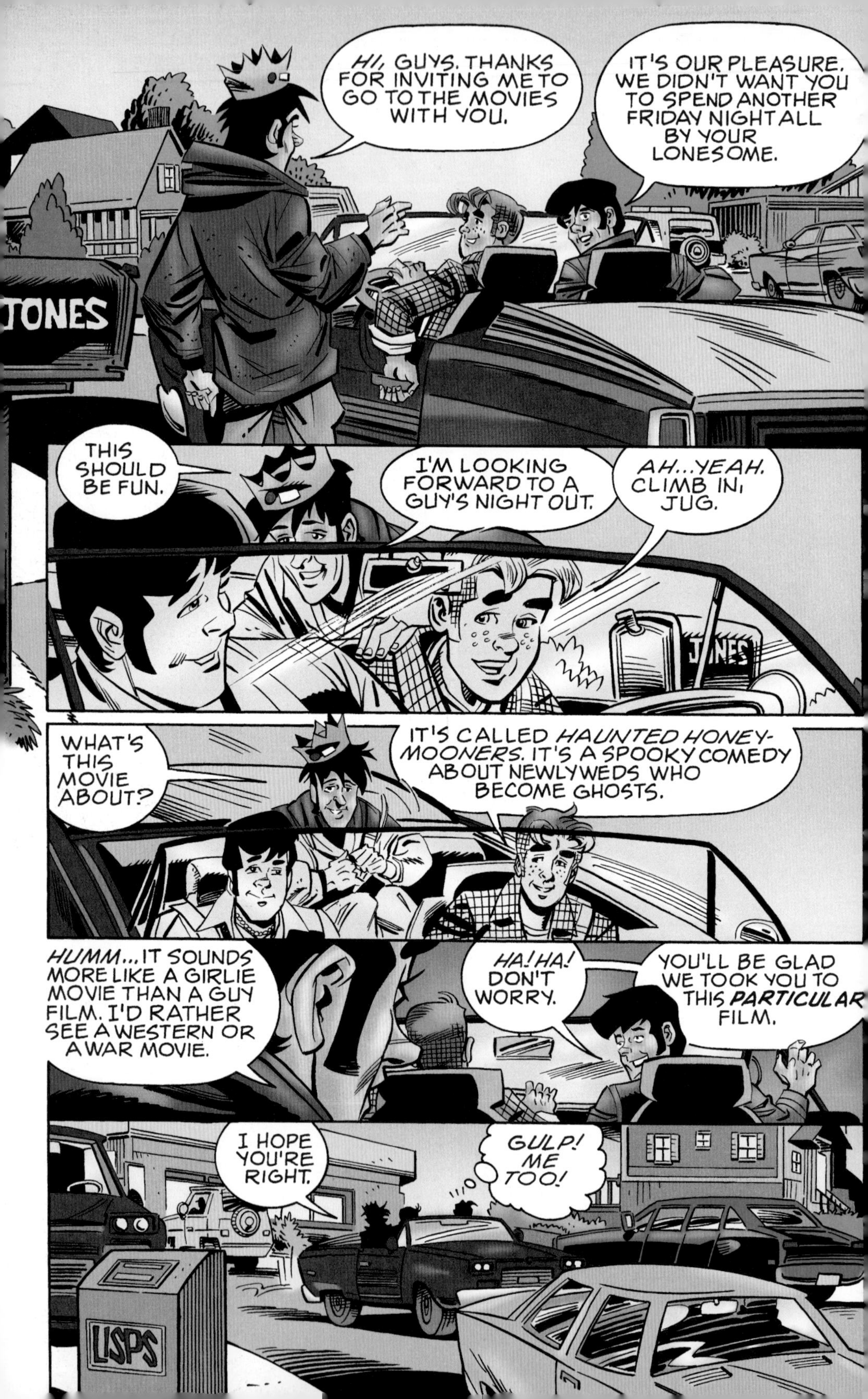
HI, GUYS. THANKS FOR INVITING ME TO GO TO THE MOVIES WITH YOU.
IT'S OUR PLEASURE. WE DIDN'T WANT YOU TO SPEND ANOTHER FRIDAY NIGHT ALL BY YOUR LONESOME.
JONES
THIS SHOULD BE FUN.
I'M LOOKING FORWARD TO A GUY'S NIGHT OUT.
AH...YEAH. CLIMB IN, JUG.
WHAT'S THIS MOVIE ABOUT?
IT'S CALLED HAUNTED HONEY-MOONERS. IT'S A SPOOKY COMEDY ABOUT NEWLYWEDS WHO BECOME GHOSTS.
HUMM... IT SOUNDS MORE LIKE A GIRLIE MOVIE THAN A GUY FILM. I'D RATHER SEE A WESTERN OR A WAR MOVIE.
HA! HA! DON'T WORRY.
YOU'LL BE GLAD WE TOOK YOU TO THIS PARTICULAR FILM.
I HOPE YOU'RE RIGHT.
GULP! ME TOO!
USPS

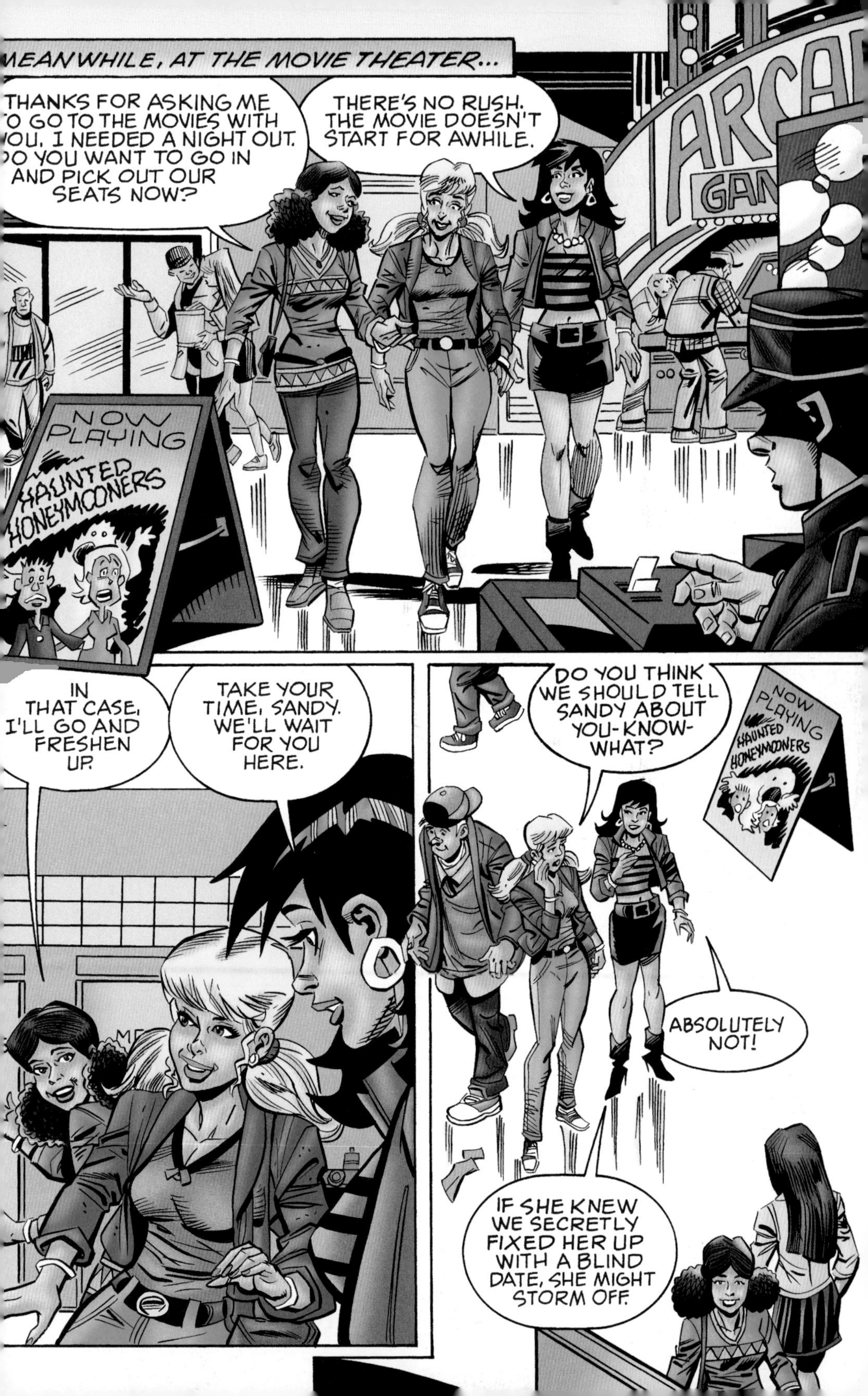
MEANWHILE, AT THE MOVIE THEATER...
THANKS FOR ASKING ME TO GO TO THE MOVIES WITH YOU. I NEEDED A NIGHT OUT. DO YOU WANT TO GO IN AND PICK OUT OUR SEATS NOW?
THERE'S NO RUSH. THE MOVIE DOESN'T START FOR AWHILE.
ARCADE GAMES
NOW PLAYING HAUNTED HONEYMOONERS
IN THAT CASE, I'LL GO AND FRESHEN UP.
TAKE YOUR TIME, SANDY. WE'LL WAIT FOR YOU HERE.
DO YOU THINK WE SHOULD TELL SANDY ABOUT YOU-KNOW-WHAT?
NOW PLAYING HAUNTED HONEYMOONERS
ABSOLUTELY NOT!
IF SHE KNEW WE SECRETLY FIXED HER UP WITH A BLIND DATE, SHE MIGHT STORM OFF.

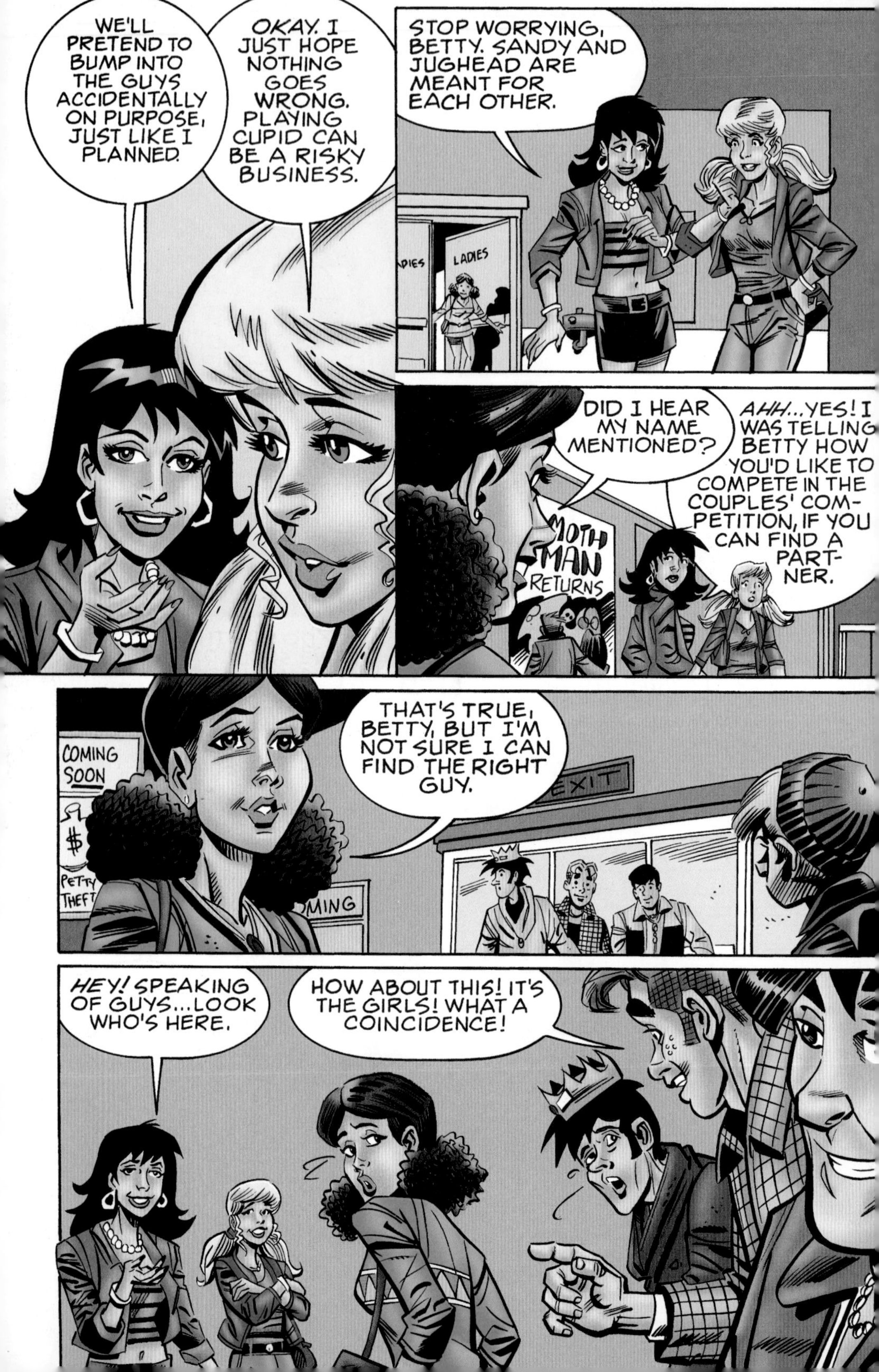
WE'LL PRETEND TO BUMP INTO THE GUYS ACCIDENTALLY ON PURPOSE, JUST LIKE I PLANNED.
OKAY. I JUST HOPE NOTHING GOES WRONG. PLAYING CUPID CAN BE A RISKY BUSINESS.
STOP WORRYING, BETTY. SANDY AND JUGHEAD ARE MEANT FOR EACH OTHER.
LADIES
DID I HEAR MY NAME MENTIONED?
AHH...YES! I WAS TELLING BETTY HOW YOU'D LIKE TO COMPETE IN THE COUPLES' COMPETITION, IF YOU CAN FIND A PARTNER.
MOTH MAN RETURNS
THAT'S TRUE, BETTY, BUT I'M NOT SURE I CAN FIND THE RIGHT GUY.
COMING SOON
PET-TY THEFT
EXIT
HEY! SPEAKING OF GUYS...LOOK WHO'S HERE.
HOW ABOUT THIS! IT'S THE GIRLS! WHAT A COINCIDENCE!

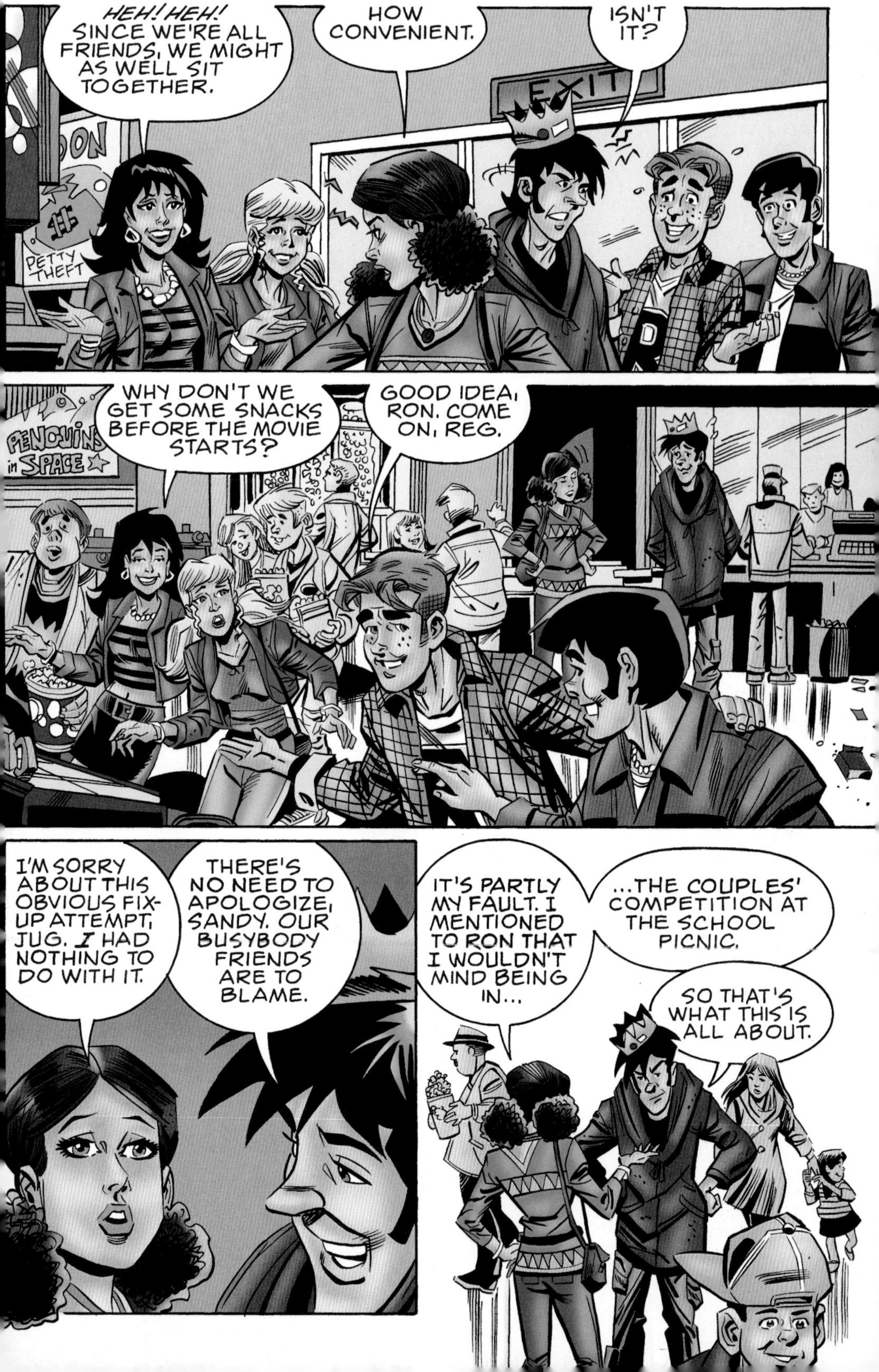
HEH! HEH! SINCE WE'RE ALL FRIENDS, WE MIGHT AS WELL SIT TOGETHER.
HOW CONVENIENT.
ISN'T IT?
EXIT
PETTY THEFT
WHY DON'T WE GET SOME SNACKS BEFORE THE MOVIE STARTS?
GOOD IDEA, RON. COME ON, REG.
PENGUINS in SPACE
I'M SORRY ABOUT THIS OBVIOUS FIX-UP ATTEMPT, JUG. I HAD NOTHING TO DO WITH IT.
THERE'S NO NEED TO APOLOGIZE, SANDY. OUR BUSYBODY FRIENDS ARE TO BLAME.
IT'S PARTLY MY FAULT. I MENTIONED TO RON THAT I WOULDN'T MIND BEING IN...
...THE COUPLES' COMPETITION AT THE SCHOOL PICNIC.
SO THAT'S WHAT THIS IS ALL ABOUT.

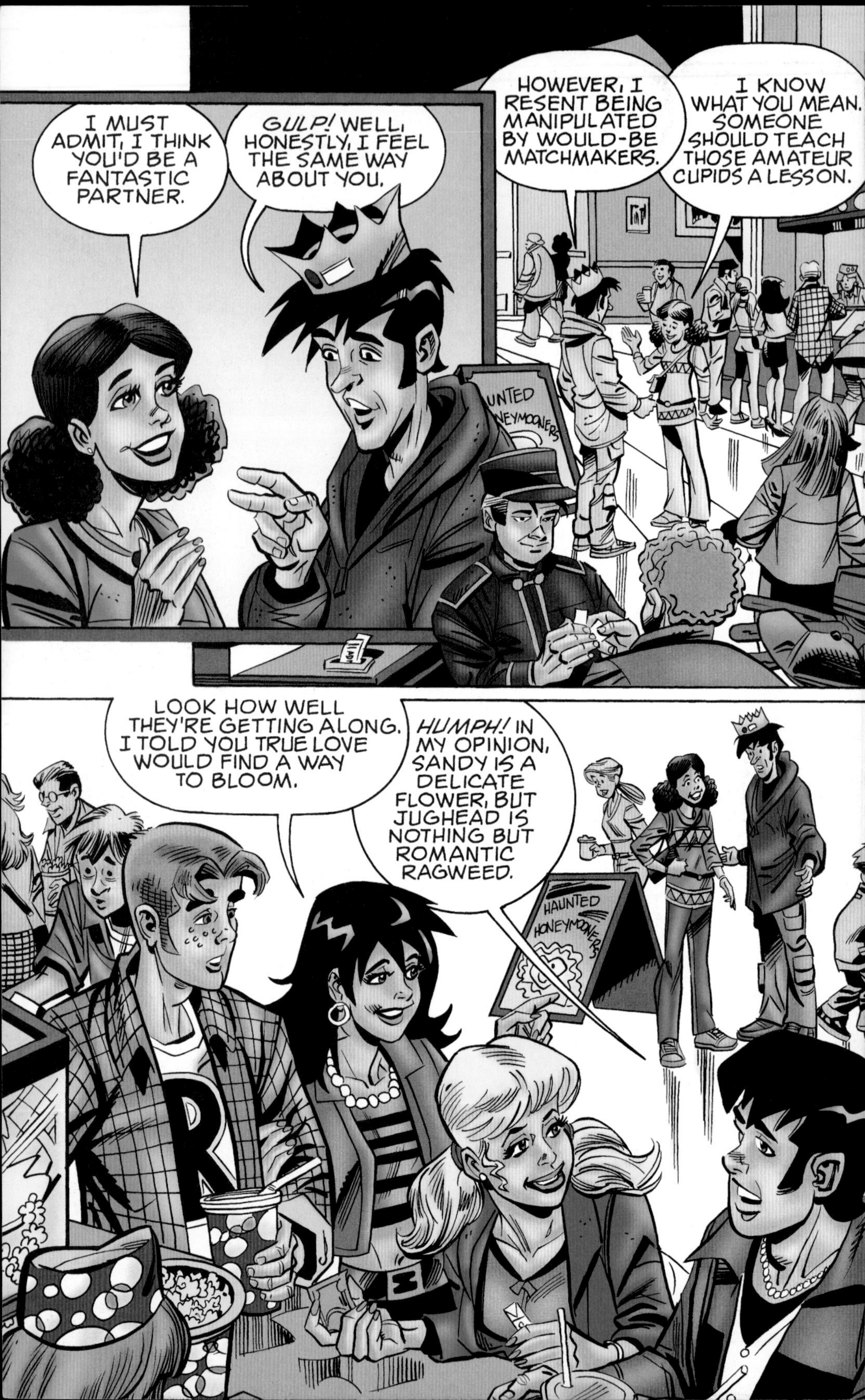
I MUST ADMIT, I THINK YOU'D BE A FANTASTIC PARTNER.
GULP! WELL, HONESTLY, I FEEL THE SAME WAY ABOUT YOU.
HOWEVER, I RESENT BEING MANIPULATED BY WOULD-BE MATCHMAKERS.
I KNOW WHAT YOU MEAN. SOMEONE SHOULD TEACH THOSE AMATEUR CUPIDS A LESSON.
UNTED
NEYMOONERS
LOOK HOW WELL THEY'RE GETTING ALONG. I TOLD YOU TRUE LOVE WOULD FIND A WAY TO BLOOM.
HUMPH! IN MY OPINION, SANDY IS A DELICATE FLOWER, BUT JUGHEAD IS NOTHING BUT ROMANTIC RAGWEED.
HAUNTED HONEYMOONERS

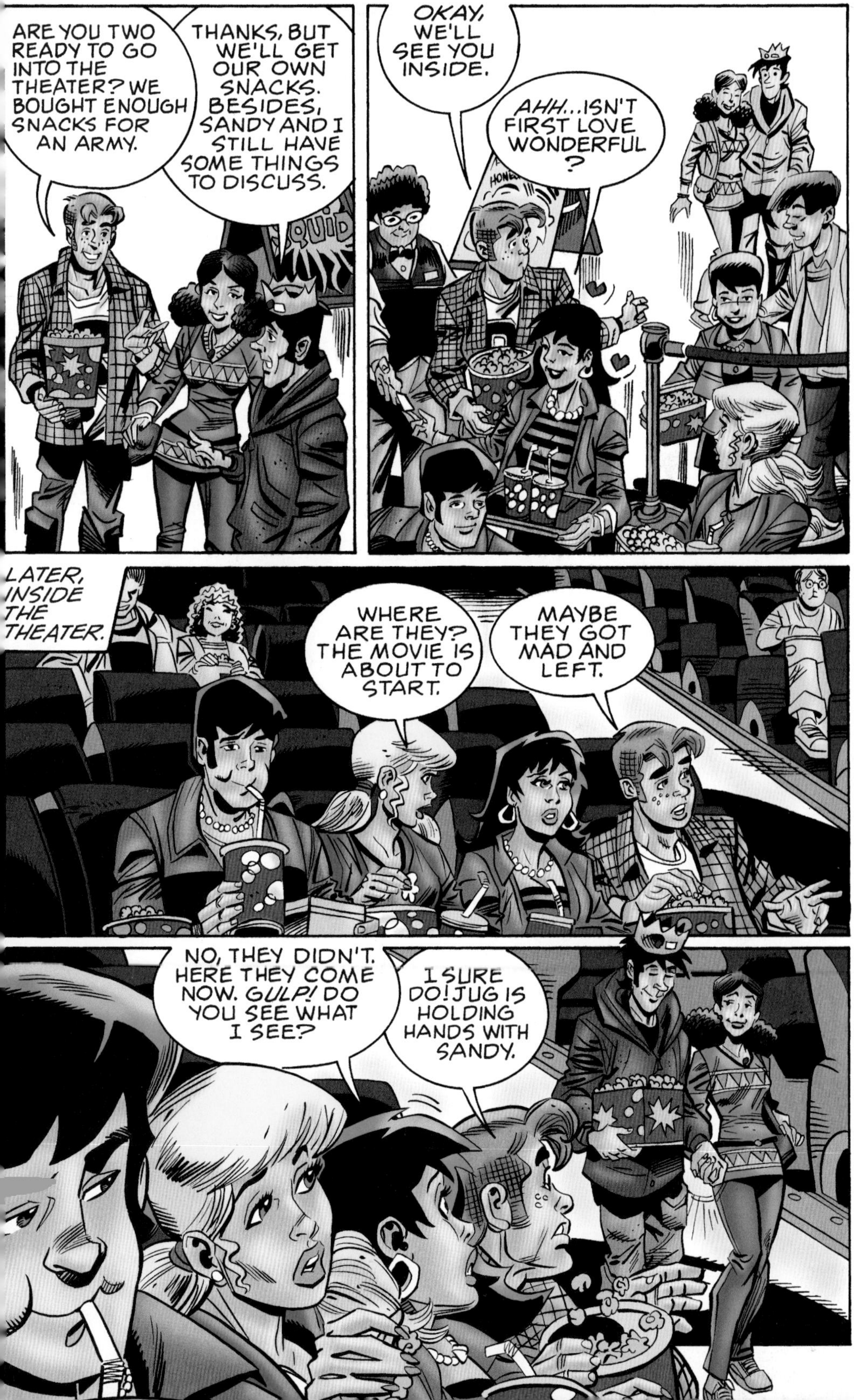
ARE YOU TWO READY TO GO INTO THE THEATER? WE BOUGHT ENOUGH SNACKS FOR AN ARMY.
THANKS, BUT WE'LL GET OUR OWN SNACKS. BESIDES, SANDY AND I STILL HAVE SOME THINGS TO DISCUSS.
OKAY, WE'LL SEE YOU INSIDE.
AHH...ISN'T FIRST LOVE WONDERFUL?
LATER, INSIDE THE THEATER.
WHERE ARE THEY? THE MOVIE IS ABOUT TO START.
MAYBE THEY GOT MAD AND LEFT.
NO, THEY DIDN'T. HERE THEY COME NOW. GULP! DO YOU SEE WHAT I SEE?
I SURE DO! JUG IS HOLDING HANDS WITH SANDY.

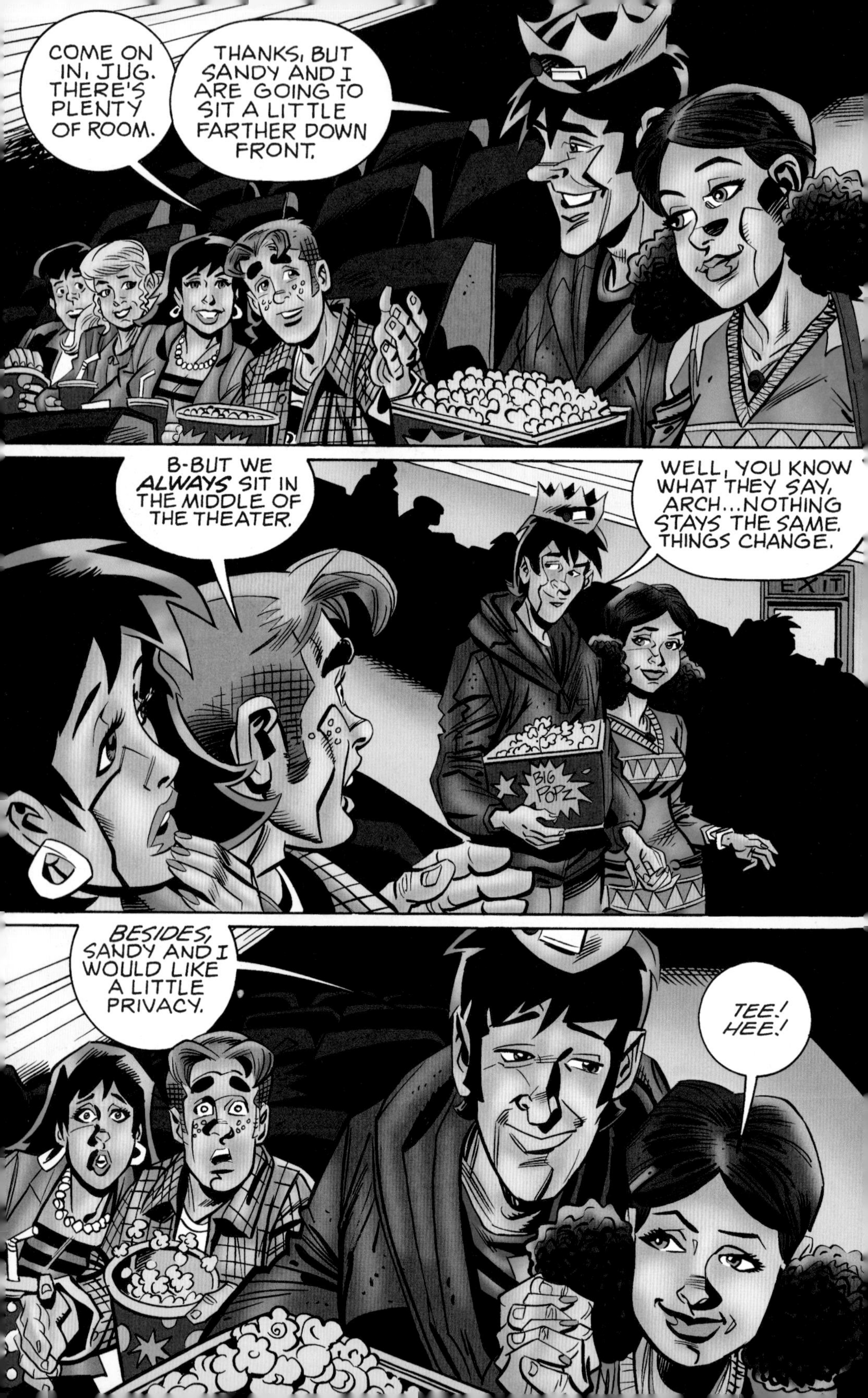
COME ON IN, JUG. THERE'S PLENTY OF ROOM.
THANKS, BUT SANDY AND I ARE GOING TO SIT A LITTLE FARTHER DOWN FRONT.
B-BUT WE *ALWAYS* SIT IN THE MIDDLE OF THE THEATER.
WELL, YOU KNOW WHAT THEY SAY, ARCH...NOTHING STAYS THE SAME. THINGS CHANGE.
EXIT
BIG POPZ
BESIDES, SANDY AND I WOULD LIKE A LITTLE PRIVACY.
TEE! HEE!

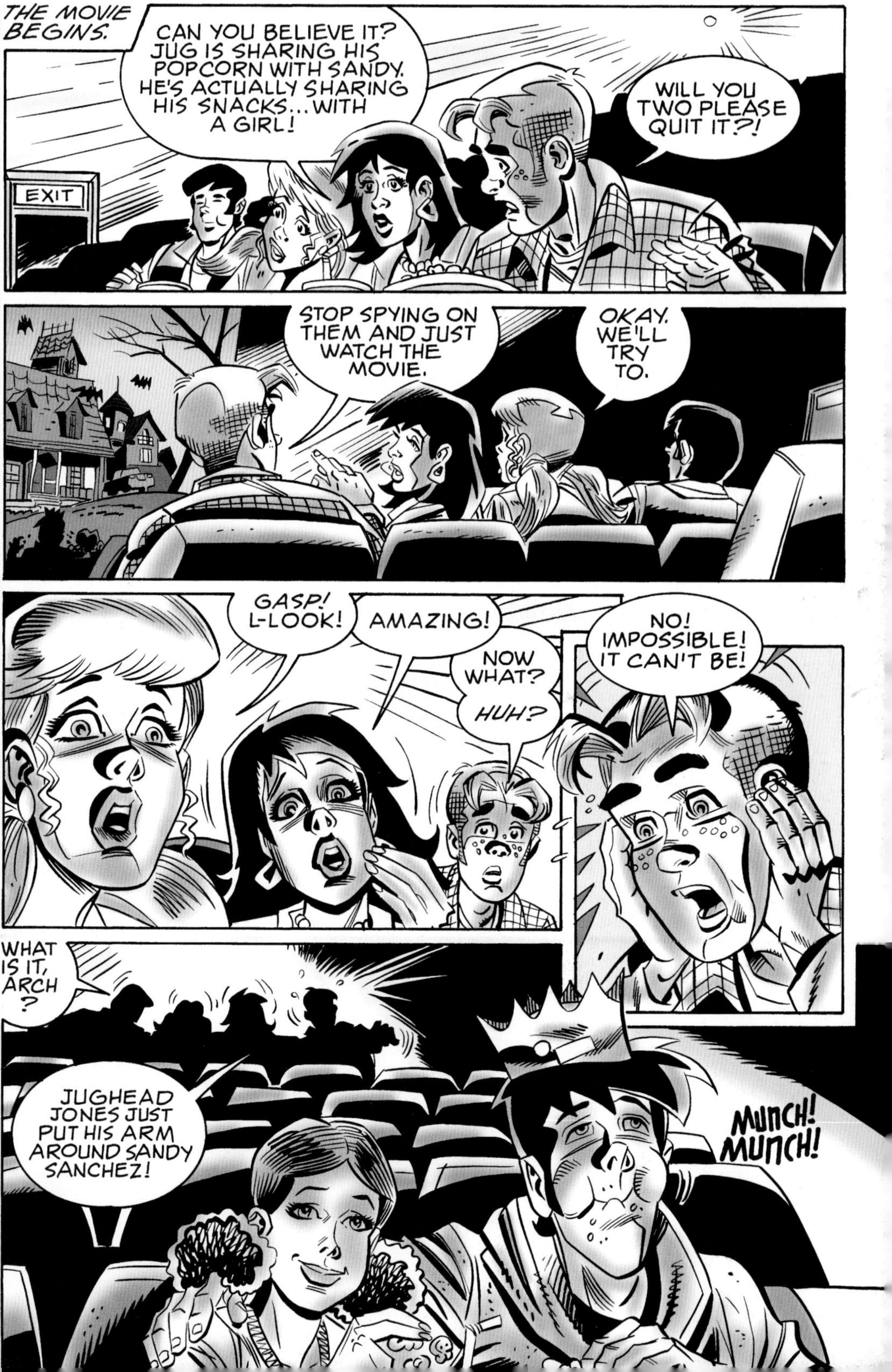
THE MOVIE BEGINS.
CAN YOU BELIEVE IT? JUG IS SHARING HIS POPCORN WITH SANDY. HE'S ACTUALLY SHARING HIS SNACKS... WITH A GIRL!
WILL YOU TWO PLEASE QUIT IT?!
EXIT
STOP SPYING ON THEM AND JUST WATCH THE MOVIE.
OKAY. WE'LL TRY TO.
GASP! L-LOOK!
AMAZING!
NOW WHAT?
HUH?
NO! IMPOSSIBLE! IT CAN'T BE!
WHAT IS IT, ARCH?
JUGHEAD JONES JUST PUT HIS ARM AROUND SANDY SANCHEZ!
MUNCH! MUNCH!

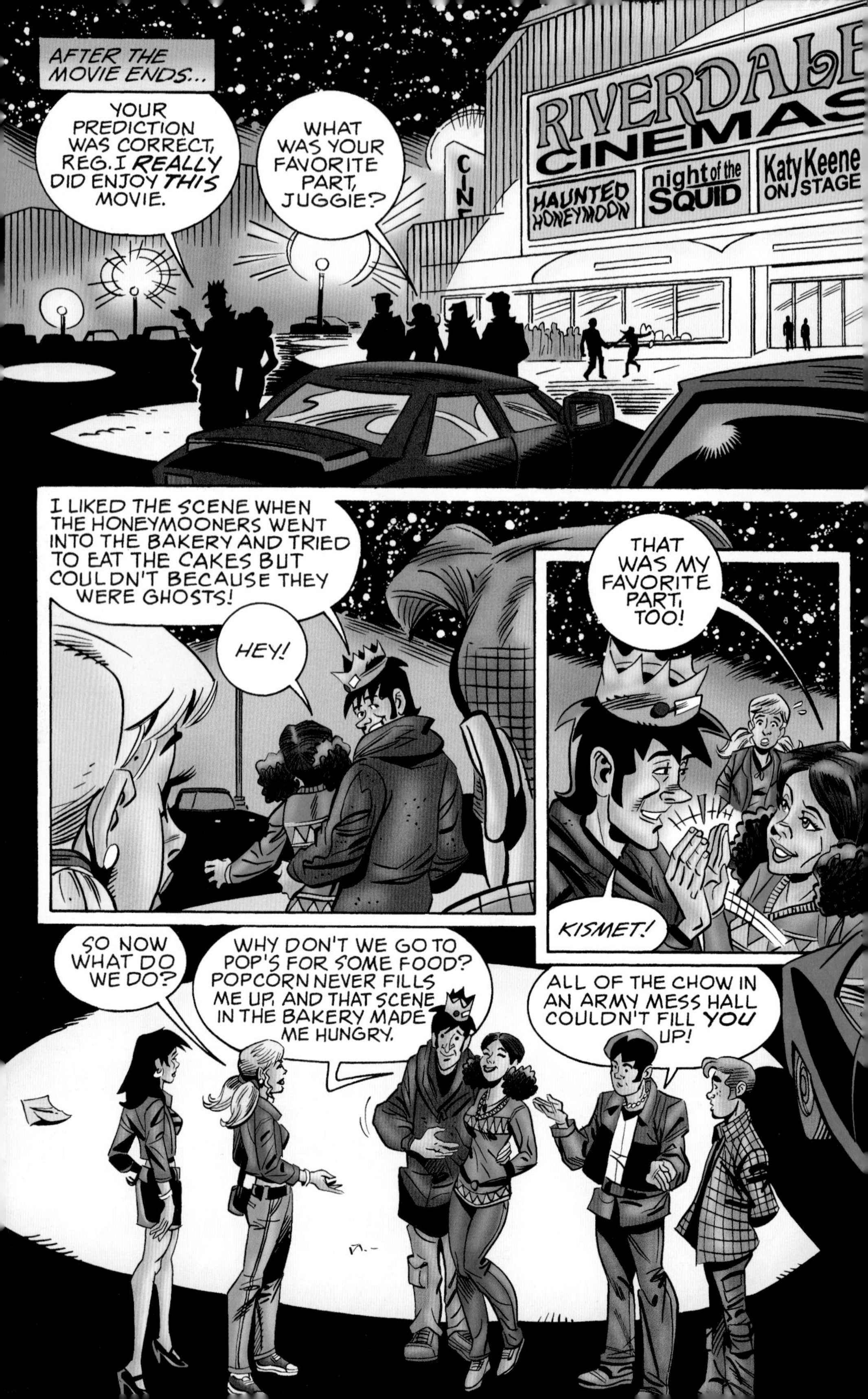
AFTER THE MOVIE ENDS...
YOUR PREDICTION WAS CORRECT, REG. I REALLY DID ENJOY THIS MOVIE.
WHAT WAS YOUR FAVORITE PART, JUGGIE?
RIVERDALE CINEMAS
HAUNTED HONEYMOON
night of the SQUID
Katy Keene ON STAGE
I LIKED THE SCENE WHEN THE HONEYMOONERS WENT INTO THE BAKERY AND TRIED TO EAT THE CAKES BUT COULDN'T BECAUSE THEY WERE GHOSTS!
HEY!
THAT WAS MY FAVORITE PART, TOO!
KISMET!
SO NOW WHAT DO WE DO?
WHY DON'T WE GO TO POP'S FOR SOME FOOD? POPCORN NEVER FILLS ME UP, AND THAT SCENE IN THE BAKERY MADE ME HUNGRY.
ALL OF THE CHOW IN AN ARMY MESS HALL COULDN'T FILL YOU UP!

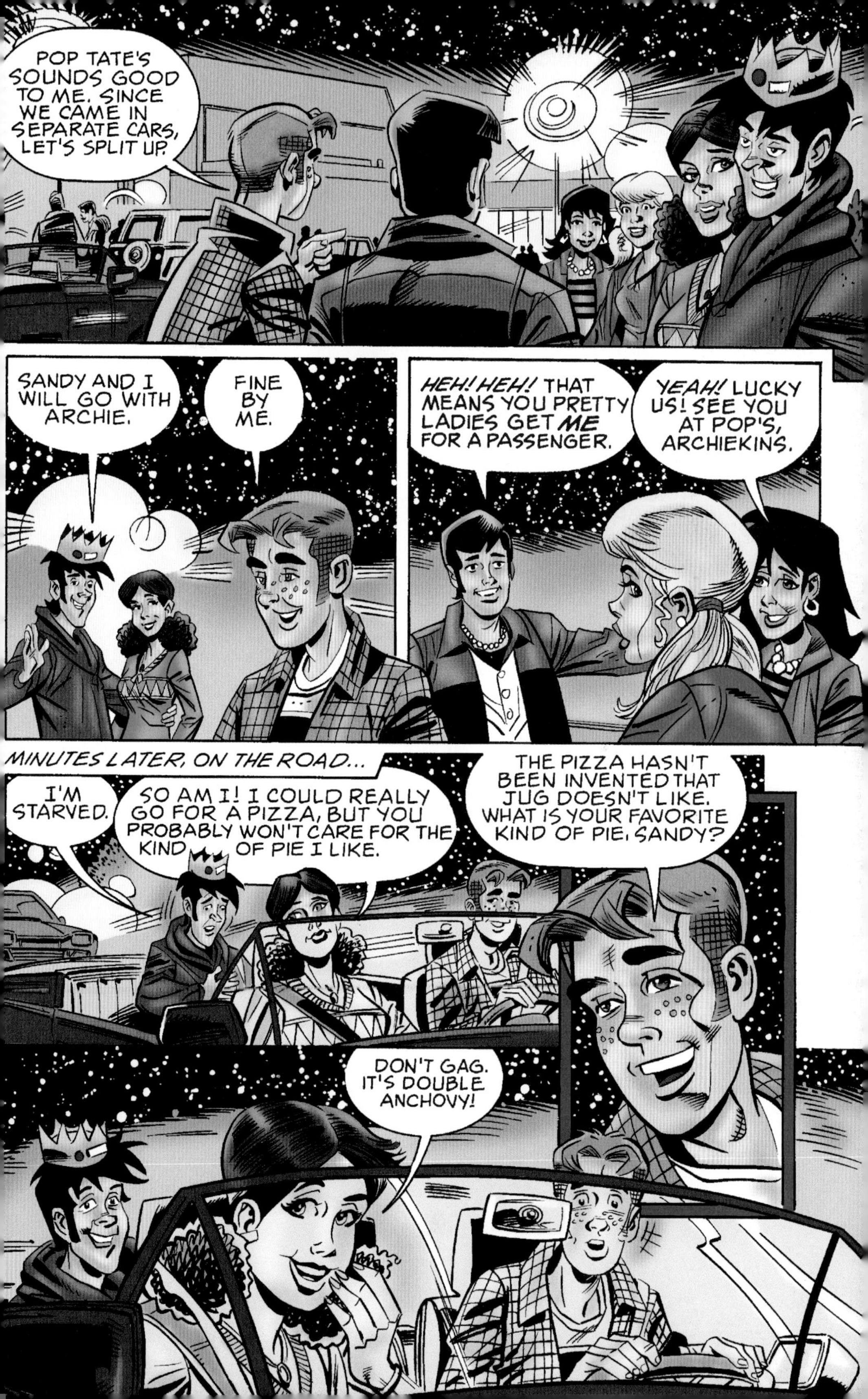
POP TATE'S SOUNDS GOOD TO ME. SINCE WE CAME IN SEPARATE CARS, LET'S SPLIT UP.
SANDY AND I WILL GO WITH ARCHIE.
FINE BY ME.
HEH! HEH! THAT MEANS YOU PRETTY LADIES GET ME FOR A PASSENGER.
YEAH! LUCKY US! SEE YOU AT POP'S, ARCHIEKINS.
MINUTES LATER, ON THE ROAD...
I'M STARVED.
SO AM I! I COULD REALLY GO FOR A PIZZA, BUT YOU PROBABLY WON'T CARE FOR THE KIND OF PIE I LIKE.
THE PIZZA HASN'T BEEN INVENTED THAT JUG DOESN'T LIKE. WHAT IS YOUR FAVORITE KIND OF PIE, SANDY?
DON'T GAG. IT'S DOUBLE ANCHOVY!

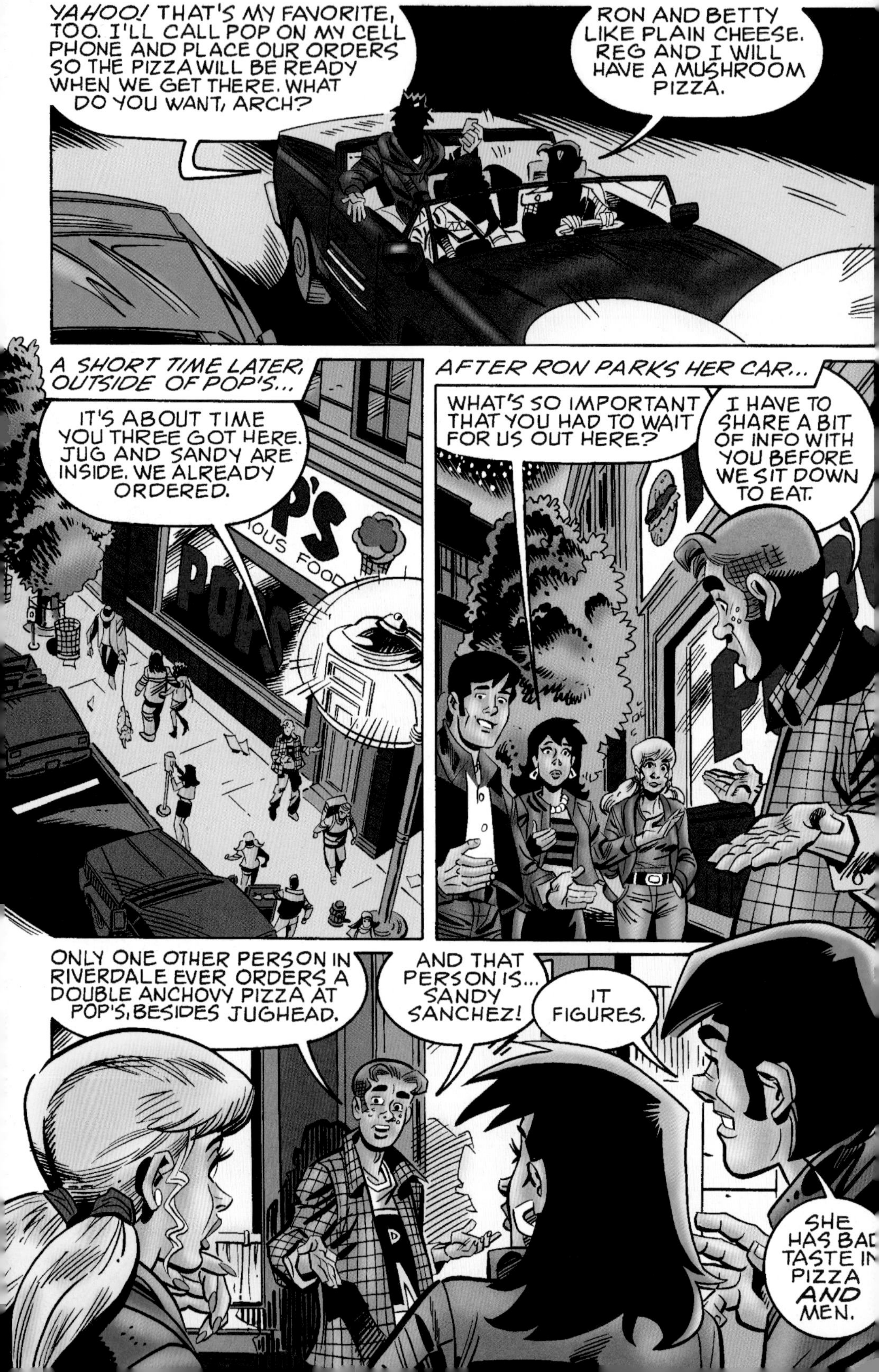
YAHOO! THAT'S MY FAVORITE, TOO. I'LL CALL POP ON MY CELL PHONE AND PLACE OUR ORDERS SO THE PIZZA WILL BE READY WHEN WE GET THERE. WHAT DO YOU WANT, ARCH?
RON AND BETTY LIKE PLAIN CHEESE. REG AND I WILL HAVE A MUSHROOM PIZZA.
A SHORT TIME LATER, OUTSIDE OF POP'S...
IT'S ABOUT TIME YOU THREE GOT HERE. JUG AND SANDY ARE INSIDE. WE ALREADY ORDERED.
AFTER RON PARKS HER CAR...
WHAT'S SO IMPORTANT THAT YOU HAD TO WAIT FOR US OUT HERE?
I HAVE TO SHARE A BIT OF INFO WITH YOU BEFORE WE SIT DOWN TO EAT.
ONLY ONE OTHER PERSON IN RIVERDALE EVER ORDERS A DOUBLE ANCHOVY PIZZA AT POP'S, BESIDES JUGHEAD.
AND THAT PERSON IS... SANDY SANCHEZ!
IT FIGURES.
SHE HAS BAD TASTE IN PIZZA AND MEN.

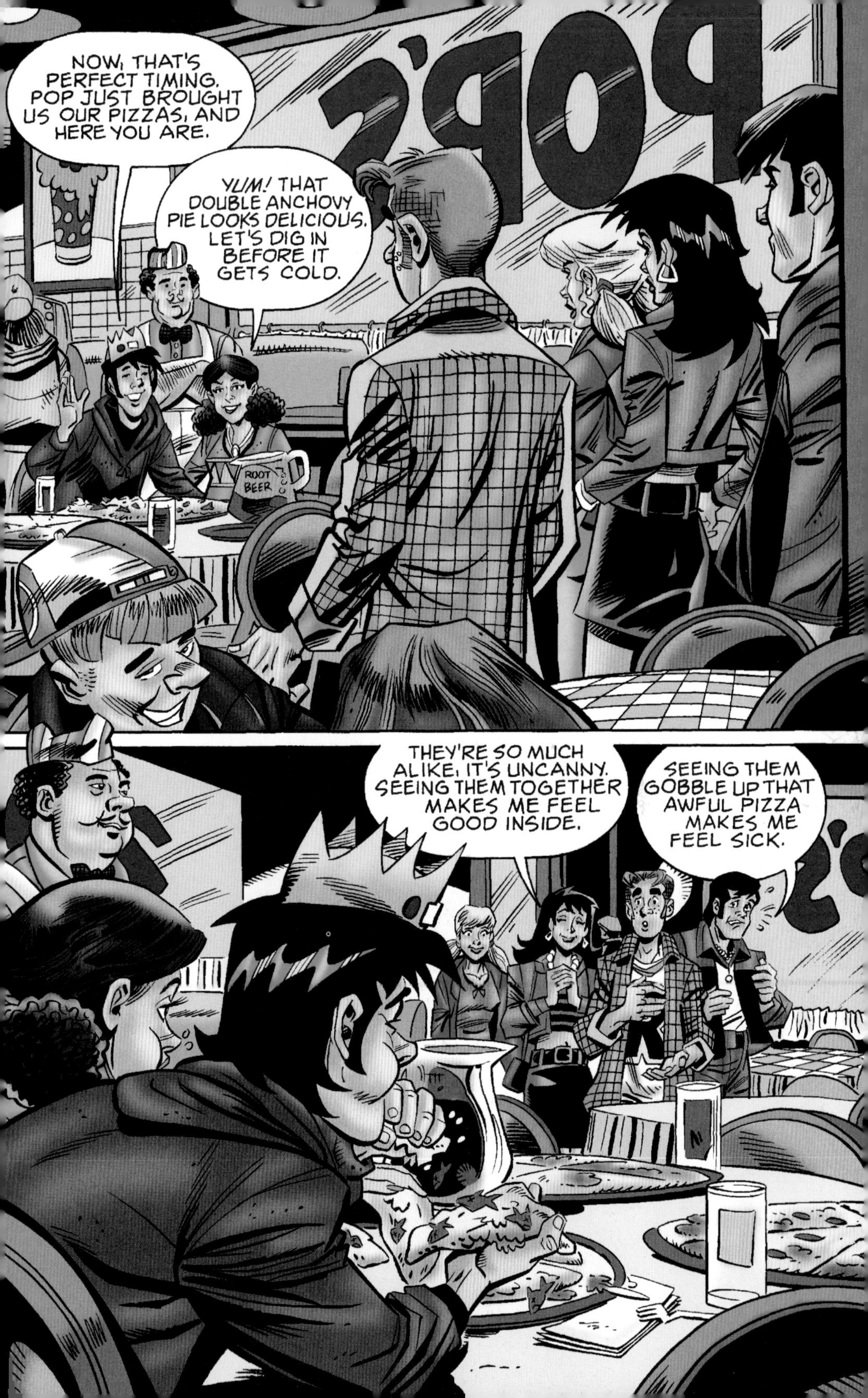
NOW, THAT'S PERFECT TIMING. POP JUST BROUGHT US OUR PIZZAS, AND HERE YOU ARE.
YUM! THAT DOUBLE ANCHOVY PIE LOOKS DELICIOUS. LET'S DIG IN BEFORE IT GETS COLD.
ROOT BEER
THEY'RE SO MUCH ALIKE, IT'S UNCANNY. SEEING THEM TOGETHER MAKES ME FEEL GOOD INSIDE.
SEEING THEM GOBBLE UP THAT AWFUL PIZZA MAKES ME FEEL SICK.

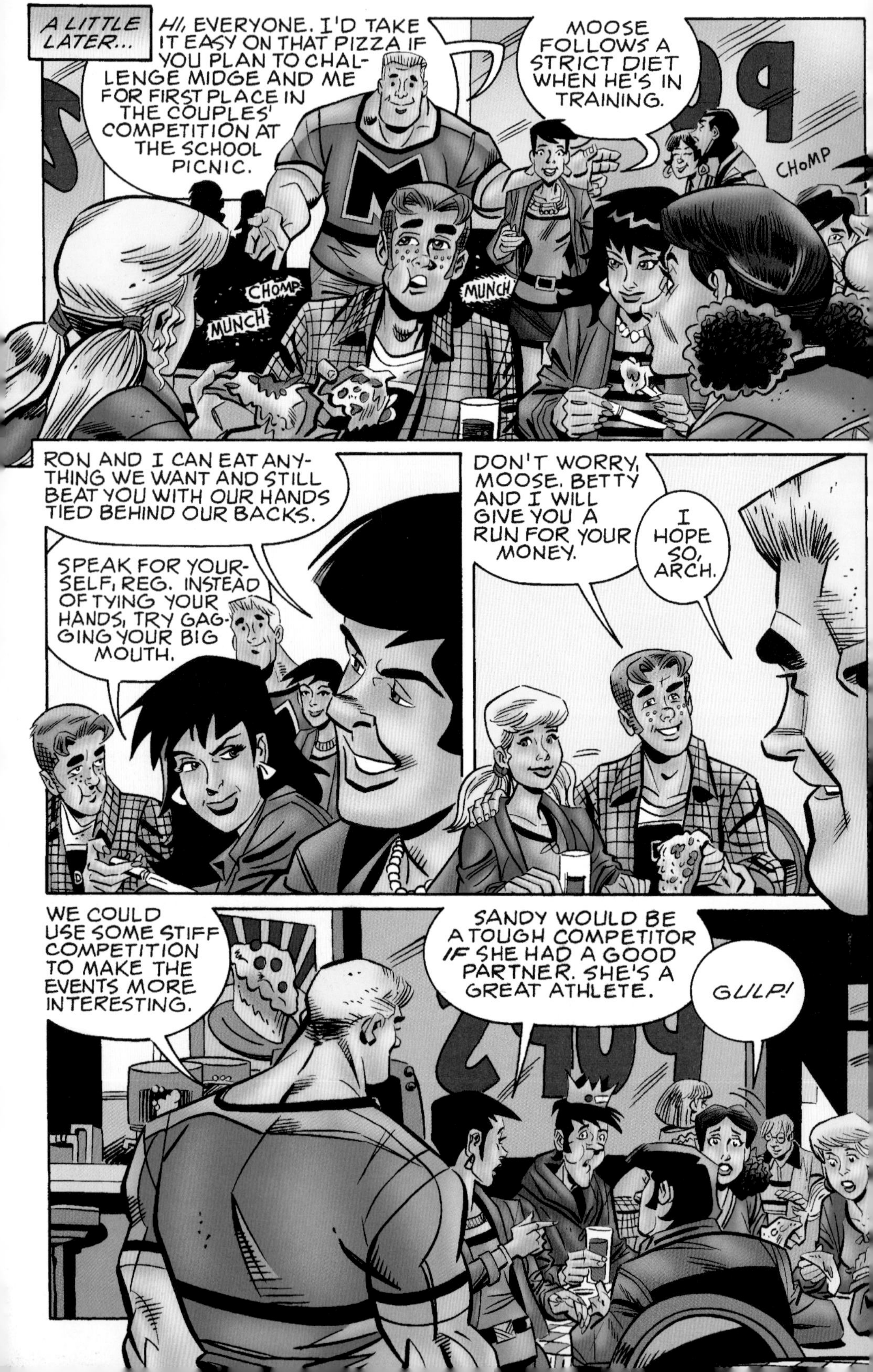
A LITTLE LATER...
HI, EVERYONE. I'D TAKE IT EASY ON THAT PIZZA IF YOU PLAN TO CHALLENGE MIDGE AND ME FOR FIRST PLACE IN THE COUPLES' COMPETITION AT THE SCHOOL PICNIC.
MOOSE FOLLOWS A STRICT DIET WHEN HE'S IN TRAINING.
CHOMP
MUNCH
MUNCH
CHOMP
RON AND I CAN EAT ANYTHING WE WANT AND STILL BEAT YOU WITH OUR HANDS TIED BEHIND OUR BACKS.
SPEAK FOR YOURSELF, REG. INSTEAD OF TYING YOUR HANDS, TRY GAGGING YOUR BIG MOUTH.
DON'T WORRY, MOOSE. BETTY AND I WILL GIVE YOU A RUN FOR YOUR MONEY.
I HOPE SO, ARCH.
WE COULD USE SOME STIFF COMPETITION TO MAKE THE EVENTS MORE INTERESTING.
SANDY WOULD BE A TOUGH COMPETITOR IF SHE HAD A GOOD PARTNER. SHE'S A GREAT ATHLETE.
GULP!

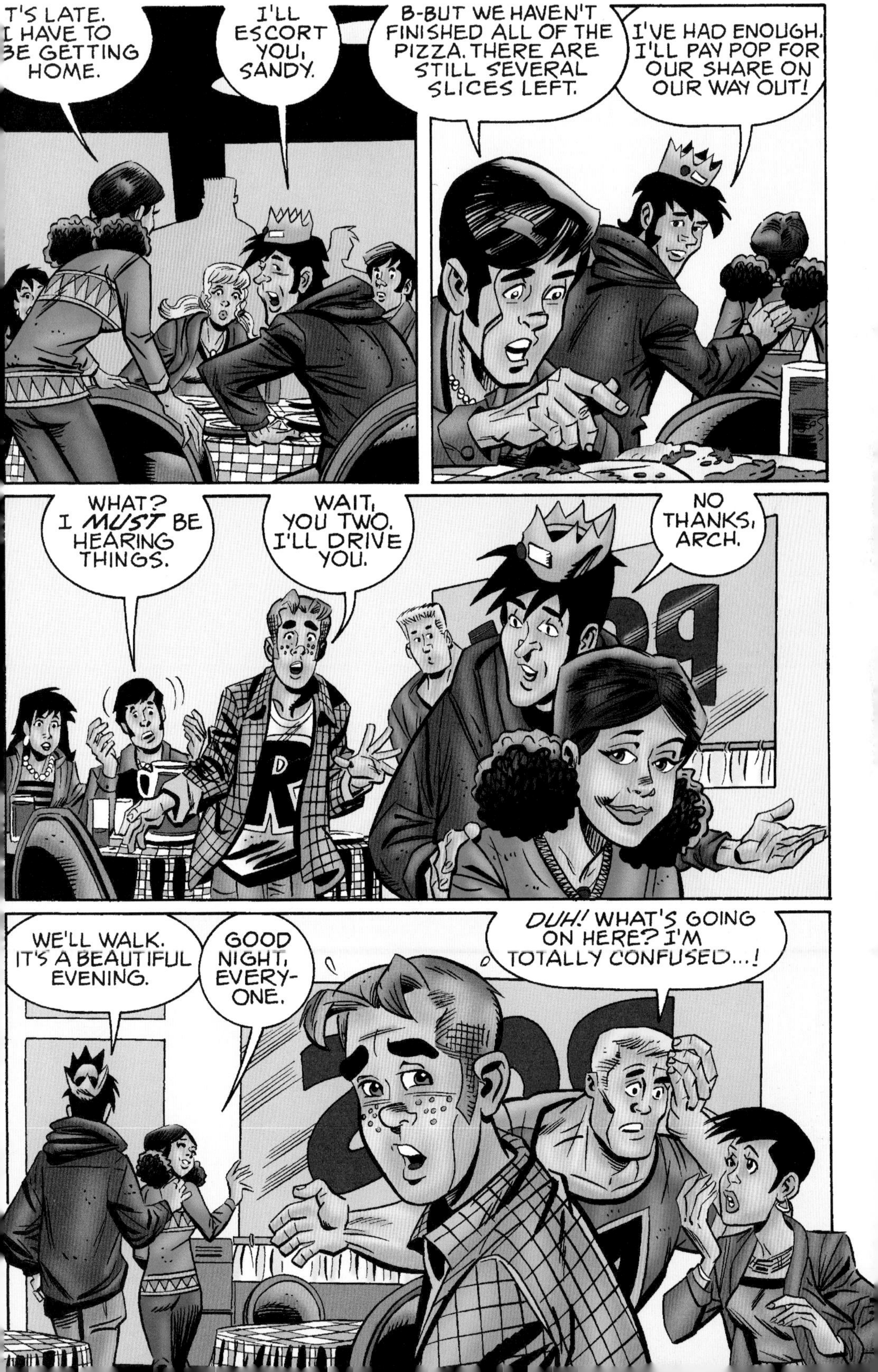
T'S LATE. I HAVE TO BE GETTING HOME.
I'LL ESCORT YOU, SANDY.
B-BUT WE HAVEN'T FINISHED ALL OF THE PIZZA. THERE ARE STILL SEVERAL SLICES LEFT.
I'VE HAD ENOUGH. I'LL PAY POP FOR OUR SHARE ON OUR WAY OUT!
WHAT? I *MUST* BE HEARING THINGS.
WAIT, YOU TWO. I'LL DRIVE YOU.
NO THANKS, ARCH.
WE'LL WALK. IT'S A BEAUTIFUL EVENING.
GOOD NIGHT, EVERY-ONE.
DUH! WHAT'S GOING ON HERE? I'M TOTALLY CONFUSED...!

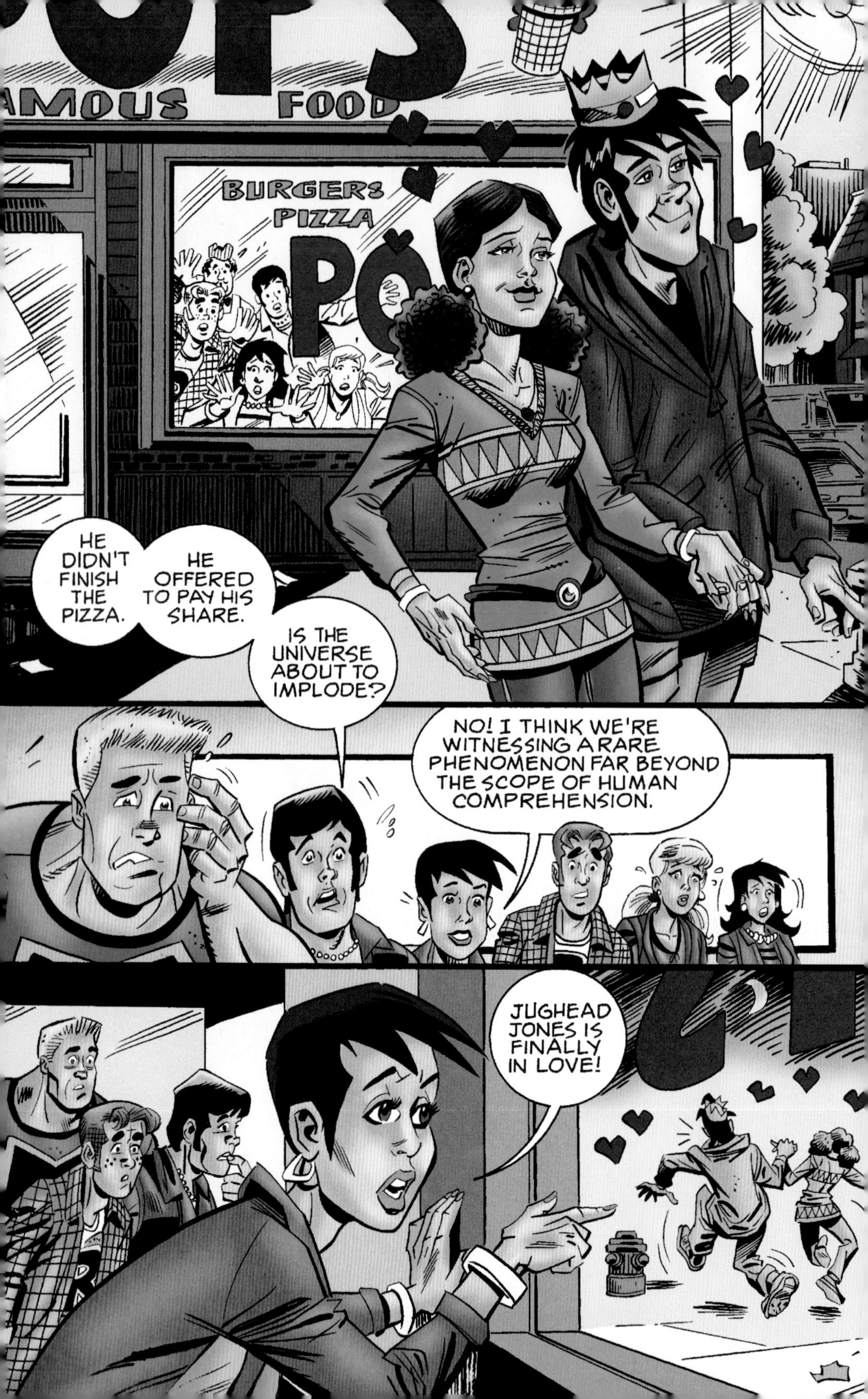

AMOUS FOOD
BURGERS PIZZA
HE DIDN'T FINISH THE PIZZA.
HE OFFERED TO PAY HIS SHARE.
IS THE UNIVERSE ABOUT TO IMPLODE?
NO! I THINK WE'RE WITNESSING A RARE PHENOMENON FAR BEYOND THE SCOPE OF HUMAN COMPREHENSION.
JUGHEAD JONES IS FINALLY IN LOVE!

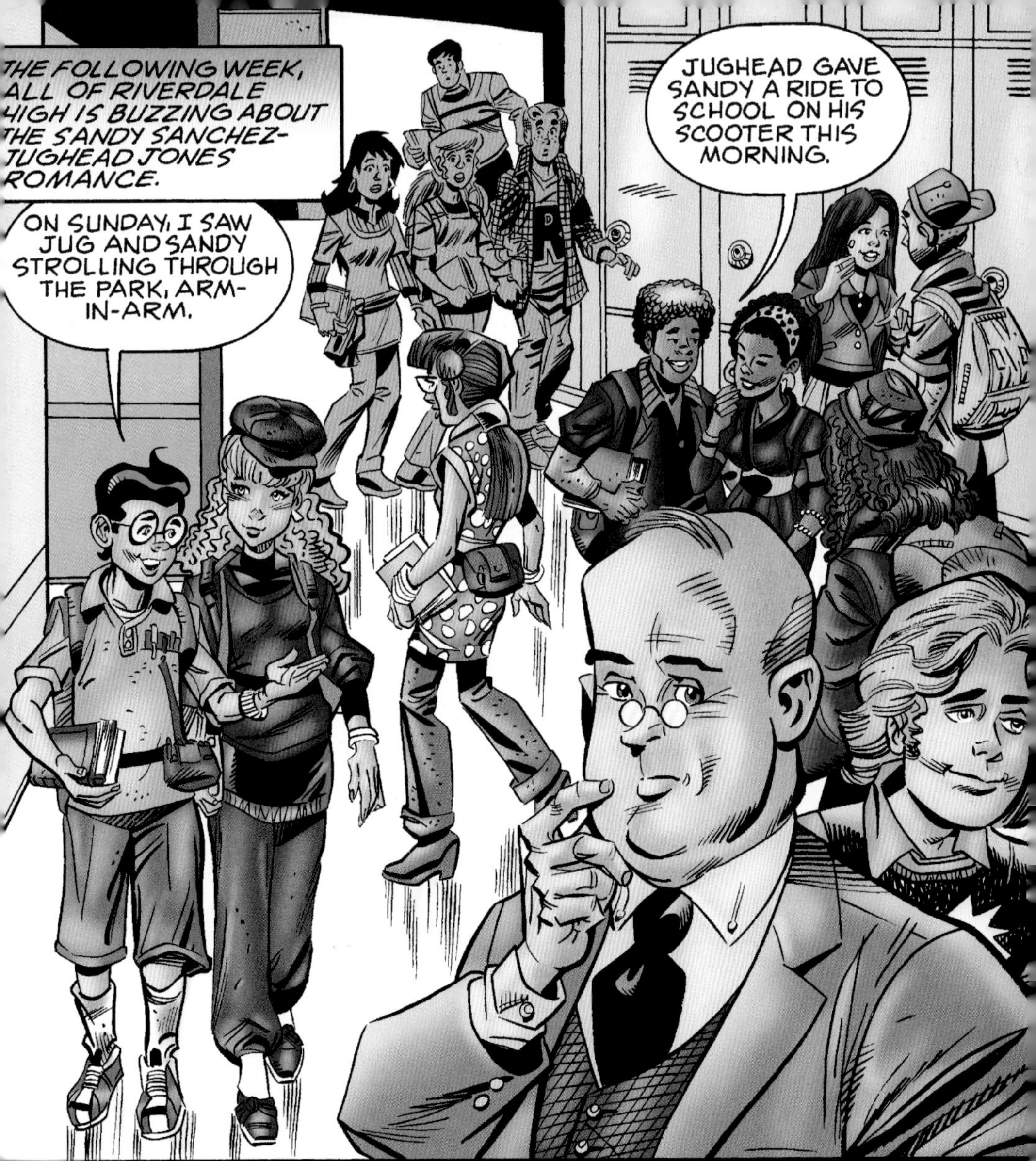
THE FOLLOWING WEEK, ALL OF RIVERDALE HIGH IS BUZZING ABOUT THE SANDY SANCHEZ-JUGHEAD JONES ROMANCE.
ON SUNDAY, I SAW JUG AND SANDY STROLLING THROUGH THE PARK, ARM-IN-ARM.
JUGHEAD GAVE SANDY A RIDE TO SCHOOL ON HIS SCOOTER THIS MORNING.

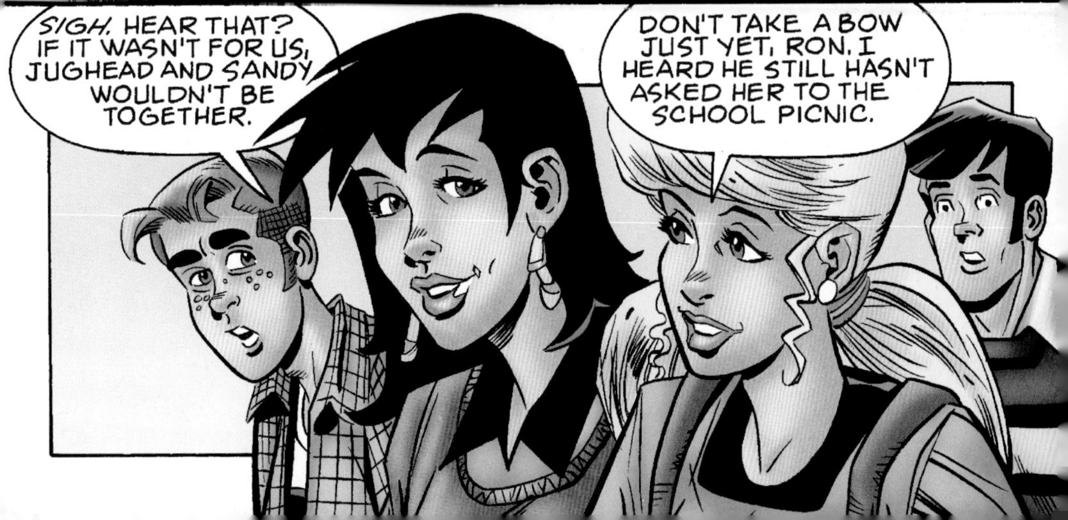
SIGH. HEAR THAT? IF IT WASN'T FOR US, JUGHEAD AND SANDY WOULDN'T BE TOGETHER.
DON'T TAKE A BOW JUST YET, RON. I HEARD HE STILL HASN'T ASKED HER TO THE SCHOOL PICNIC.

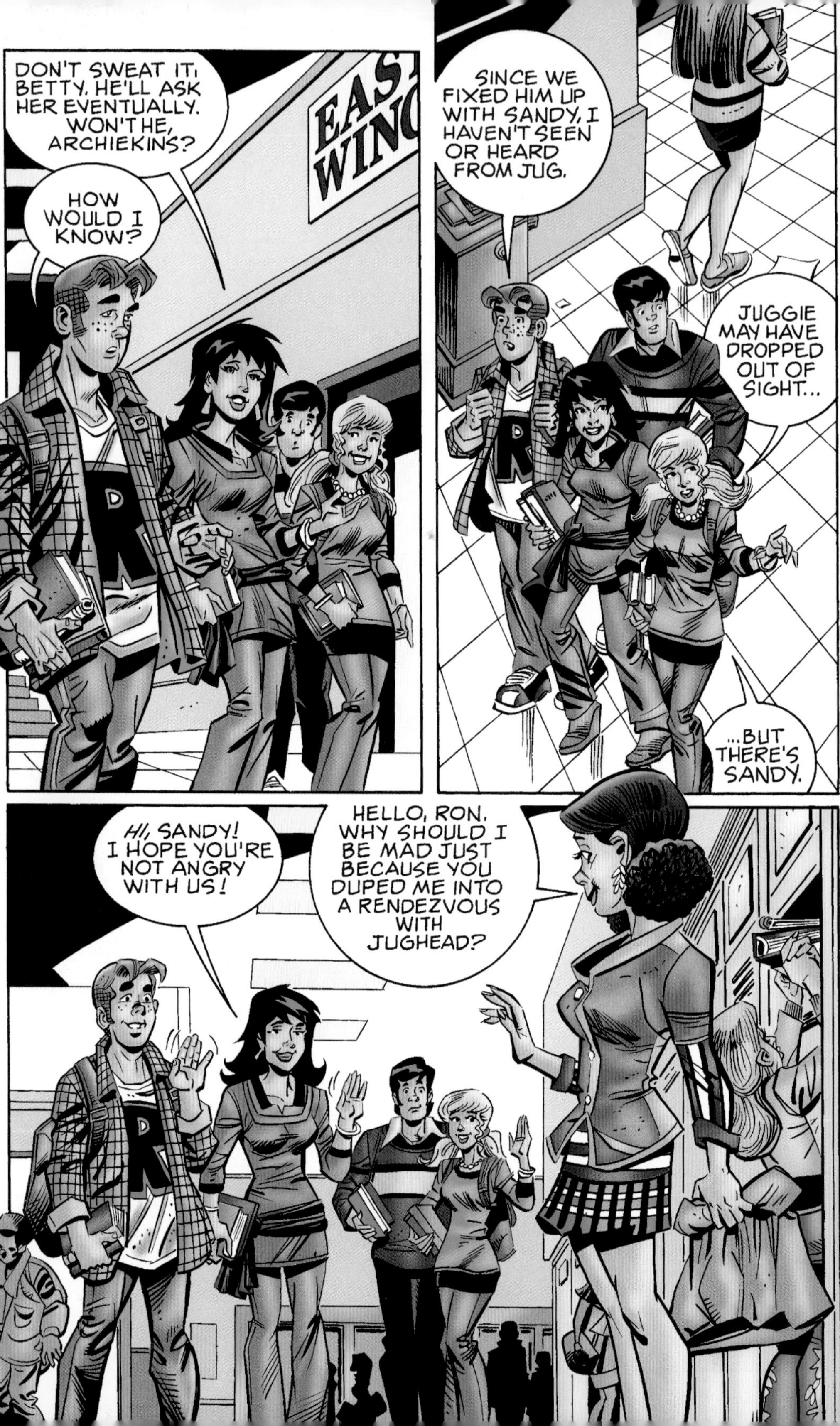
DON'T SWEAT IT, BETTY. HE'LL ASK HER EVENTUALLY. WON'T HE, ARCHIEKINS?
EAST WING
HOW WOULD I KNOW?
SINCE WE FIXED HIM UP WITH SANDY, I HAVEN'T SEEN OR HEARD FROM JUG.
JUGGIE MAY HAVE DROPPED OUT OF SIGHT...
...BUT THERE'S SANDY.
HI, SANDY! I HOPE YOU'RE NOT ANGRY WITH US!
HELLO, RON. WHY SHOULD I BE MAD JUST BECAUSE YOU DUPED ME INTO A RENDEZVOUS WITH JUGHEAD?

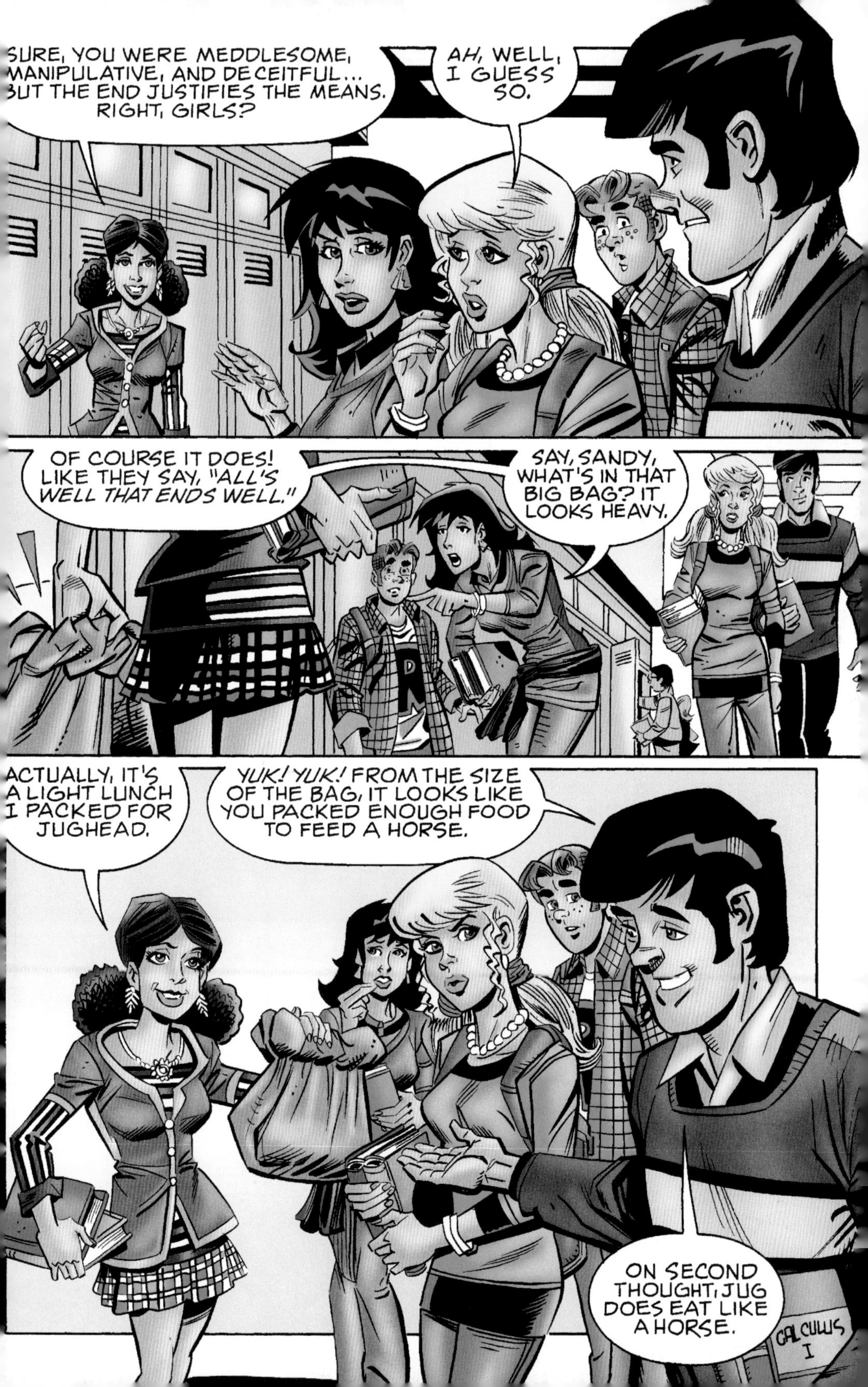

SURE, YOU WERE MEDDLESOME, MANIPULATIVE, AND DECEITFUL... BUT THE END JUSTIFIES THE MEANS. RIGHT, GIRLS?
AH, WELL, I GUESS SO.
OF COURSE IT DOES! LIKE THEY SAY, "ALL'S WELL THAT ENDS WELL."
SAY, SANDY, WHAT'S IN THAT BIG BAG? IT LOOKS HEAVY.
ACTUALLY, IT'S A LIGHT LUNCH I PACKED FOR JUGHEAD.
YUK! YUK! FROM THE SIZE OF THE BAG, IT LOOKS LIKE YOU PACKED ENOUGH FOOD TO FEED A HORSE.
ON SECOND THOUGHT, JUG DOES EAT LIKE A HORSE.
CALCULUS I

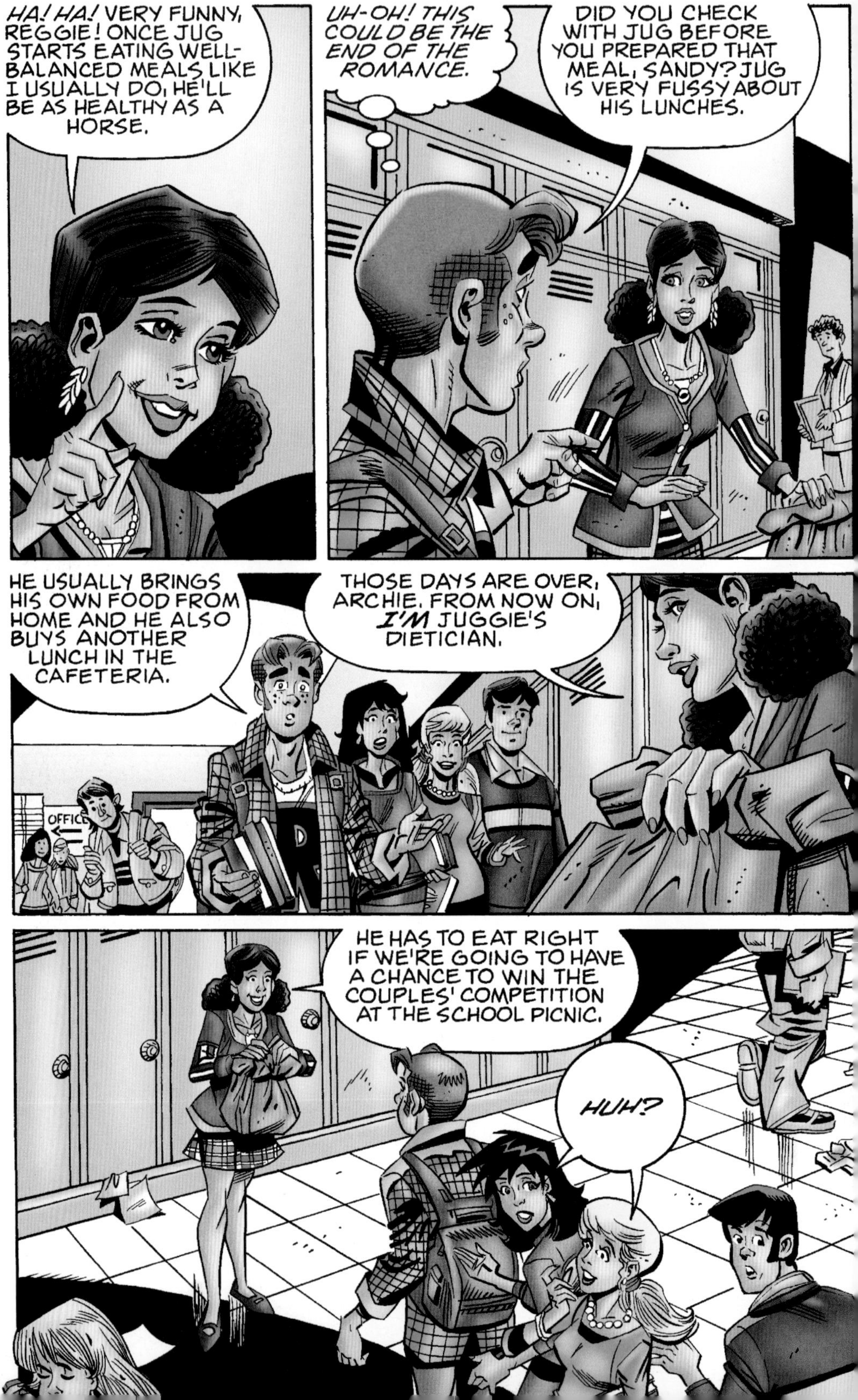
HA! HA! VERY FUNNY, REGGIE! ONCE JUG STARTS EATING WELL-BALANCED MEALS LIKE I USUALLY DO, HE'LL BE AS HEALTHY AS A HORSE.
UH-OH! THIS COULD BE THE END OF THE ROMANCE.
DID YOU CHECK WITH JUG BEFORE YOU PREPARED THAT MEAL, SANDY? JUG IS VERY FUSSY ABOUT HIS LUNCHES.
HE USUALLY BRINGS HIS OWN FOOD FROM HOME AND HE ALSO BUYS ANOTHER LUNCH IN THE CAFETERIA.
THOSE DAYS ARE OVER, ARCHIE. FROM NOW ON, I'M JUGGIE'S DIETICIAN.
OFFICE
HE HAS TO EAT RIGHT IF WE'RE GOING TO HAVE A CHANCE TO WIN THE COUPLES' COMPETITION AT THE SCHOOL PICNIC.
HUH?

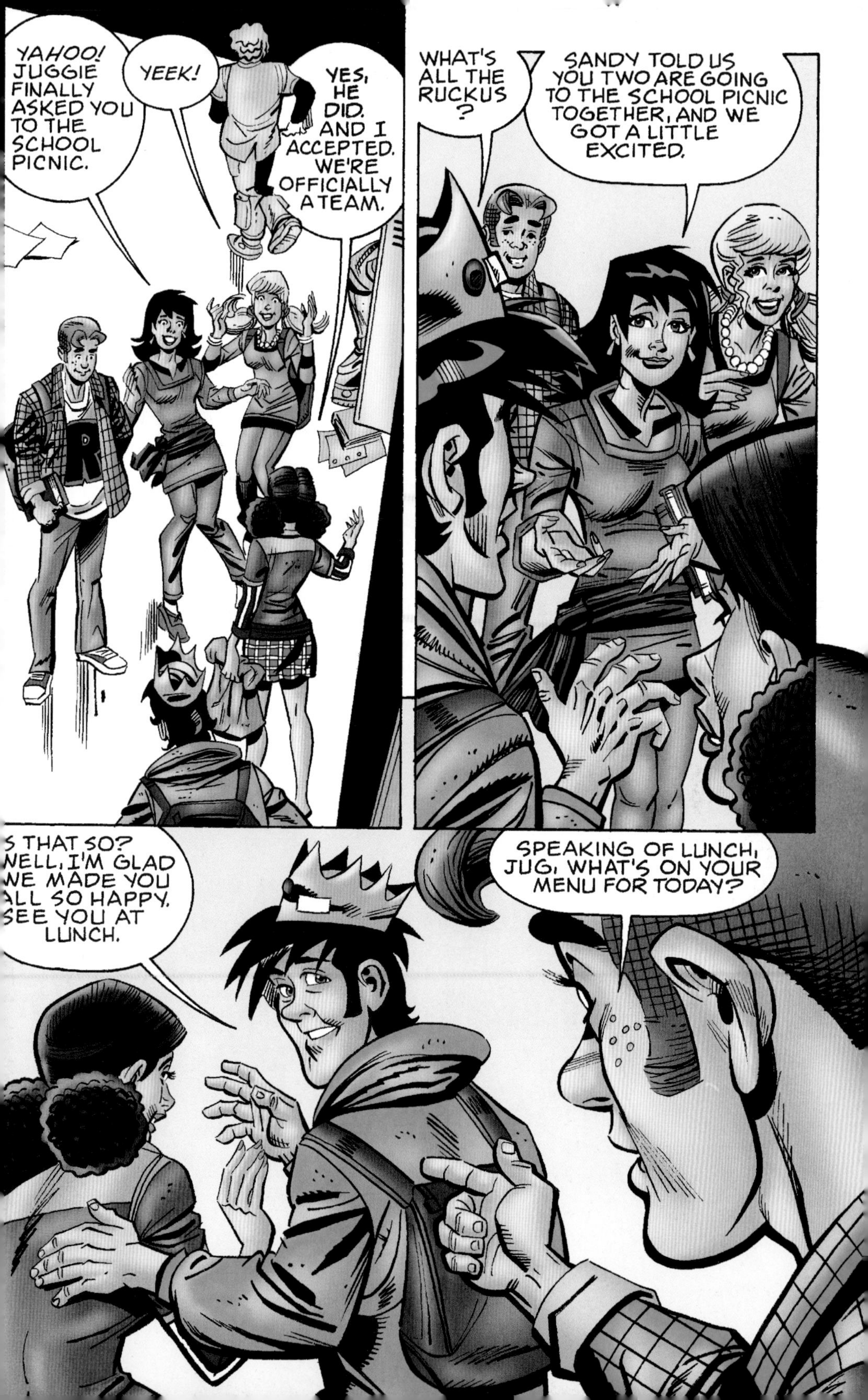
YAHOO! JUGGIE FINALLY ASKED YOU TO THE SCHOOL PICNIC.
YEEK!
YES, HE DID. AND I ACCEPTED. WE'RE OFFICIALLY A TEAM.
WHAT'S ALL THE RUCKUS ?
SANDY TOLD US YOU TWO ARE GOING TO THE SCHOOL PICNIC TOGETHER, AND WE GOT A LITTLE EXCITED.
S THAT SO? NELL, I'M GLAD NE MADE YOU ALL SO HAPPY. SEE YOU AT LUNCH.
SPEAKING OF LUNCH, JUG, WHAT'S ON YOUR MENU FOR TODAY?

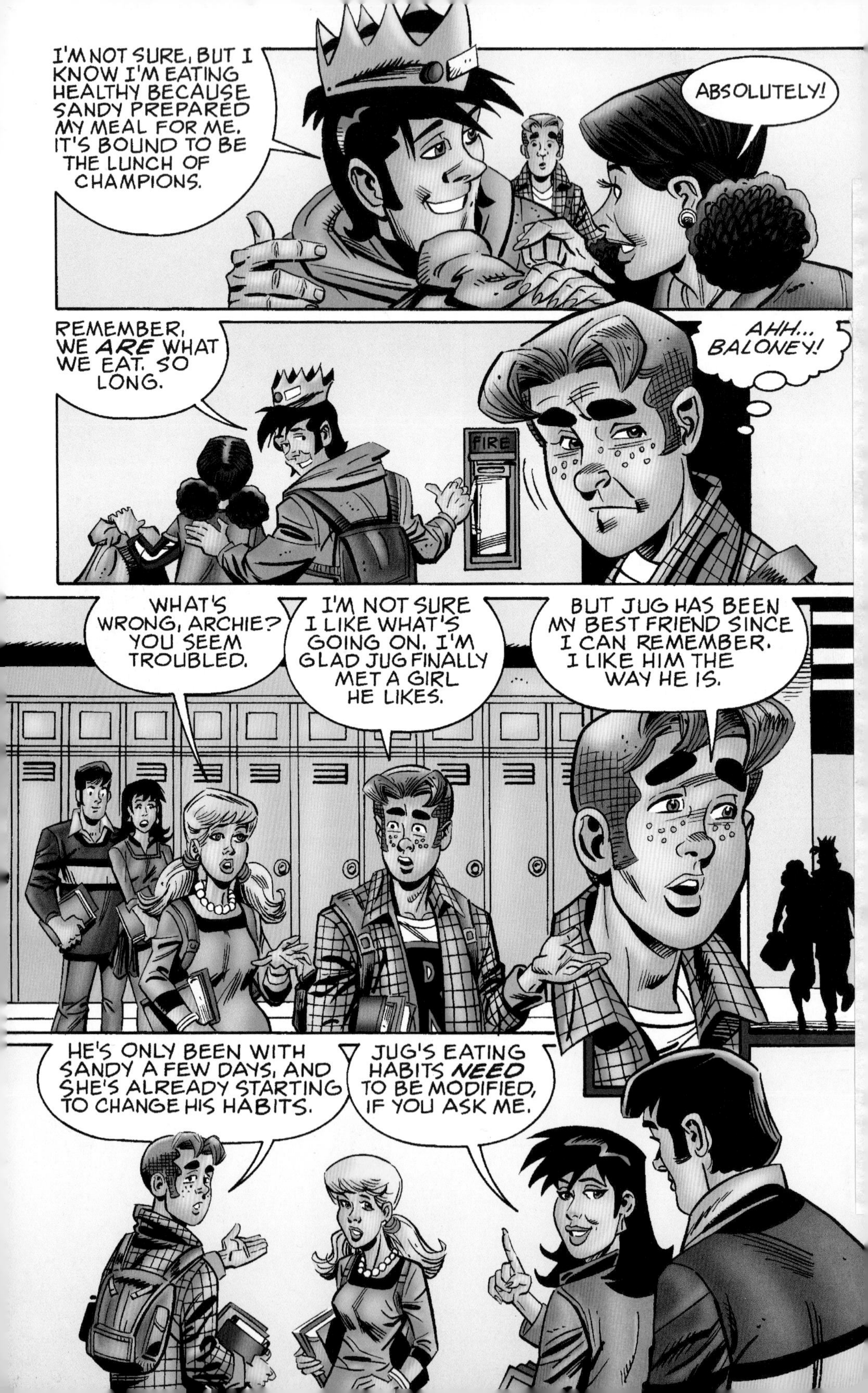
I'M NOT SURE, BUT I KNOW I'M EATING HEALTHY BECAUSE SANDY PREPARED MY MEAL FOR ME. IT'S BOUND TO BE THE LUNCH OF CHAMPIONS.
ABSOLUTELY!
REMEMBER, WE *ARE* WHAT WE EAT. SO LONG.
FIRE
AHH... BALONEY!
WHAT'S WRONG, ARCHIE? YOU SEEM TROUBLED.
I'M NOT SURE I LIKE WHAT'S GOING ON. I'M GLAD JUG FINALLY MET A GIRL HE LIKES.
BUT JUG HAS BEEN MY BEST FRIEND SINCE I CAN REMEMBER. I LIKE HIM THE WAY HE IS.
HE'S ONLY BEEN WITH SANDY A FEW DAYS, AND SHE'S ALREADY STARTING TO CHANGE HIS HABITS.
JUG'S EATING HABITS *NEED* TO BE MODIFIED, IF YOU ASK ME.

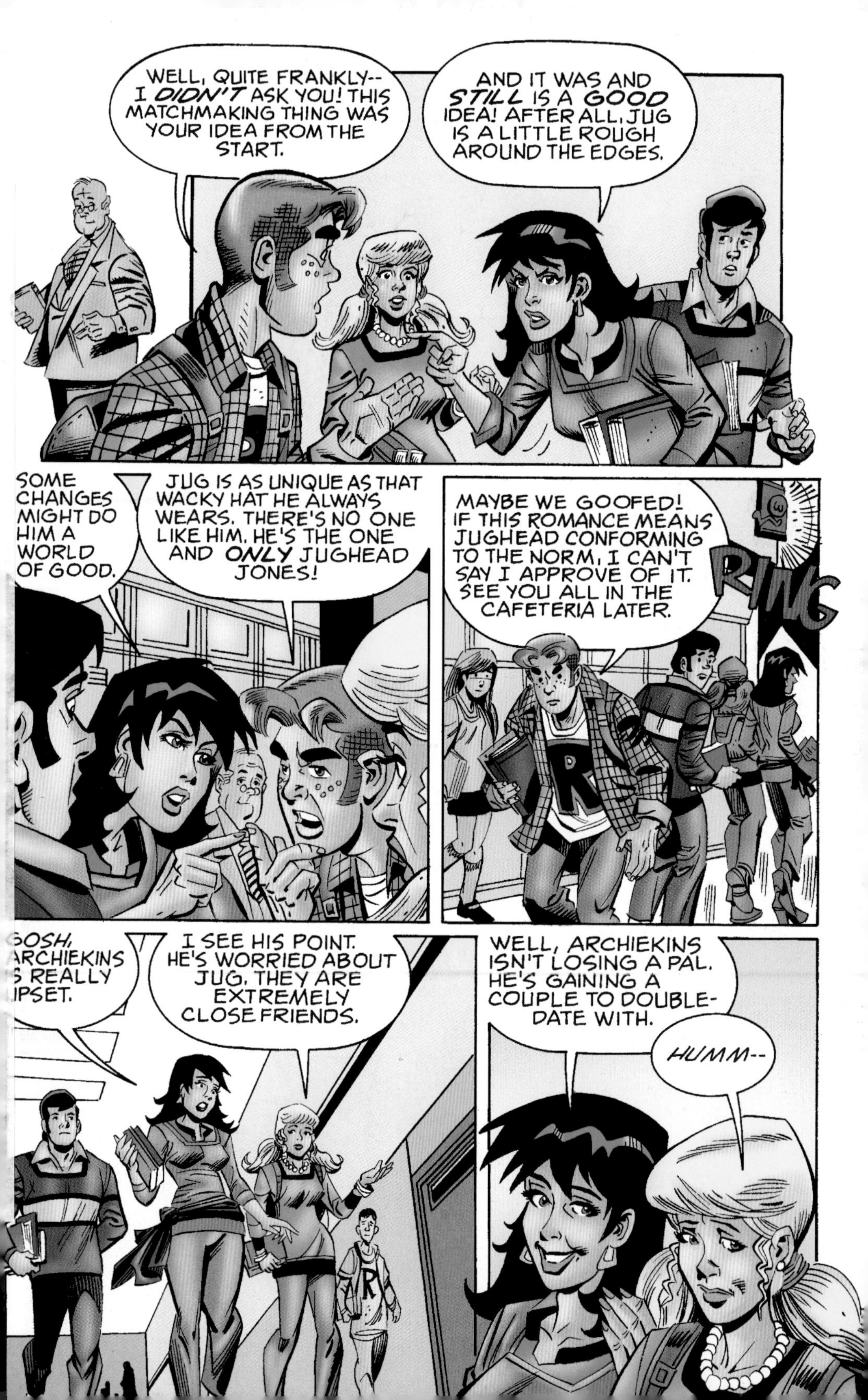
WELL, QUITE FRANKLY-- I DIDN'T ASK YOU! THIS MATCHMAKING THING WAS YOUR IDEA FROM THE START.
AND IT WAS AND STILL IS A GOOD IDEA! AFTER ALL, JUG IS A LITTLE ROUGH AROUND THE EDGES.
SOME CHANGES MIGHT DO HIM A WORLD OF GOOD.
JUG IS AS UNIQUE AS THAT WACKY HAT HE ALWAYS WEARS. THERE'S NO ONE LIKE HIM. HE'S THE ONE AND ONLY JUGHEAD JONES!
MAYBE WE GOOFED! IF THIS ROMANCE MEANS JUGHEAD CONFORMING TO THE NORM, I CAN'T SAY I APPROVE OF IT. SEE YOU ALL IN THE CAFETERIA LATER.
RING
I SEE HIS POINT. HE'S WORRIED ABOUT JUG. THEY ARE EXTREMELY CLOSE FRIENDS.
WELL, ARCHIEKINS ISN'T LOSING A PAL. HE'S GAINING A COUPLE TO DOUBLE-DATE WITH.
HUMM--

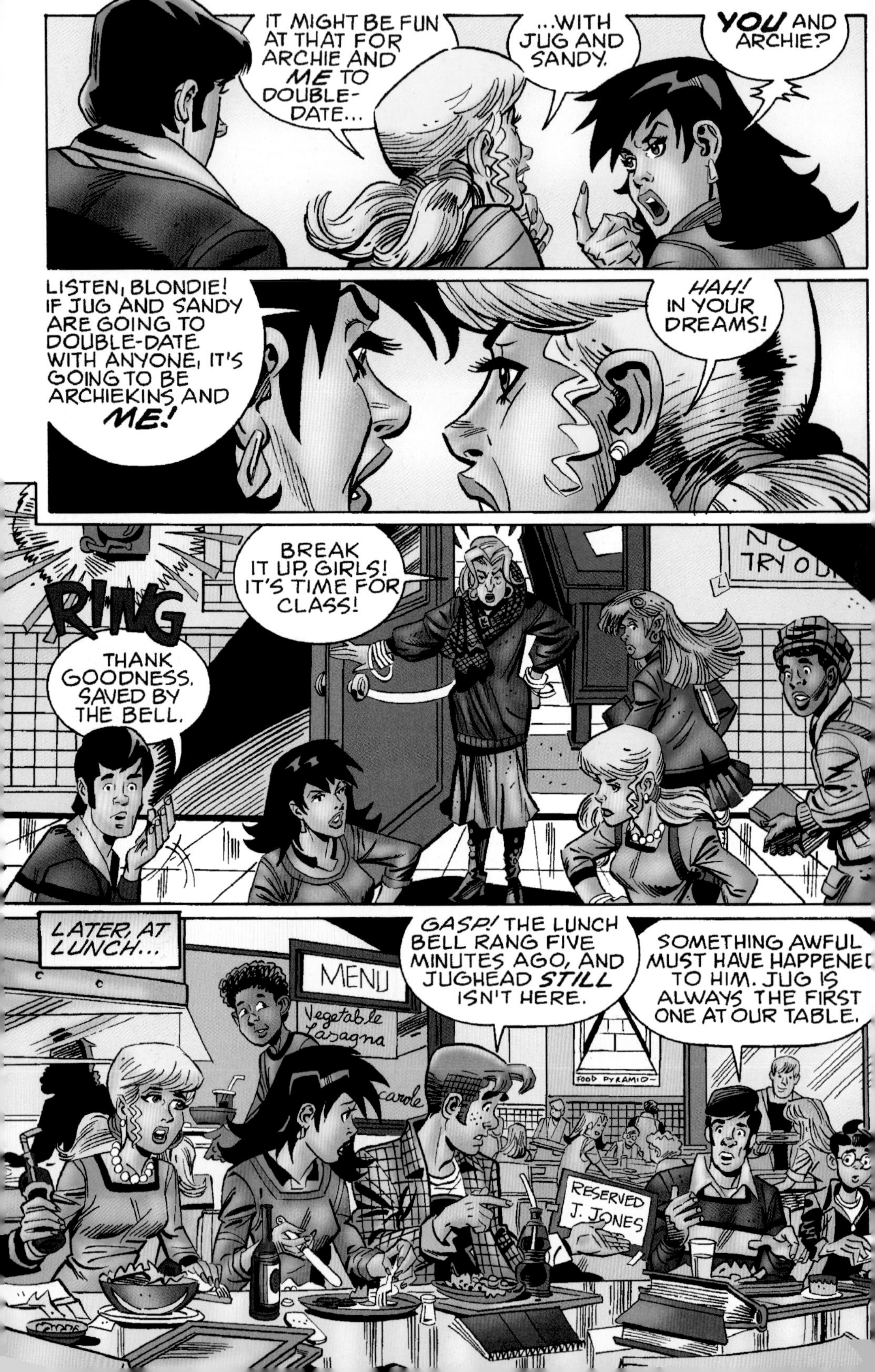
IT MIGHT BE FUN AT THAT FOR ARCHIE AND ME TO DOUBLE-DATE...
...WITH JUG AND SANDY.
YOU AND ARCHIE?
LISTEN, BLONDIE! IF JUG AND SANDY ARE GOING TO DOUBLE-DATE WITH ANYONE, IT'S GOING TO BE ARCHIEKINS AND ME!
HAH! IN YOUR DREAMS!
RING
BREAK IT UP, GIRLS! IT'S TIME FOR CLASS!
THANK GOODNESS. SAVED BY THE BELL.
LATER, AT LUNCH...
MENU
Vegetable Lasagna
GASP! THE LUNCH BELL RANG FIVE MINUTES AGO, AND JUGHEAD STILL ISN'T HERE.
SOMETHING AWFUL MUST HAVE HAPPENED TO HIM. JUG IS ALWAYS THE FIRST ONE AT OUR TABLE.
FOOD PYRAMID
RESERVED J. JONES

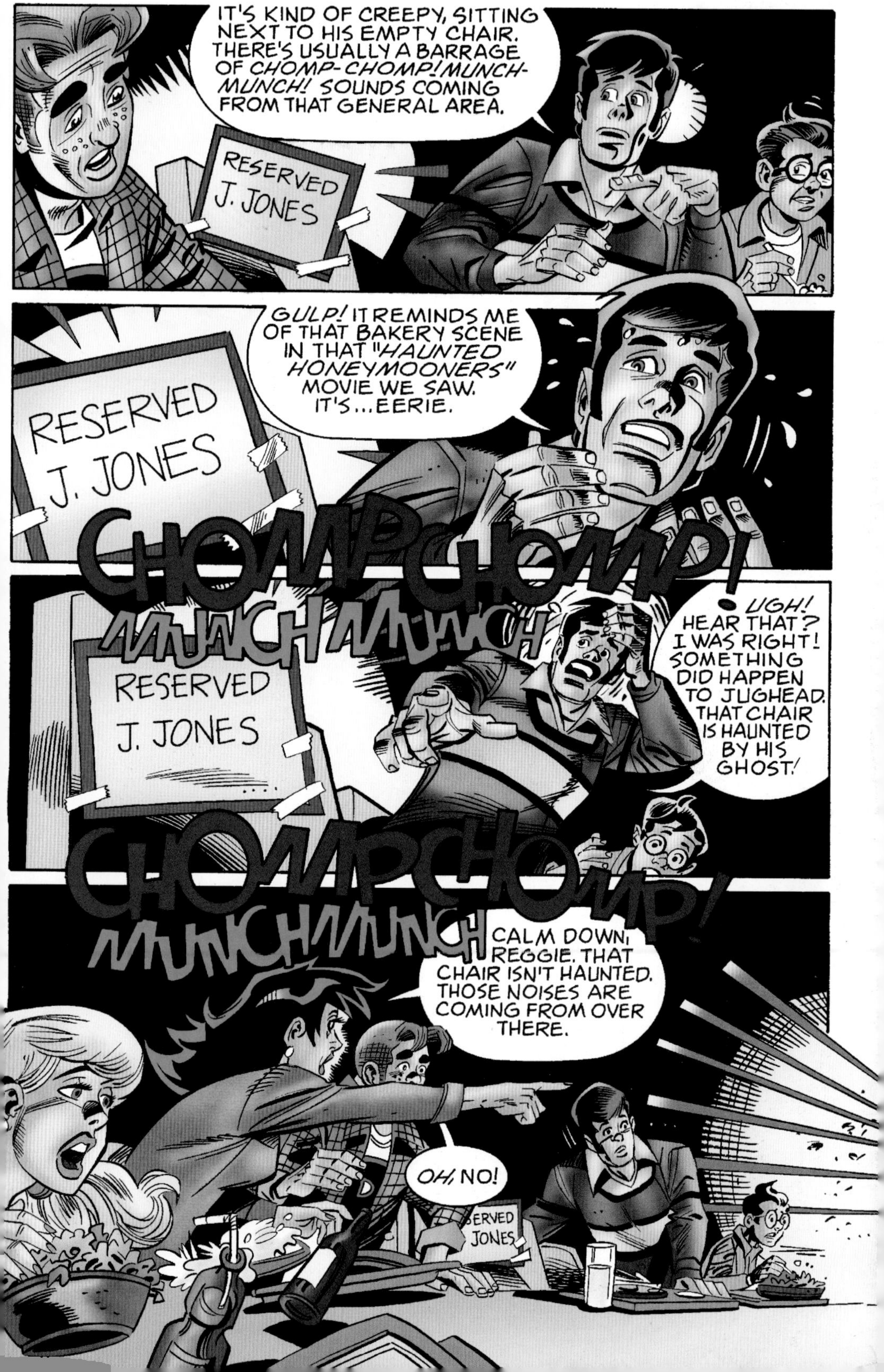
IT'S KIND OF CREEPY, SITTING NEXT TO HIS EMPTY CHAIR. THERE'S USUALLY A BARRAGE OF CHOMP-CHOMP! MUNCH-MUNCH! SOUNDS COMING FROM THAT GENERAL AREA.
RESERVED J. JONES
GULP! IT REMINDS ME OF THAT BAKERY SCENE IN THAT "HAUNTED HONEYMOONERS" MOVIE WE SAW. IT'S...EERIE.
RESERVED J. JONES
CHOMP CHOMP!
MUNCH MUNCH
RESERVED J. JONES
UGH! HEAR THAT? I WAS RIGHT! SOMETHING DID HAPPEN TO JUGHEAD. THAT CHAIR IS HAUNTED BY HIS GHOST!
CHOMP CHOMP!
MUNCH MUNCH
CALM DOWN, REGGIE. THAT CHAIR ISN'T HAUNTED. THOSE NOISES ARE COMING FROM OVER THERE.
OH, NO!
ERVED JONES

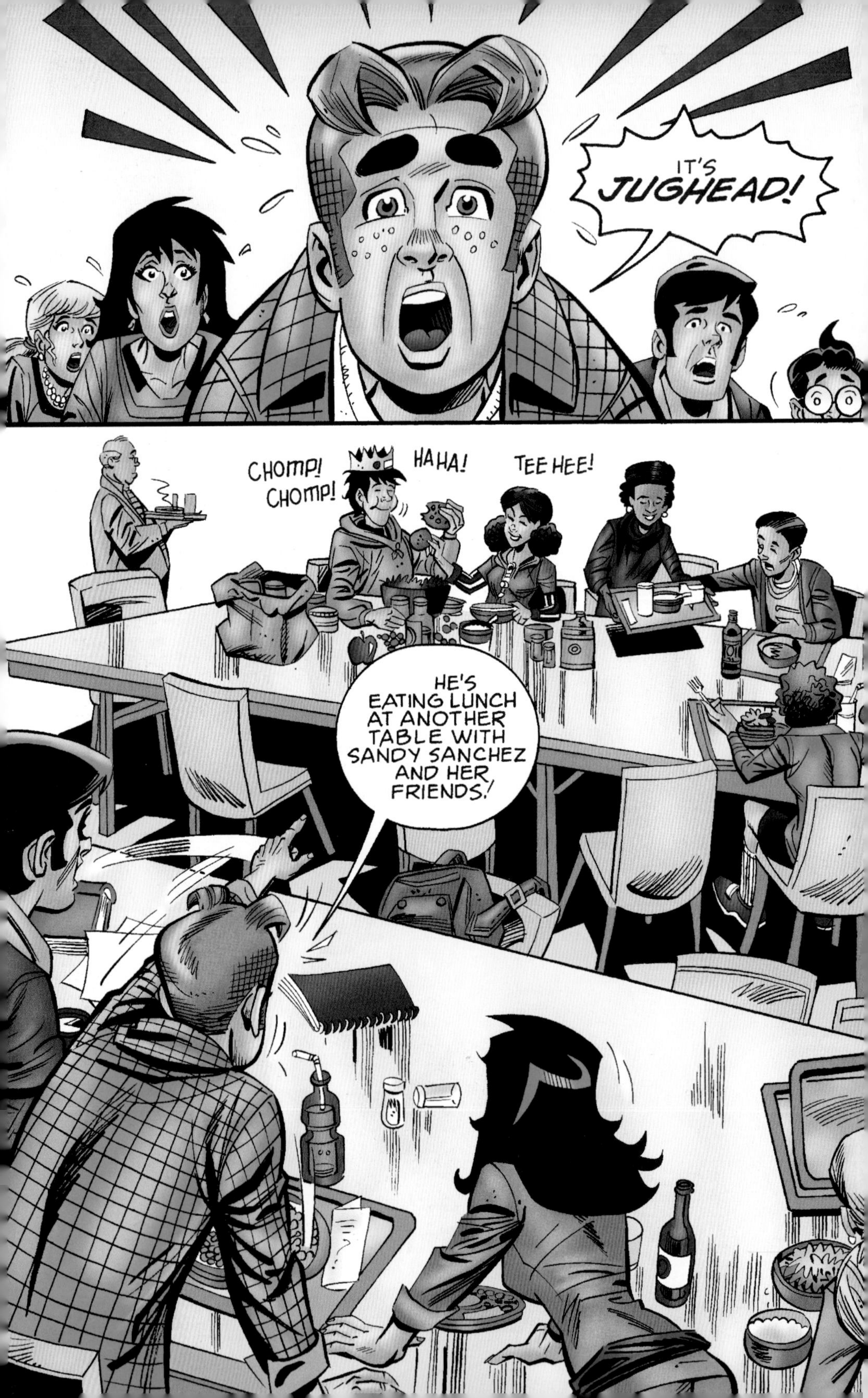
IT'S JUGHEAD!
CHOMP! CHOMP!
HAHA!
TEE HEE!
HE'S EATING LUNCH AT ANOTHER TABLE WITH SANDY SANCHEZ AND HER FRIENDS!

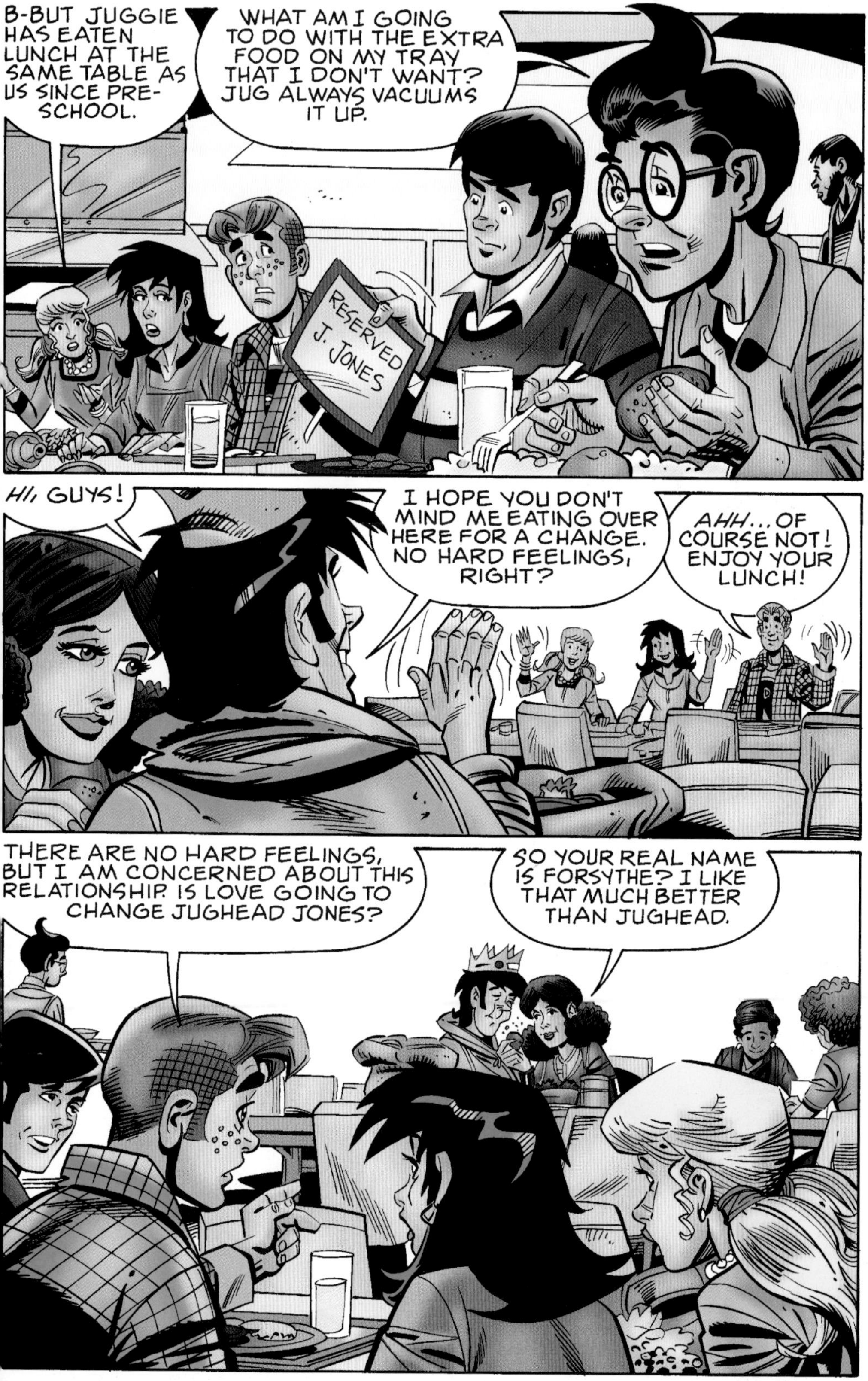
B-BUT JUGGIE HAS EATEN LUNCH AT THE SAME TABLE AS US SINCE PRE-SCHOOL.
WHAT AM I GOING TO DO WITH THE EXTRA FOOD ON MY TRAY THAT I DON'T WANT? JUG ALWAYS VACUUMS IT UP.
RESERVED J. JONES
HI, GUYS!
I HOPE YOU DON'T MIND ME EATING OVER HERE FOR A CHANGE. NO HARD FEELINGS, RIGHT?
AHH... OF COURSE NOT! ENJOY YOUR LUNCH!
THERE ARE NO HARD FEELINGS, BUT I AM CONCERNED ABOUT THIS RELATIONSHIP. IS LOVE GOING TO CHANGE JUGHEAD JONES?
SO YOUR REAL NAME IS FORSYTHE? I LIKE THAT MUCH BETTER THAN JUGHEAD.

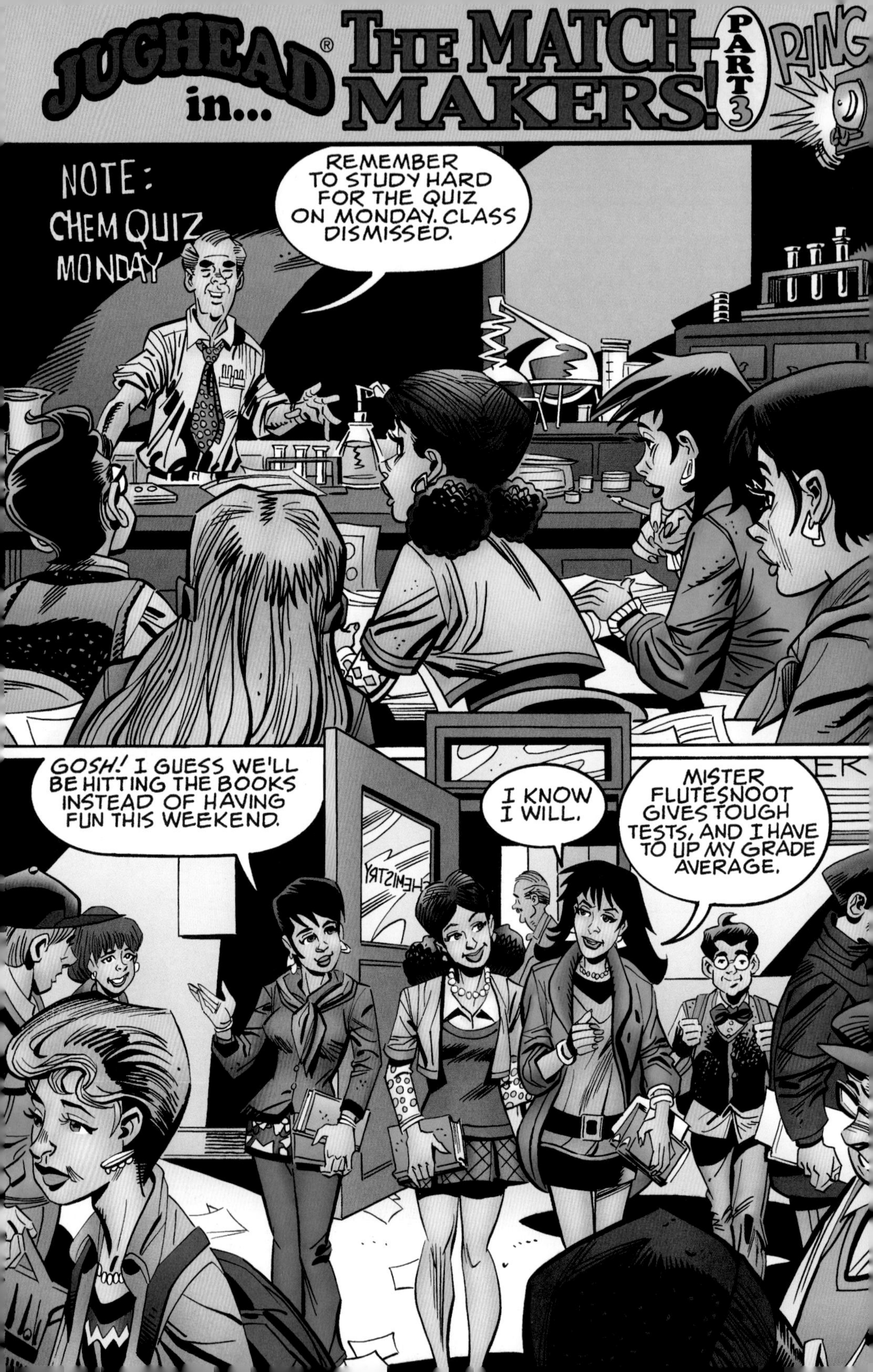
JUGHEAD® in...
THE MATCH-MAKERS!
PART 3
RING
NOTE: CHEM QUIZ MONDAY
REMEMBER TO STUDY HARD FOR THE QUIZ ON MONDAY. CLASS DISMISSED.
GOSH! I GUESS WE'LL BE HITTING THE BOOKS INSTEAD OF HAVING FUN THIS WEEKEND.
I KNOW I WILL.
MISTER FLUTESNOOT GIVES TOUGH TESTS, AND I HAVE TO UP MY GRADE AVERAGE.

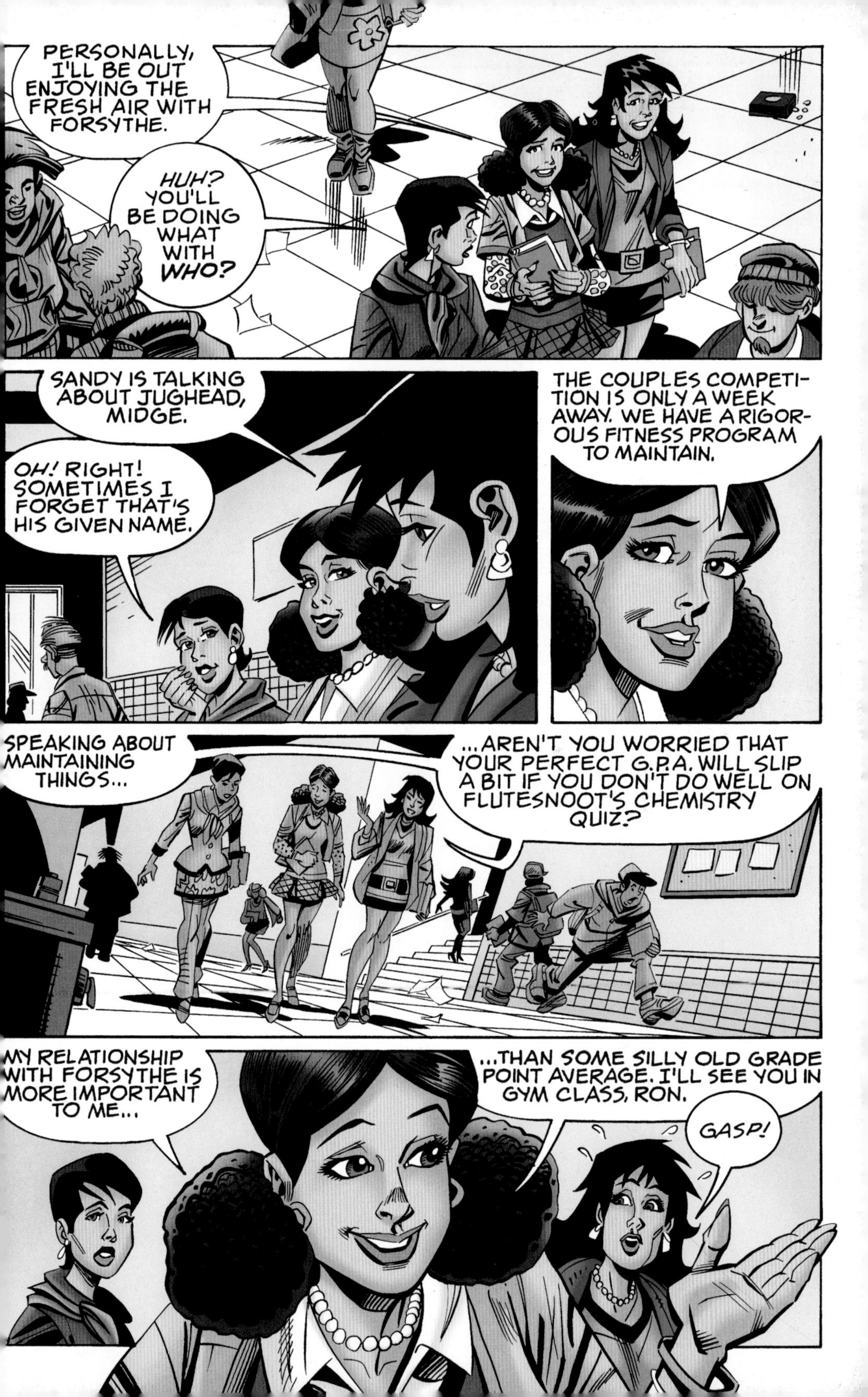
PERSONALLY, I'LL BE OUT ENJOYING THE FRESH AIR WITH FORSYTHE.
HUH? YOU'LL BE DOING WHAT WITH WHO?
SANDY IS TALKING ABOUT JUGHEAD, MIDGE.
OH! RIGHT! SOMETIMES I FORGET THAT'S HIS GIVEN NAME.
THE COUPLES COMPETITION IS ONLY A WEEK AWAY. WE HAVE A RIGOROUS FITNESS PROGRAM TO MAINTAIN.
SPEAKING ABOUT MAINTAINING THINGS...
...AREN'T YOU WORRIED THAT YOUR PERFECT G.P.A. WILL SLIP A BIT IF YOU DON'T DO WELL ON FLUTESNOOT'S CHEMISTRY QUIZ?
MY RELATIONSHIP WITH FORSYTHE IS MORE IMPORTANT TO ME...
...THAN SOME SILLY OLD GRADE POINT AVERAGE. I'LL SEE YOU IN GYM CLASS, RON.
GASP!

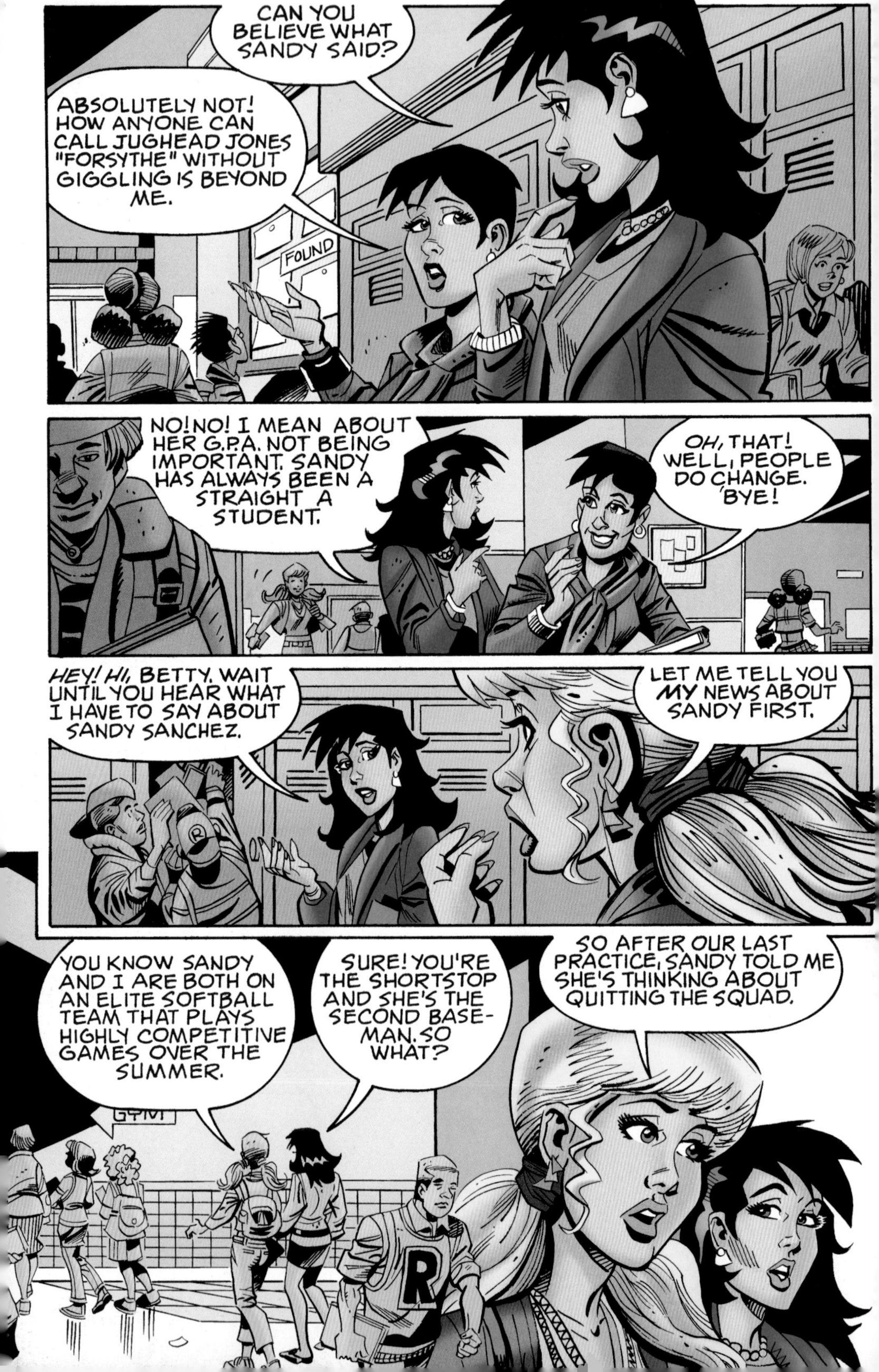

CAN YOU BELIEVE WHAT SANDY SAID?
ABSOLUTELY NOT! HOW ANYONE CAN CALL JUGHEAD JONES "FORSYTHE" WITHOUT GIGGLING IS BEYOND ME.
FOUND
NO! NO! I MEAN ABOUT HER G.P.A. NOT BEING IMPORTANT. SANDY HAS ALWAYS BEEN A STRAIGHT A STUDENT.
OH, THAT! WELL, PEOPLE DO CHANGE. 'BYE!
HEY! HI, BETTY. WAIT UNTIL YOU HEAR WHAT I HAVE TO SAY ABOUT SANDY SANCHEZ.
LET ME TELL YOU MY NEWS ABOUT SANDY FIRST.
YOU KNOW SANDY AND I ARE BOTH ON AN ELITE SOFTBALL TEAM THAT PLAYS HIGHLY COMPETITIVE GAMES OVER THE SUMMER.
SURE! YOU'RE THE SHORTSTOP AND SHE'S THE SECOND BASE-MAN. SO WHAT?
SO AFTER OUR LAST PRACTICE, SANDY TOLD ME SHE'S THINKING ABOUT QUITTING THE SQUAD.
GYM

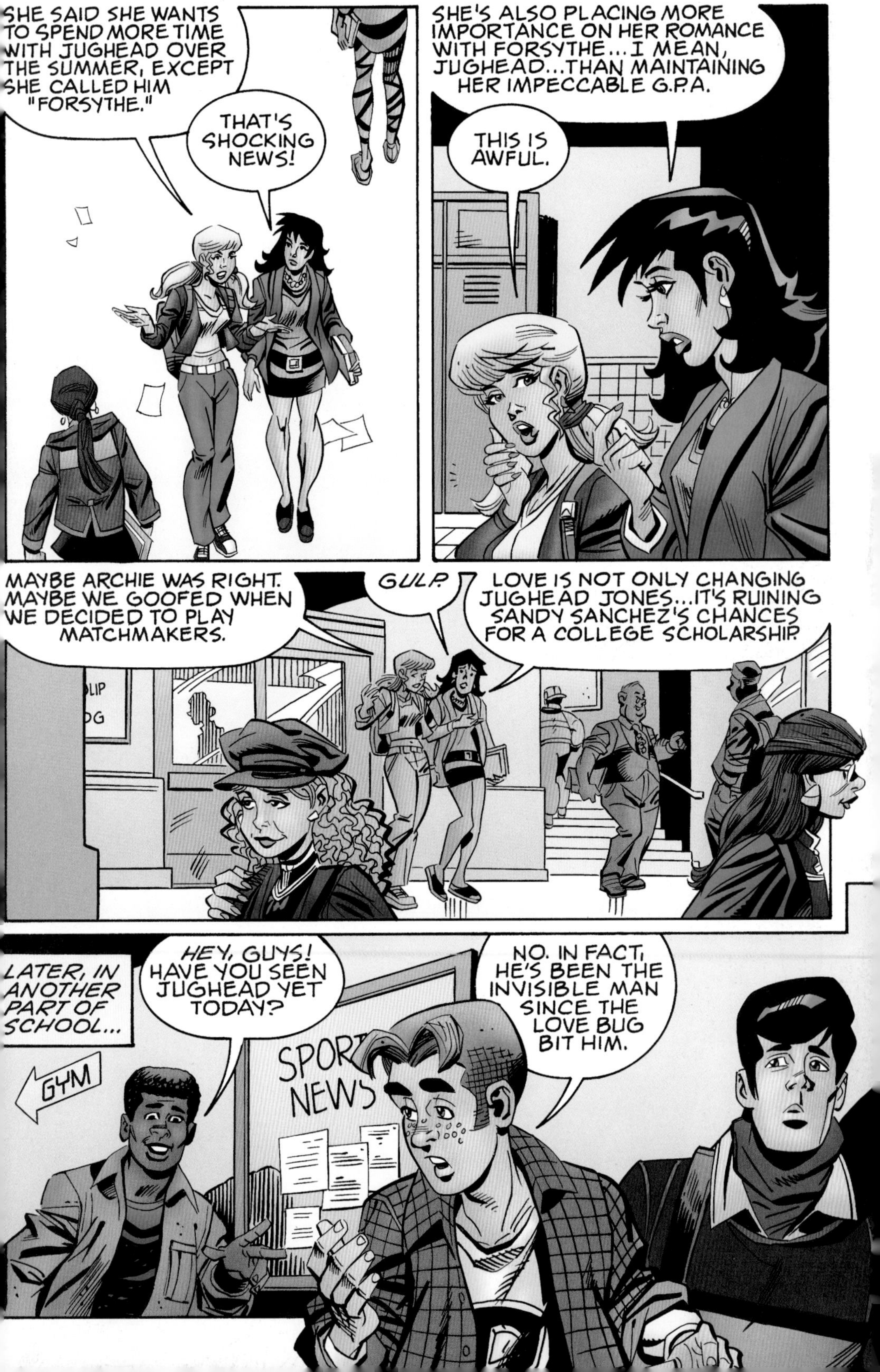
SHE SAID SHE WANTS TO SPEND MORE TIME WITH JUGHEAD OVER THE SUMMER, EXCEPT SHE CALLED HIM "FORSYTHE."
THAT'S SHOCKING NEWS!
SHE'S ALSO PLACING MORE IMPORTANCE ON HER ROMANCE WITH FORSYTHE... I MEAN, JUGHEAD...THAN MAINTAINING HER IMPECCABLE G.P.A.
THIS IS AWFUL.
MAYBE ARCHIE WAS RIGHT. MAYBE WE GOOFED WHEN WE DECIDED TO PLAY MATCHMAKERS.
GULP!
LOVE IS NOT ONLY CHANGING JUGHEAD JONES...IT'S RUINING SANDY SANCHEZ'S CHANCES FOR A COLLEGE SCHOLARSHIP!
LATER, IN ANOTHER PART OF SCHOOL...
HEY, GUYS! HAVE YOU SEEN JUGHEAD YET TODAY?
NO. IN FACT, HE'S BEEN THE INVISIBLE MAN SINCE THE LOVE BUG BIT HIM.
GYM
SPORT NEWS

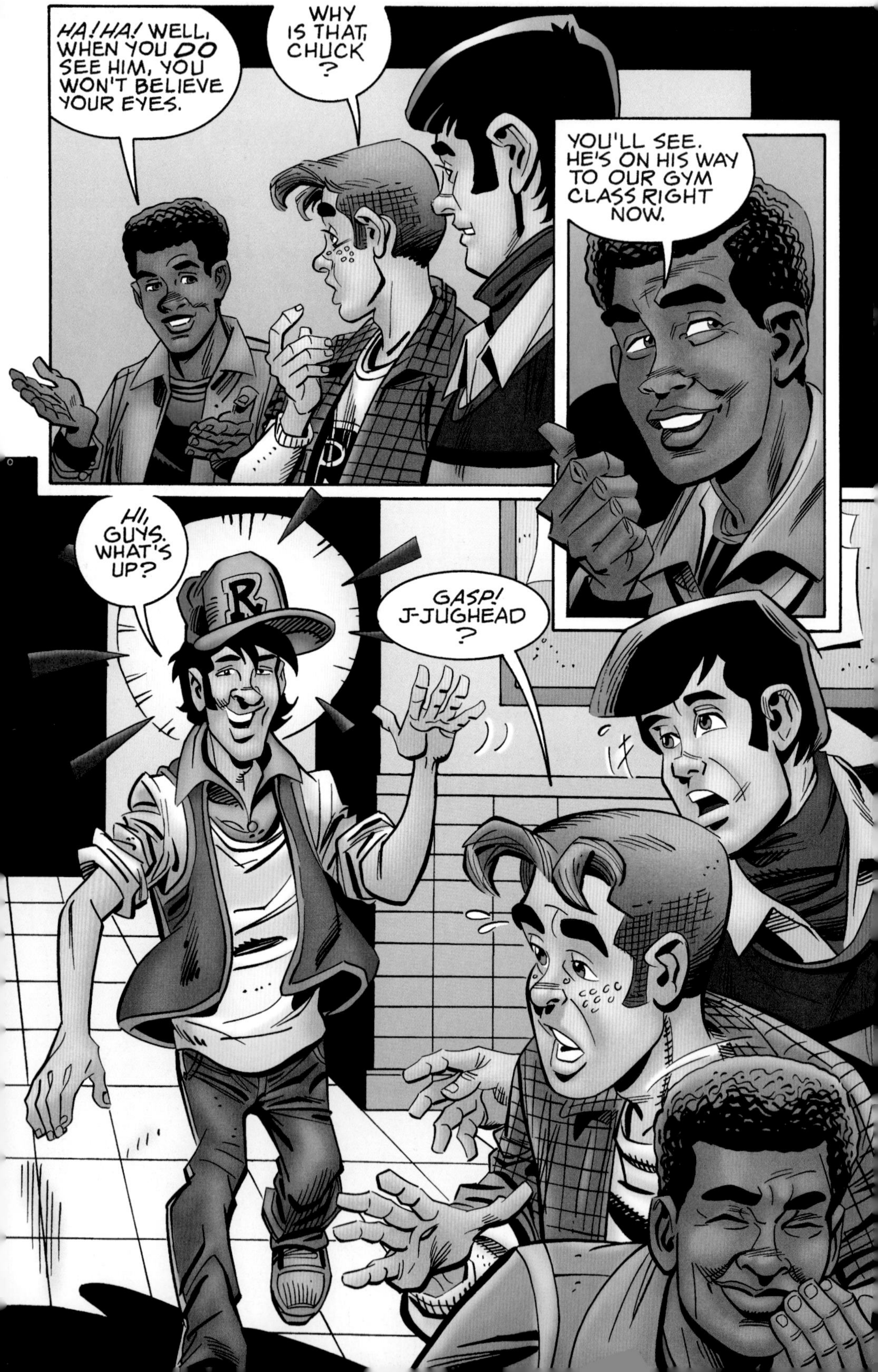
HA! HA! WELL, WHEN YOU DO SEE HIM, YOU WON'T BELIEVE YOUR EYES.
WHY IS THAT, CHUCK ?
YOU'LL SEE. HE'S ON HIS WAY TO OUR GYM CLASS RIGHT NOW.
HI, GUYS. WHAT'S UP?
GASP! J-JUGHEAD ?

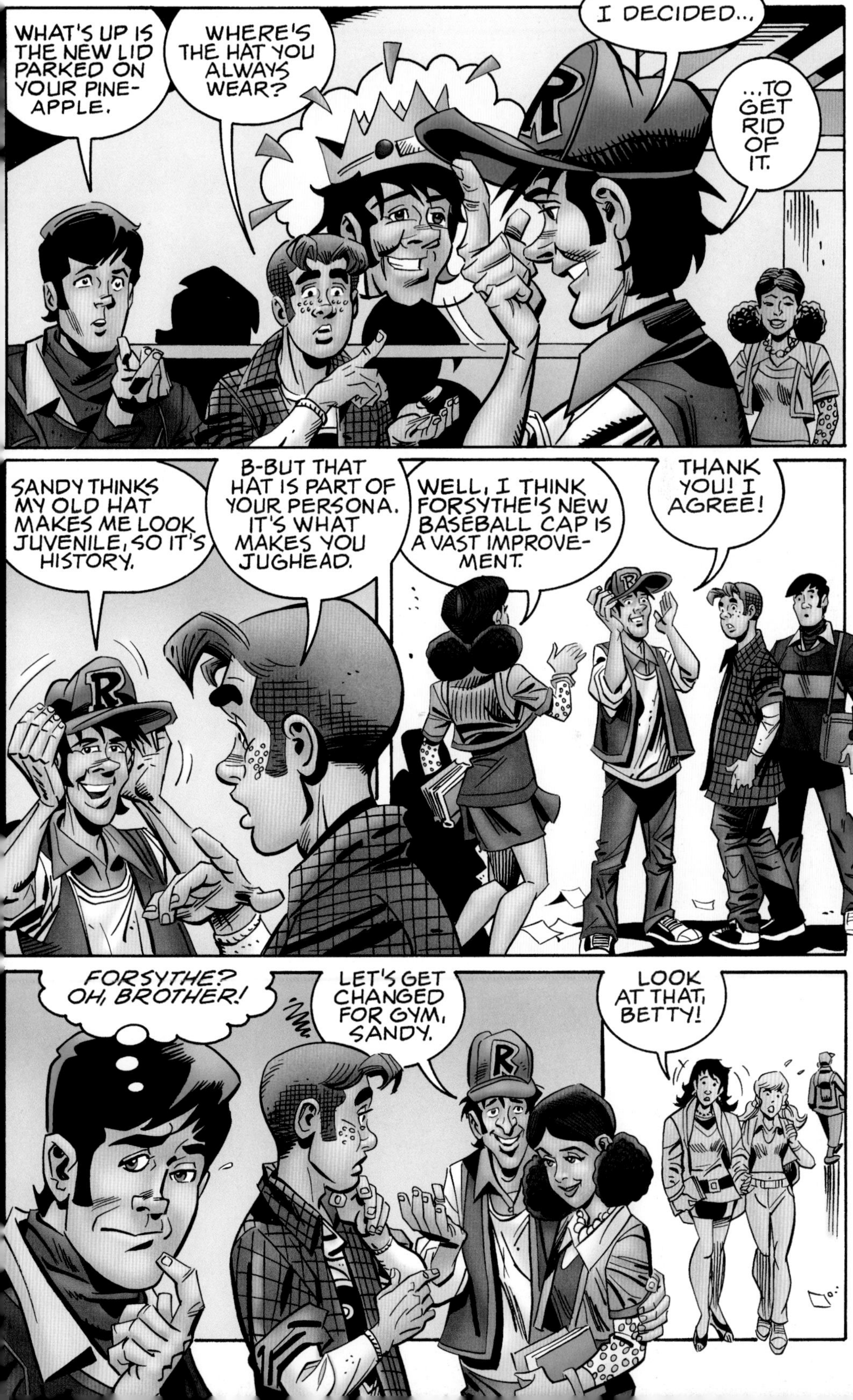
WHAT'S UP IS THE NEW LID PARKED ON YOUR PINE-APPLE.
WHERE'S THE HAT YOU ALWAYS WEAR?
I DECIDED...
...TO GET RID OF IT.
SANDY THINKS MY OLD HAT MAKES ME LOOK JUVENILE, SO IT'S HISTORY.
B-BUT THAT HAT IS PART OF YOUR PERSONA. IT'S WHAT MAKES YOU JUGHEAD.
WELL, I THINK FORSYTHE'S NEW BASEBALL CAP IS A VAST IMPROVE-MENT.
THANK YOU! I AGREE!
FORSYTHE? OH, BROTHER!
LET'S GET CHANGED FOR GYM, SANDY.
LOOK AT THAT, BETTY!

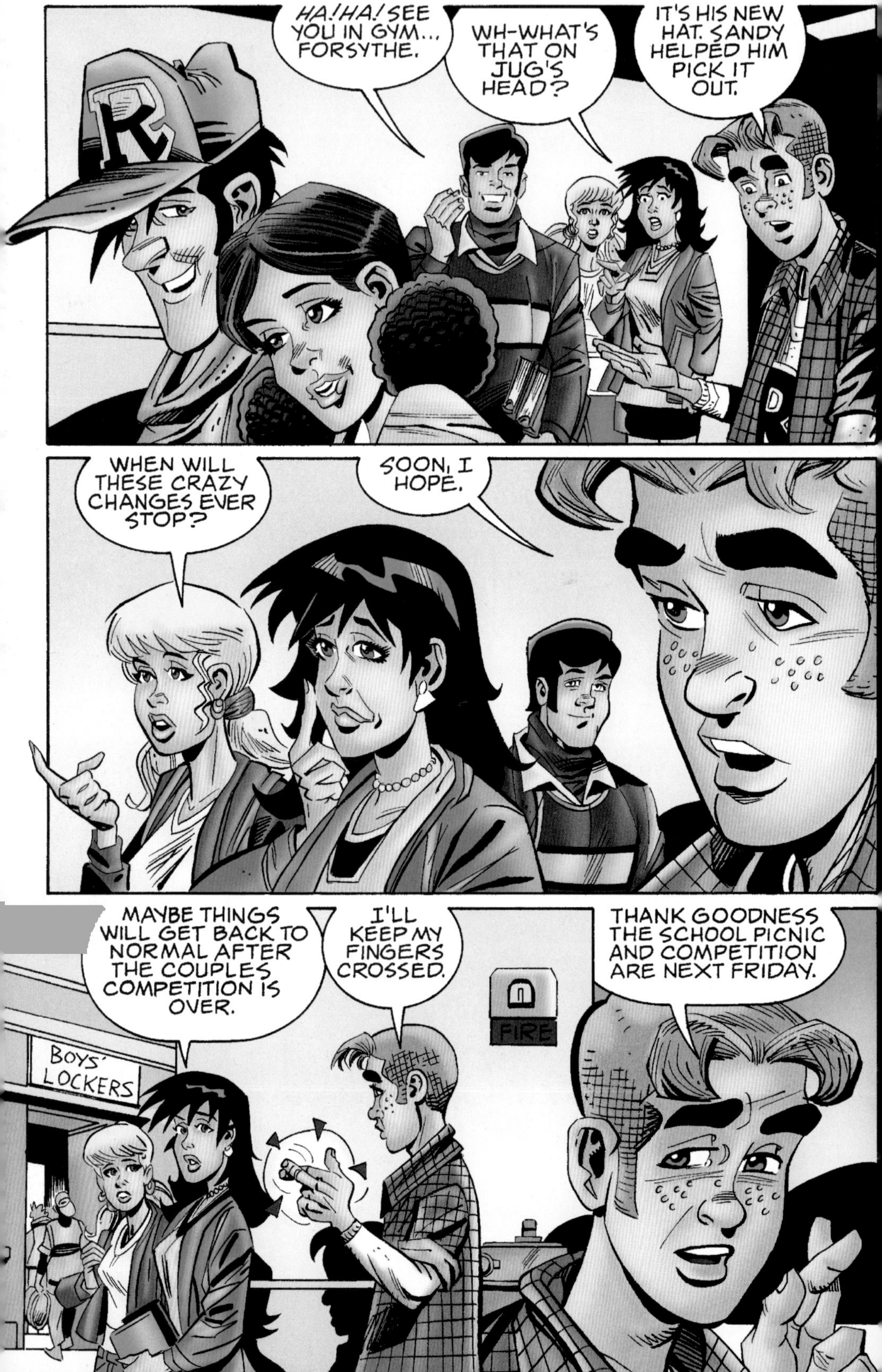
HA! HA! SEE YOU IN GYM... FORSYTHE.
WH-WHAT'S THAT ON JUG'S HEAD?
IT'S HIS NEW HAT. SANDY HELPED HIM PICK IT OUT.
WHEN WILL THESE CRAZY CHANGES EVER STOP?
SOON, I HOPE.
MAYBE THINGS WILL GET BACK TO NORMAL AFTER THE COUPLES COMPETITION IS OVER.
I'LL KEEP MY FINGERS CROSSED.
THANK GOODNESS THE SCHOOL PICNIC AND COMPETITION ARE NEXT FRIDAY.
BOYS' LOCKERS
FIRE

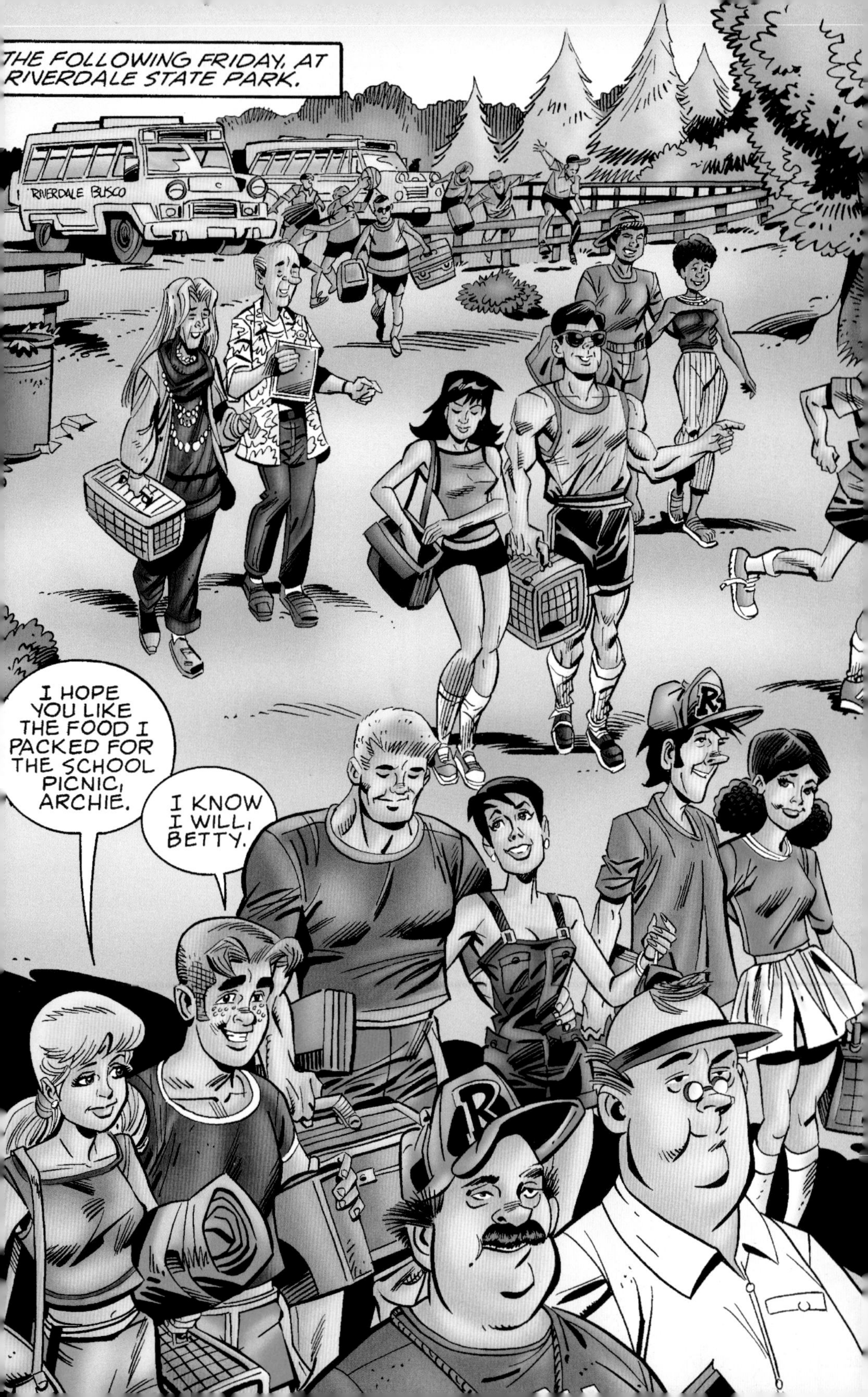
THE FOLLOWING FRIDAY, AT RIVERDALE STATE PARK.
RIVERDALE BUSCO
I HOPE YOU LIKE THE FOOD I PACKED FOR THE SCHOOL PICNIC, ARCHIE.
I KNOW I WILL, BETTY.

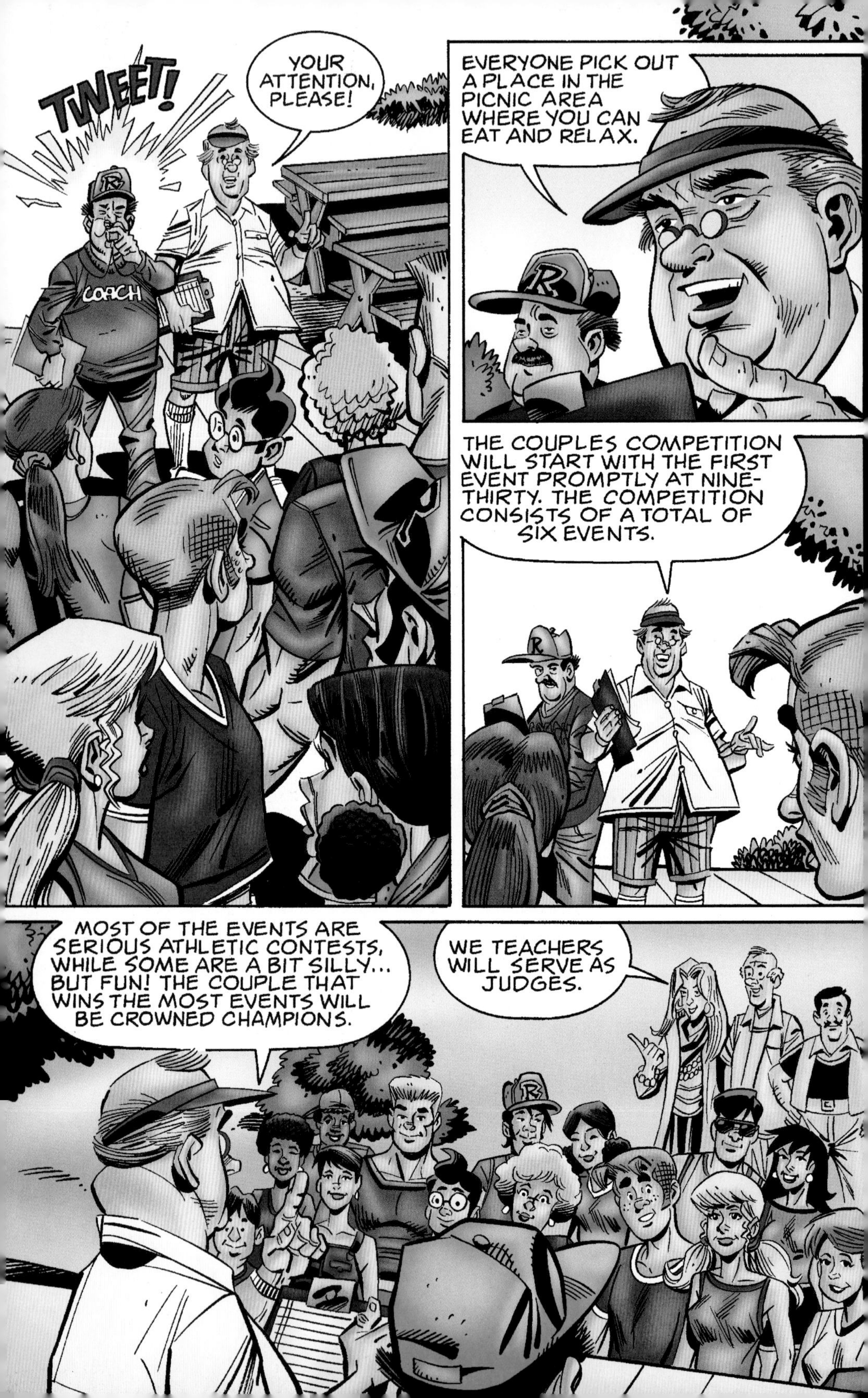
TWEET!
YOUR ATTENTION, PLEASE!
COACH
EVERYONE PICK OUT A PLACE IN THE PICNIC AREA WHERE YOU CAN EAT AND RELAX.
THE COUPLES COMPETITION WILL START WITH THE FIRST EVENT PROMPTLY AT NINE-THIRTY. THE COMPETITION CONSISTS OF A TOTAL OF SIX EVENTS.
MOST OF THE EVENTS ARE SERIOUS ATHLETIC CONTESTS, WHILE SOME ARE A BIT SILLY... BUT FUN! THE COUPLE THAT WINS THE MOST EVENTS WILL BE CROWNED CHAMPIONS.
WE TEACHERS WILL SERVE AS JUDGES.

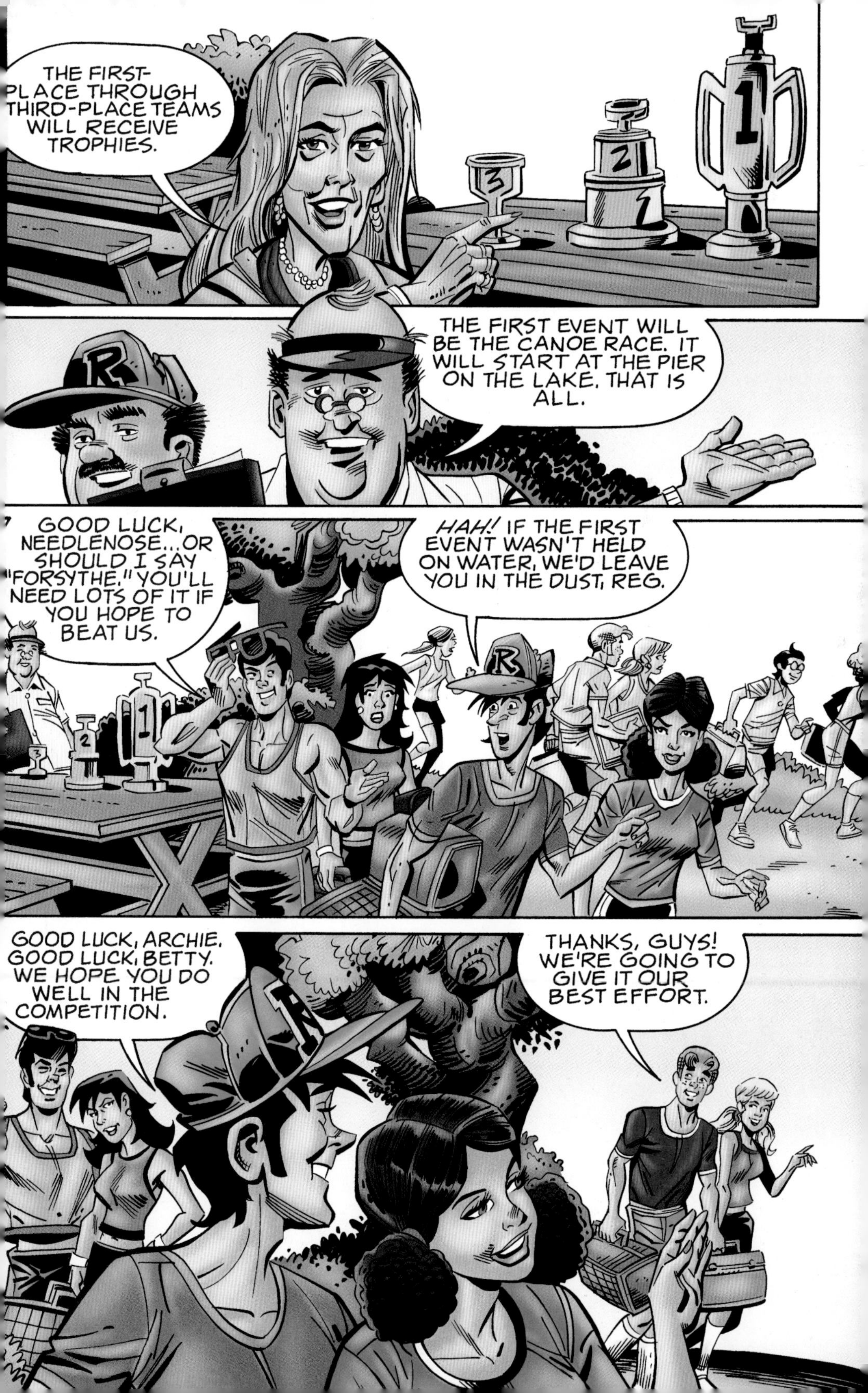
THE FIRST-PLACE THROUGH THIRD-PLACE TEAMS WILL RECEIVE TROPHIES.
1
2
3
THE FIRST EVENT WILL BE THE CANOE RACE. IT WILL START AT THE PIER ON THE LAKE. THAT IS ALL.
GOOD LUCK, NEEDLENOSE...OR SHOULD I SAY "FORSYTHE." YOU'LL NEED LOTS OF IT IF YOU HOPE TO BEAT US.
HAH! IF THE FIRST EVENT WASN'T HELD ON WATER, WE'D LEAVE YOU IN THE DUST, REG.
GOOD LUCK, ARCHIE. GOOD LUCK, BETTY. WE HOPE YOU DO WELL IN THE COMPETITION.
THANKS, GUYS! WE'RE GOING TO GIVE IT OUR BEST EFFORT.

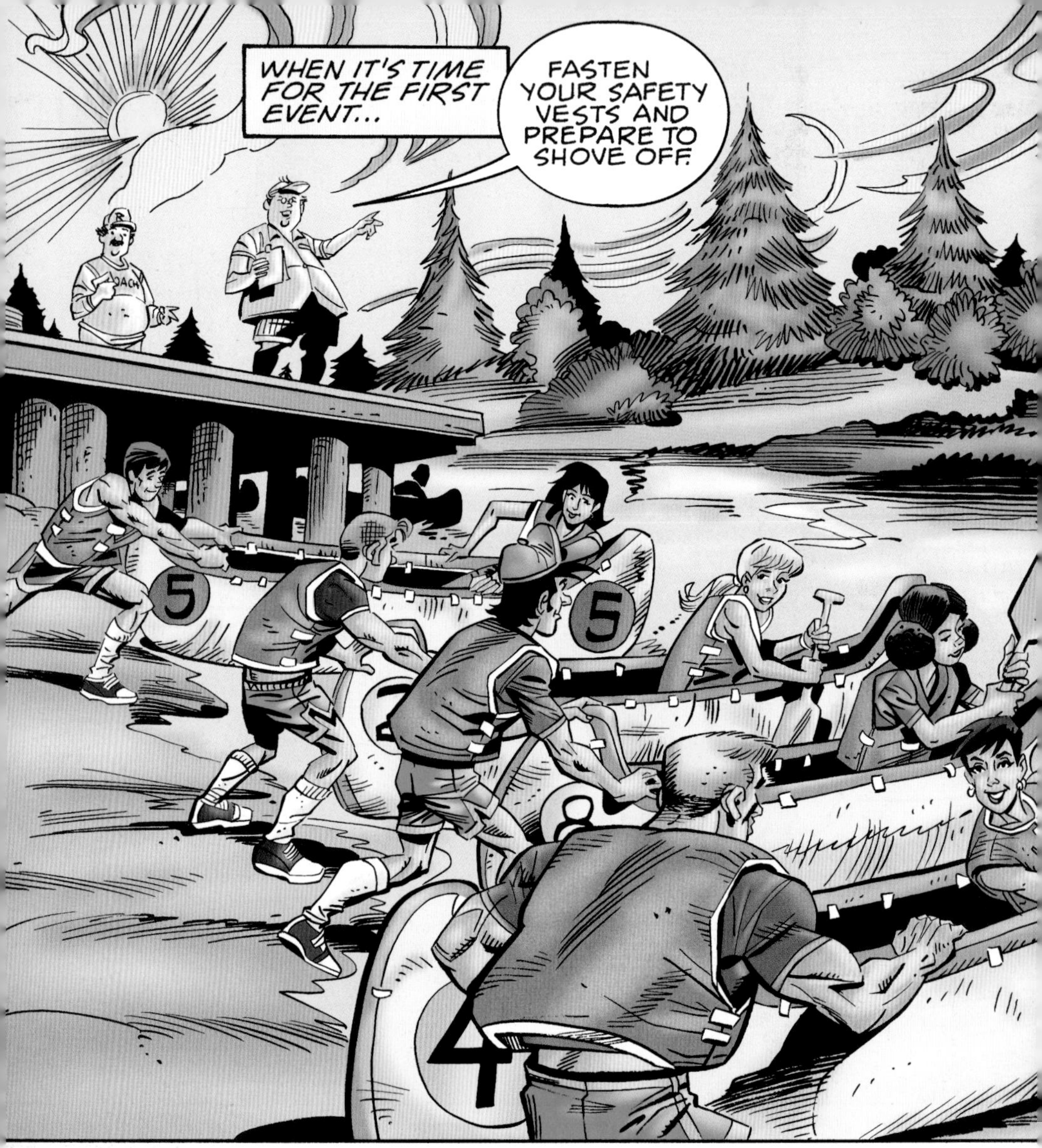
WHEN IT'S TIME FOR THE FIRST EVENT...
FASTEN YOUR SAFETY VESTS AND PREPARE TO SHOVE OFF.
5
5
8
4

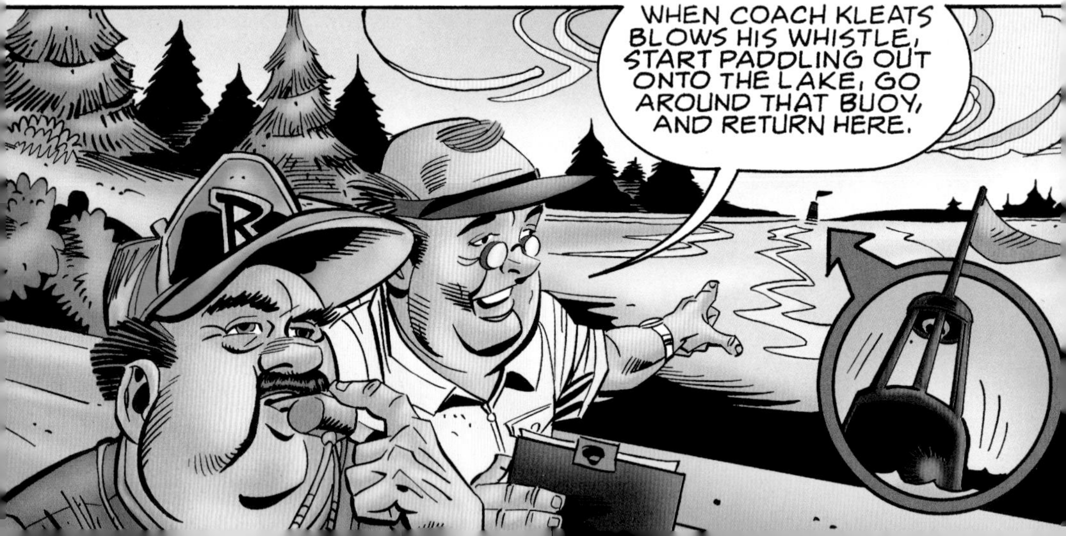
WHEN COACH KLEATS BLOWS HIS WHISTLE, START PADDLING OUT ONTO THE LAKE, GO AROUND THAT BUOY, AND RETURN HERE.

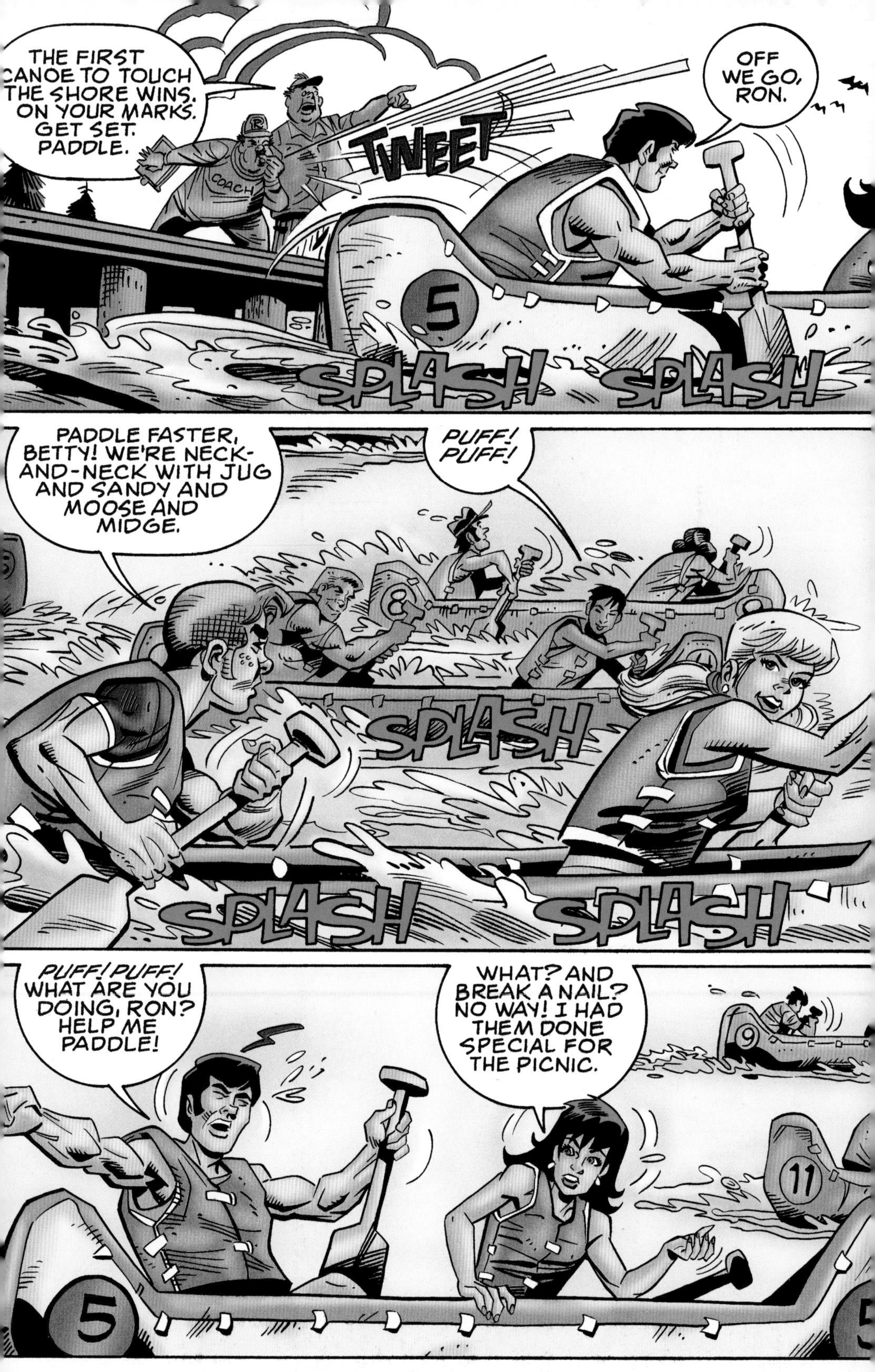
THE FIRST CANOE TO TOUCH THE SHORE WINS. ON YOUR MARKS. GET SET. PADDLE.
COACH
TWEET
OFF WE GO, RON.
5
SPLASH SPLASH
PADDLE FASTER, BETTY! WE'RE NECK-AND-NECK WITH JUG AND SANDY AND MOOSE AND MIDGE.
PUFF! PUFF!
SPLASH
SPLASH SPLASH
PUFF! PUFF! WHAT ARE YOU DOING, RON? HELP ME PADDLE!
WHAT? AND BREAK A NAIL? NO WAY! I HAD THEM DONE SPECIAL FOR THE PICNIC.
9
11
5

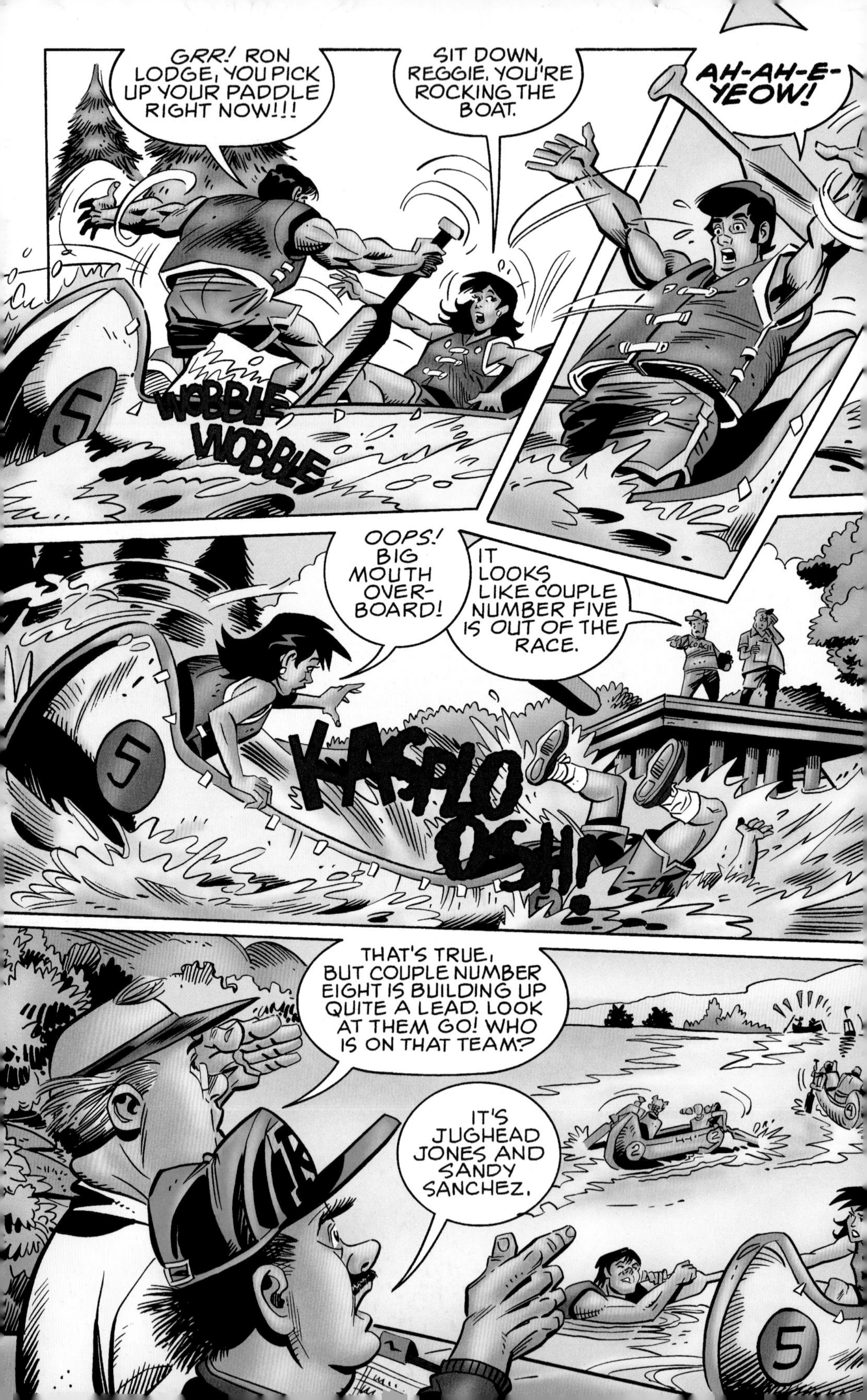
GRR! RON LODGE, YOU PICK UP YOUR PADDLE RIGHT NOW!!!
SIT DOWN, REGGIE. YOU'RE ROCKING THE BOAT.
WOBBLE WOBBLE
AH-AH-E-YEOW!
OOPS! BIG MOUTH OVER-BOARD!
IT LOOKS LIKE COUPLE NUMBER FIVE IS OUT OF THE RACE.
KASPLOOSH!
THAT'S TRUE, BUT COUPLE NUMBER EIGHT IS BUILDING UP QUITE A LEAD. LOOK AT THEM GO! WHO IS ON THAT TEAM?
IT'S JUGHEAD JONES AND SANDY SANCHEZ.

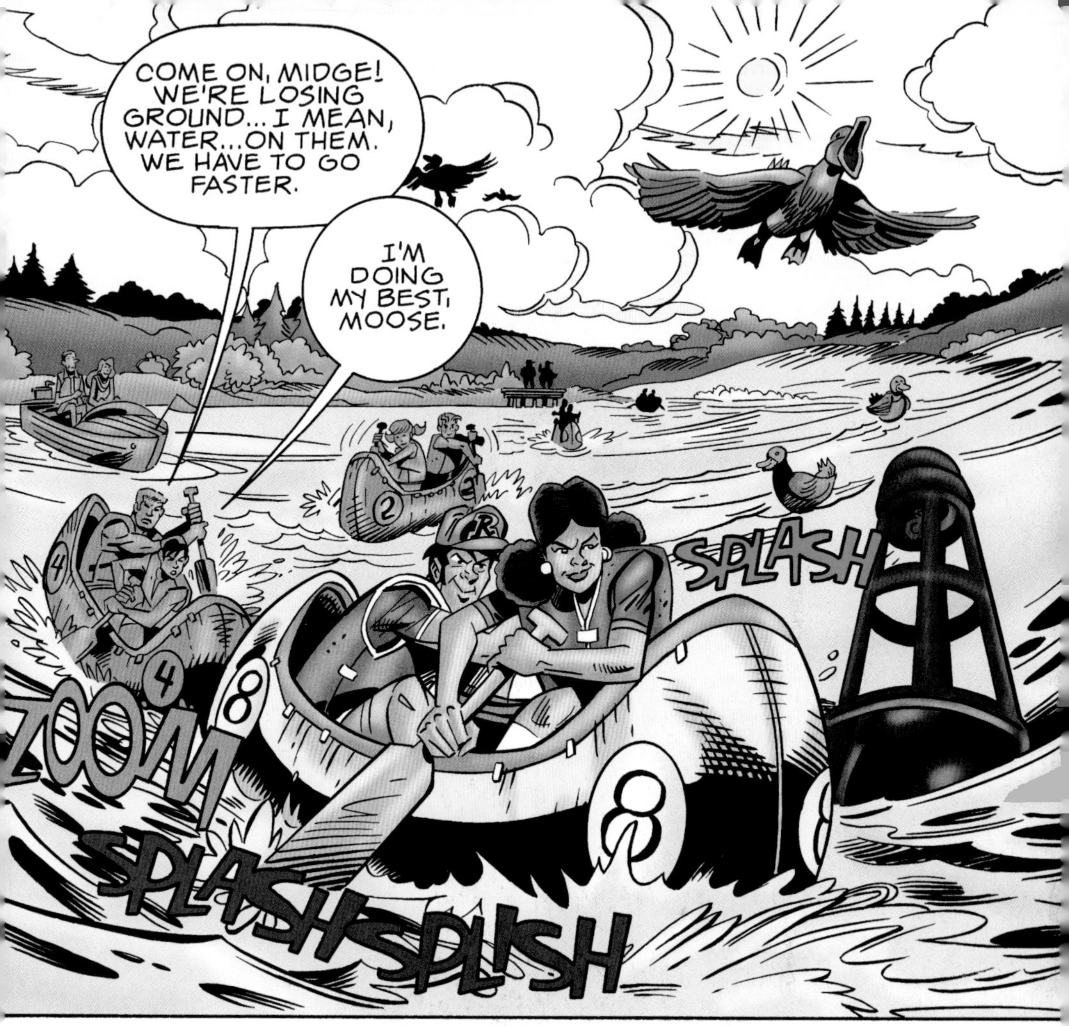
COME ON, MIDGE! WE'RE LOSING GROUND... I MEAN, WATER...ON THEM. WE HAVE TO GO FASTER.
I'M DOING MY BEST, MOOSE.
SPLASH
ZOOM
SPLASH SPLISH

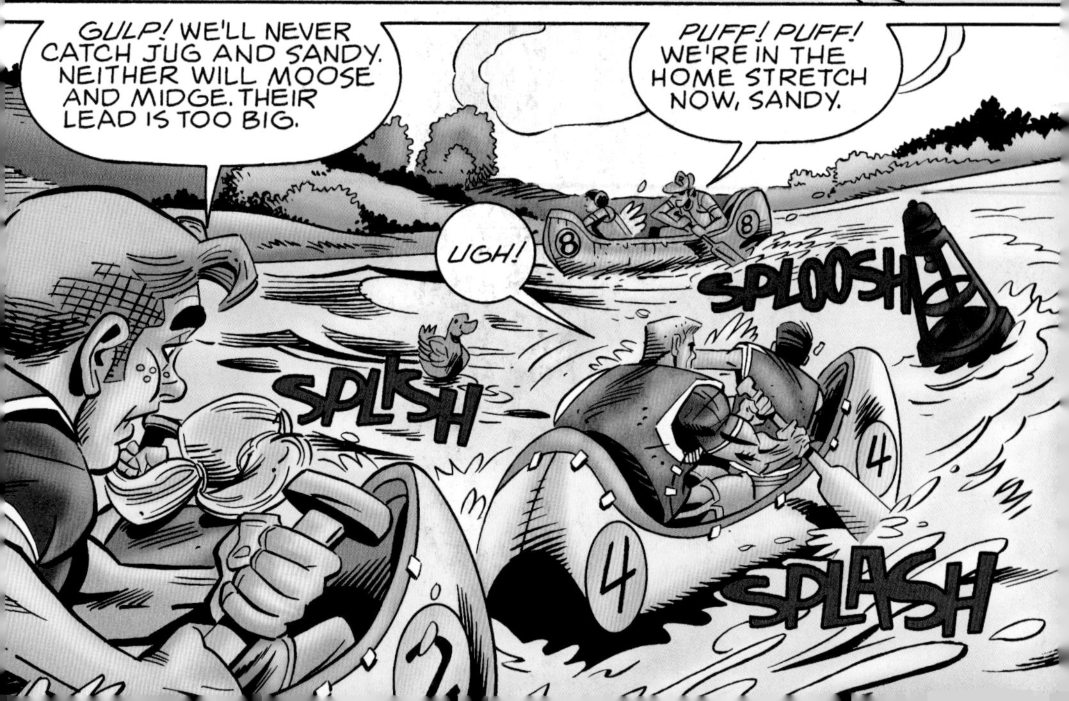
GULP! WE'LL NEVER CATCH JUG AND SANDY. NEITHER WILL MOOSE AND MIDGE. THEIR LEAD IS TOO BIG.
PUFF! PUFF! WE'RE IN THE HOME STRETCH NOW, SANDY.
UGH!
SPLOOSH
SPLISH
SPLASH

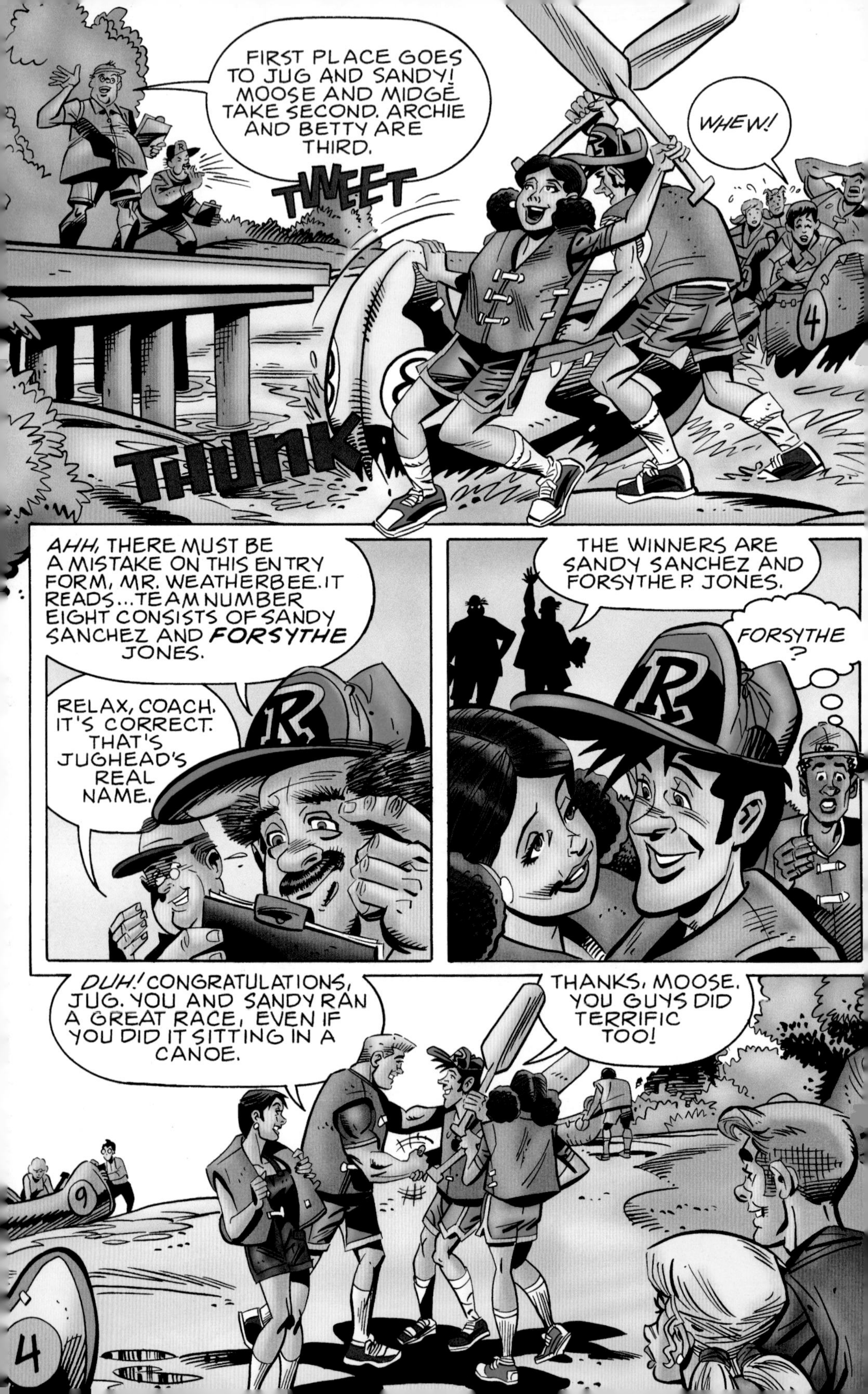
FIRST PLACE GOES TO JUG AND SANDY! MOOSE AND MIDGE TAKE SECOND. ARCHIE AND BETTY ARE THIRD.
TWEET
WHEW!
THUNK
AHH, THERE MUST BE A MISTAKE ON THIS ENTRY FORM, MR. WEATHERBEE. IT READS...TEAM NUMBER EIGHT CONSISTS OF SANDY SANCHEZ AND FORSYTHE JONES.
RELAX, COACH. IT'S CORRECT. THAT'S JUGHEAD'S REAL NAME.
THE WINNERS ARE SANDY SANCHEZ AND FORSYTHE P. JONES.
FORSYTHE ?
DUH! CONGRATULATIONS, JUG. YOU AND SANDY RAN A GREAT RACE, EVEN IF YOU DID IT SITTING IN A CANOE.
THANKS, MOOSE. YOU GUYS DID TERRIFIC TOO!

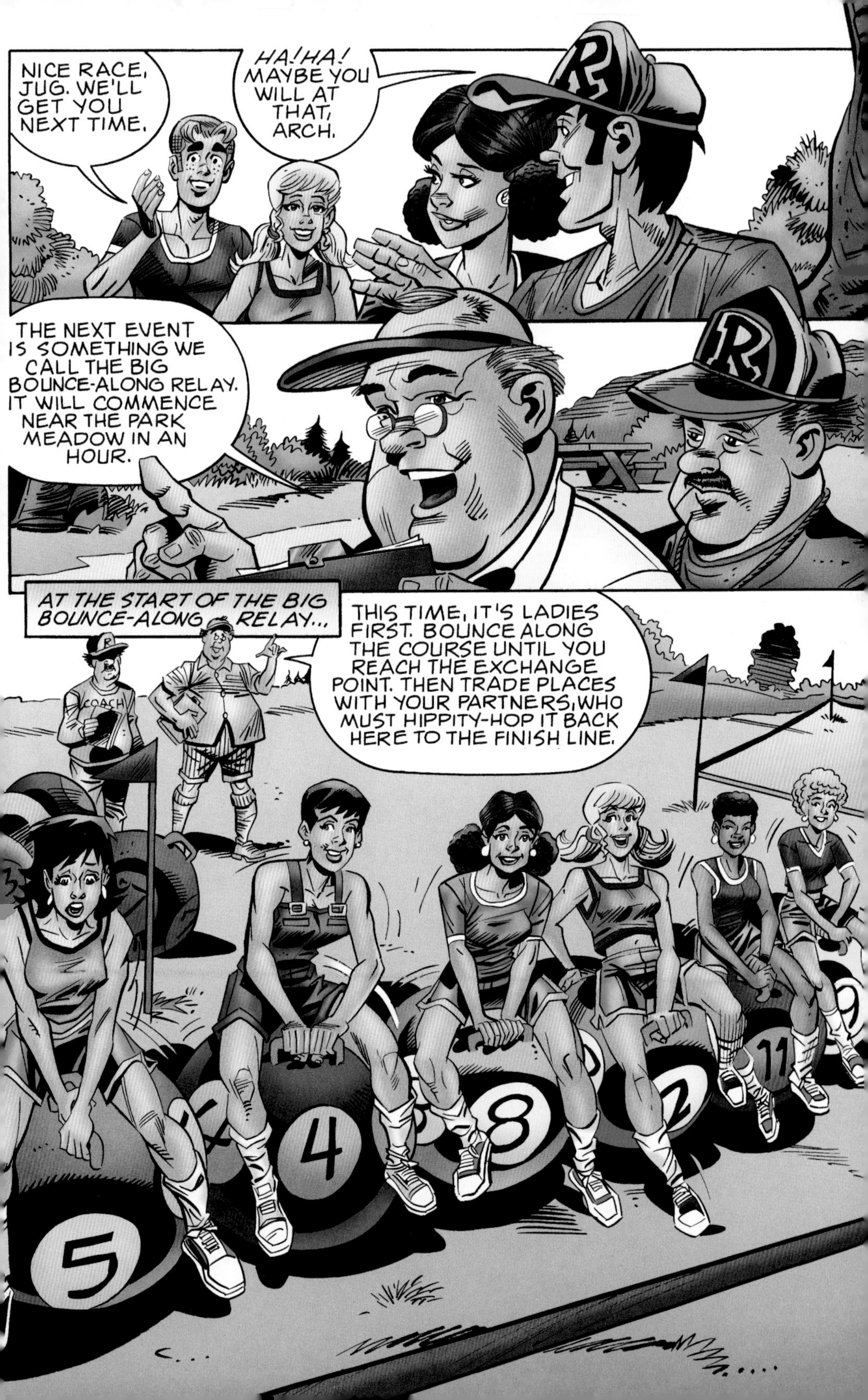
NICE RACE, JUG. WE'LL GET YOU NEXT TIME.
HA! HA! MAYBE YOU WILL AT THAT, ARCH.
THE NEXT EVENT IS SOMETHING WE CALL THE BIG BOUNCE-ALONG RELAY. IT WILL COMMENCE NEAR THE PARK MEADOW IN AN HOUR.
AT THE START OF THE BIG BOUNCE-ALONG RELAY...
THIS TIME, IT'S LADIES FIRST. BOUNCE ALONG THE COURSE UNTIL YOU REACH THE EXCHANGE POINT. THEN TRADE PLACES WITH YOUR PARTNERS, WHO MUST HIPPITY-HOP IT BACK HERE TO THE FINISH LINE.
COACH

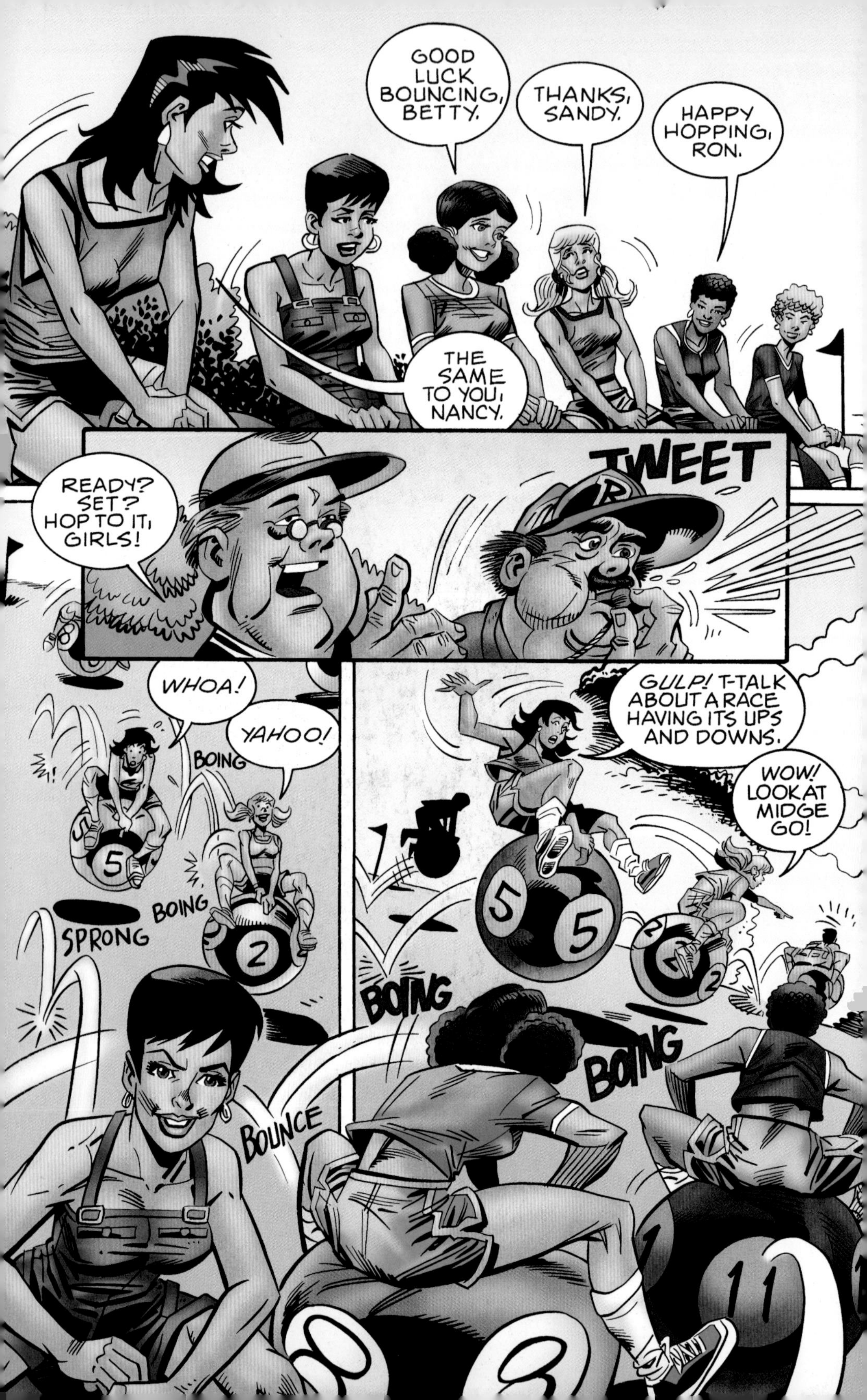

GOOD LUCK BOUNCING, BETTY.
THANKS, SANDY.
HAPPY HOPPING, RON.
THE SAME TO YOU, NANCY.
READY? SET? HOP TO IT, GIRLS!
TWEET
WHOA!
YAHOO!
BOING
BOING
SPRONG
GULP! T-TALK ABOUT A RACE HAVING ITS UPS AND DOWNS.
WOW! LOOK AT MIDGE GO!
BOING
BOING
BOUNCE

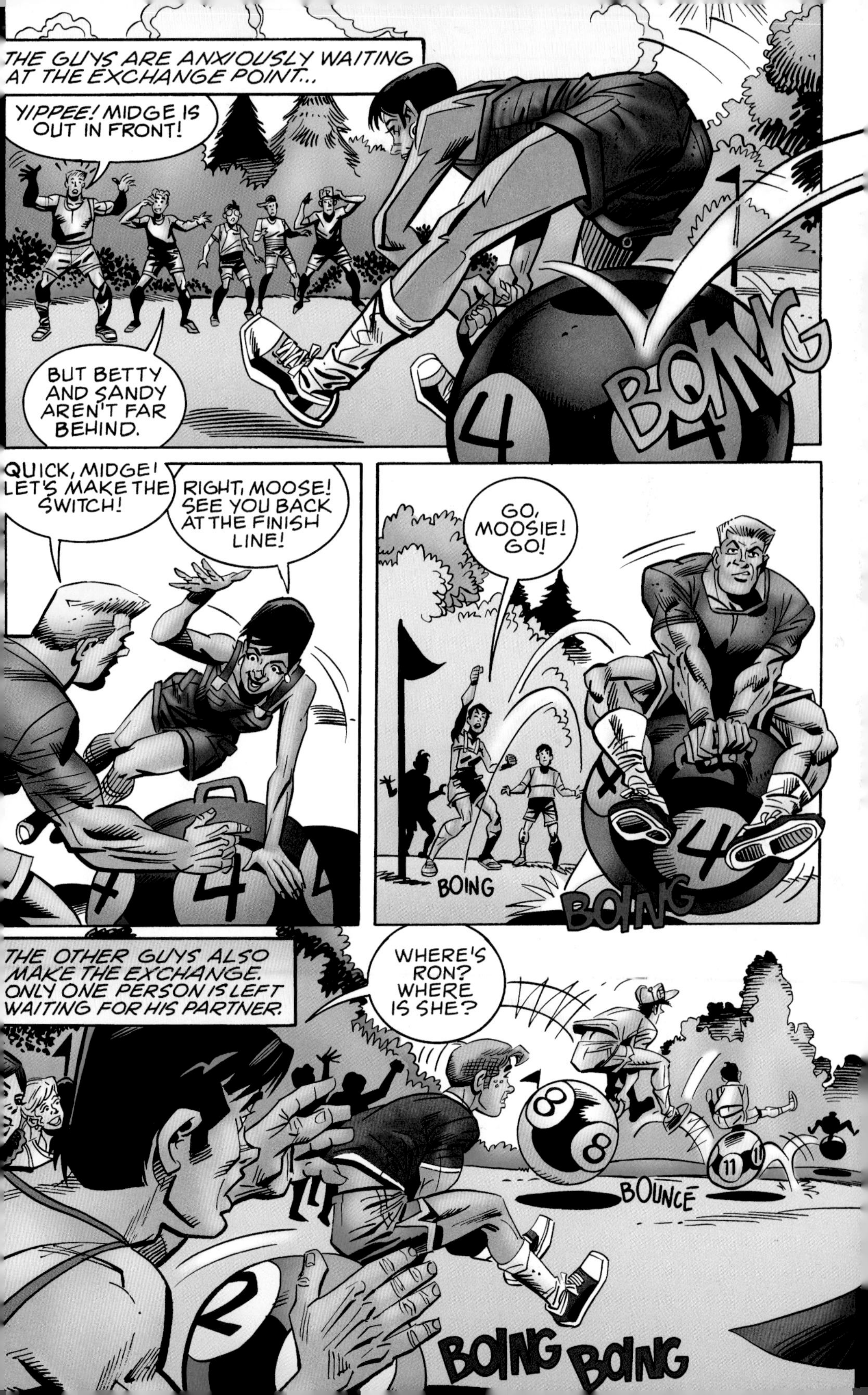
THE GUYS ARE ANXIOUSLY WAITING AT THE EXCHANGE POINT...
YIPPEE! MIDGE IS OUT IN FRONT!
BUT BETTY AND SANDY AREN'T FAR BEHIND.
BOING
QUICK, MIDGE! LET'S MAKE THE SWITCH!
RIGHT, MOOSE! SEE YOU BACK AT THE FINISH LINE!
GO, MOOSIE! GO!
BOING
BOING
THE OTHER GUYS ALSO MAKE THE EXCHANGE. ONLY ONE PERSON IS LEFT WAITING FOR HIS PARTNER.
WHERE'S RON? WHERE IS SHE?
BOUNCE
BOING BOING

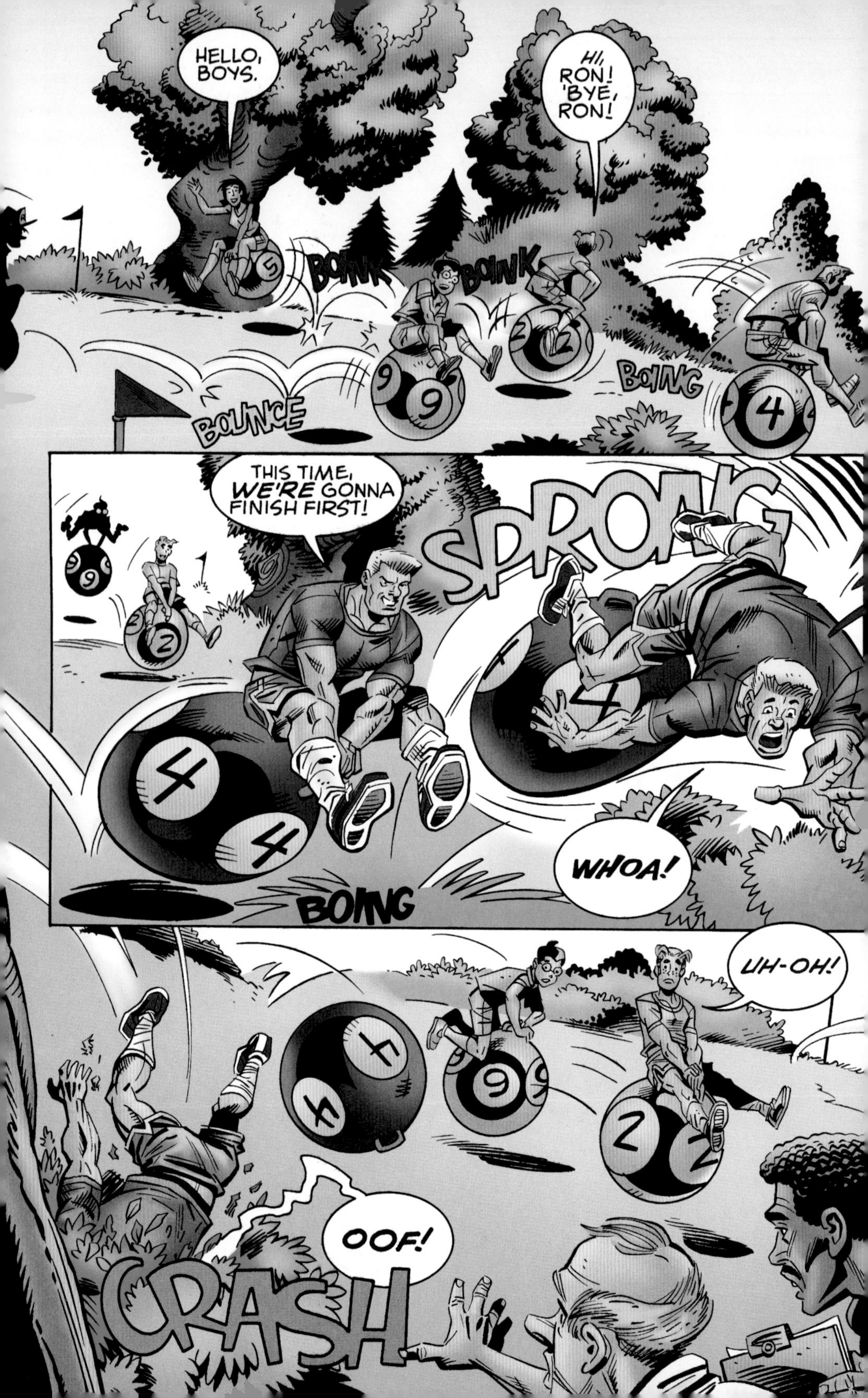

HELLO, BOYS.
HI, RON! 'BYE, RON!
BOINK
BOINK
BOING
BOUNCE
THIS TIME, WE'RE GONNA FINISH FIRST!
SPROING
WHOA!
BOING
UH-OH!
OOF!
CRASH

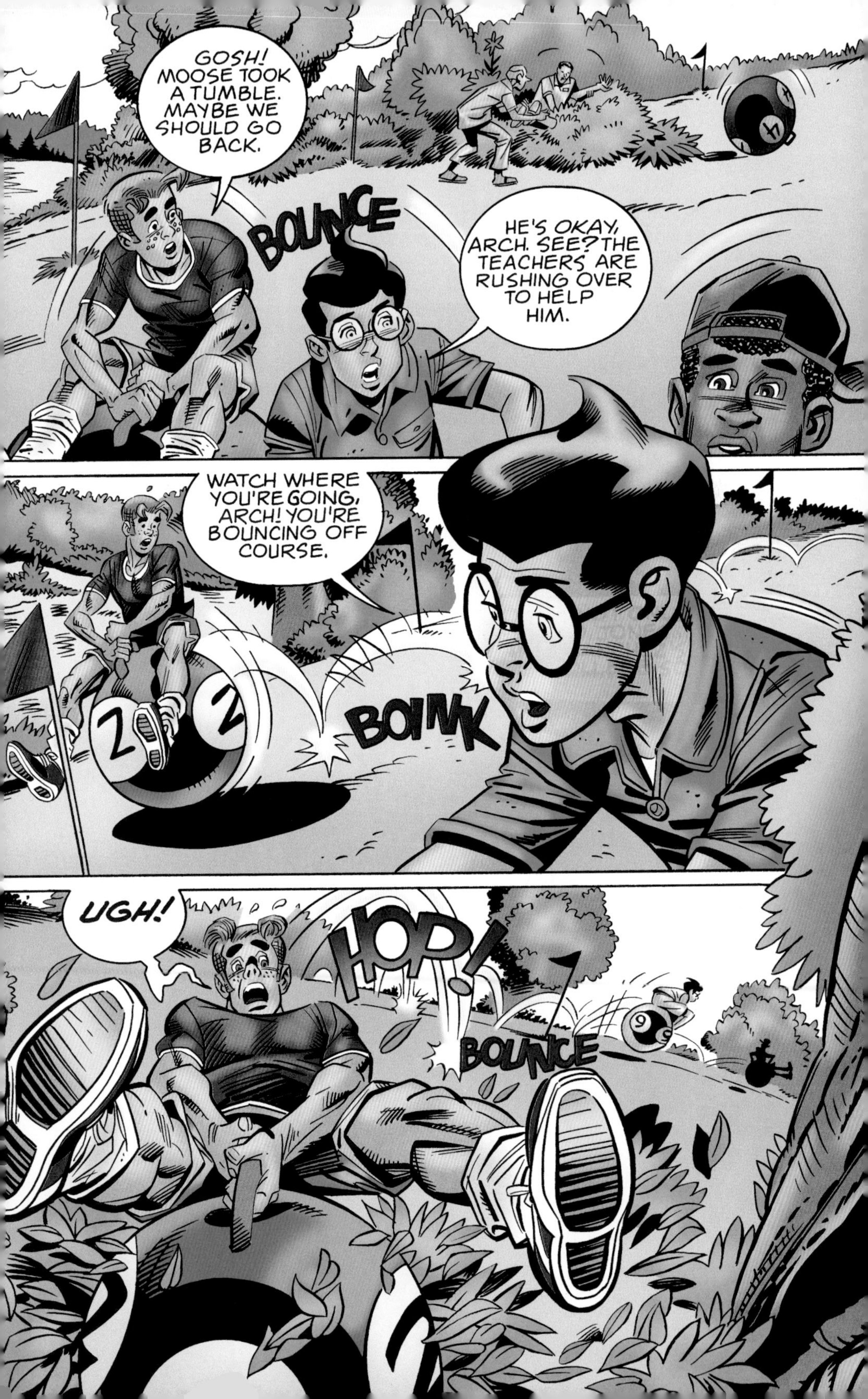
GOSH! MOOSE TOOK A TUMBLE. MAYBE WE SHOULD GO BACK.
BOUNCE
HE'S OKAY, ARCH. SEE? THE TEACHERS ARE RUSHING OVER TO HELP HIM.
WATCH WHERE YOU'RE GOING, ARCH! YOU'RE BOUNCING OFF COURSE.
BOINK
UGH!
HOP!
BOUNCE

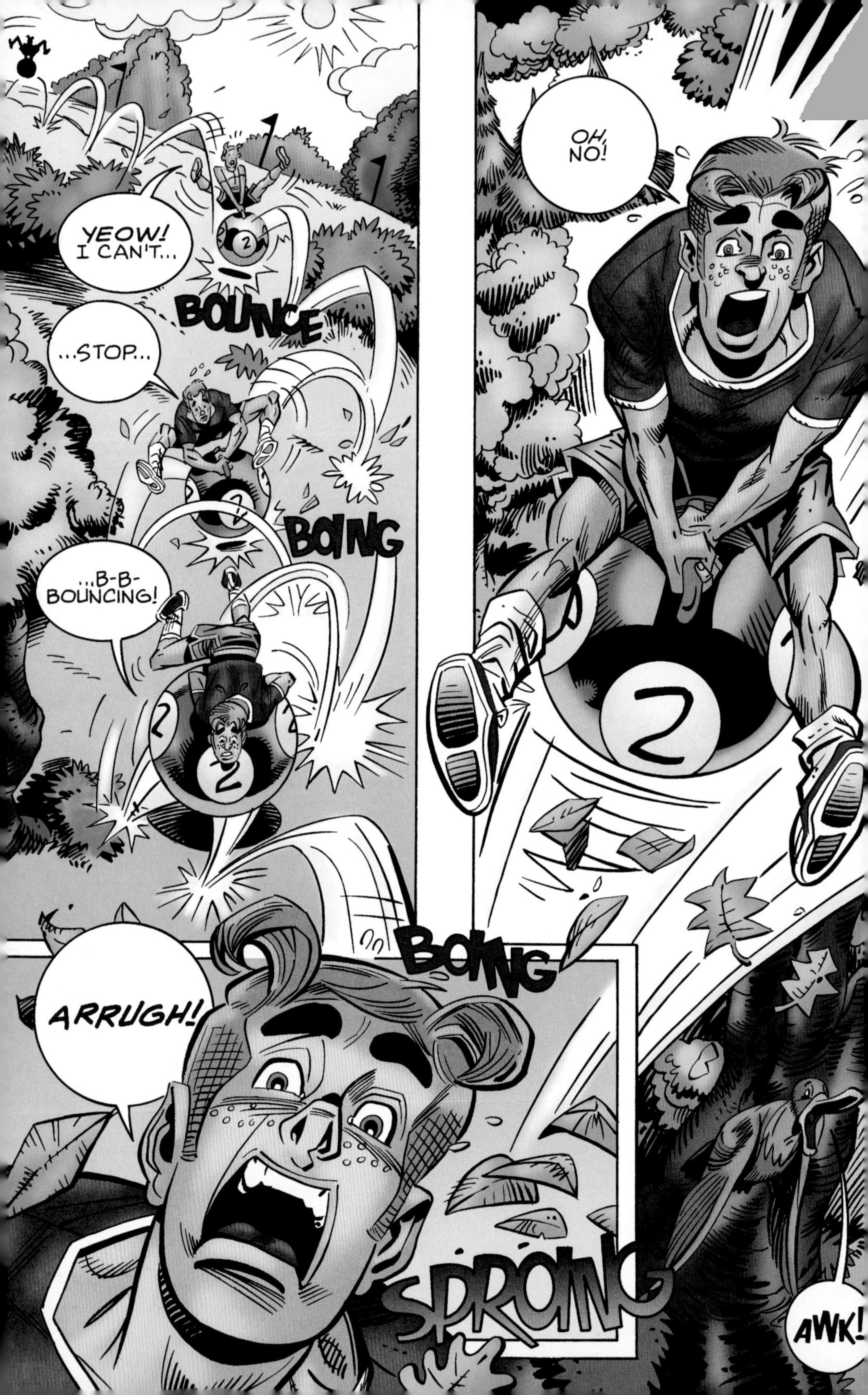
YEOW! I CAN'T...
BOUNCE
...STOP...
BOING
...B-B-BOUNCING!
OH, NO!
ARRUGH!
BOING
SPROING
AWK!

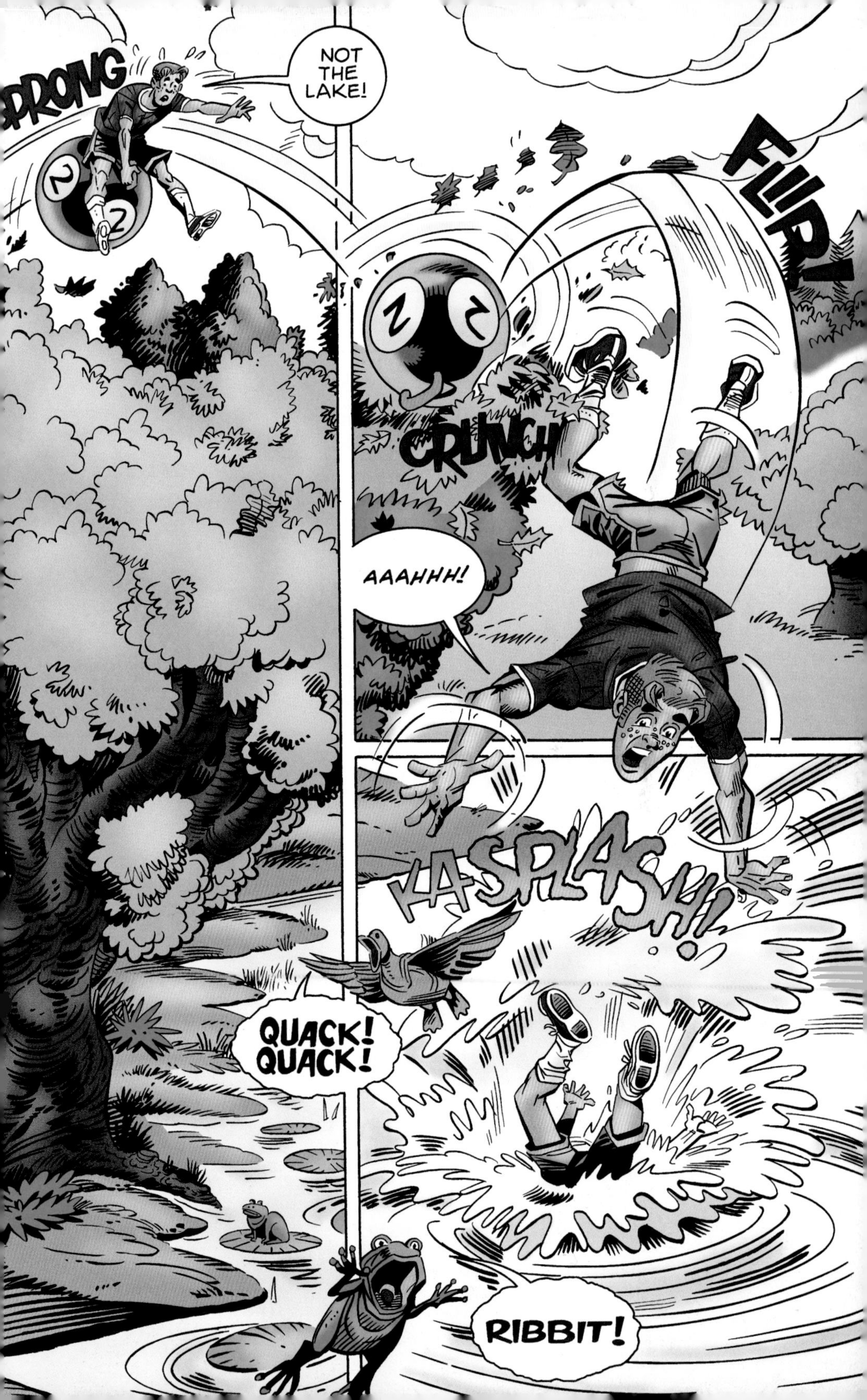
PRONG
NOT THE LAKE!
FLIP!
CRUNCH
AAAHHH!
KASPLASH!
QUACK! QUACK!
RIBBIT!

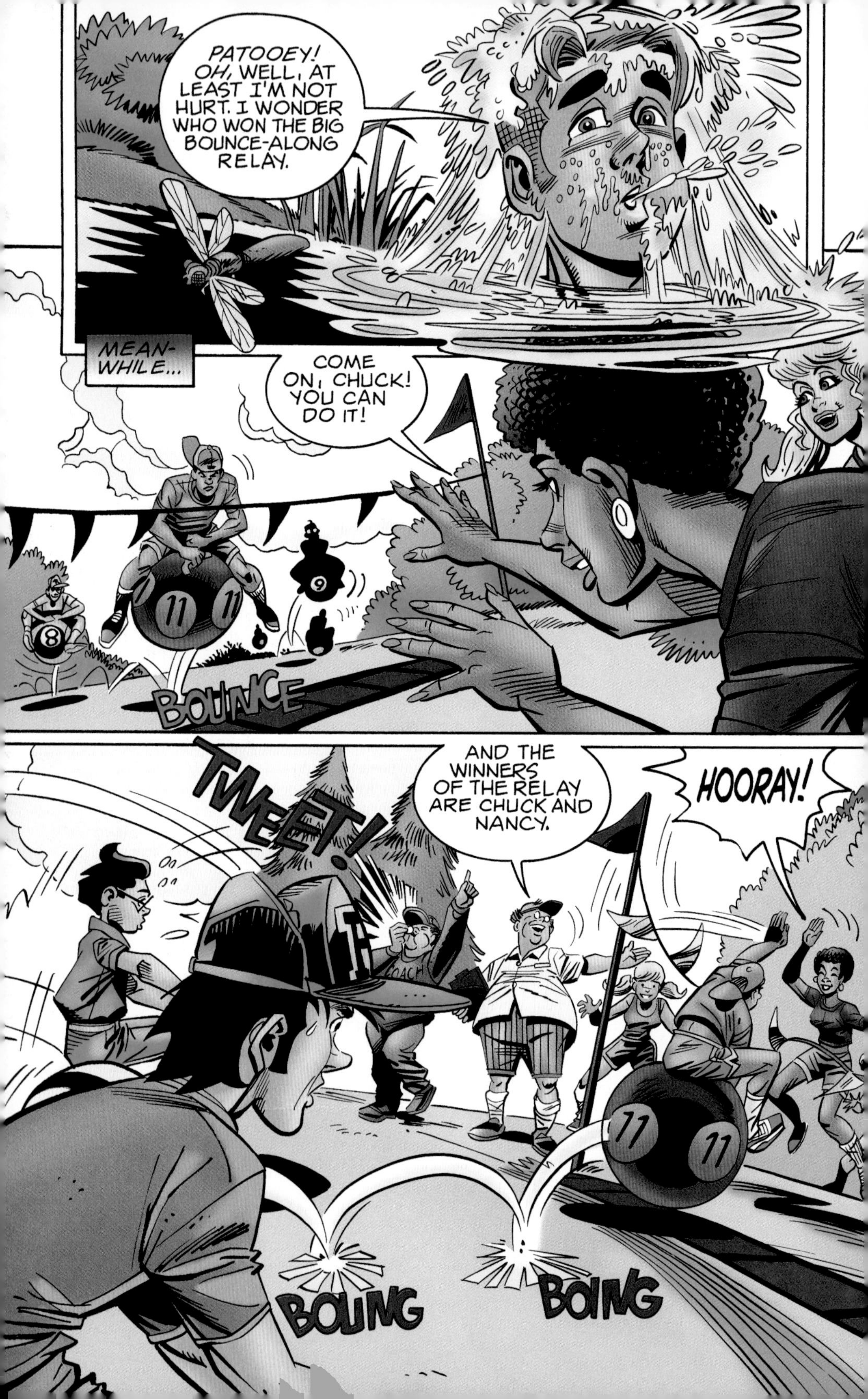
PATOOEY! OH, WELL, AT LEAST I'M NOT HURT. I WONDER WHO WON THE BIG BOUNCE-ALONG RELAY.
MEAN-WHILE...
COME ON, CHUCK! YOU CAN DO IT!
BOUNCE
TWEET!
AND THE WINNERS OF THE RELAY ARE CHUCK AND NANCY.
HOORAY!
BOING
BOING

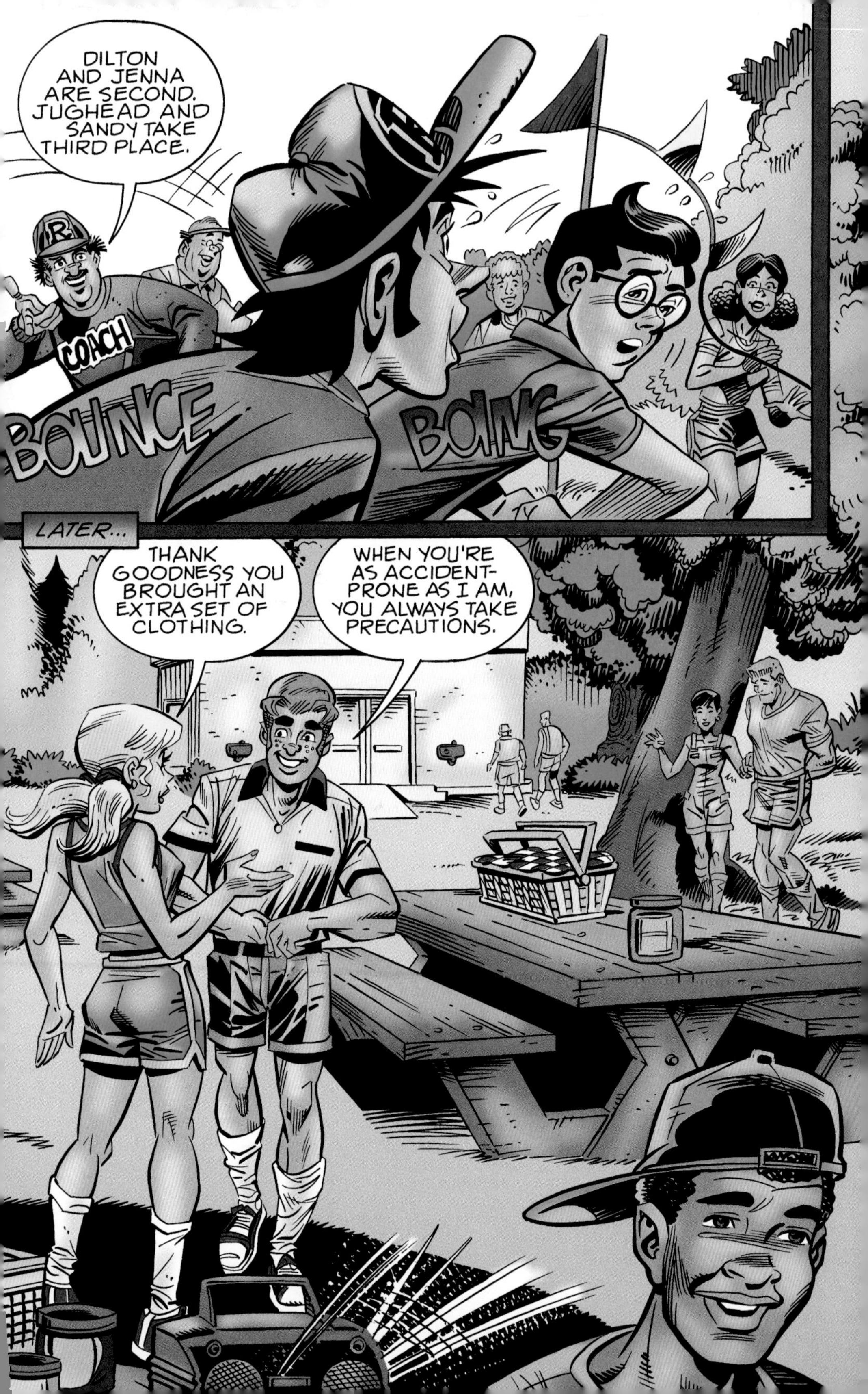
DILTON AND JENNA ARE SECOND. JUGHEAD AND SANDY TAKE THIRD PLACE.
COACH
BOUNCE
BOING
LATER...
THANK GOODNESS YOU BROUGHT AN EXTRA SET OF CLOTHING.
WHEN YOU'RE AS ACCIDENT-PRONE AS I AM, YOU ALWAYS TAKE PRECAUTIONS.

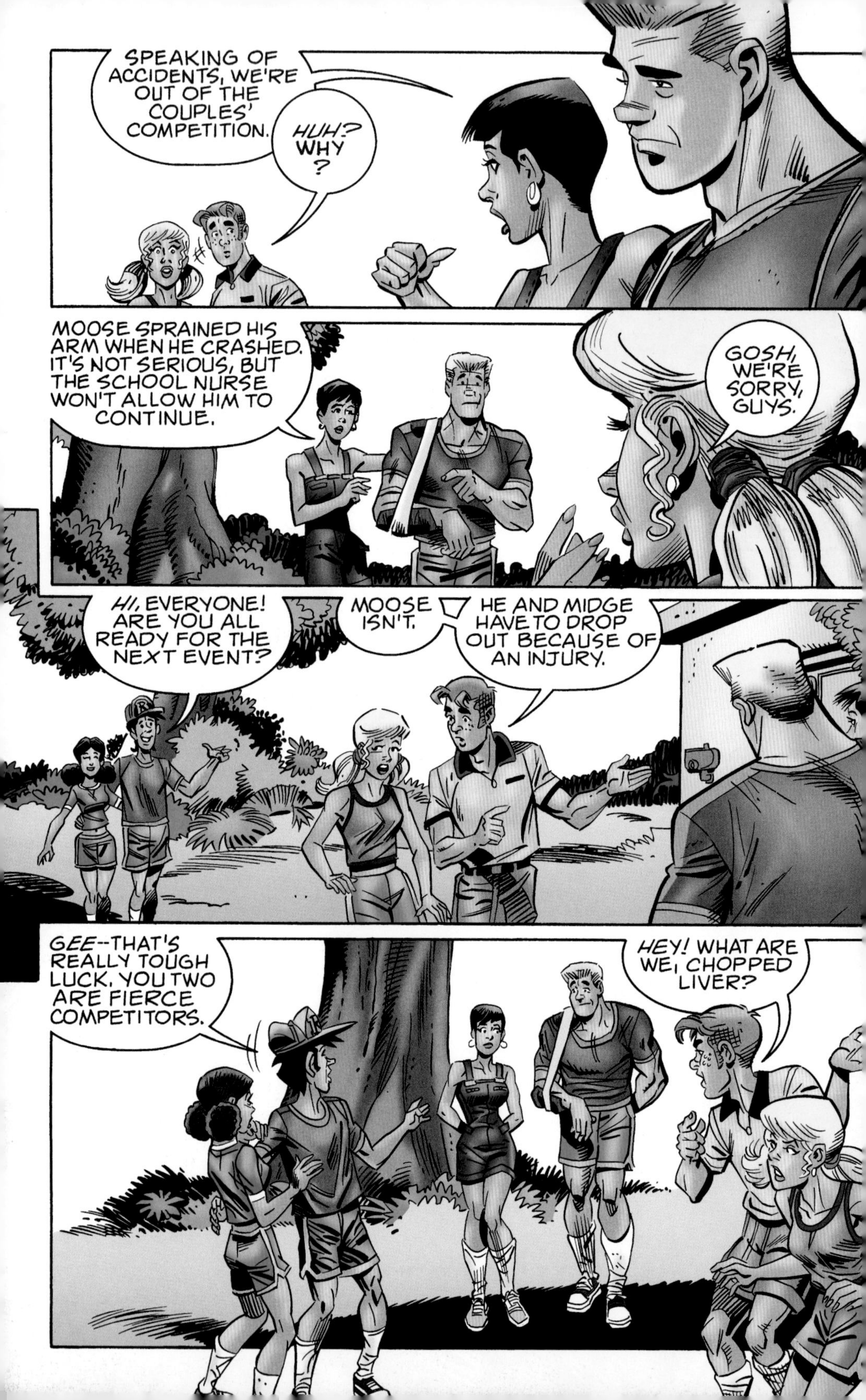
SPEAKING OF ACCIDENTS, WE'RE OUT OF THE COUPLES' COMPETITION.
HUH? WHY?
MOOSE SPRAINED HIS ARM WHEN HE CRASHED. IT'S NOT SERIOUS, BUT THE SCHOOL NURSE WON'T ALLOW HIM TO CONTINUE.
GOSH, WE'RE SORRY, GUYS.
HI, EVERYONE! ARE YOU ALL READY FOR THE NEXT EVENT?
MOOSE ISN'T.
HE AND MIDGE HAVE TO DROP OUT BECAUSE OF AN INJURY.
GEE--THAT'S REALLY TOUGH LUCK. YOU TWO ARE FIERCE COMPETITORS.
HEY! WHAT ARE WE, CHOPPED LIVER?

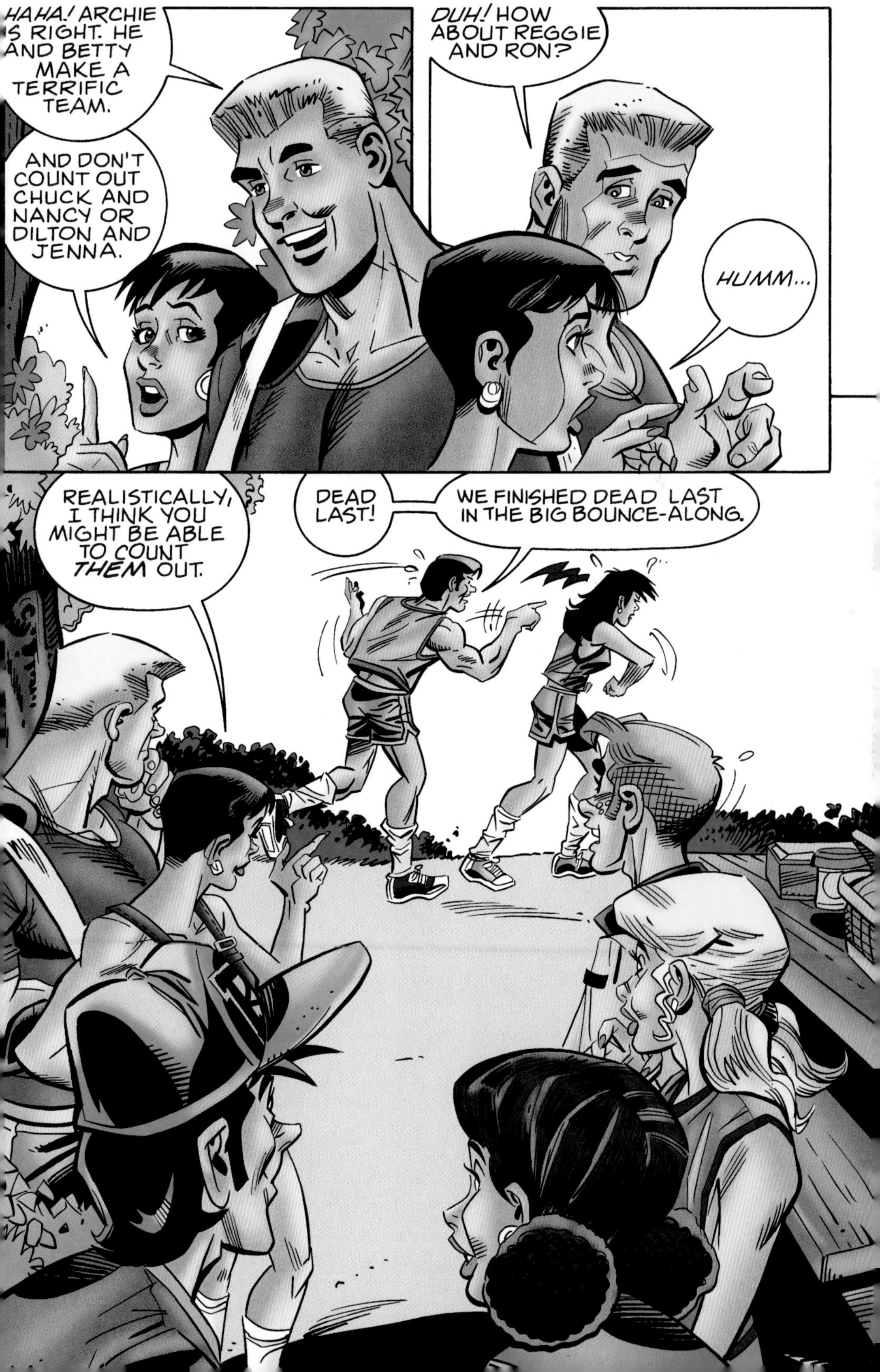
HAHA! ARCHIE'S RIGHT. HE AND BETTY MAKE A TERRIFIC TEAM.
AND DON'T COUNT OUT CHUCK AND NANCY OR DILTON AND JENNA.
DUH! HOW ABOUT REGGIE AND RON?
HUMM...
REALISTICALLY, I THINK YOU MIGHT BE ABLE TO COUNT *THEM* OUT.
DEAD LAST!
WE FINISHED DEAD LAST IN THE BIG BOUNCE-ALONG.

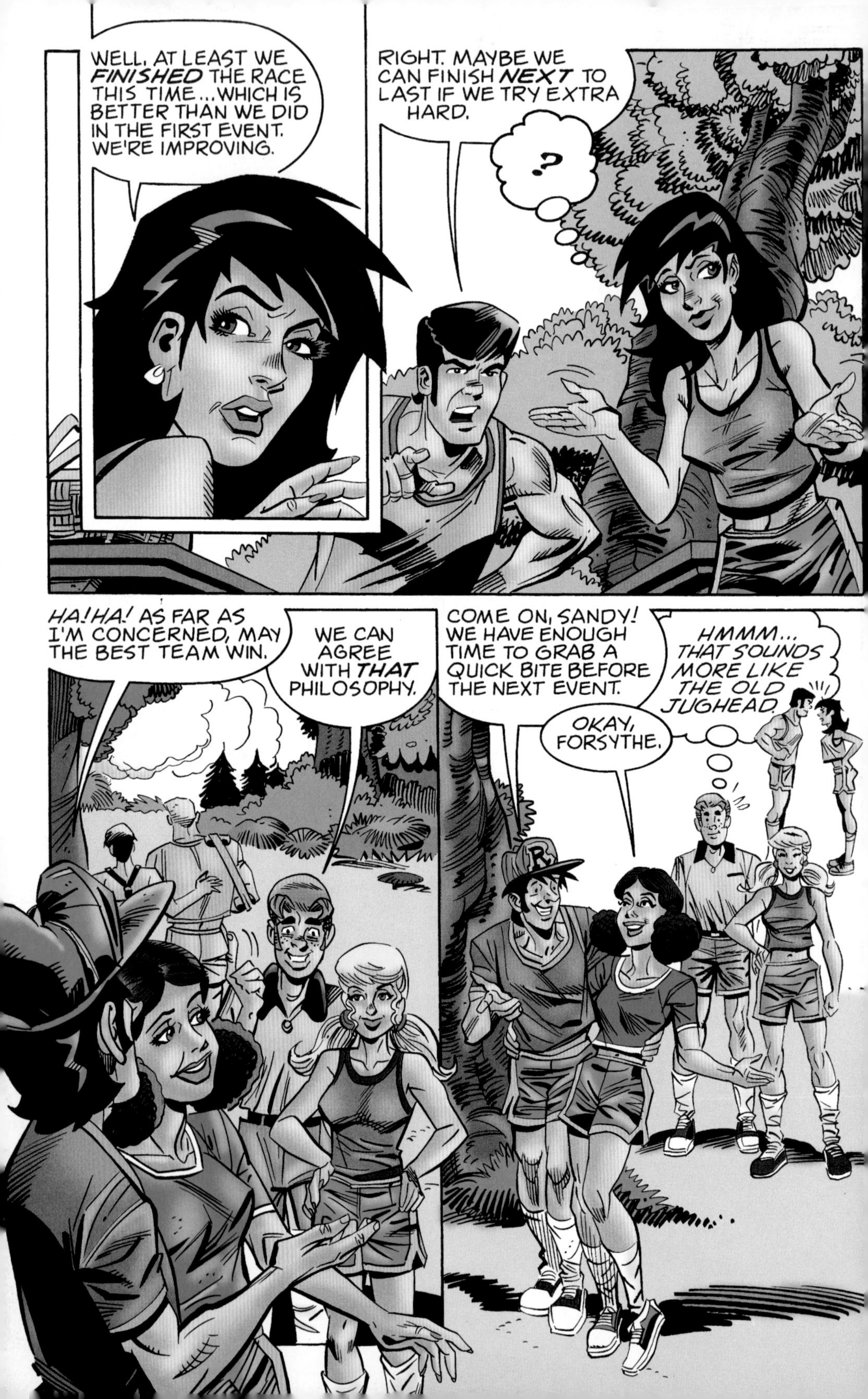

WELL, AT LEAST WE FINISHED THE RACE THIS TIME... WHICH IS BETTER THAN WE DID IN THE FIRST EVENT. WE'RE IMPROVING.
RIGHT. MAYBE WE CAN FINISH NEXT TO LAST IF WE TRY EXTRA HARD.
?
HA! HA! AS FAR AS I'M CONCERNED, MAY THE BEST TEAM WIN.
WE CAN AGREE WITH THAT PHILOSOPHY.
COME ON, SANDY! WE HAVE ENOUGH TIME TO GRAB A QUICK BITE BEFORE THE NEXT EVENT.
OKAY, FORSYTHE.
HMMM... THAT SOUNDS MORE LIKE THE OLD JUGHEAD.

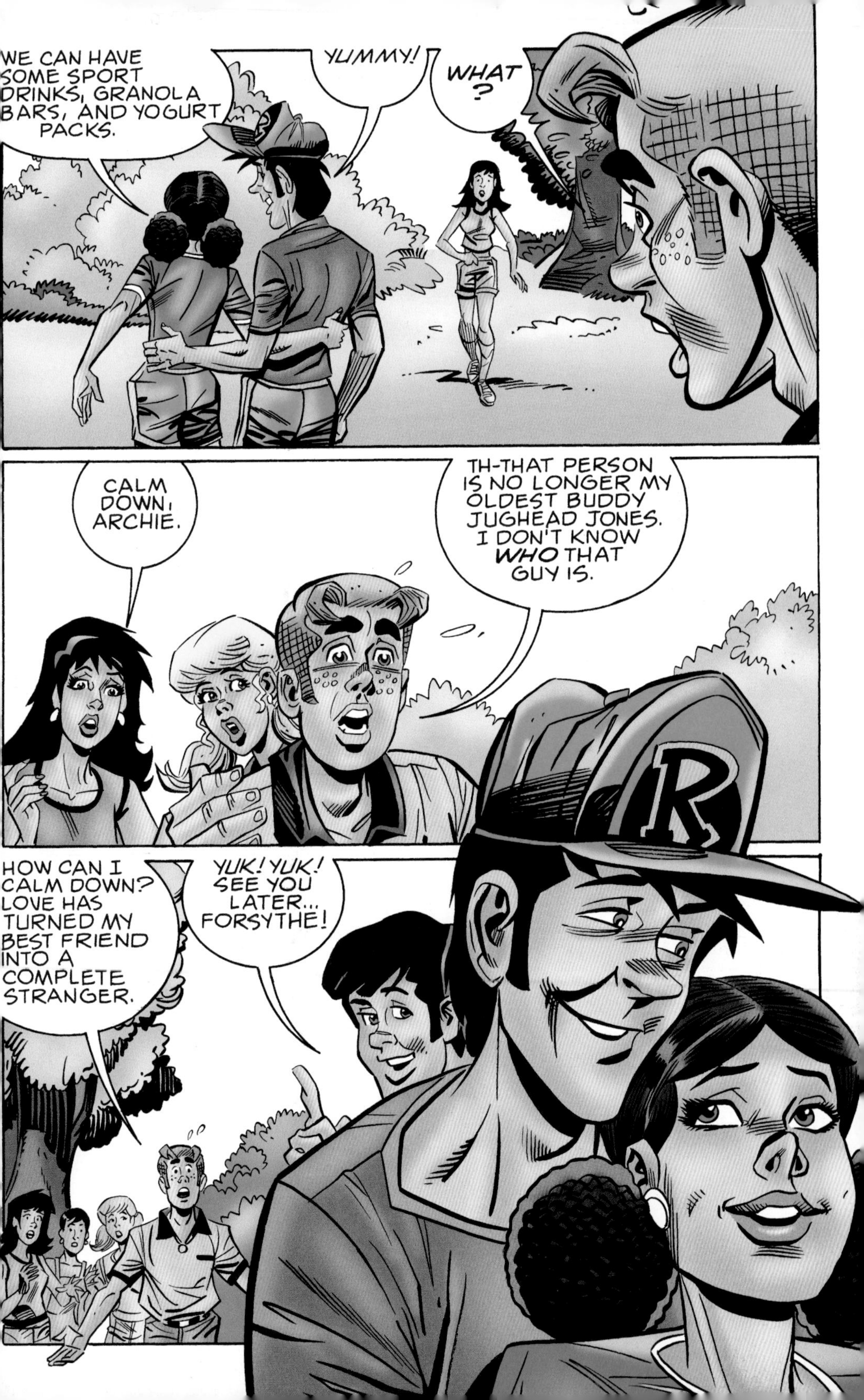
WE CAN HAVE SOME SPORT DRINKS, GRANOLA BARS, AND YOGURT PACKS.
YUMMY!
WHAT?
CALM DOWN, ARCHIE.
TH-THAT PERSON IS NO LONGER MY OLDEST BUDDY JUGHEAD JONES. I DON'T KNOW WHO THAT GUY IS.
HOW CAN I CALM DOWN? LOVE HAS TURNED MY BEST FRIEND INTO A COMPLETE STRANGER.
YUK! YUK! SEE YOU LATER... FORSYTHE!

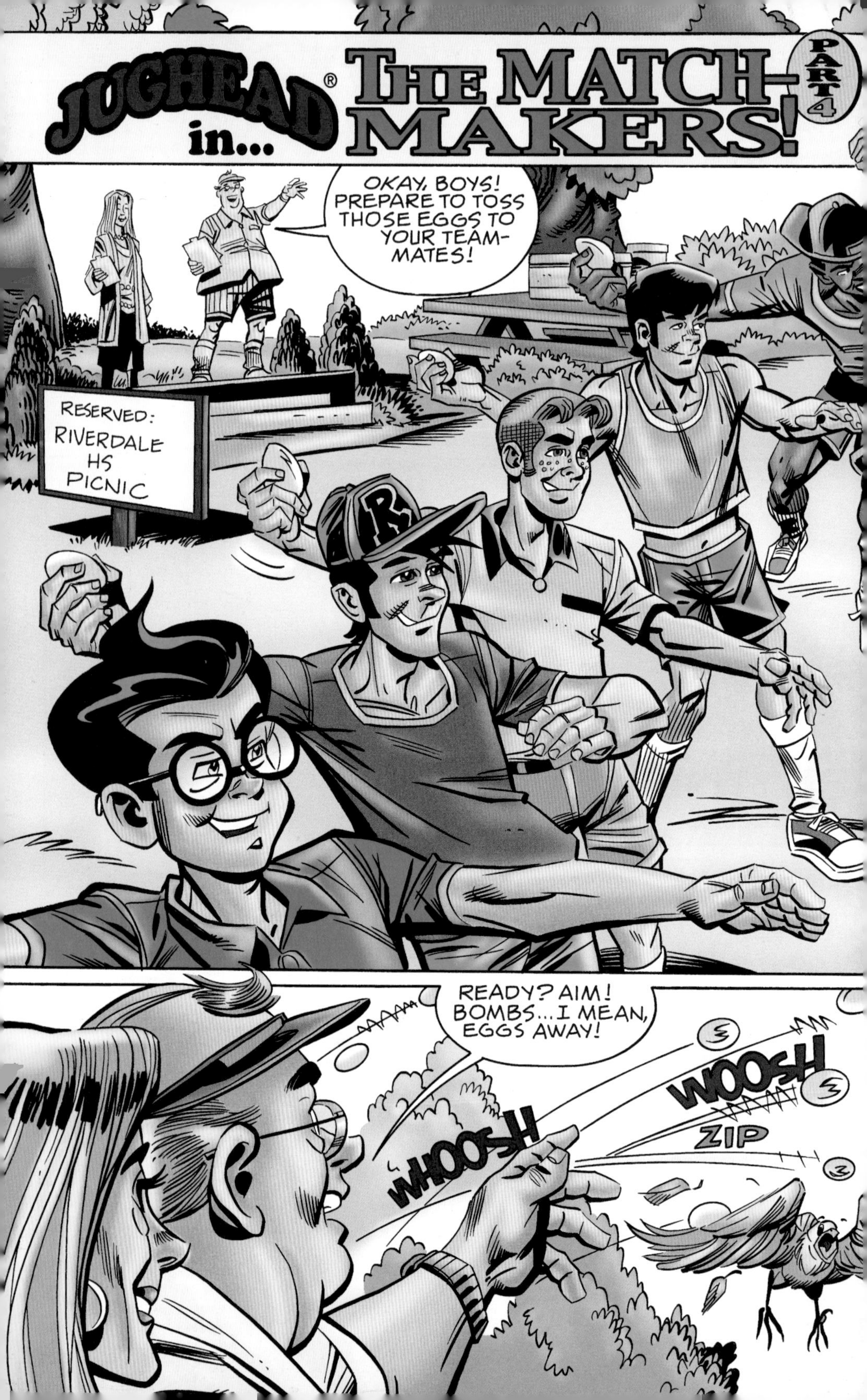
JUGHEAD® in...
THE MATCH-MAKERS! PART 4
OKAY, BOYS! PREPARE TO TOSS THOSE EGGS TO YOUR TEAM-MATES!
RESERVED: RIVERDALE HS PICNIC
READY? AIM! BOMBS... I MEAN, EGGS AWAY!
WOOSH
ZIP
WHOOSH

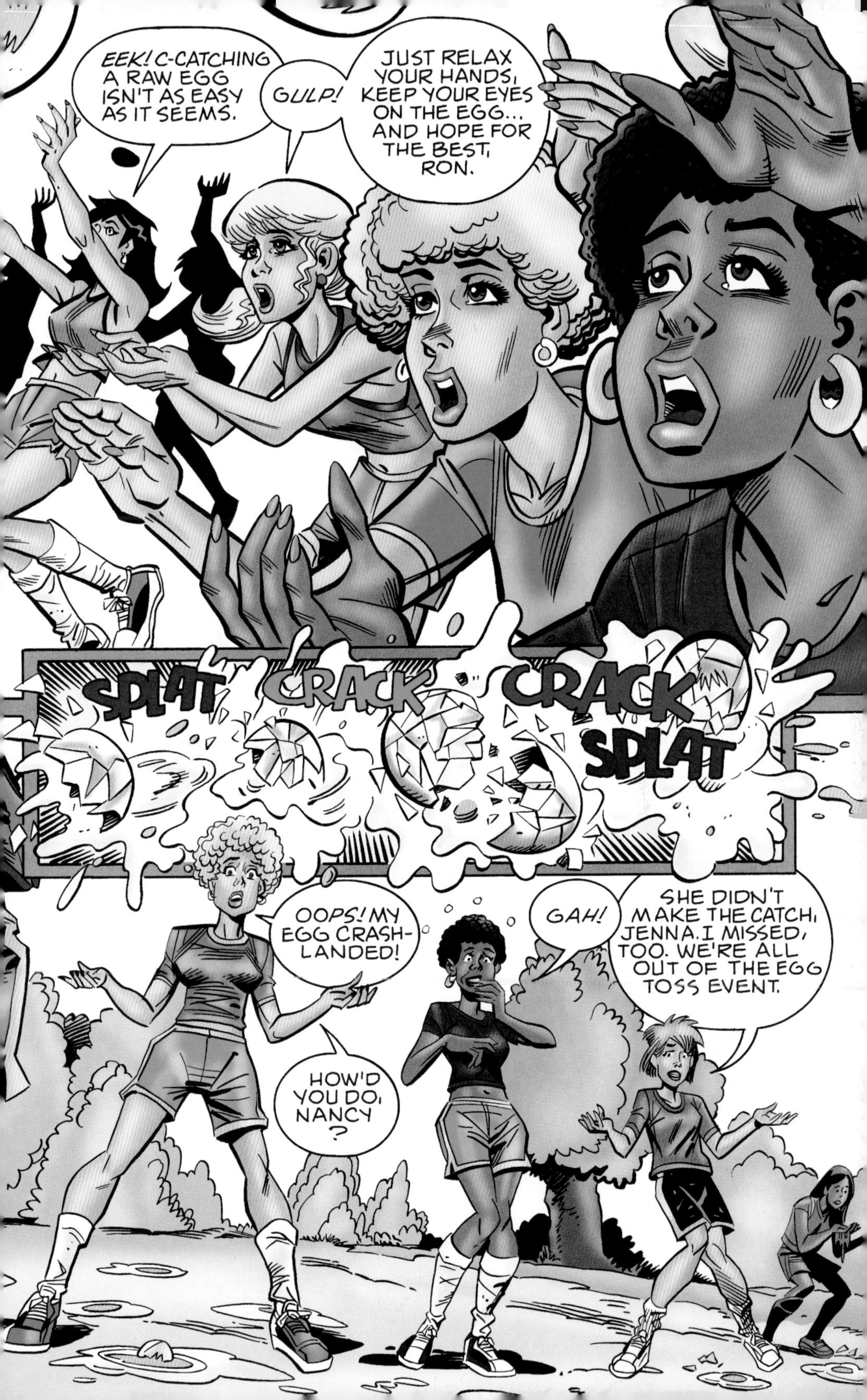
EEK! C-CATCHING A RAW EGG ISN'T AS EASY AS IT SEEMS.
GULP!
JUST RELAX YOUR HANDS, KEEP YOUR EYES ON THE EGG... AND HOPE FOR THE BEST, RON.
SPLAT
CRACK
CRACK
SPLAT
OOPS! MY EGG CRASH-LANDED!
HOW'D YOU DO, NANCY?
GAH!
SHE DIDN'T MAKE THE CATCH, JENNA. I MISSED, TOO. WE'RE ALL OUT OF THE EGG TOSS EVENT.

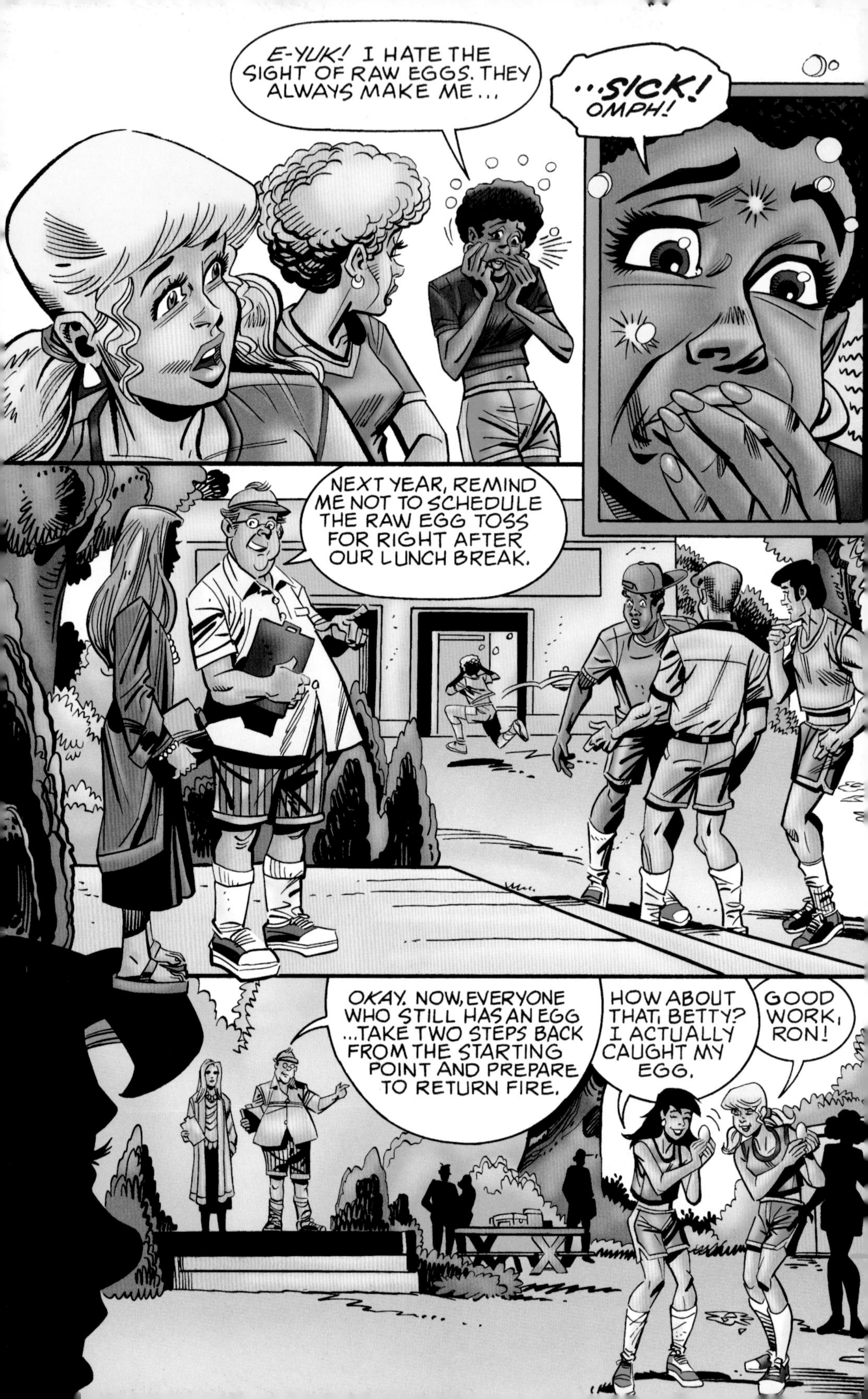

E-YUK! I HATE THE SIGHT OF RAW EGGS. THEY ALWAYS MAKE ME...
...SICK! OMPH!
NEXT YEAR, REMIND ME NOT TO SCHEDULE THE RAW EGG TOSS FOR RIGHT AFTER OUR LUNCH BREAK.
OKAY. NOW, EVERYONE WHO STILL HAS AN EGG ...TAKE TWO STEPS BACK FROM THE STARTING POINT AND PREPARE TO RETURN FIRE.
HOW ABOUT THAT, BETTY? I ACTUALLY CAUGHT MY EGG.
GOOD WORK, RON!

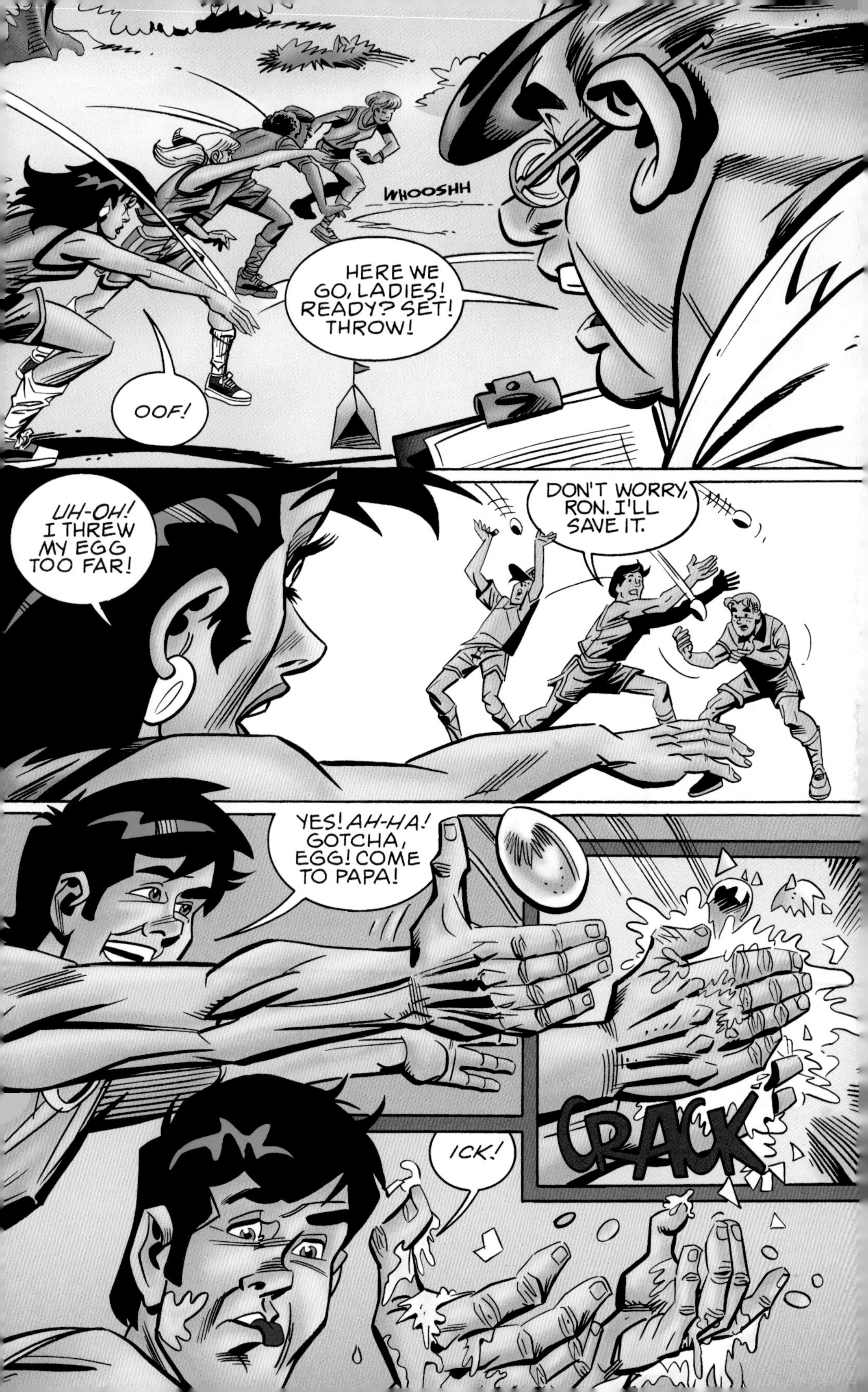
WHOOSHH
HERE WE GO, LADIES! READY? SET! THROW!
OOF!
UH-OH! I THREW MY EGG TOO FAR!
DON'T WORRY, RON. I'LL SAVE IT.
YES! AH-HA! GOTCHA, EGG! COME TO PAPA!
CRACK
ICK!

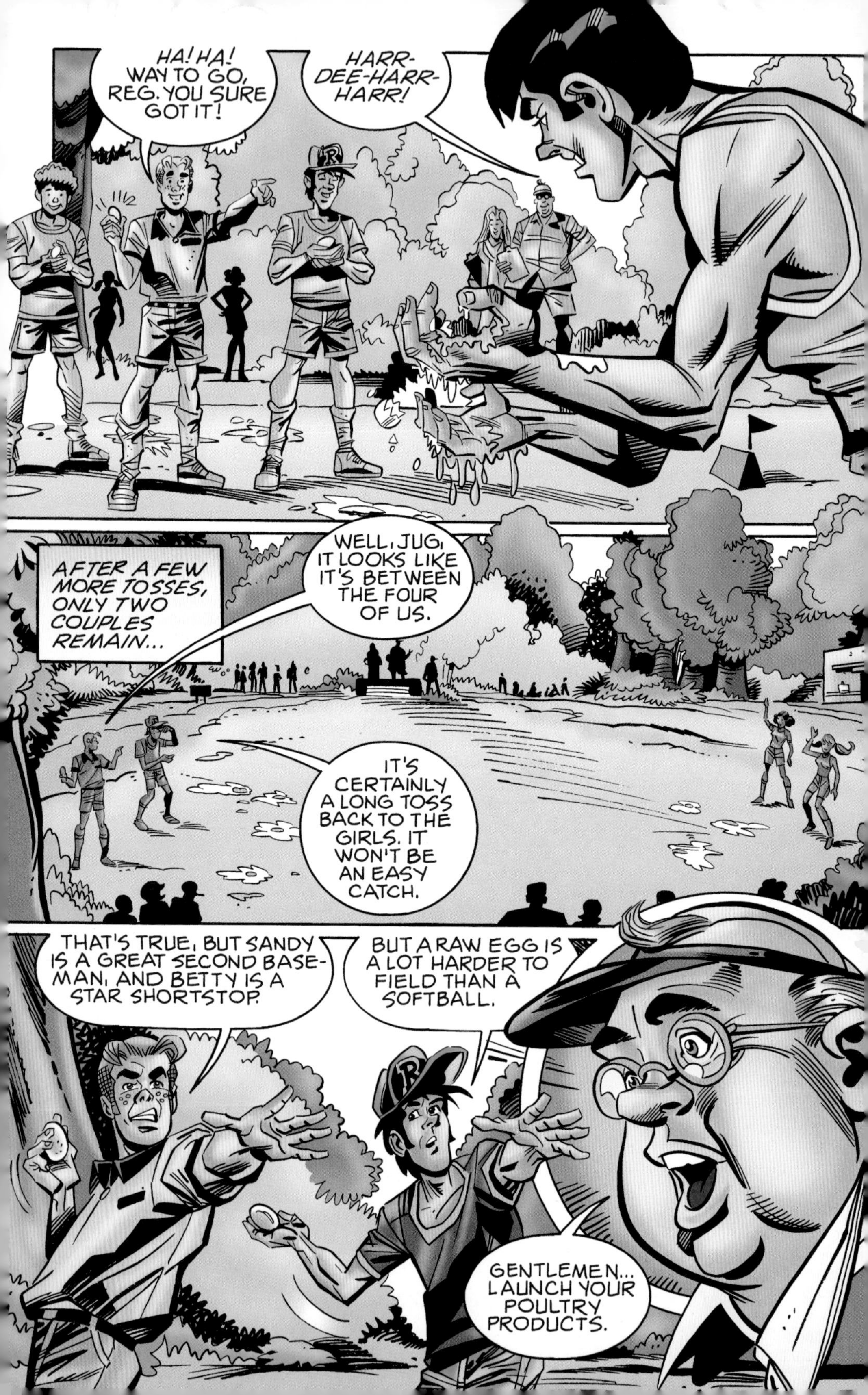
HA! HA! WAY TO GO, REG. YOU SURE GOT IT!
HARR-DEE-HARR-HARR!
AFTER A FEW MORE TOSSES, ONLY TWO COUPLES REMAIN...
WELL, JUG, IT LOOKS LIKE IT'S BETWEEN THE FOUR OF US.
IT'S CERTAINLY A LONG TOSS BACK TO THE GIRLS. IT WON'T BE AN EASY CATCH.
THAT'S TRUE, BUT SANDY IS A GREAT SECOND BASE-MAN, AND BETTY IS A STAR SHORTSTOP.
BUT A RAW EGG IS A LOT HARDER TO FIELD THAN A SOFTBALL.
GENTLEMEN... LAUNCH YOUR POULTRY PRODUCTS.

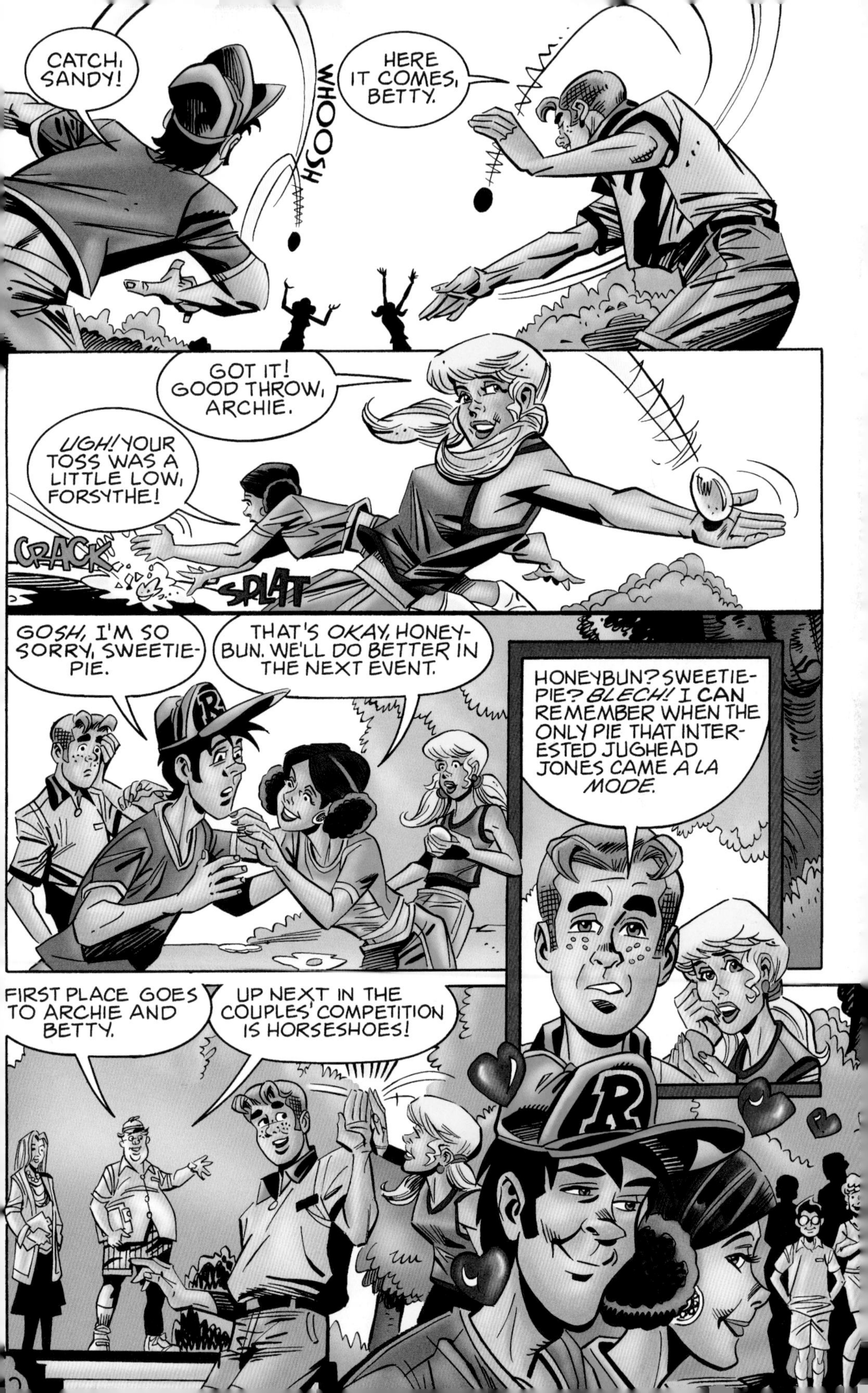
CATCH, SANDY!
WHOOSH
HERE IT COMES, BETTY.
GOT IT! GOOD THROW, ARCHIE.
UGH! YOUR TOSS WAS A LITTLE LOW, FORSYTHE!
CRACK
SPLAT
GOSH, I'M SO SORRY, SWEETIE-PIE.
THAT'S OKAY, HONEY-BUN. WE'LL DO BETTER IN THE NEXT EVENT.
HONEYBUN? SWEETIE-PIE? BLECH! I CAN REMEMBER WHEN THE ONLY PIE THAT INTERESTED JUGHEAD JONES CAME A LA MODE.
FIRST PLACE GOES TO ARCHIE AND BETTY.
UP NEXT IN THE COUPLES' COMPETITION IS HORSESHOES!

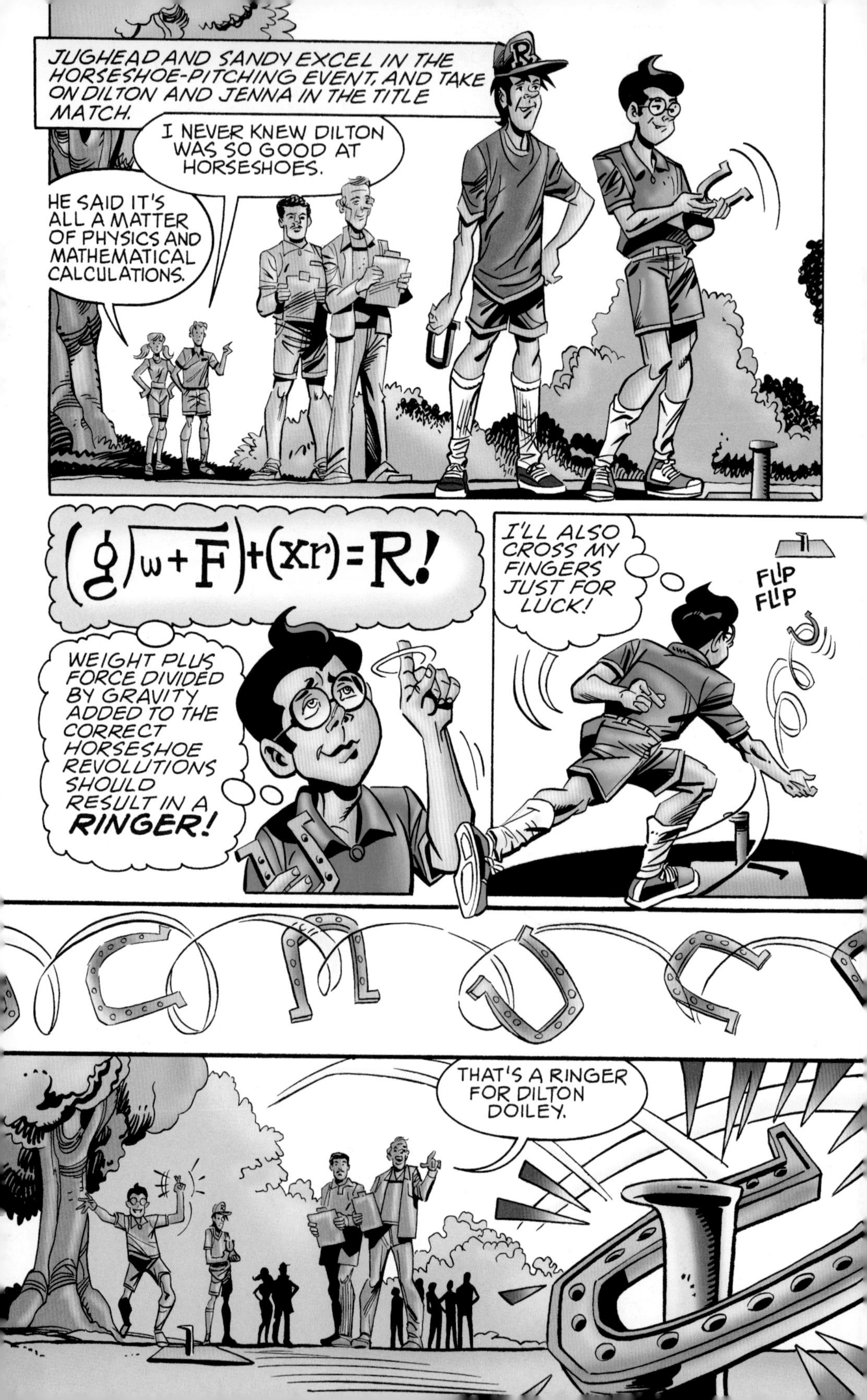
JUGHEAD AND SANDY EXCEL IN THE HORSESHOE-PITCHING EVENT, AND TAKE ON DILTON AND JENNA IN THE TITLE MATCH.
I NEVER KNEW DILTON WAS SO GOOD AT HORSESHOES.
HE SAID IT'S ALL A MATTER OF PHYSICS AND MATHEMATICAL CALCULATIONS.
(g/w+F)+(xr)=R!
WEIGHT PLUS FORCE DIVIDED BY GRAVITY ADDED TO THE CORRECT HORSESHOE REVOLUTIONS SHOULD RESULT IN A RINGER!
I'LL ALSO CROSS MY FINGERS JUST FOR LUCK!
FLIP FLIP
THAT'S A RINGER FOR DILTON DOILEY.

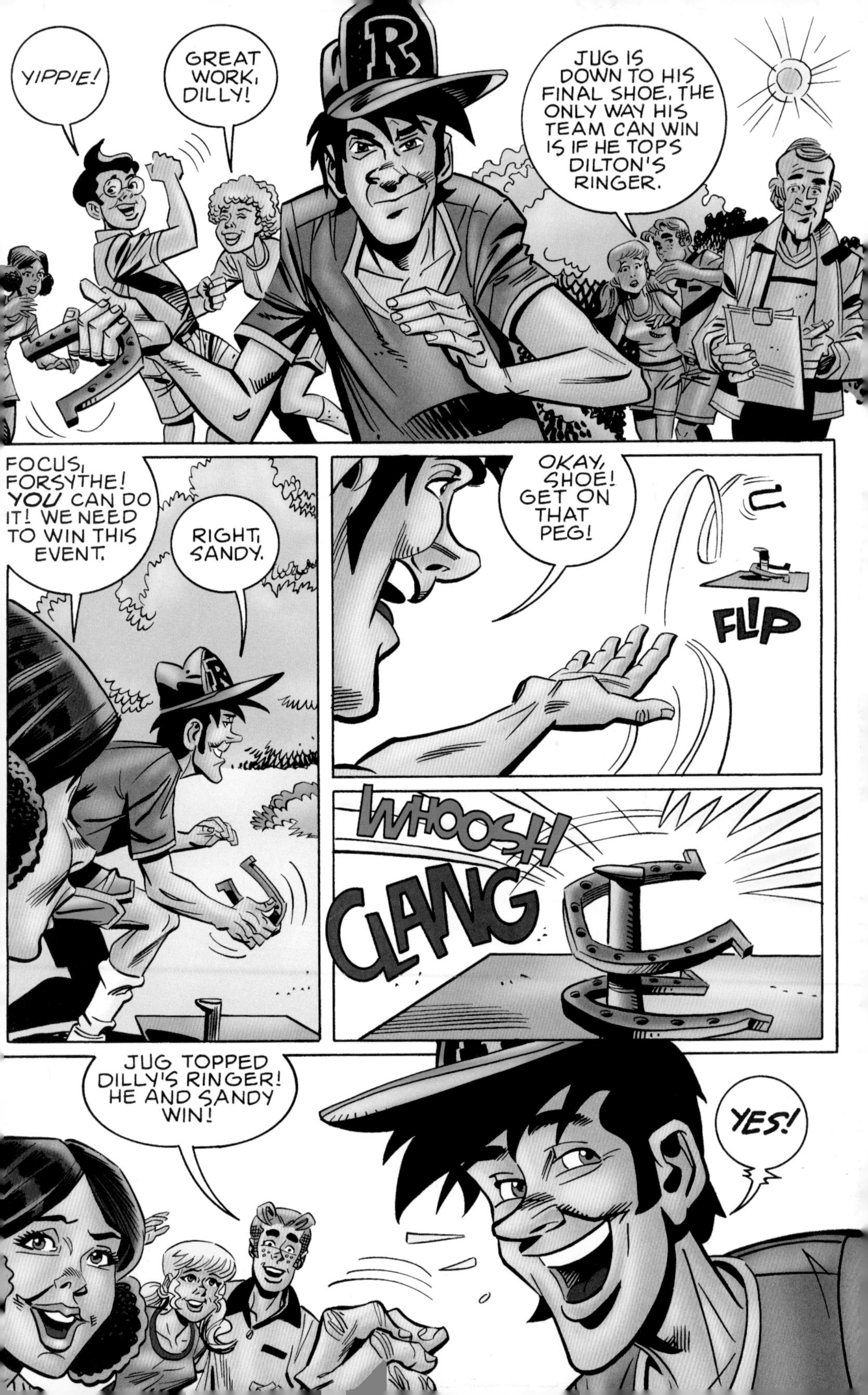
YIPPIE!
GREAT WORK, DILLY!
JUG IS DOWN TO HIS FINAL SHOE. THE ONLY WAY HIS TEAM CAN WIN IS IF HE TOPS DILTON'S RINGER.
FOCUS, FORSYTHE! YOU CAN DO IT! WE NEED TO WIN THIS EVENT.
RIGHT, SANDY.
OKAY, SHOE! GET ON THAT PEG!
FLIP
WHOOSH
CLANG
JUG TOPPED DILLY'S RINGER! HE AND SANDY WIN!
YES!

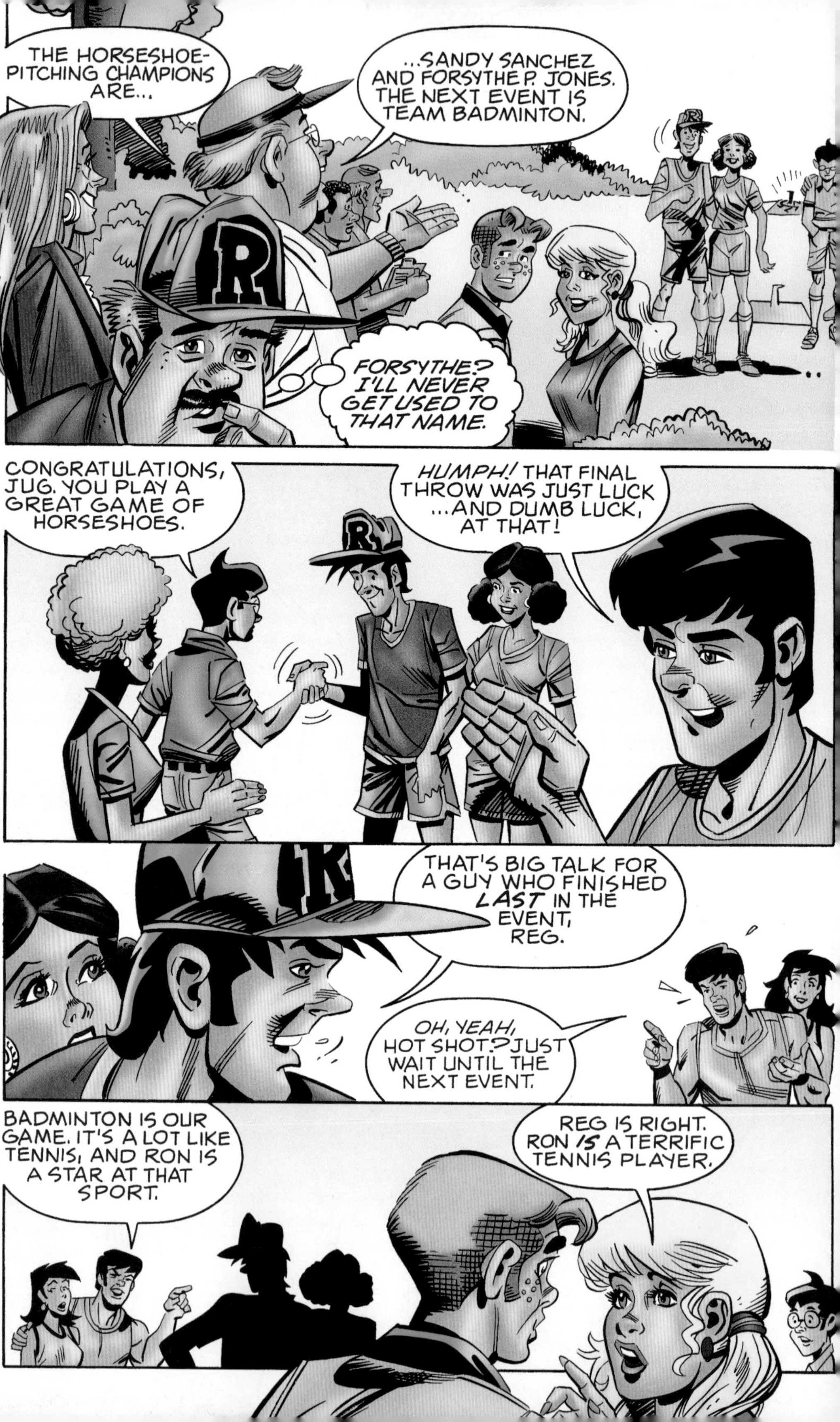
THE HORSESHOE-PITCHING CHAMPIONS ARE...
...SANDY SANCHEZ AND FORSYTHE P. JONES. THE NEXT EVENT IS TEAM BADMINTON.
FORSYTHE? I'LL NEVER GET USED TO THAT NAME.
CONGRATULATIONS, JUG. YOU PLAY A GREAT GAME OF HORSESHOES.
HUMPH! THAT FINAL THROW WAS JUST LUCK ...AND DUMB LUCK, AT THAT!
THAT'S BIG TALK FOR A GUY WHO FINISHED LAST IN THE EVENT, REG.
OH, YEAH, HOT SHOT? JUST WAIT UNTIL THE NEXT EVENT.
BADMINTON IS OUR GAME. IT'S A LOT LIKE TENNIS, AND RON IS A STAR AT THAT SPORT.
REG IS RIGHT. RON IS A TERRIFIC TENNIS PLAYER.

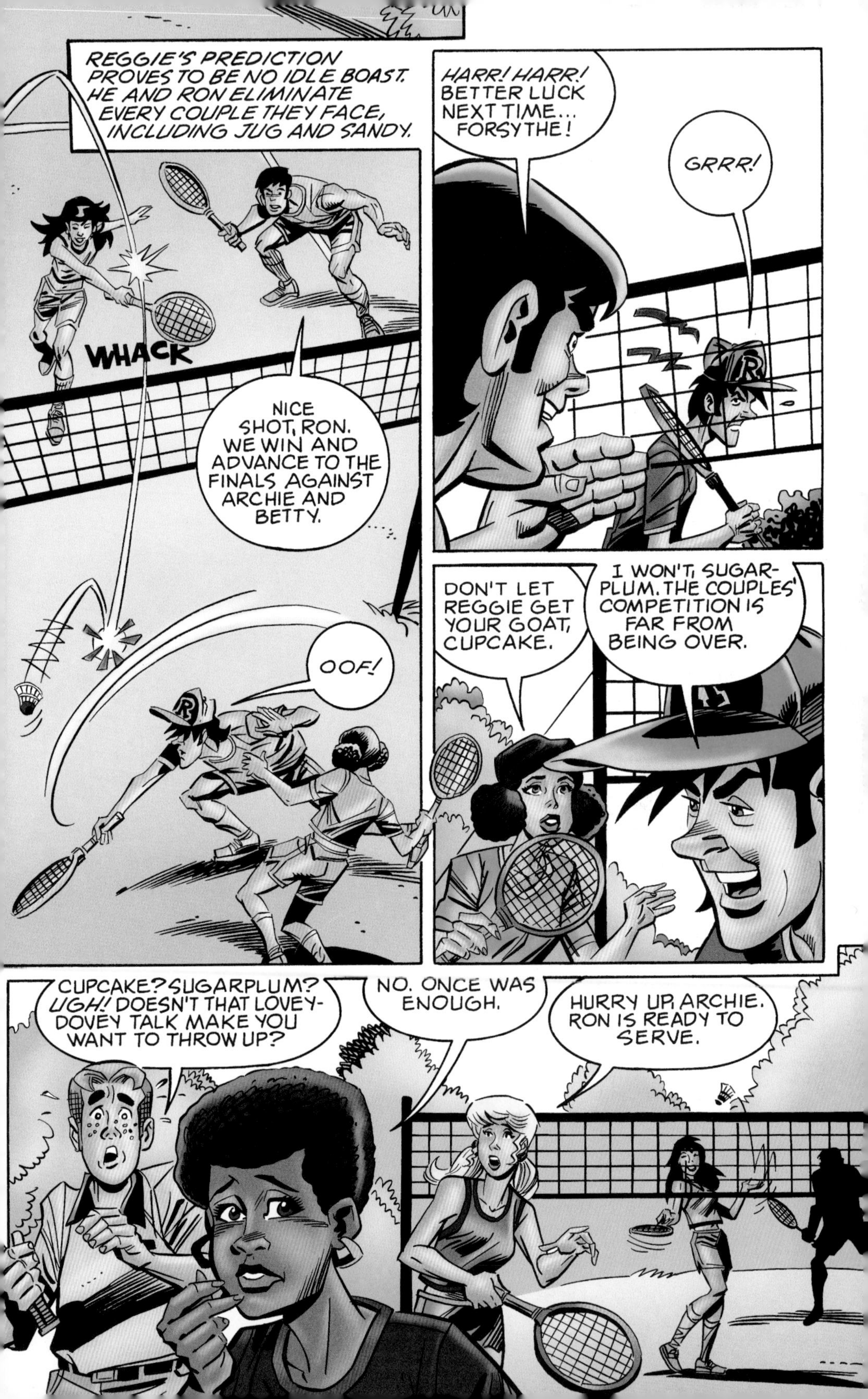
REGGIE'S PREDICTION PROVES TO BE NO IDLE BOAST. HE AND RON ELIMINATE EVERY COUPLE THEY FACE, INCLUDING JUG AND SANDY.
WHACK
NICE SHOT, RON. WE WIN AND ADVANCE TO THE FINALS AGAINST ARCHIE AND BETTY.
OOF!
HARR! HARR! BETTER LUCK NEXT TIME... FORSYTHE!
GRRR!
DON'T LET REGGIE GET YOUR GOAT, CUPCAKE.
I WON'T, SUGAR-PLUM. THE COUPLES' COMPETITION IS FAR FROM BEING OVER.
CUPCAKE? SUGARPLUM? UGH! DOESN'T THAT LOVEY-DOVEY TALK MAKE YOU WANT TO THROW UP?
NO. ONCE WAS ENOUGH.
HURRY UP, ARCHIE. RON IS READY TO SERVE.

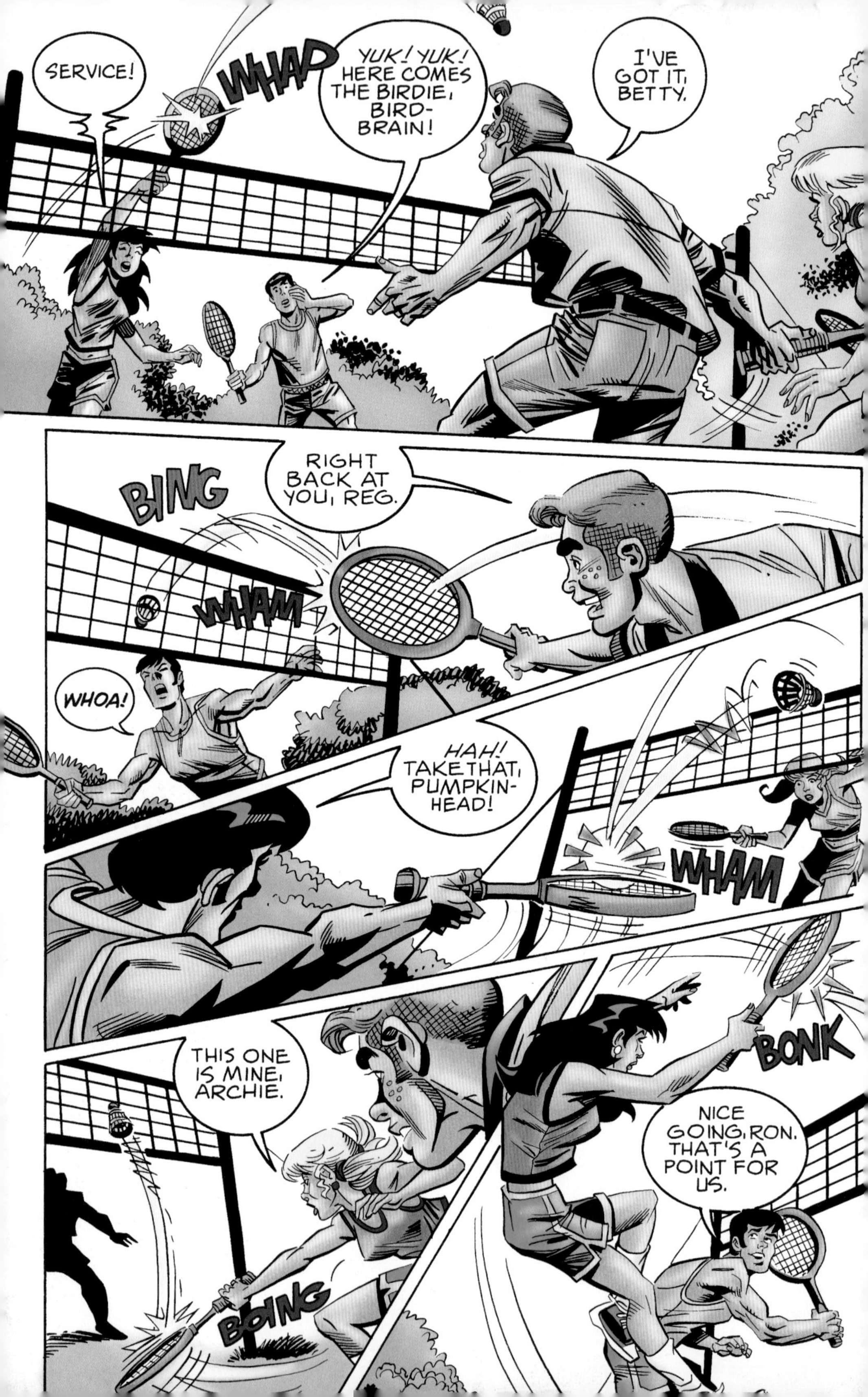
SERVICE!
WHAP
YUK! YUK! HERE COMES THE BIRDIE, BIRD-BRAIN!
I'VE GOT IT, BETTY.
BING
RIGHT BACK AT YOU, REG.
WHAM
WHOA!
HAH! TAKE THAT, PUMPKIN-HEAD!
WHAM
BONK
THIS ONE IS MINE, ARCHIE.
NICE GOING, RON. THAT'S A POINT FOR US.
BOING

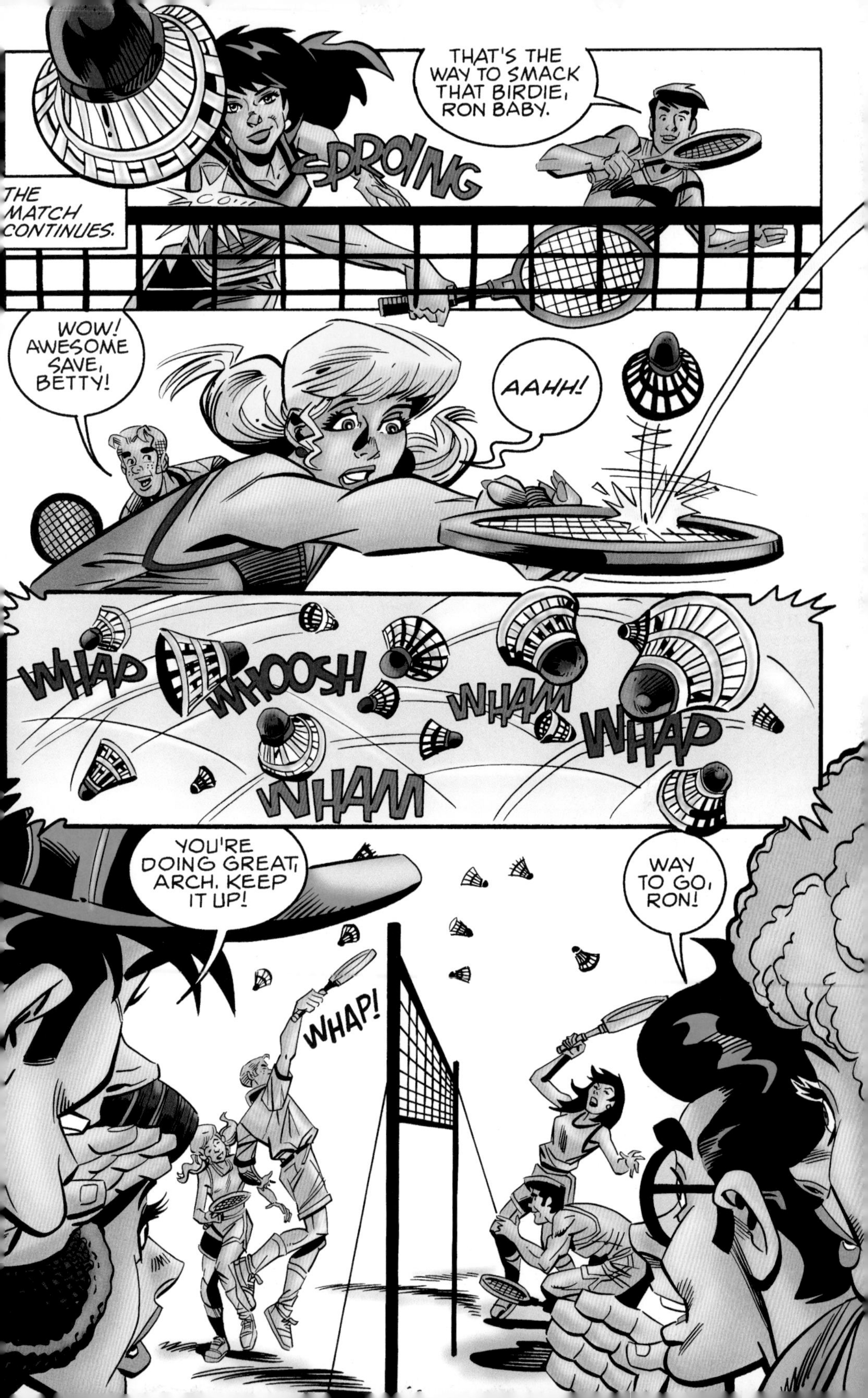
THAT'S THE WAY TO SMACK THAT BIRDIE, RON BABY.
THE MATCH CONTINUES.
SPROING
WOW! AWESOME SAVE, BETTY!
AAHH!
WHAP
WHOOSH
WHAM
WHAP
WHAM
YOU'RE DOING GREAT, ARCH. KEEP IT UP!
WAY TO GO, RON!
WHAP!

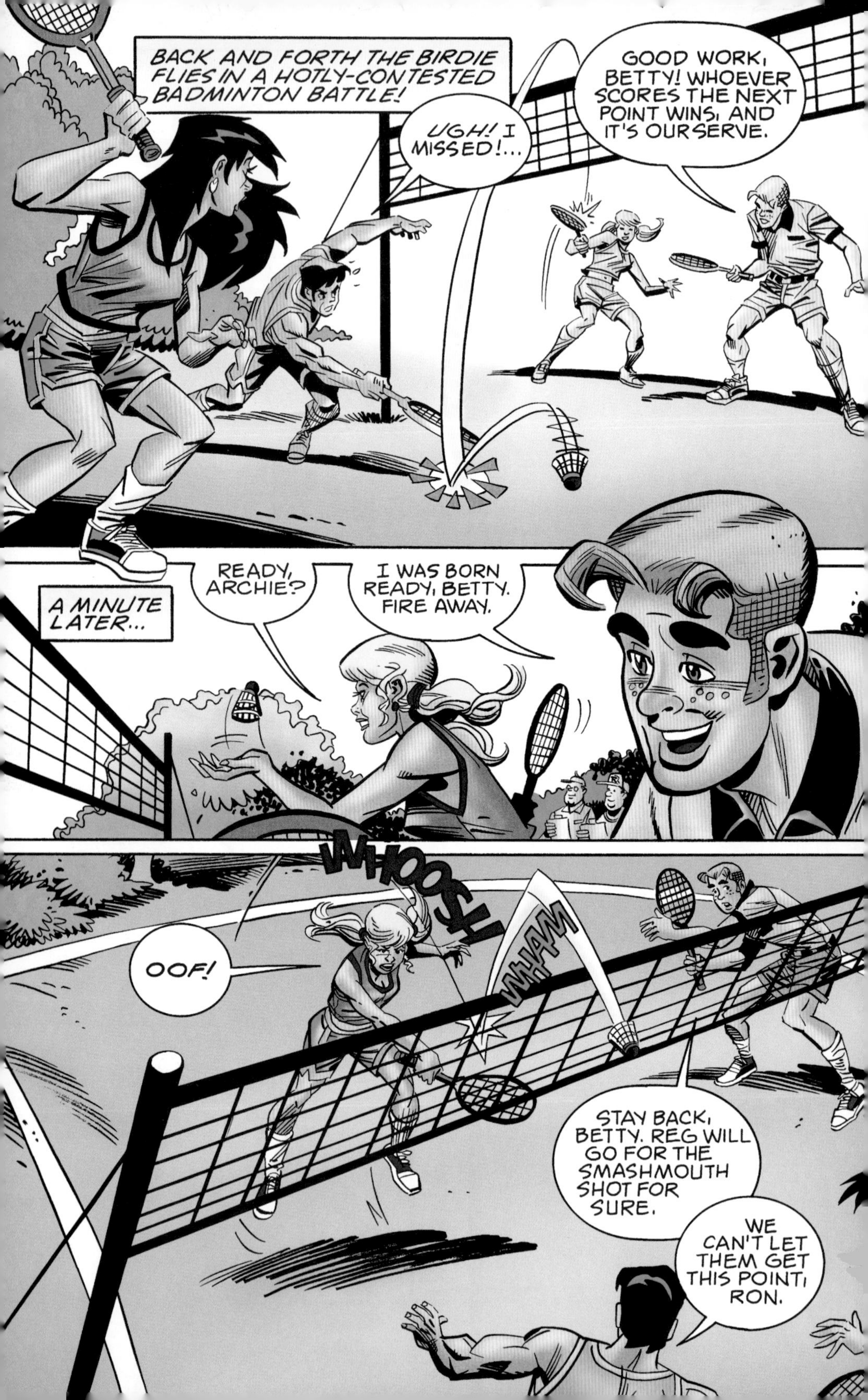
BACK AND FORTH THE BIRDIE FLIES IN A HOTLY-CONTESTED BADMINTON BATTLE!
UGH! I MISSED!...
GOOD WORK, BETTY! WHOEVER SCORES THE NEXT POINT WINS, AND IT'S OUR SERVE.
A MINUTE LATER...
READY, ARCHIE?
I WAS BORN READY, BETTY. FIRE AWAY.
WHOOSH
WHAM
OOF!
STAY BACK, BETTY. REG WILL GO FOR THE SMASHMOUTH SHOT FOR SURE.
WE CAN'T LET THEM GET THIS POINT, RON.

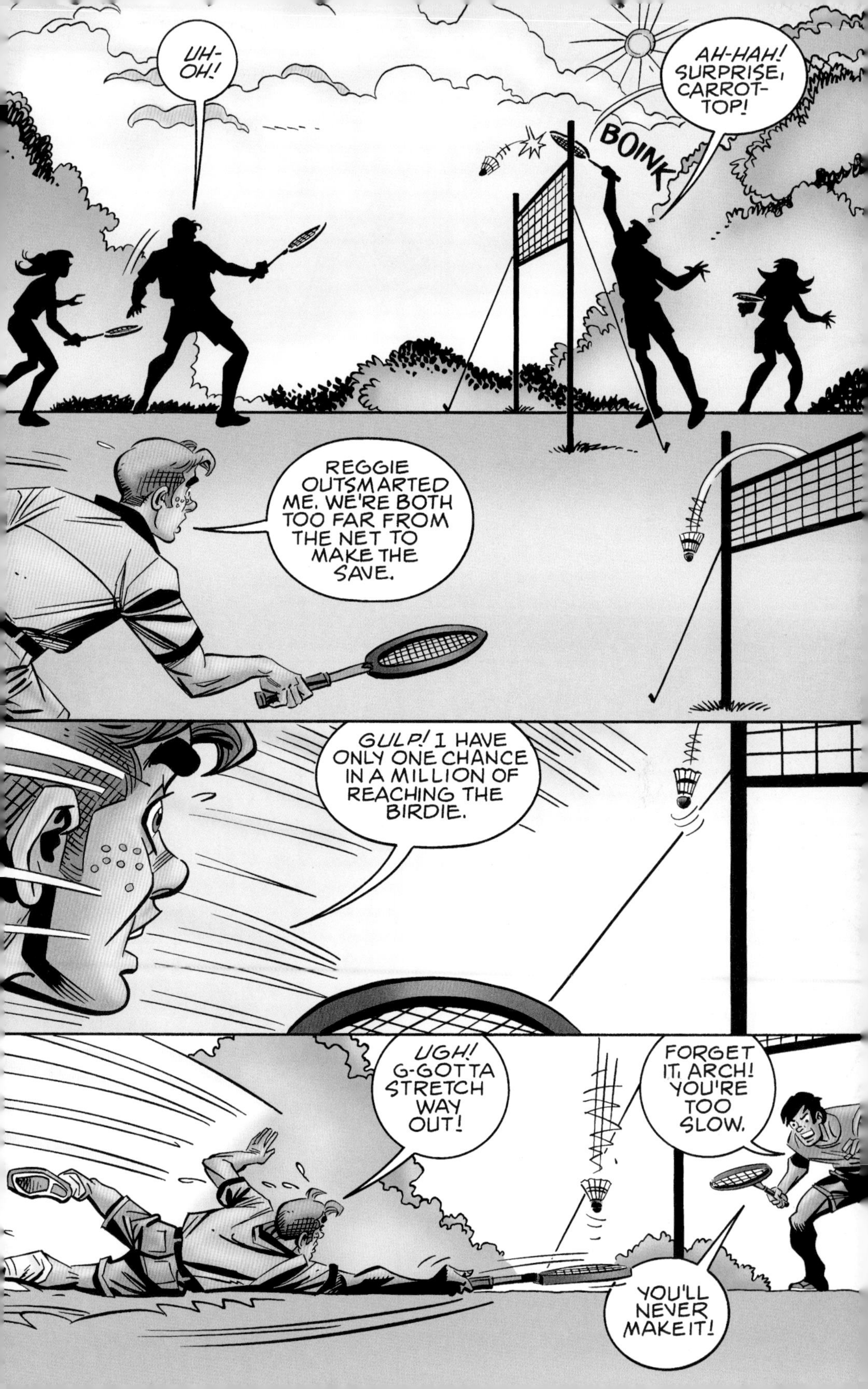
UH-OH!
AH-HAH! SURPRISE, CARROT-TOP!
BOINK
REGGIE OUTSMARTED ME. WE'RE BOTH TOO FAR FROM THE NET TO MAKE THE SAVE.
GULP! I HAVE ONLY ONE CHANCE IN A MILLION OF REACHING THE BIRDIE.
UGH! G-GOTTA STRETCH WAY OUT!
FORGET IT, ARCH! YOU'RE TOO SLOW.
YOU'LL NEVER MAKE IT!

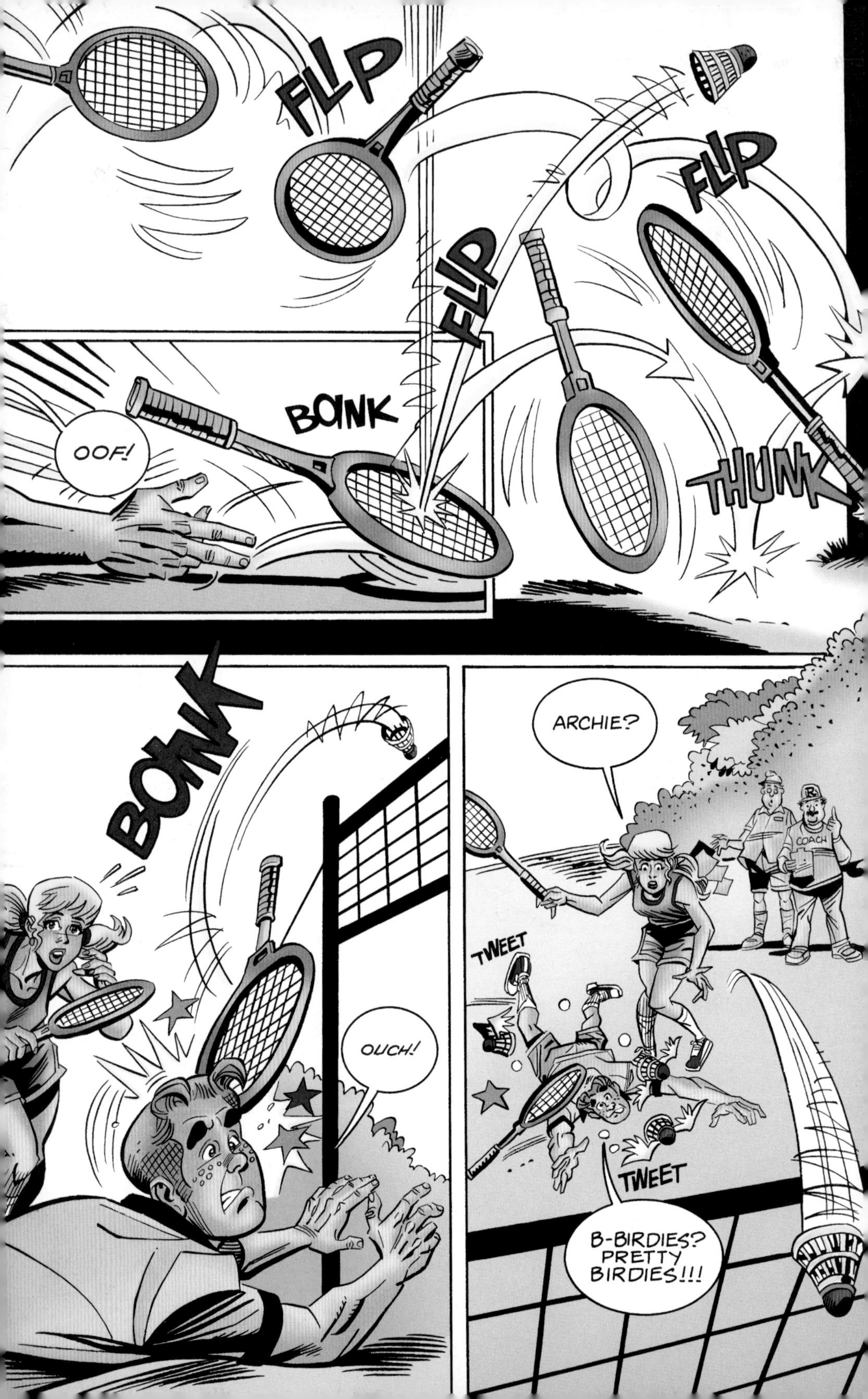
FLIP
FLIP
FLIP
OOF!
BOINK
THUNK
BOINK
OUCH!
ARCHIE?
COACH
TWEET
TWEET
B-BIRDIES? PRETTY BIRDIES!!!

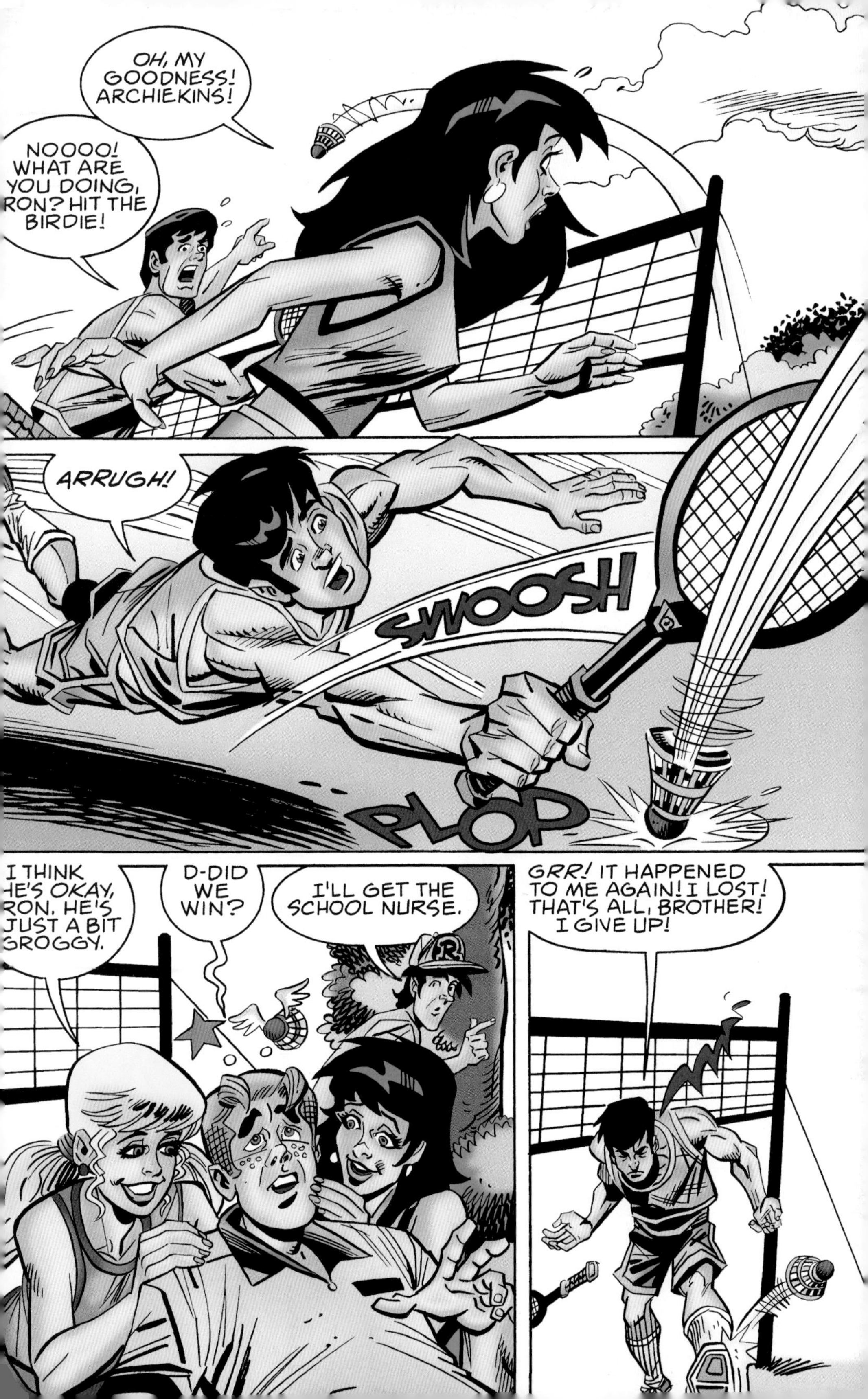
OH, MY GOODNESS! ARCHIEKINS!
NOOOO! WHAT ARE YOU DOING, RON? HIT THE BIRDIE!
ARRUGH!
SWOOSH
PLOP
I THINK HE'S OKAY, RON. HE'S JUST A BIT GROGGY.
D-DID WE WIN?
I'LL GET THE SCHOOL NURSE.
GRR! IT HAPPENED TO ME AGAIN! I LOST! THAT'S ALL, BROTHER! I GIVE UP!

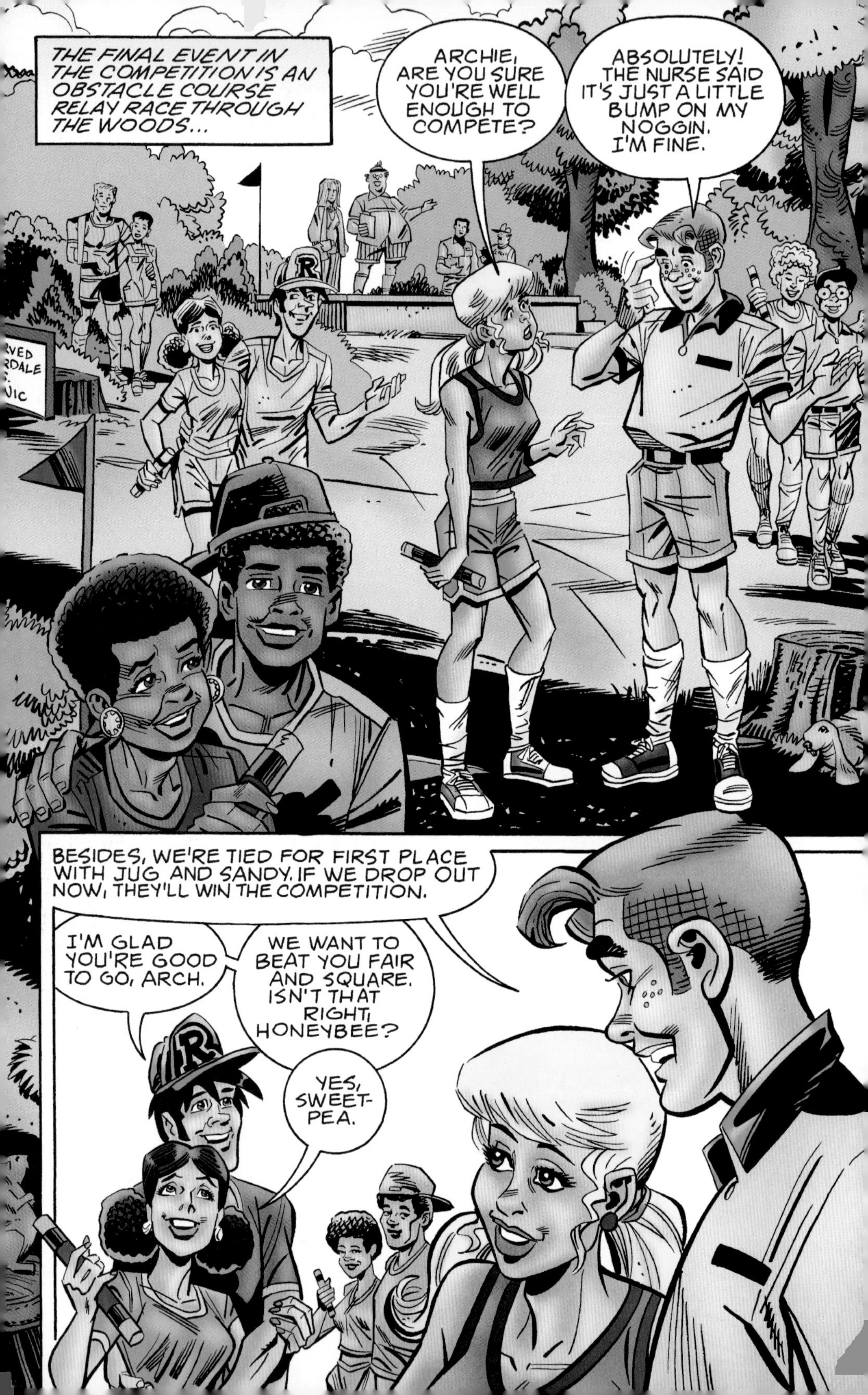
THE FINAL EVENT IN THE COMPETITION IS AN OBSTACLE COURSE RELAY RACE THROUGH THE WOODS...
ARCHIE, ARE YOU SURE YOU'RE WELL ENOUGH TO COMPETE?
ABSOLUTELY! THE NURSE SAID IT'S JUST A LITTLE BUMP ON MY NOGGIN. I'M FINE.
BESIDES, WE'RE TIED FOR FIRST PLACE WITH JUG AND SANDY. IF WE DROP OUT NOW, THEY'LL WIN THE COMPETITION.
I'M GLAD YOU'RE GOOD TO GO, ARCH.
WE WANT TO BEAT YOU FAIR AND SQUARE. ISN'T THAT RIGHT, HONEYBEE?
YES, SWEET-PEA.

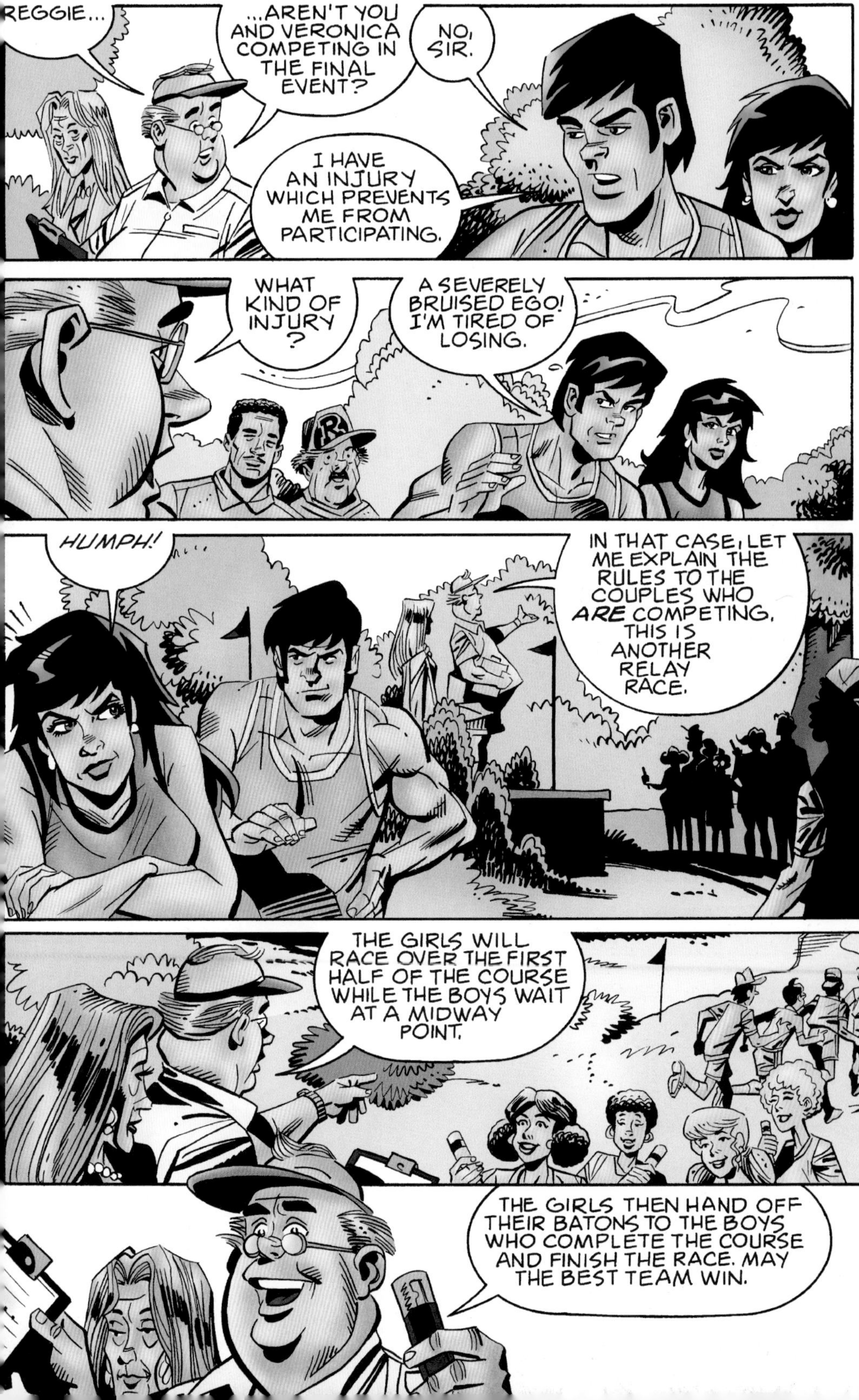
REGGIE...
...AREN'T YOU AND VERONICA COMPETING IN THE FINAL EVENT?
NO, SIR.
I HAVE AN INJURY WHICH PREVENTS ME FROM PARTICIPATING.
WHAT KIND OF INJURY?
A SEVERELY BRUISED EGO! I'M TIRED OF LOSING.
HUMPH!
IN THAT CASE, LET ME EXPLAIN THE RULES TO THE COUPLES WHO ARE COMPETING. THIS IS ANOTHER RELAY RACE.
THE GIRLS WILL RACE OVER THE FIRST HALF OF THE COURSE WHILE THE BOYS WAIT AT A MIDWAY POINT.
THE GIRLS THEN HAND OFF THEIR BATONS TO THE BOYS WHO COMPLETE THE COURSE AND FINISH THE RACE. MAY THE BEST TEAM WIN.

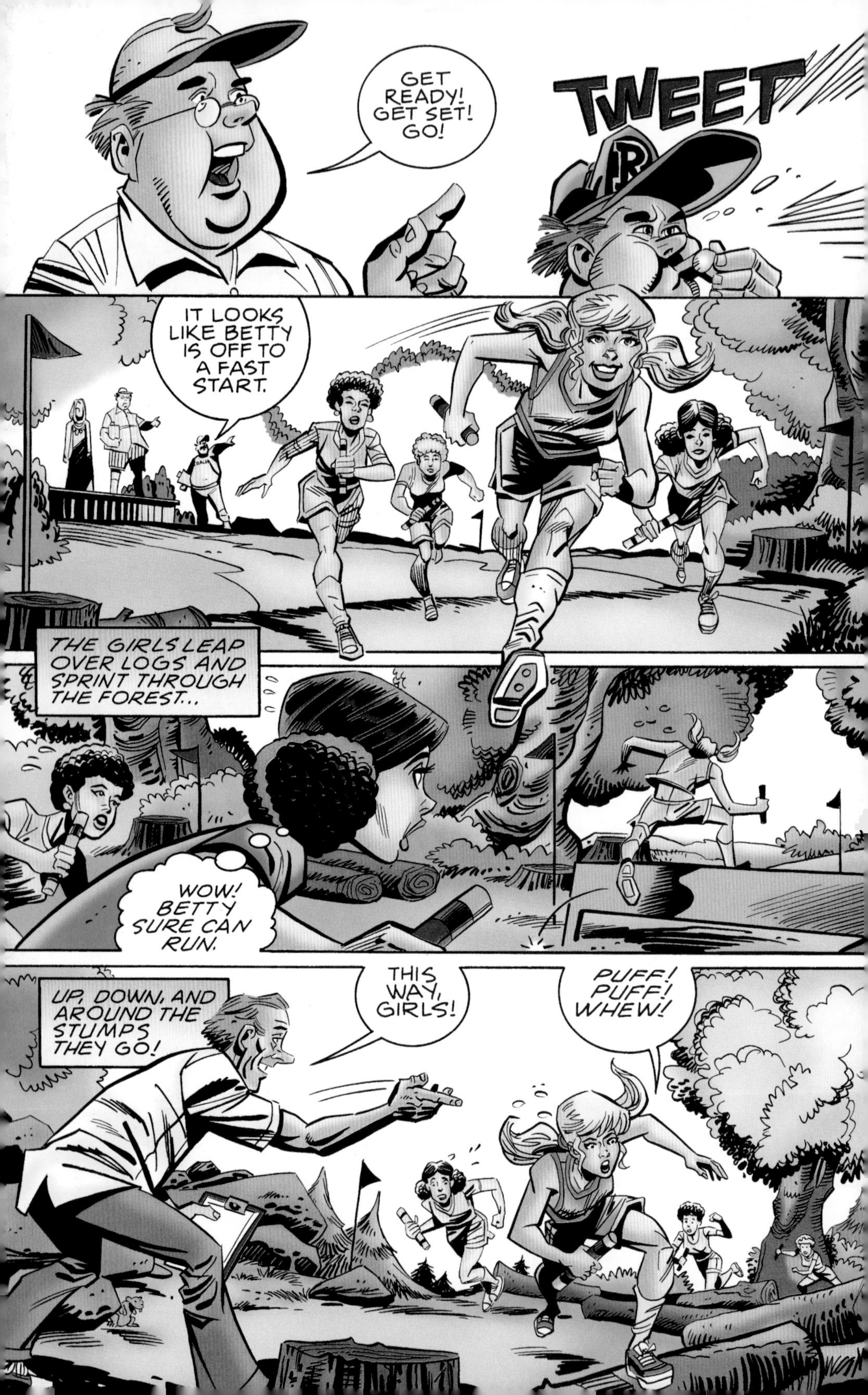
GET READY! GET SET! GO!
TWEET
IT LOOKS LIKE BETTY IS OFF TO A FAST START.
COACH
THE GIRLS LEAP OVER LOGS AND SPRINT THROUGH THE FOREST...
WOW! BETTY SURE CAN RUN.
UP, DOWN, AND AROUND THE STUMPS THEY GO!
THIS WAY, GIRLS!
PUFF! PUFF! WHEW!

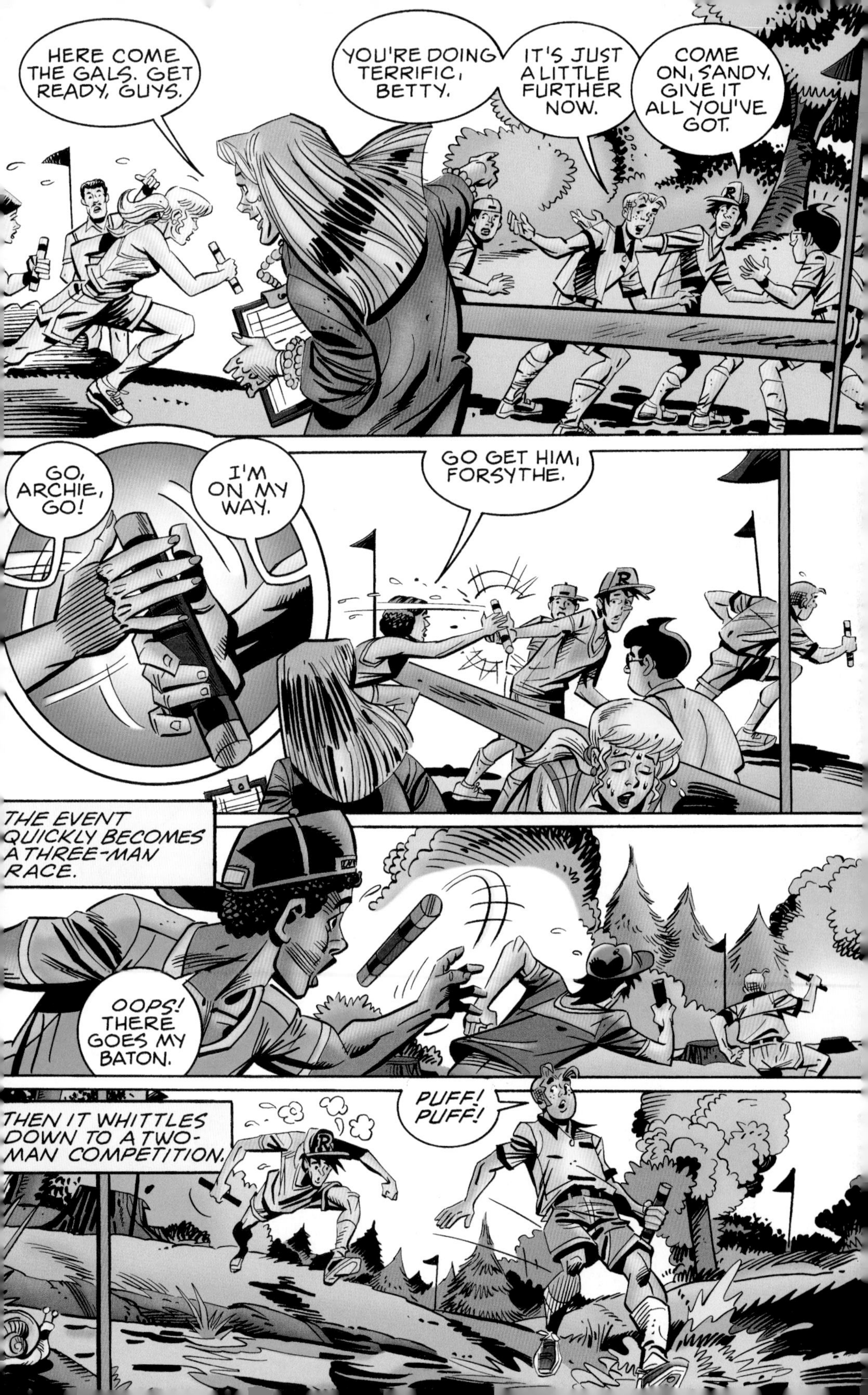
HERE COME THE GALS. GET READY, GUYS.
YOU'RE DOING TERRIFIC, BETTY.
IT'S JUST A LITTLE FURTHER NOW.
COME ON, SANDY. GIVE IT ALL YOU'VE GOT.
GO, ARCHIE, GO!
I'M ON MY WAY.
GO GET HIM, FORSYTHE.
THE EVENT QUICKLY BECOMES A THREE-MAN RACE.
OOPS! THERE GOES MY BATON.
THEN IT WHITTLES DOWN TO A TWO-MAN COMPETITION.
PUFF! PUFF!

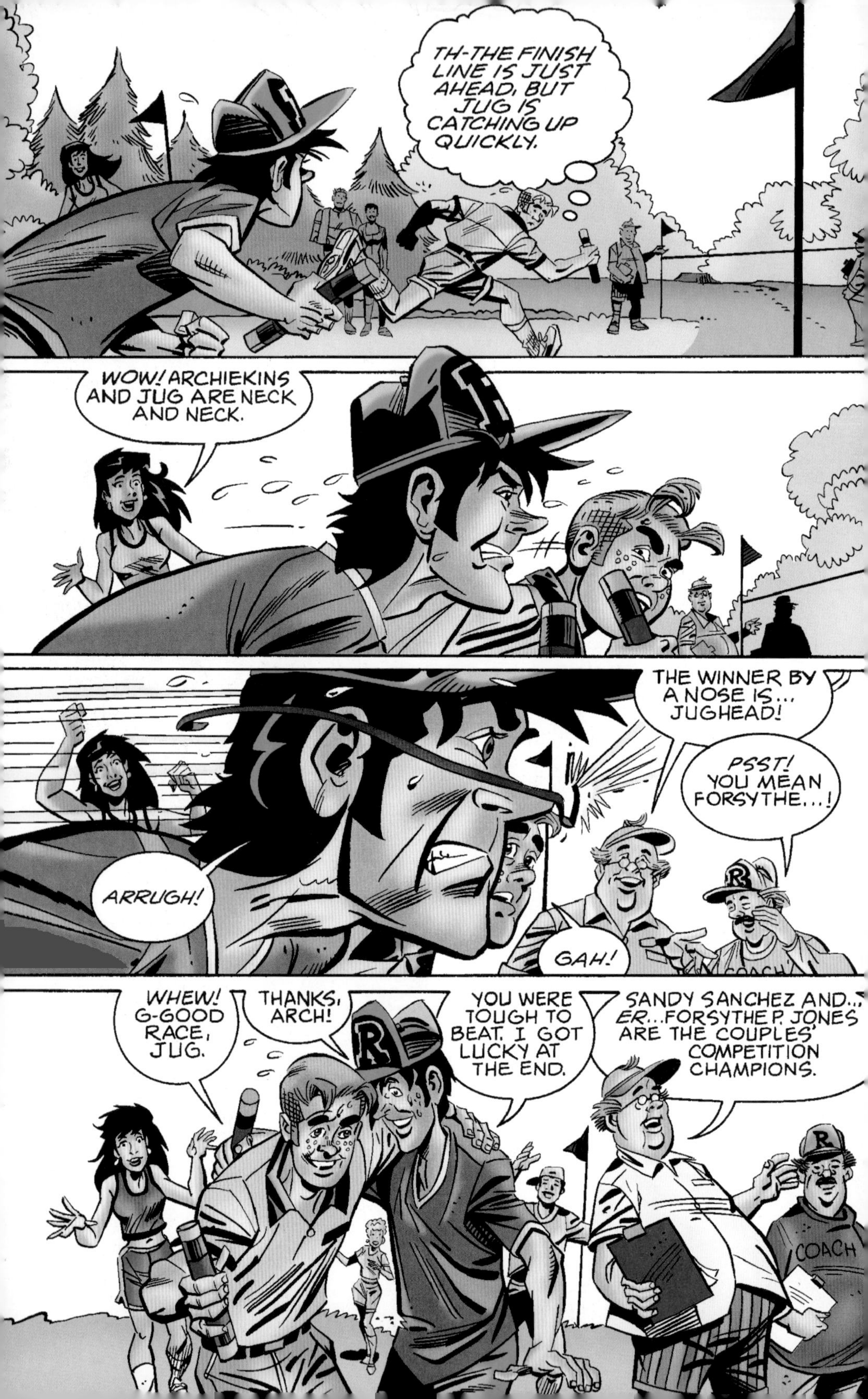
TH-THE FINISH LINE IS JUST AHEAD, BUT JUG IS CATCHING UP QUICKLY.
WOW! ARCHIEKINS AND JUG ARE NECK AND NECK.
THE WINNER BY A NOSE IS... JUGHEAD!
PSST! YOU MEAN FORSYTHE...!
ARRUGH!
GAH!
WHEW! G-GOOD RACE, JUG.
THANKS, ARCH!
YOU WERE TOUGH TO BEAT. I GOT LUCKY AT THE END.
SANDY SANCHEZ AND... ER...FORSYTHE P. JONES ARE THE COUPLES' COMPETITION CHAMPIONS.
COACH
COACH

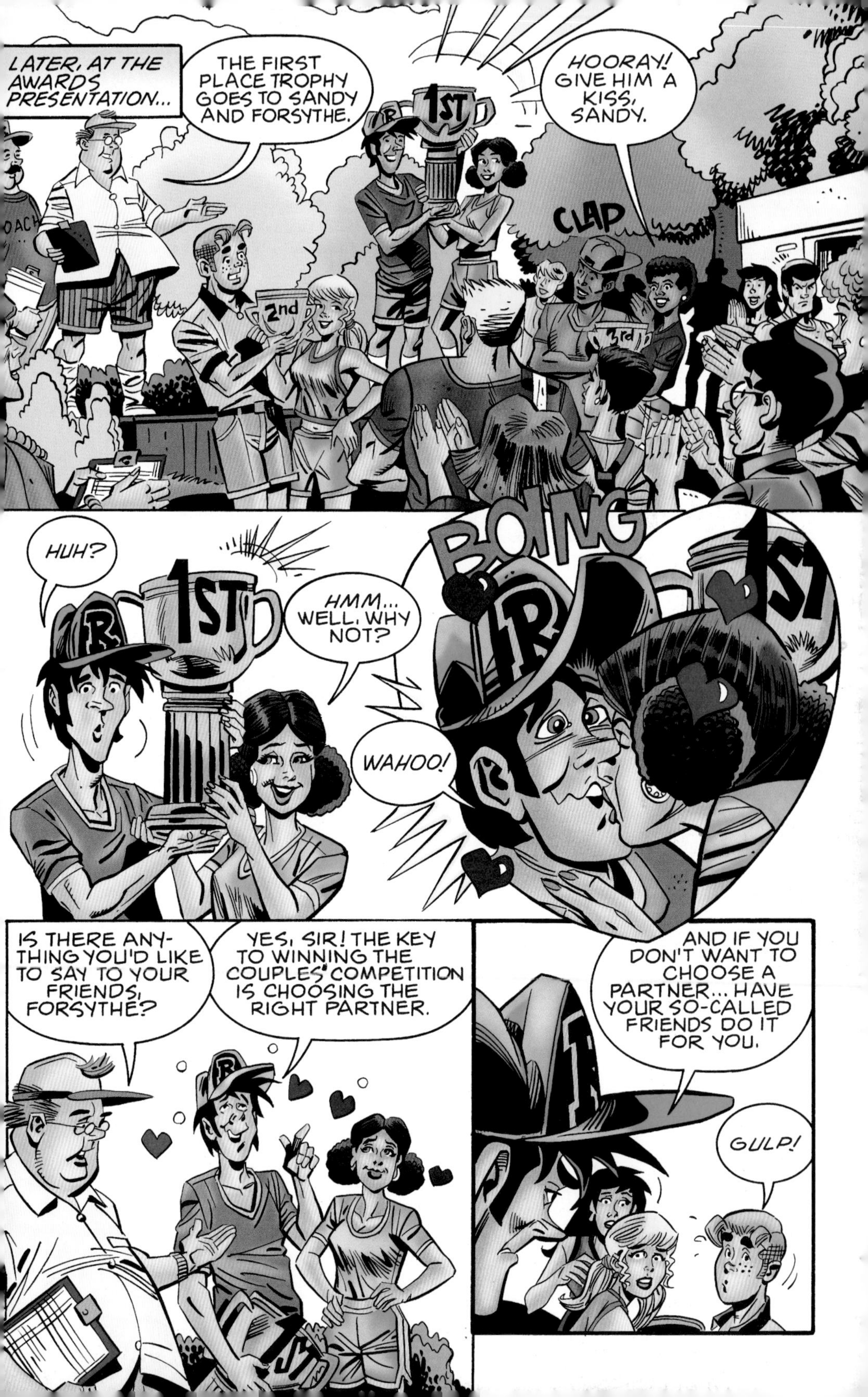
LATER, AT THE AWARDS PRESENTATION...
THE FIRST PLACE TROPHY GOES TO SANDY AND FORSYTHE.
HOORAY! GIVE HIM A KISS, SANDY.
CLAP
1ST
2nd
3rd
HUH?
HMM... WELL, WHY NOT?
BOING
WAHOO!
IS THERE ANY-THING YOU'D LIKE TO SAY TO YOUR FRIENDS, FORSYTHE?
YES, SIR! THE KEY TO WINNING THE COUPLES' COMPETITION IS CHOOSING THE RIGHT PARTNER.
AND IF YOU DON'T WANT TO CHOOSE A PARTNER... HAVE YOUR SO-CALLED FRIENDS DO IT FOR YOU.
GULP!

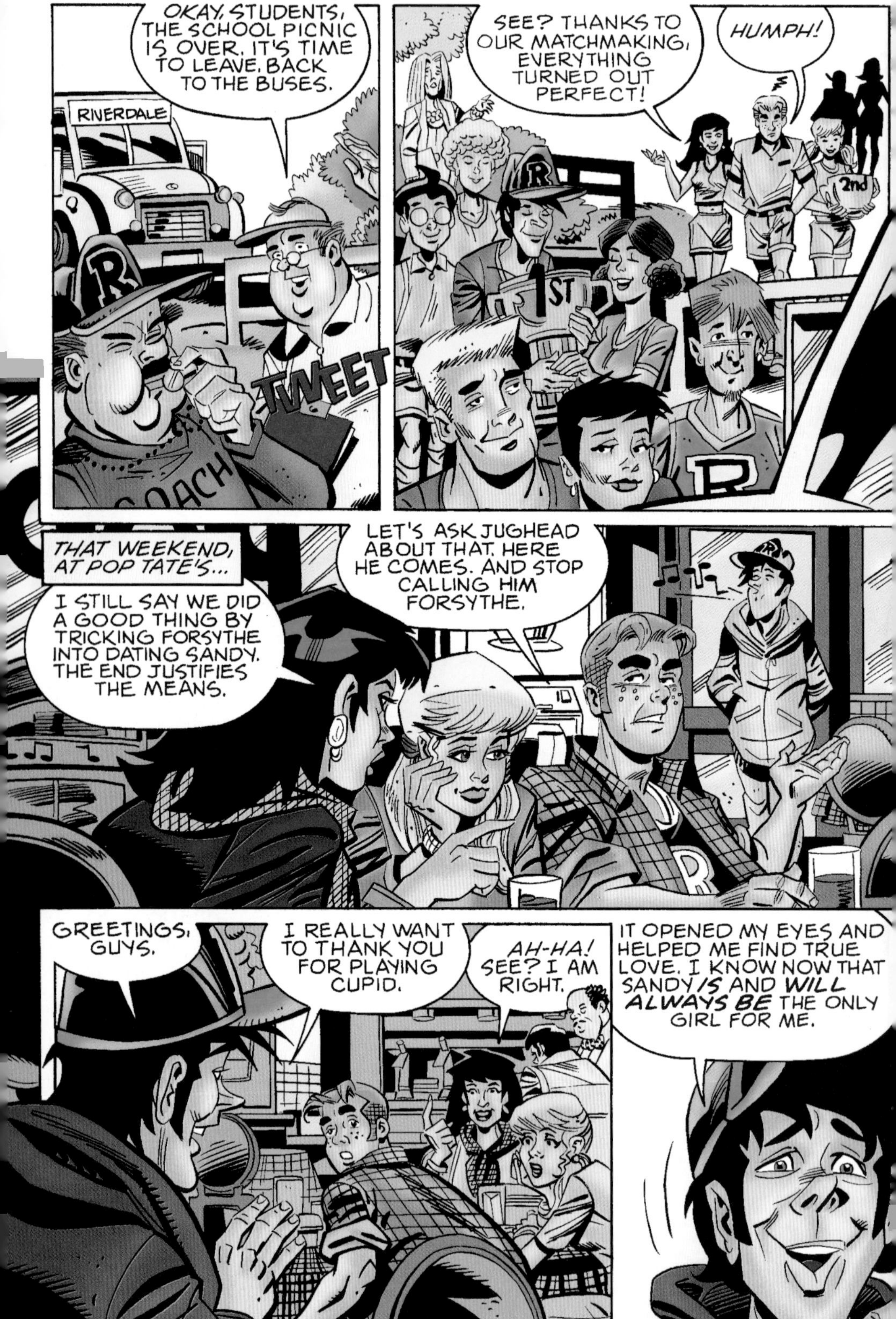
OKAY, STUDENTS, THE SCHOOL PICNIC IS OVER. IT'S TIME TO LEAVE. BACK TO THE BUSES.
RIVERDALE
TWEET
COACH
SEE? THANKS TO OUR MATCHMAKING, EVERYTHING TURNED OUT PERFECT!
HUMPH!
1ST
2nd
THAT WEEKEND, AT POP TATE'S...
I STILL SAY WE DID A GOOD THING BY TRICKING FORSYTHE INTO DATING SANDY. THE END JUSTIFIES THE MEANS.
LET'S ASK JUGHEAD ABOUT THAT. HERE HE COMES. AND STOP CALLING HIM FORSYTHE.
GREETINGS, GUYS.
I REALLY WANT TO THANK YOU FOR PLAYING CUPID.
AH-HA! SEE? I AM RIGHT.
IT OPENED MY EYES AND HELPED ME FIND TRUE LOVE. I KNOW NOW THAT SANDY *IS* AND ***WILL ALWAYS BE*** THE ONLY GIRL FOR ME.

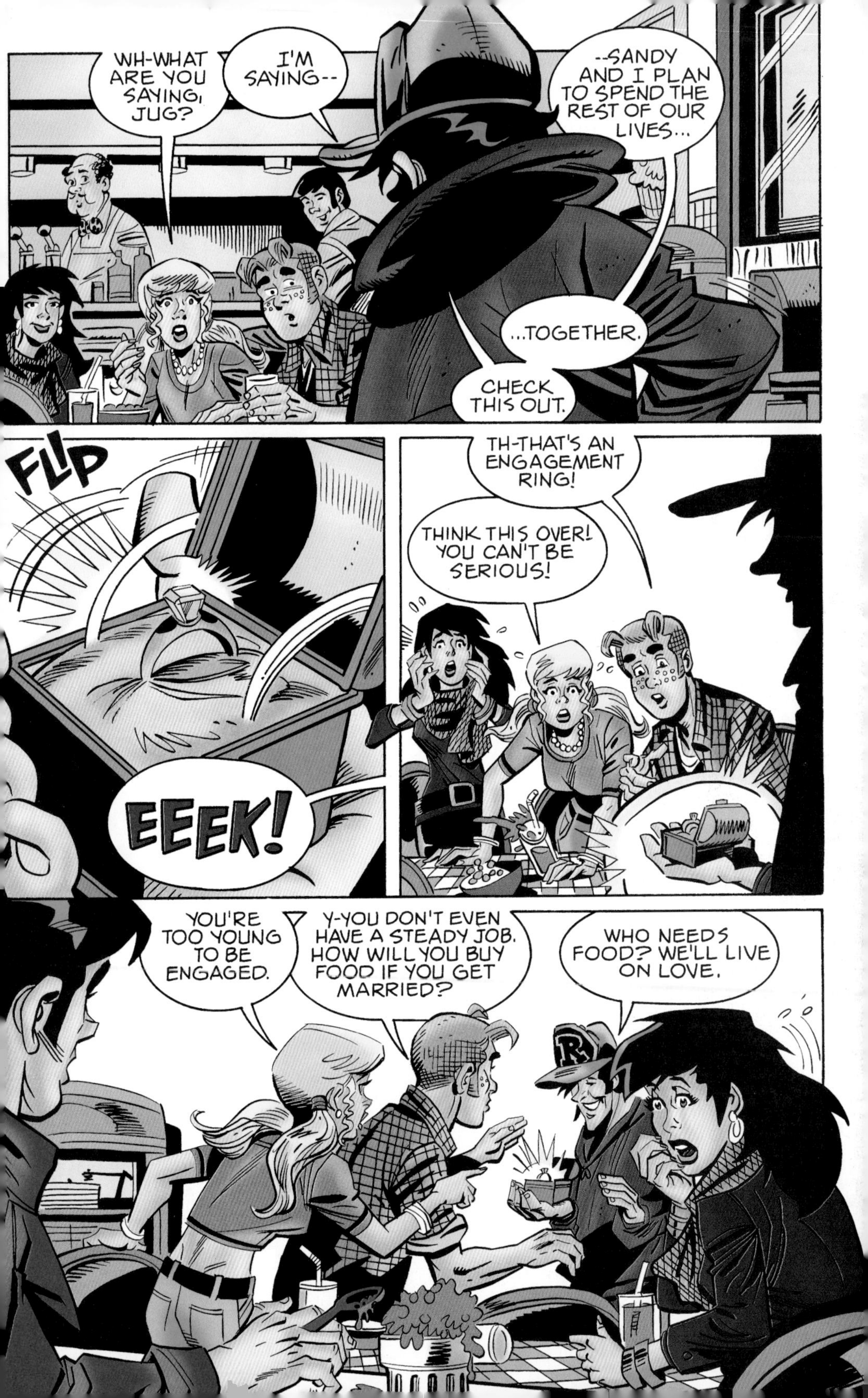
WH-WHAT ARE YOU SAYING, JUG?
I'M SAYING--
--SANDY AND I PLAN TO SPEND THE REST OF OUR LIVES...
...TOGETHER.
CHECK THIS OUT.
FLIP
EEEK!
TH-THAT'S AN ENGAGEMENT RING!
THINK THIS OVER! YOU CAN'T BE SERIOUS!
YOU'RE TOO YOUNG TO BE ENGAGED.
Y-YOU DON'T EVEN HAVE A STEADY JOB. HOW WILL YOU BUY FOOD IF YOU GET MARRIED?
WHO NEEDS FOOD? WE'LL LIVE ON LOVE.

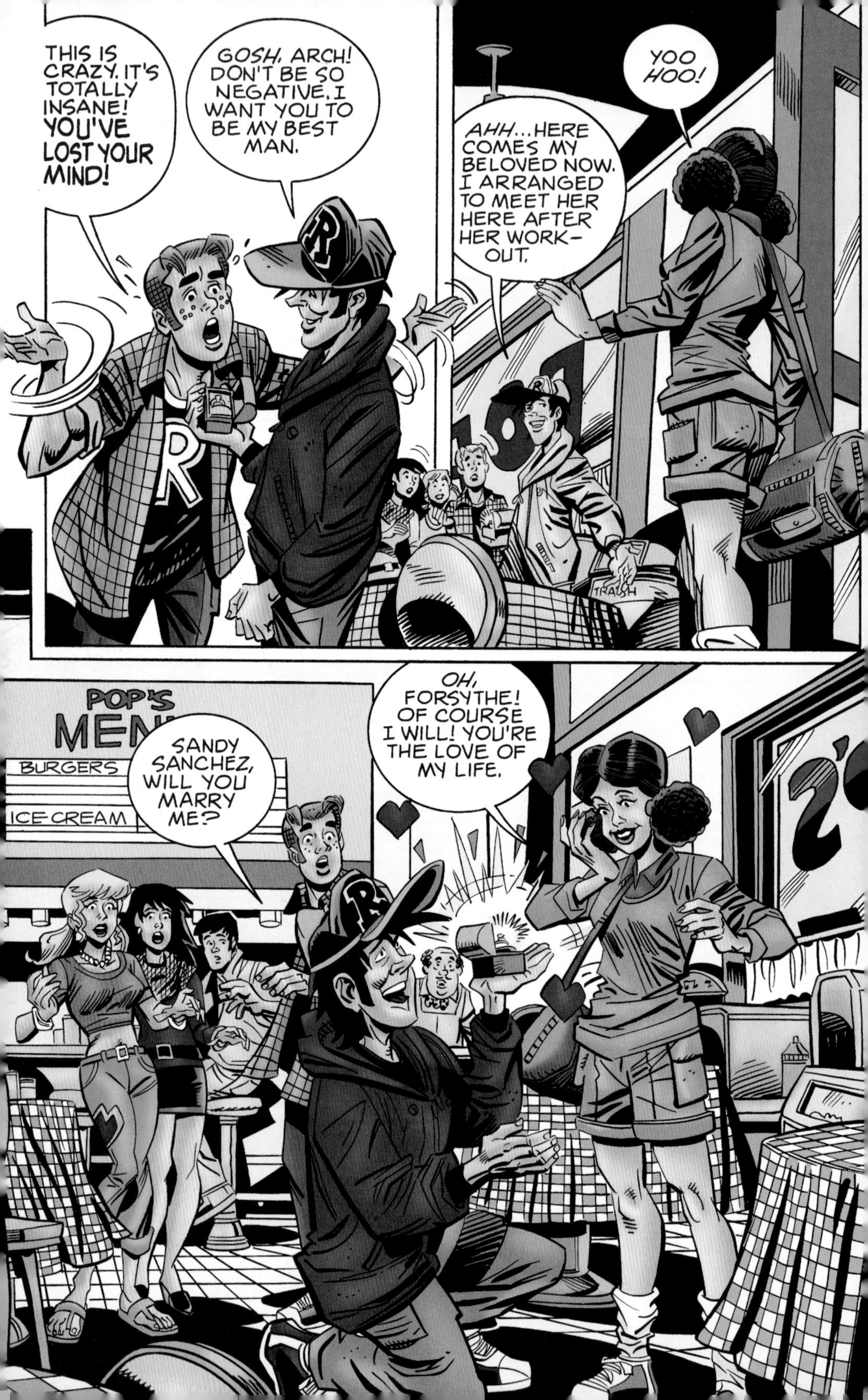

THIS IS CRAZY. IT'S TOTALLY INSANE! YOU'VE LOST YOUR MIND!
GOSH, ARCH! DON'T BE SO NEGATIVE. I WANT YOU TO BE MY BEST MAN.
YOO HOO!
AHH...HERE COMES MY BELOVED NOW. I ARRANGED TO MEET HER HERE AFTER HER WORK-OUT.
TRASH
POP'S MEN
BURGERS
ICE-CREAM
SANDY SANCHEZ, WILL YOU MARRY ME?
OH, FORSYTHE! OF COURSE I WILL! YOU'RE THE LOVE OF MY LIFE.

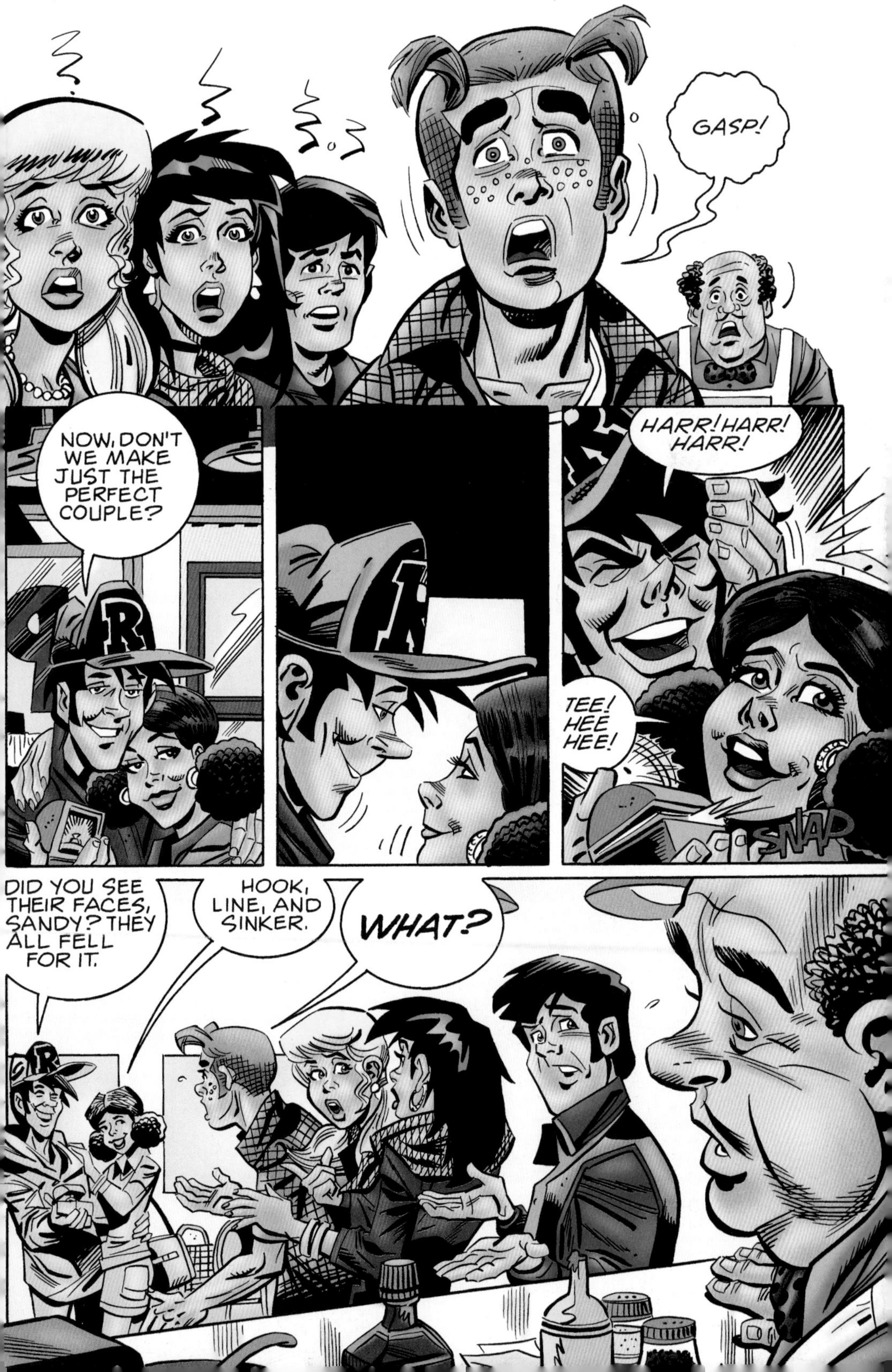
GASP!
NOW, DON'T WE MAKE JUST THE PERFECT COUPLE?
HARR! HARR! HARR!
TEE! HEE HEE!
SNAP
DID YOU SEE THEIR FACES, SANDY? THEY ALL FELL FOR IT.
HOOK, LINE, AND SINKER.
WHAT?

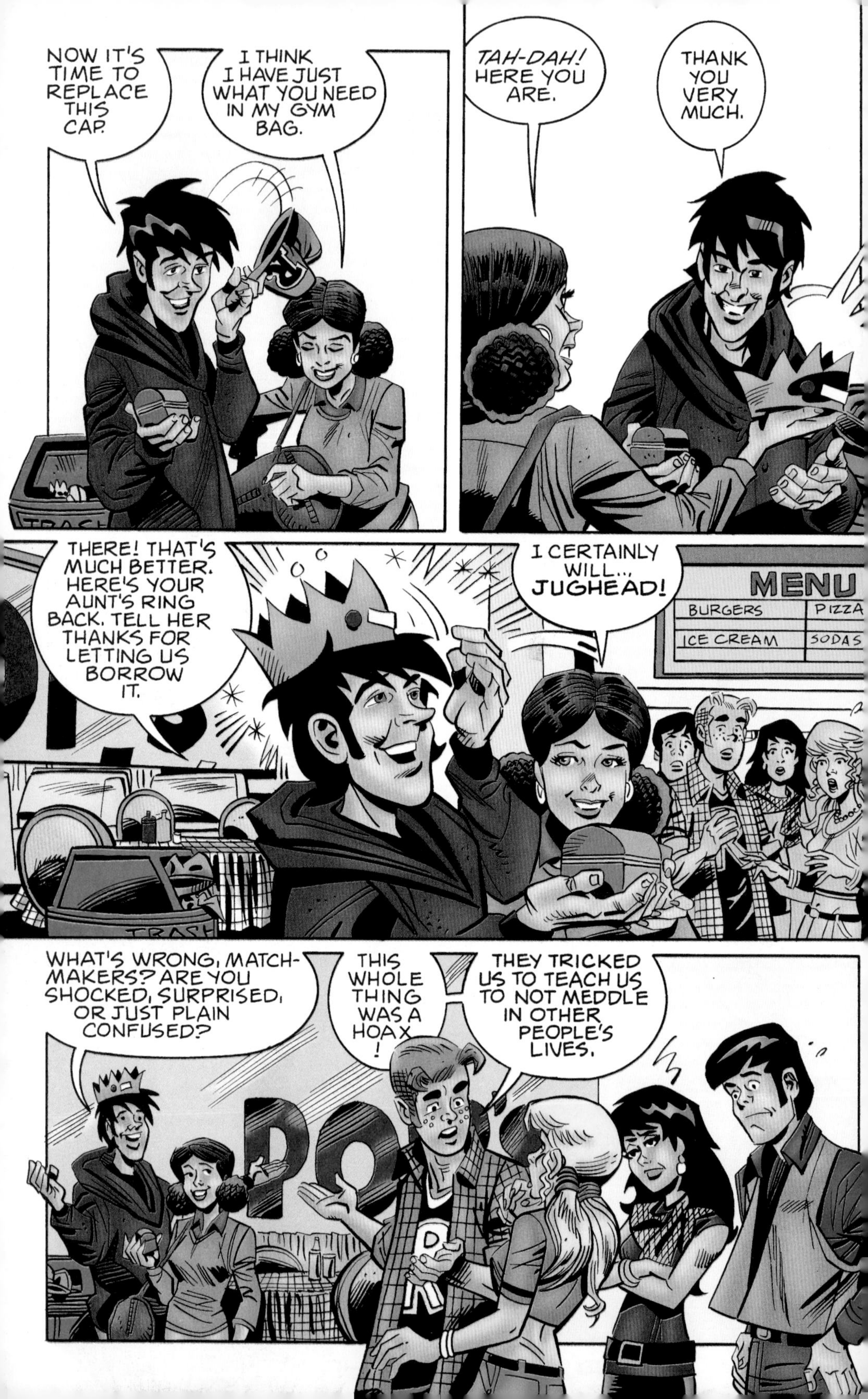
NOW IT'S TIME TO REPLACE THIS CAP.
I THINK I HAVE JUST WHAT YOU NEED IN MY GYM BAG.
TAH-DAH! HERE YOU ARE.
THANK YOU VERY MUCH.
THERE! THAT'S MUCH BETTER. HERE'S YOUR AUNT'S RING BACK. TELL HER THANKS FOR LETTING US BORROW IT.
I CERTAINLY WILL... JUGHEAD!
MENU
BURGERS
PIZZA
ICE CREAM
SODAS
WHAT'S WRONG, MATCH-MAKERS? ARE YOU SHOCKED, SURPRISED, OR JUST PLAIN CONFUSED?
THIS WHOLE THING WAS A HOAX!
THEY TRICKED US TO TEACH US TO NOT MEDDLE IN OTHER PEOPLE'S LIVES.

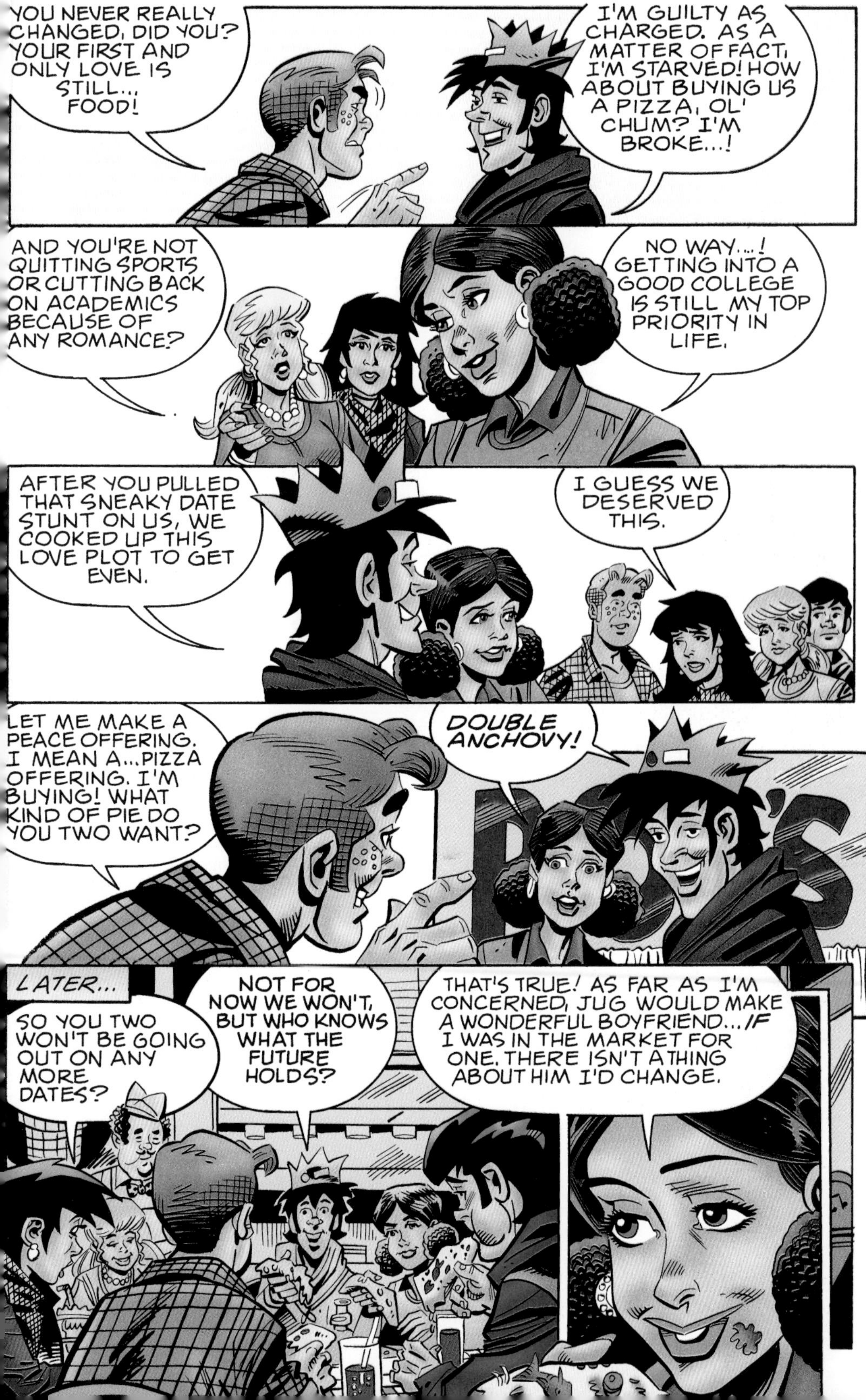
YOU NEVER REALLY CHANGED, DID YOU? YOUR FIRST AND ONLY LOVE IS STILL... FOOD!
I'M GUILTY AS CHARGED. AS A MATTER OF FACT, I'M STARVED! HOW ABOUT BUYING US A PIZZA, OL' CHUM? I'M BROKE...!
AND YOU'RE NOT QUITTING SPORTS OR CUTTING BACK ON ACADEMICS BECAUSE OF ANY ROMANCE?
NO WAY...! GETTING INTO A GOOD COLLEGE IS STILL MY TOP PRIORITY IN LIFE.
AFTER YOU PULLED THAT SNEAKY DATE STUNT ON US, WE COOKED UP THIS LOVE PLOT TO GET EVEN.
I GUESS WE DESERVED THIS.
LET ME MAKE A PEACE OFFERING. I MEAN A...PIZZA OFFERING. I'M BUYING! WHAT KIND OF PIE DO YOU TWO WANT?
DOUBLE ANCHOVY!
LATER...
SO YOU TWO WON'T BE GOING OUT ON ANY MORE DATES?
NOT FOR NOW WE WON'T, BUT WHO KNOWS WHAT THE FUTURE HOLDS?
THAT'S TRUE! AS FAR AS I'M CONCERNED, JUG WOULD MAKE A WONDERFUL BOYFRIEND... IF I WAS IN THE MARKET FOR ONE. THERE ISN'T A THING ABOUT HIM I'D CHANGE.

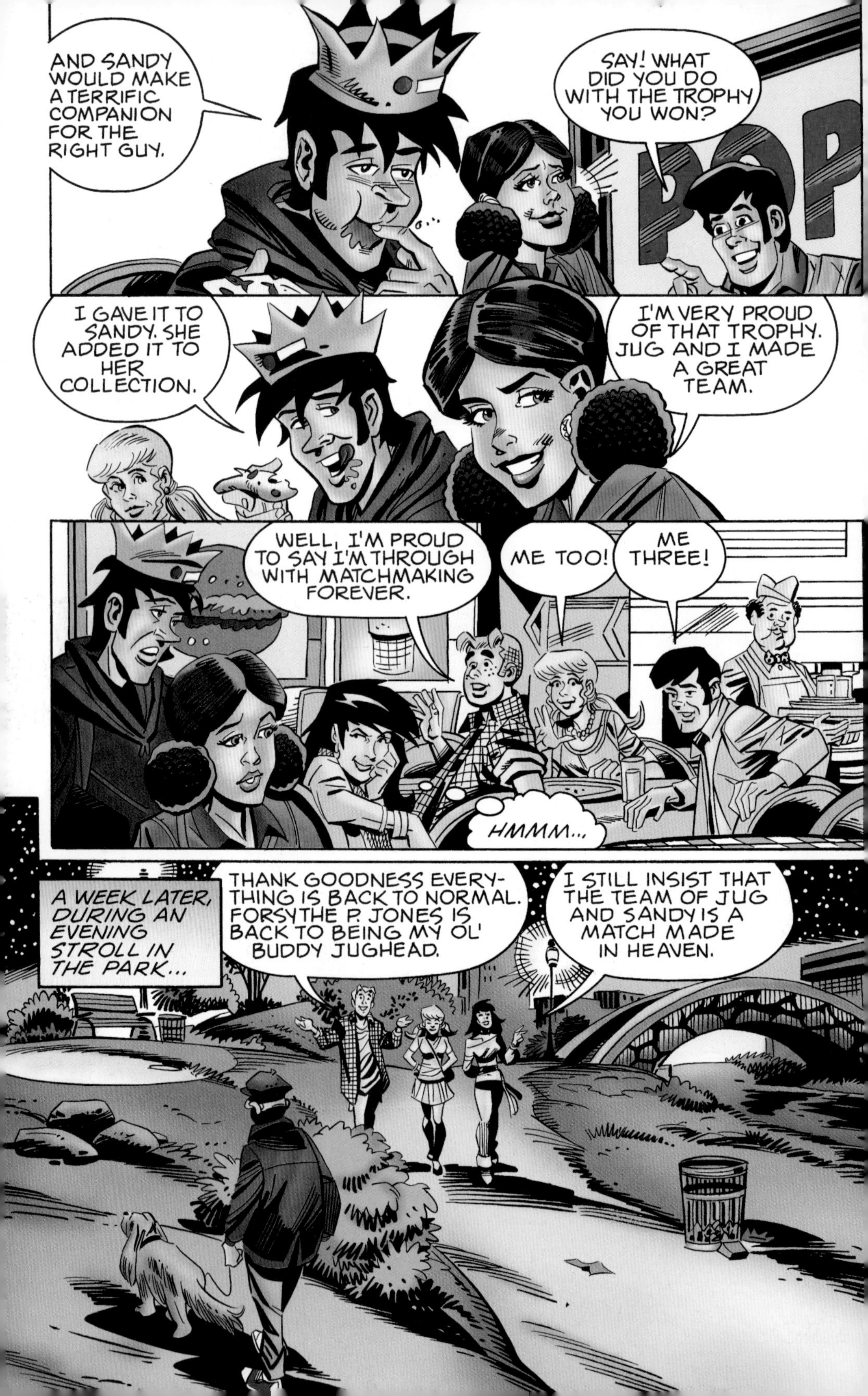
AND SANDY WOULD MAKE A TERRIFIC COMPANION FOR THE RIGHT GUY.
SAY! WHAT DID YOU DO WITH THE TROPHY YOU WON?
POP
I GAVE IT TO SANDY. SHE ADDED IT TO HER COLLECTION.
I'M VERY PROUD OF THAT TROPHY. JUG AND I MADE A GREAT TEAM.
WELL, I'M PROUD TO SAY I'M THROUGH WITH MATCHMAKING FOREVER.
ME TOO!
ME THREE!
HMMM...
A WEEK LATER, DURING AN EVENING STROLL IN THE PARK...
THANK GOODNESS EVERY-THING IS BACK TO NORMAL. FORSYTHE P. JONES IS BACK TO BEING MY OL' BUDDY JUGHEAD.
I STILL INSIST THAT THE TEAM OF JUG AND SANDY IS A MATCH MADE IN HEAVEN.

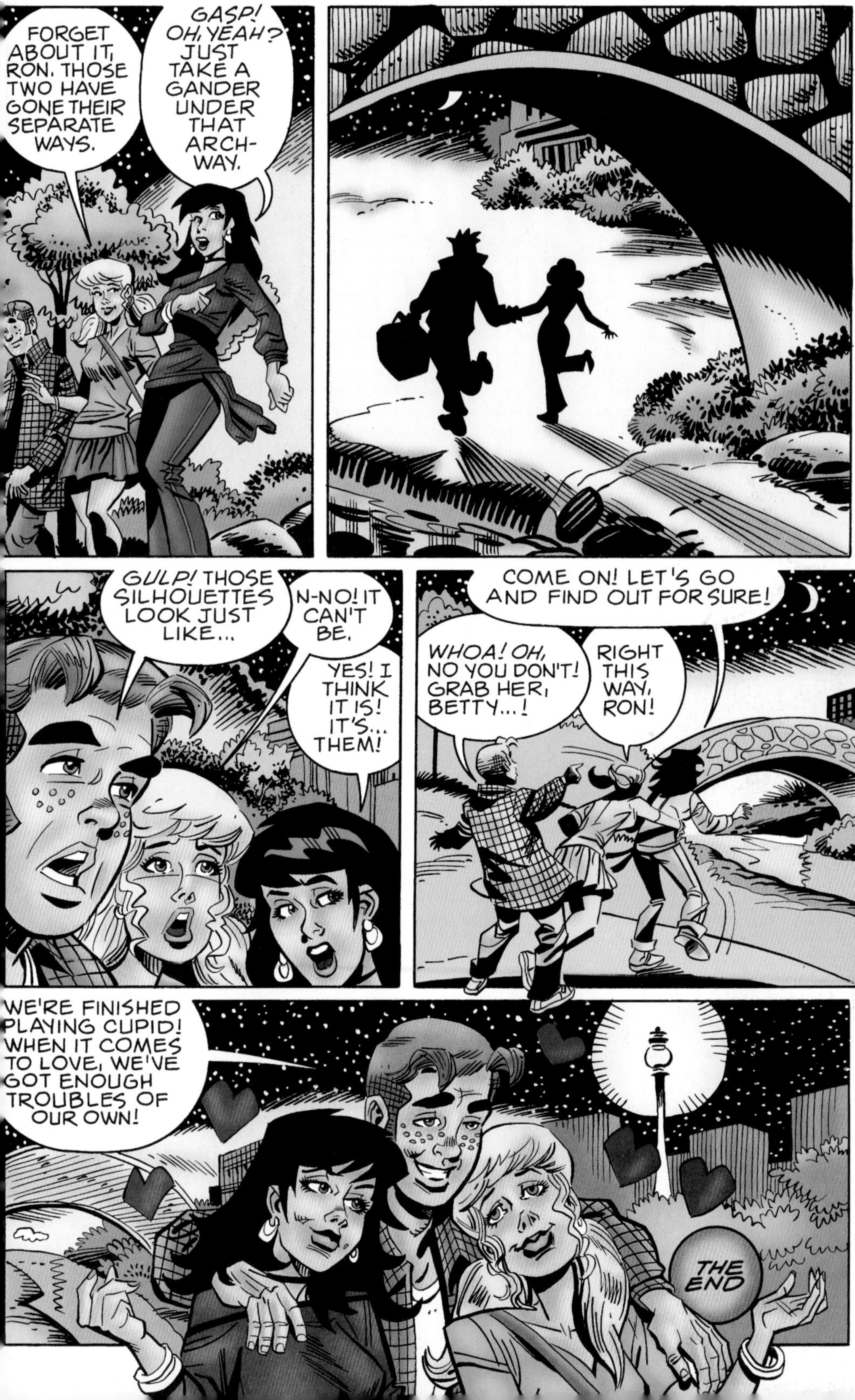
FORGET ABOUT IT, RON. THOSE TWO HAVE GONE THEIR SEPARATE WAYS.
GASP! OH, YEAH? JUST TAKE A GANDER UNDER THAT ARCH-WAY.
GULP! THOSE SILHOUETTES LOOK JUST LIKE...
N-NO! IT CAN'T BE.
YES! I THINK IT IS! IT'S... THEM!
COME ON! LET'S GO AND FIND OUT FOR SURE!
WHOA! OH, NO YOU DON'T! GRAB HER, BETTY...!
RIGHT THIS WAY, RON!
WE'RE FINISHED PLAYING CUPID! WHEN IT COMES TO LOVE, WE'VE GOT ENOUGH TROUBLES OF OUR OWN!
THE END